Amanda's Eyes

KATHY DISANTO

Cover design by Tatiana Vila

ISBN: 978-0-615-87162-2
ISBN-061587162-3

For Leo and Nick, with all my love

Man looks on the outward appearance, but the LORD
looks on the heart.
1 Samuel 16:7

He seemed like such a nice guy.
Famous Last Words

PROLOGUE

September 2075

In the beginning, it was pitch black.

And there was pain. But distant, like a memory. Or a threat, prowling the far reaches of the darkness.

Weightless. Suspended in the void. No up, no down. Nowhere.

Beyond the blackness, time passed. Snatches of sound began to drift in. Patchy. Disconnected. A rhythmic, pneumatic sigh. Hollow beep. Voices murmuring words without context.

"Count ... three .... "

"Family .... outside ...."

"Lucky ...."

" .... dead .... "

A warm touch, tenderly reaching through the darkness. A whisper. Close, very close.

"… going to be all right ... fine ... listen ... mother now."

Listen to your mother now.

Hours crept by. Mental synapses sputtered dimly to life as the brain began to reboot. Thought sparked, flickered, died. Cut in again. Shorted out. Coalesced laboriously, one syllable at a time.

The memory came together in fits and starts—a kaleidoscope of disjointed fragments and gaping holes, arranging, then rearranging, until the pieces finally fell into place. At long last, a scene unspooled against the blackness, like a movie in a darkened theater.

"A police reporter, Amanda Joy?" She shook her head, giving her blue eyes that where-did-I-go-wrong roll that still managed to make me feel like I was a scabby kneed five-year-old tracking mud across the marble floor. "Call me an optimistic old woman, but I was

hoping you would choose a more ... well, a more dignified profession."

"Come on, Mom. Nobody would call you old."

"Don't change the subject." But she was pleased. I could tell by the slight smile and the way she lightly touched her glossy black chignon as she glanced around the crowded restaurant.

Lunch at the extremely pricey Henri's was Mom's idea, billed as a girls-only celebration of my brand-new college degree. If I had been in my right mind, I would have shut my trap and gone along for the eats and used Dad as a buffer. Told him and let him tell her. Less flack for me that way. But under the influence of that post-commencement high and further intoxicated by raspberry grilled salmon, basmati rice, and steamed vegetables, telling Mom about my new job seemed like a good idea. Now I was in for it.

"We were discussing your poor choice in career tracks," she reminded me.

"I've wanted to be a reporter since I was sixteen. You know that."

"Yes," she said, deliberately studying her flawless manicure. The violet nail polish matched her off-the-shoulder silk blouse. A delicate bracelet – diamonds strung like tiny, winking stars – glittered when she flexed her wrist. Her eyes lifted again. "But I had deluded myself into thinking that was a phase. I hoped you might grow out of it."

"Before or after I got my degree in journalism?"

She shot me a look. "Don't rub it in. I was wrong, and I admit it. Still, if you're determined to be a reporter, why not choose a more conservative approach for once in your life?"

"Like what, for example?"

"Oh ..." She considered briefly, head tilted to one side. "Like the society page."

"Mom. This is me, Amanda, remember? Can you honestly see me in three-inch heels, playing nice with the rich and famous?"

"You would break your neck," she sighed.

"If I didn't die of boredom first," I agreed, forking up a hefty bite of Henri's world-famous Chocolate Thunder Cake.

Her unlined forehead creased in thought for a moment. When her expression brightened, I braced myself.

"Politics! It's perfect! And if you were assigned to cover the Assembly, you could see your father more often. I'm sure we can make it happen! Hal must have some media connections who would hire you in – "

I pointed my fork. "Nice try, but no. I mean it, Mom, stay out of this. If you and Dad have your way, I'll be a talking-airhead by morning. One more rich kid living off her connections. Nobody would take me seriously, not even me. I want to make a difference."

"But a police reporter? *Good heavens, Amanda, nobody likes those people! They're ...." She hesitated, obviously searching for a sufficiently damning turn of phrase. "Brash. Tactless. Headstrong and reckless!"*

Trying not to laugh, I held my arms out to my sides. "Remind you of anyone you know?"

That earned me a glare and a ladylike growl of frustration. "I blame your brothers for that."

"You wish. Jim, Kev, and Bri didn't force me to act like one of the guys. The truth is, they couldn't keep me from tagging along."

"Maybe," she conceded reluctantly, then her gaze filled with concern. "This could be dangerous, Amanda. Please reconsider."

I should have listened to my mother.

"I'll tell her you said so."

A man's voice, quietly amused, quickly swallowed by the resurgent void. Touch again, a gentle but insistent prodding.

"Oh, no you don't. Time to wake up, Ms. Gregson."

Chapter 1

The mind stirred unwillingly, groped groggily, struggled sluggishly to process emerging data.

Dark. Unbelievably dark.

Pain crept closer, prompting a moan of protest.

"Atta girl! Let me see you move your legs. Come on, Ms. Gregson, move those long legs."

The long legs in question shifted obediently as the drift toward consciousness picked up speed. Signals started to trickle in from the body, none of them pleasant: thick, cottony tongue; heavy, inert limbs; one arm stiffly immobile. Pain. Everywhere.

The eyelids that should have fluttered open at that point didn't.

"Can' ...." The thought tailed away.

"Say again? Hey!" More prodding. "Don't fade out on me. The Tramadine I added to your drip should be bringing you around pretty quickly now. Talk to me, lady."

Fumbling for the errant thought. "Can' ... open m'eyes."

"Okay, still with us. Good enough. As for not being able to open your eyes .... They're .... The upper part of your face is bandaged."

"M'face?" The tremor of concern—weak, muffled, and distant—danced away before it fully registered.

"Yeah. Not to worry, though. You'll be fine."

A dry swallow as awareness continued to flood in. "Thirsty."

"I'm sure you are." The unseen stranger picked up my wrist, his touch reaching through the merciful mists of oblivion, to drag me farther into the throbbing here and now. He took my pulse swiftly and expertly, laying my hand back on the bed and giving it a sympathetic pat. "No fluids allowed yet, I'm afraid, but I'll get you some ice chips as soon as the doctor answers my page and gives the okay. Meanwhile, let's raise your head up a bit. We don't want you going back under, do we?"

Speak for yourself, buster.

I was, indeed, coming around quickly. But the more awake I got, the more I could feel; and the more I could feel, the better "going back under" sounded. Besides, I had figured out where I was, and I wasn't happy about it.

"Hospiddle," I groaned.

"Right. UCSF Mount Zion."

I hate hospitals. Not that I had ever needed one before, but I've visited enough of them in the line of duty to learn all I need to know. Hospitals are full of sick, hurt people with stories guaranteed to break your heart. Pale, rumpled relatives roam the hallways and hover in cramped waiting rooms like apprehensive-yet-hopeful ghosts, their bloodshot eyes constantly searching for some bearer of glad tidings. Meanwhile, so-called angels of mercy stalk the same halls, looking for any excuse to *practice medicine*. Based on my observations, I would define *practicing medicine* as inflicting pain and discomfort on helpless people who already have their fair share of both. Thanks, but no thanks, has always been my attitude toward hospitals.

Except nobody was asking my opinion as the bed hummed quietly, elevating my upper body. I felt the mattress contours silently readjust to cradle me in my new position.

"So, our patient is awake." A new voice—smooth, rich alto. "How long?"

"Started coming out of it about five minutes ago, Doctor Ramirez," replied the nurse. "She says she's thirsty. Now that you're here, I'll go get her some ice chips, if that's all right with you."

"That will be fine, Dennis. While you're at it," added the woman, "call down to her brothers and call her parents at the hotel."

"Which hotel?"

"The Les Grandes. They went back to their room shortly after midnight to catch a few hours of sleep. Tell the family she's awake and can have visitors." She sounded close now, right next to the bed.

"Fam'ly?" I interjected weakly.

"Yes, your family is here. Your parents and two brothers flew in from the East Coast five days ago. Another brother arrived from Los Angeles the same day. I take it that's everyone?" I must have nodded, because she said, "Quite a crowd. They were here around the clock, taking turns at your bedside while you were on the fourth floor. After we moved you into this room late last night, I was finally able to convince the Senator to take your mother back to the hotel to get some rest. Your brothers I only managed to chase as far as the cafeteria."

I was completely disoriented, unable to see, and had one foot still in LaLa Land, but this was beginning to sound serious.

"Wha' —" I ran my fat, gummy tongue over dry, cracked lips and tried again. "Wha' happen'd?" Then, with the closest thing to urgency I could muster, "Why'm I here?"

She laid a gloved hand on my left forearm, her touch steady and reassuring. "Amanda, listen to me. I know you have questions, and I intend to answer them as soon as I'm convinced you're aware enough to understand what I tell you. Right now, I'm going to check your vitals and scan for signs of infection. While I do that, I want you to answer some questions. We don't want you to fall asleep again. All right? Good." She checked my pulse. "What's your name?"

"'Manda."

"Your *full* name."

"'Manda. Joygregson." But because I slurred the last two into one word, and getting it right struck me as important, I tried again. "Joy. Gregson."

"Parents' first names?"

"Hal an' Ruth."

"How old are you?"

"Thirdy-two."

She pulled back the blanket. Her fingers gently explored my abdomen. "You stay in shape. How?"

How? Oh, yeah. "Run."

"Can you tell me what you do for a living?"

"Reporter."

"Well, you may not be up to complex sentences yet," she said, tugging the covers back into place, "but I've heard enough to rule out global amnesia. Ah, here's Dennis with your ice chips."

Something nudged my lips—a plastic spoon. I opened wide and felt two blessedly icy disks slide onto my parched tongue.

"Don't chew," warned the invisible nurse. "Let 'em melt."

Way easier said than done when you're practically dying of thirst, but I managed, rolling the rapidly shrinking chips around in my mouth. All too soon, they were nothing but a cool aftertaste. I opened again, instinctively trusting Dennis to be on the ball and shovel in two more. He didn't let me down.

"Pain?" asked Doctor Ramirez.

No, thanks. I've got plenty.

She had moved to the other side of the bed, and I automatically turned my head toward the sound of her voice, only to be rudely reminded I couldn't see her. That was when it suddenly dawned on me. If I couldn't see these people, I had no way to prepare myself for whatever they might be planning to do to me. My fight or flight response shot right off the scale as I realized I was absolutely defenseless, completely at their mercy.

And as anyone with a lick of sense knows, doctors don't *have* any mercy.

It was enough to make me gag on my ice chips.

I coughed, "What?"

"Do you have pain? If you do, can you describe it? How would you rate it on a scale of one to ten, one being mild and ten being unbearable?"

I could hardly hear her over the roar in my head. I felt like I was trapped in one of those nightmares where *you know you're going to die if you don't wake up*. So you try to claw your way out of the dream, willing your eyelids to open, but you can't, and they won't. Except this nightmare was no dream, because you don't feel pain in dreams, and my head was pounding like "The Anvil Chorus."

"Relax, Amanda." The doc stroked my arm. "You're going to hyperventilate. Take a deep breath, let it out slowly ... that's right, all the way out. Again. Good. I know this is difficult, and you must be frightened. But trust me, you're going to be fine."

"I wanna see."

Great. My first complete sentence was a whine.

"And you will. Soon. But first things first, all right? I need you to relax and focus. The scanner and monitors can tell me a great deal, but they can't describe your pain. You'll have to do that yourself."

Nothing like a massive surge of adrenaline to sharpen the old thought processes, right? My brief panic attack catapulted me to complete lucidity. Forcing myself to draw another calming breath, I concentrated on answering the doc's question.

"Five," I finally estimated unsteadily. "Except here." I reached up to touch the bandages swathing my head, finally registering the IV running into the back of my shaky hand.

"How bad is your headache?"

"Eight, maybe. Going on nine."

"All right, hold on. I'm going to add a medication to your IV that will help." I heard her move around the bed, felt her gloved fingers lightly grasp the catheter taped to my left hand. A second later, coolness flooded my vein. "There. The pain should start to ease quickly now."

"Thanks." I straightened my head on the pillow. "Sorry about the sniveling."

"Under the circumstances, I'd say you're entitled to a snivel or two," Doctor Ramirez decided, as her fingers lightly checked my headgear.

Okay, so maybe not *all* doctors are heartless fiends.

"Yeah, well, I'll try to hold it to a minimum just the same." I licked my lips. "Could I please have some more ice?"

"You bet," said Dennis. "Say, 'Ah.'"

"Ahhh."

"Sort of reminds me of a baby bird," drawled a deep voice.

"It's the mouth," added another.

Chapter 2

I choked on my ice again, then gasped, "Bri? Kev?"

Tears threatened, but I dammed the spillway, because *Never let them see you cry, never let them see you sweat* is one of my three unbreakable rules, the other two being *Dig until you find the truth*, and *Tell it like it is.*

My brothers and I grew up on our family's sprawling estate in the Sierra Nevada foothills. We may be spread all over the globe now—me in New Frisco; Jim in the D of C; Kevin in Connecticut; and Brian the California equivalent of a nomad, with penthouses in L.A., Rio, and Porto-Vecchio—but no matter where we hang our hats, when we say *home*, we mean the ranch. Mom and Dad still live there when Congress isn't in session, and that's where we all gather for Christmas and such.

As soon as I could walk, the guys decided to raise me right. They took me under their collective wing and included me in all their adventures. Rambling up rocky rises and plunging through dry, brush-choked ravines in the wake of three older brothers definitely gave me an athletic, rough-and-tumble skill set. Also a personal style I like to think of as assertive, although I can be, and have been, described as in your face. What can I say? My brothers helped make me the woman I am today—a natural-born swashbuckler and unapologetic tomboy. I love them so much it hurts.

"I'm here, too, Stretch."

A hint of sandalwood, the warm grasp of long, strong fingers. My oldest brother, Jim. I pictured his chiseled features—tanned and clean-shaven with Dad's square jaw and piercing, amber gaze under arched black eyebrows. A face unreadable to defense attorneys trying to poke holes in his prosecution but an open book to me.

"Hey," I murmured, curling my fingers gratefully around

his.

He leaned down to kiss my left cheek. "Hey, yourself. About time you woke up."

"Remember what I told you, gentlemen." Ramirez's voice sounded different—softer, less professional, sort of ... honeyed. Despite the circumstances, one corner of my mouth kicked up wryly. "Keep the conversation light. How she got here and the extent of her injuries are strictly off limits for now. We'll go over all that when your parents arrive. Dennis and I will give you some privacy, but we'll be right down the hall, if you need us."

"I don't get it," I muttered when I was fairly sure the four of us were alone.

Kevin's voice to my right: "What? The fact that she thinks we're gentlemen?" He ruffled my hair—which was how I discovered the bandages didn't cover my whole head—and I caught a whiff of the cherry tobacco he favored.

The scent called up a quick mental image of my youngest brother leaning back in his office chair, feet crossed atop the leather blotter on his scarred cherry wood desk as he packed his pipe and contemplated the mysteries of the universe. Jet-black hair curling down to his collar, sparkling blue eyes, lethal dimples beneath high, sculpted cheekbones. Six feet, three inches of lean, muscled male and a long step removed from your stereotypical philosophy professor. But doctor of philosophy he is, and he has the Mensa IQ, the list of publications as long as your arm, and the office at prestigious Chandler University in Waterbury, Connecticut, to prove it.

"That, too. But what I honestly don't get is what women see in you guys."

"Well, I know what they see in *me*," Brian offered. "But these two clowns? It's a mystery, little sister. A complete mystery."

At six-two, Bri is an inch shorter than Jim and Kev and four inches taller than my five-ten. He's the only one of us kids to inherit Dad's dishwater blond hair. But unlike Dad, who's always impeccably groomed, Brian wears his hair finger-combed, if combed at all. That, his easy-going manner, and his broad-shouldered, lean-hipped build are classic surfer dude; but my brother's interest in waves is purely commercial and limited to those lapping the immaculate, white-sand beaches fronting his highly profitable string of luxury hotels.

"Never mind him. How are you feeling?" asked Jim.

I licked my lips. "A little rocky."

"Yeah, well, you look a little rocky," he agreed with a blunt, brotherly candor I found oddly reassuring. "Here, have some more ice."

"Mm."

"Did they give you something for the pain?"

"Um-hm. Head's not thumping so bad now," I mumbled around the ice.

"That's good." He lifted my hand to kiss my knuckles. "I talked to Dad right before we came up. You know they're at the Les Grandes, right?"

"So I hear."

"Well, they're on the way." He gave it a beat before adding, "Dickson is driving."

Another beat passed while they waited for me to pick up on my cue.

"What's the pool look like?" I murmured, belatedly.

Betting on Dickson's no-holds-barred piloting is a time-honored Gregson sibling tradition. I wasn't so far out in left field that I didn't get what my brothers were up to, of course. They had been giving me the unruffled and ready-to-push-your-buttons treatment since they walked through the door. Like I wouldn't pick up on the undercurrents. They were worried about me, but they would keep the conversation light, if it killed them. No wonder I'm crazy about these guys.

"Twenty credits each. You in?" I nodded. "Okay, I have it fifteen minutes from the time I called, Brian puts it at seventeen, Kev figures twenty."

"It's rush hour," Kevin pointed out a tad defensively, and I was forced to admit he had a point.

In the fifty years since the Big One weighed in at 10.5 on the Richter Scale and reduced eighty percent of old San Fran to a smoking pile of rubble, New Frisco has been growing by leaps and bounds. With two strikes against them, a less *Carpe diem, baby!* populace would have taken the hint and rebuilt the city further inland. But San Franciscans have been teetering on the San Andreas brink for so long, they've developed a taste for life on the edge. Besides, *City by the San Joaquin* doesn't have the same ring to it.

The new infrastructure is supposed to be quake-proof. Nobody actually buys that, but we're not a million Chicken Littles waiting for the skyscrapers to fall again, either. Fog City has always attracted the free spirit and the risk-taker like a magnet attracts pig iron. We're a boom town at heart—a little bit rough and ready, a little bit anything goes. Knowing what's here today could be gone tomorrow only adds spice to the mix.

But with civic growth at an all-time high, air traffic control has been hard pressed to keep up with the influx. Hence, the legendary multilevel snarl known as Golden Gate Gridlock.

Mile-high traffic jam notwithstanding, I shook my head. "Ten minutes. Tops."

"From the Les Grandes at this time of day?" scoffed Bri. "Never happen."

"Unless Dickson uses the first-responder tier," Jim mused slowly. "Fast lane at a thousand feet, then a quick dive to street level."

"That maneuver is only for emergencies!" Kevin protested.

"Yeah, but Stretch is Dickson's pet," Bri countered.

"Damn. You may be right. He's been worried sick about her."

"How can you tell?" asked Bri. "He's only got the one dour expression."

Picturing the expression in question brought a faint smile to my face.

Dad's bodyguard cum chauffeur, Bart Dickson, is a hard, square slab of a man with one of those don't-mess-with-me faces that encourages would-be assailants to think twice. His hawk-like nose was obviously broken more than once in his special forces career. A jagged scar zigzags down his left cheek, slicing whitely through perpetual five-o'clock shadow. The grim, determined line of his lips rarely softens.

"He asked about her," Kevin replied glumly. "Twice."

"And you waited until now to tell us? We're toast."

As silly as it was, their banter was a lifeline in my darkness. If it hadn't been for my brothers' voices, their touches, their mingled scents, and the offbeat normalcy of the whole conversation, I don't know what I would have done. I was awake enough at that point to have questions. A ton of them. Coherent enough to understand something terrible had happened, aware enough to sense the world-tilt of events gone horribly wrong. Memories threatened to surface, and given my present predicament, it was safe to assume they wouldn't be pretty. So be it. Better an ugly story, than no story at all.

" — all right? Stretch! I said, are you all right?"

Brian's agitated tone captured my wandering attention. "Sorry. Guess I zoned out for a minute. I'm fine, Bri."

"Well, don't do it again. You were quiet for so long, we thought you went back under."

I fingered the bandages around my eyes. "I guess it's hard to tell if I'm awake with—"

"Oh, *Amanda!*"

At the sound of Mom's voice, unsteady but brimming with relief, Jim let go of my hand. I sensed him make room, and before I knew it, I was enveloped in the familiar scent of gardenias, and her small, soft hands were cradling my face.

Chapter 3

"Thank God," she breathed against my cheek. "Thank God!"

"How's my girl?" Dad murmured tenderly in his aristocratic Tidewater drawl. I felt him lean close, felt his lips touch the crown of my head. His cologne was light, clean, citrusy. "You gave us quite a scare, daughter."

"I'm okay, Dad."

"She's a tough nut," growled Dickson in his gravelly bass. *Tough nut* was Bart's highest compliment.

Mom reclaimed my attention when she let go of my face to take my left hand, her fingers carefully skirting the IV. "How do you feel? What did the doctor say?"

"I've felt better and not much. I hope she unwraps me pretty soon, so I can keep an eye on her. I want to be able to see what she's up to." Dead silence. "Mom?"

"I heard you, sweetheart."

But she sounded uneasy now. On edge. I started to get one of those bad feelings you hear so much about.

"What's wrong?"

Dad stroked my hair. "Not a thing, darlin'. Your mother has been worried about you, that's all. As were your brothers and I. Now, what did Doctor Ramirez say?"

He gave it his best shot, but he sounded exactly the way he had when that twerp Billy Jackson, whose head came maybe to my chin, dumped me in front of the whole school on eighth-grade prom night. I believe Billy's exact words on that never-to-be-forgotten occasion were, "Take a hike, Beanpole!" Dad held me while I cried, murmuring endearments and reassurances the way people do when they know they can't take away the hurt. Hearing that tone now wasn't a good sign.

"Like I said, not much," I replied slowly. "Claimed she

didn't want to get into the details until I was firing on all cylinders. Promised to give me the whole rundown when the rest of you got here."

Again with the silence. Okay, either being blindfolded was playing games with my head, or there was something they weren't telling me. If it was the latter—and my well-honed instincts jangled a warning that it was—that could only spell one thing: *bad news*. I didn't want to hear it, but I *had* to know. Call it an occupational hazard.

"You're all here now," I pointed out.

After what felt like a highly charged pause, Dad cleared his throat. "So we are. James, would you ask the doctor to join us?"

"Sure, Dad."

"Now you listen to me, Amanda Joy Gregson," Mom ordered in a fierce undertone, tightening her grip on my fingers. "You're going to be fine, do you hear? You're going to be just fine."

"That's what they tell me." Over and over. Which meant we weren't talking *bad news*. I swallowed hard. *We're talking very bad news.*

Maybe two minutes later, Doctor Ramirez said, "I hear our patient is ready for some information."

"I don't know how ready I am," I admitted, "but I think it's time I got the story."

"I agree. How do you want it?"

My brow furrowed under the bandages. "Excuse me?"

"Do you want the executive summary, or would you prefer a Q&A?"

She was offering me a measure of control, I realized with a surge of gratitude. "I live for Q&A, Doc. You can fill in the blanks afterwards. Okay?"

"All right." I heard the scrape of a chair being drawn up on the right side of the bed, opposite Mom. "You may fire when ready, Gridley."

It's amazing how quickly you learn to read voices when you can't read facial expressions. Ramirez didn't sound flip, but she didn't sound funereal, either. So why all the familial tiptoeing around? My condition wasn't dire, only serious bordering on dire? Slightly reassured without knowing why, I got down to business.

"How did I get hurt?"

"There was an explosion."

"You're kidding! When did this happen? Where?"

"The night of September fourth. Near Pier One. Down where all those old warehouses are."

An explosion near Pier One, down where all those old warehouses are. The words roused the dark memory coiled in the recesses of my mind; but when I tried to grab it, it shrank back into its hole.

"What was I doing down there?" I wondered absently, still probing the fissure in my consciousness.

"The authorities refuse to part with the specifics, but it appears you were either with, or had followed, two CIIS agents."

CIIS being shorthand for Continental Intelligence and Investigative Service. Sixty years ago—before the global economic meltdown and rampant cross-border drug wars forced Mexico, Canada, and the United States into the ultimate merger, giving birth to the country now known as Tri-America—the U.S. tossed a mishmash of law enforcement and intelligence services into a pot watched by an umbrella agency called Homeland Security. But day-to-day operations were herky-jerky, turf wars were common, and vital intelligence continued to fall through the cracks. When the three countries joined hands to become one big, happy family, all law enforcement and intelligence organizations were combined. One agency with two fluid divisions under one chain of command equals zero competition. That's the theory, anyway.

The question was, how and why had I crossed paths with the feds on steroids this time?

I flashed on an image: a man's face. Round, coffee-dark, young. Skin smooth and unscarred.

"I think I remember one of them," I said. "He had dreadlocks and a gold stud in his left ear."

"Do you remember anything else?"

"I'm trying." I shook my head. "It's there, but when I try to pin it down ...."

"You can't force it, Amanda. With the physical and psychological trauma you've sustained, you may never remember the events leading up to your injury."

Oh, no. I would remember, all right. I would remember,

because I had to, for reasons that went way beyond personal. I didn't understand how I knew that, but I was sure of it. Still, the doc was right–no use trying to force it. Not yet, anyway.

"Tell me about the explosion."

"All I know is, it was powerful enough to ignite the entire block. Police and fire departments from all over the city responded. Even with so many first responders on hand, they almost missed you. You were dressed in dark clothing, crumpled unconscious against a brick wall five feet beyond the entrance to an alley almost a block away from the explosion's point of origin. The buildings on either side of the alley were fully involved." She paused. "As precarious as that sounds, the location actually saved your life by protecting you from the full force of the blast and the worst of the debris and shrapnel."

"And the two agents?"

"As I said, it was an extremely powerful explosion. And they were evidently very close to the source."

"Oh, God." Emotion rolled over me in waves. Sadness because two people were dead, the realization of how close I had come to joining them, the guilt because I hadn't. I bore the brunt of it, then blew out a shaky breath. *Let's get this over with.* The sooner I knew the rest of the facts, the sooner I could start to deal with them. I turned my head toward the doctor. "How long have I been here? How badly am I hurt?"

"You were admitted a week ago and until last night, you were in the ICU. You have multiple contusions and abrasions, some of them quite severe. Two gashes, one on your right shoulder and another on your forehead, required nanosutures. You suffered a concussion, probably as a result of being thrown against the wall by the blast. Your right arm was broken, as well. Fortunately, it was a clean, closed fracture of the ulna. Barring complications, you should be in the ultrasonic cast for another week."

In other words, I looked as beat up as I felt. I would have shrugged it off as could-have-been-worse, but Mom's hand was still clamped around my fingers, which pretty much ruled out the subjunctive. It *was* worse.

"What about the bandages around my head?"

"You were apparently watching the agents from your hiding place in the alley when the blast occurred. Frankly, it's a miracle your eardrums didn't rupture. Perhaps you screamed, your open mouth equalizing the pressure." Imagining it, I shuddered inwardly, as she continued, "In any case, the upper half of your face and your right shoulder were peppered by shrapnel, some of it large, accounting for the gashes."

"Am I ... disfigured?" That would explain the half-turban.

"Not in the way you mean, no. The collagen bonds formed quickly, and the wound edges knitted together seamlessly. You won't even have scars. The most serious damage was to your eyes."

My stomach slid queasily. "My eyes?"

"Yes."

"How bad?"

"Catastrophic, I'm afraid. We had to remove both of them."

Chapter 4

For once in my life, I was speechless. I simply shut down. Didn't make a peep, didn't so much as twitch, for I don't know how long.

Too long, evidently.

"Maybe she passed out," Bri whispered. "You know, fainted from shock."

"Stretch?" scoffed Kev. "No way!"

"Not a chance in He—" Dickson coughed. "Not a chance."

Mom tightened her grip on my fingers. "Amanda?"

When I was ten, I climbed the big willow in our back yard. Didn't get high enough to break my neck when I fell, but I landed flat on my back and got the wind knocked out of me. The doc's big announcement produced that same tight, suffocating sensation.

I mean, we were talking about my *eyes* here. As in, those soft, delicate organs hardwired directly into the brain? As in, sliced out and tossed who knows where? As in, me lying there with empty eye sockets? Gruesome didn't *begin* to cover it.

"Amanda Joy?" Mom had a death grip on my fingers now. If I didn't speak up soon, I would have a few more bruises to add to what was evidently an already impressive collection.

I finally managed to draw enough breath to ask, "How—" Had to stop to clear my throat. "How soon can I get the transplant, doctor?"

Mom released a quiet sigh of relief as her strangle-hold eased.

"Your new eyes are already under construction, so to speak. We've harvested stem cells from your bone marrow and misted them onto the biodegradable scaffolds. In the meantime, volume in the eye sockets will be maintained by implants we inserted during surgery. In three weeks, your new eyes will be fully formed, identical to your former pair in every respect. That's when we'll do the transplant."

"And how long before I'm able to see again?"

"If all goes well, another three weeks after surgery. It will take your body that long to regenerate axons programmed to grow into the optic nerve, fusing the new and previously existing segments and connecting your eyes to the appropriate brain centers."

Six weeks, total. Not so long. Unless ....

"Do I have to stay here the whole time?"

"I'm afraid so," the doctor replied, not without sympathy. "We don't want to risk an infection that might delay surgery or cause post-operative complications. There's no way to definitively control that risk beyond hospital confines. Unless your home is equipped with decon ports, of course."

No such luck. Unlike facilities where maintaining a sterile atmosphere is important—like, oh, hospitals, for instance— your average, well-adjusted homeowner doesn't lose much sleep over possible contamination by friends and neighbors. Anybody entering or leaving Mount Zion, on the other hand, passes through tunnel-like ports where a micro-fine mist kills viruses and harmful bacteria externally, on contact, and internally, by inhalation. Abandon pathogens, all ye who enter here.

My heart sank. I might have been able to argue my way to freedom, if she had said I had to stay because they wanted to keep an eye on me. Keeping eyes on people is what private nurses are all about, right? But a sterile environment? Not even round, redheaded Penny, Mom's full-time housekeeper and part-time Captain Bligh, was that picky.

I was trapped.

My dismay must have been obvious, because the doctor patted my arm. "Time will pass more quickly than you think. You'll probably sleep for long stretches over the next few days, and you'll be up and around before you know it. Meanwhile, I'm sure you'll have visitors who can help you while away your waking hours."

"Best not overdo the company," Dad interjected. "You mustn't tire yourself out. We want you well rested for the surgery."

"Don't worry, Senator," replied the doctor, "We'll monitor the guest traffic."

"Speaking of monitoring," said Jim, "if her editor shows his face, you'll want to watch him like a hawk. Don't leave Tug Maxwell alone with her for a minute. CIIS is trying to keep a lid on this for now. As far as the public is concerned, the explosion is still under investigation and my sister was critically injured in a hit and run halfway across the city. But Maxwell knows where she was and why she was there, and he's not above badgering her for the story."

Doctor Ramirez evidently felt constrained to remind my brother of the obvious. "She doesn't remember what happened."

"That won't stop the interrogation. He would grill his ninety-year-old mother, if it would increase the ratings."

"Sounds like a prince among men. I'll make sure Dennis sits in on his visits."

"That ought'a do it," Bri figured. "Guy looks like he eats nails frosted with ground glass for breakfast. Where did you find him?"

"He came to us from the Special Forces."

"Good man to have on the job," Dickson decided.

The conversation swirled above and around my bed, but even though it concerned me, none of it seemed to touch me— not even the surprising revelation about my faithful nurse, Dennis, gentle of touch but evidently daunting to behold. The weight of recent revelations was pressing down on me. Meanwhile, memory both eluded and threatened. When I tried to sort it all out, my thoughts became impossibly tangled. All at once, I realized I was exhausted.

Mom picked up on it immediately. She squeezed my hand, gently this time. "Getting tired, sweetheart?"

"Yeah, kind of."

"Kind of, my Aunt Hattie." She squeezed again, then announced in her patented don't-give-me-any-guff voice, "All right, you bunch of hooligans, time to go and let Amanda get some rest."

Conversation screeched to an immediate halt. No surprise there. When Ruth Gregson used that tone, *everybody* listened. Never mind the fact that most of the world towered over her dainty five-foot frame. One by one, the men in my family obediently said their good-byes.

"See you tomorrow, Sis," said Bri, kissing my cheek. "Do

what the doctor tells you."

"Do I have a choice?"

"No." Kevin kissed my cheek, too. "See if you can get her number for me," he whispered before making room for Jim.

"I have a teleconference in the morning," said Jim, "but I'll come by around one. Guess you know you won the pool. Ten minutes on the nose."

"Pay up."

"We'll transfer the loot into your account as soon as we get back to the hotel." He kissed my bandaged forehead. "Love you. Now mind Mom and get some rest."

"Your mother and I can stay, if you like," Dad told me, once my brothers had taken their leave. "Sit right here beside you while you sleep."

I shook my head. "No, you go on. I'll be fine."

"I don't like leaving you here alone, darlin'."

"Alone? Dad, in case you haven't noticed, there are a couple thousand doctors and nurses hanging around this place. Go back to the hotel and catch up on your messages, Mister Speaker." I gave him a tired smile. "I wouldn't want the country to fall apart on my account. Three governments on one continent didn't work so well the last time they tried it."

"Bother the government," he grumbled.

"Come on, Hal," Mom said, pushing back her chair with one last squeeze of my fingers. "Amanda is in good hands."

"I suppose so. No offense, doctor," he quickly added. "It's simply that—"

"No need to explain, Senator Gregson, I understand perfectly."

My parents both leaned down to kiss me, then I sensed them moving away, heard Mom's heels tapping toward the door.

I also heard Dad murmur slyly, "Speaking of good hands, Ruth, will you give me one of your special back rubs when we get back to the hotel?" She laughed softly in reply.

Doctor Ramirez moved around the bed, taking my pulse, checking various tubes and patches. "You have an impressive family."

"My brother wants your number."

"Oh?" If she was aiming for nonchalant, she missed by a mile. "Which brother?"

"Kevin. Black hair, on the longish side. Killer dimples."

"Ohhh. *That* brother."

"Uh-huh. Listen, is it okay if I go to sleep now?"

"What? Oh, yes. Dennis will be in to check on you every half hour or so, but he'll try not to wake you."

"Thanks," I mumbled, already drifting off.

Chapter 5

Doc Ramirez was right. I slept big chunks of next few days away. Most of my sleep was deep and dreamless. But once in a while, I would jerk awake in a cold sweat to the echo of some fading catastrophe, my mind swimming with vague, blood-red mists. Whenever that happened, I swore I would cheerfully give my broken right arm to be able to open my eyes. As it was, I could only lie there, locked in darkness, probing that crimson haze. Trying to catch the tail of the maddeningly elusive dragon haunting my dreams.

I needed to remember.

Between naps, I learned a lot about humility and helplessness and good stuff like that — which is another way of saying I learned a lot about myself. Like most adults, I guess, I had taken certain basic skills for granted. Feeding myself, getting dressed, and going to the bathroom, for example. Only now I couldn't manage any of those tasks without help.

I'll be the first to admit my adjustment was bumpier than it should have been, but what can you do when you're cursed with a stubborn independent streak a mile wide? I've been working on mine since kindergarten. Refusing to rely on anyone is probably my way of bucking the assumption that I must have it easy, because my family is wealthy and well connected.

Don't get me wrong, I'm all for self-reliance. But *I can do it myself* wasn't a realistic option under present circumstances. If I had any doubts on that score, day one and Dennis laid them to rest.

I wasn't pain free when I woke up the morning after my return to the living, but I was a mile closer than I had been. The soreness in my arms, legs, and ribs was subsiding, and the pounding in my head had subsided to a mild ache. The most pressing problems I had at the moment were acute hunger pangs and an urgent need to use the ladies' room. I fumbled for, and finally found, the call button.

A minute or two later, I heard sneakers squeak against linoleum. "Morning, Sleeping Beauty," Dennis greeted me cheerfully. "You rang?"

"Morning. Yeah. I, uh, need to use the bathroom."

"No problem." I smelled his woodsy aftershave when he stopped next to the bed. Heard a drawer open and close. "Okay, lift up," he said.

"Huh?"

"Your hips. Lift up your hips, so I can slide the bedpan under you."

"You're kidding."

"Would I kid about high-tech medical equipment like this bedpan?"

"Just help me up, okay? I can make it to the bathroom."

"Not until Ramirez says you can."

"Come on, Dennis, do I really have to use that thing?"

"Well, I *could* put the catheter back in." I lifted my hips. "Thought you would see it my way. No need to be embarrassed," he said, sliding the bedpan into place, "I do this kind of stuff all the time."

"Who said I was embarrassed?" I muttered, settling gingerly on the cool plastic.

"You're blushing. Look, why don't I give you some space? Ring when you're done."

"Now, that wasn't so bad, was it?" Dennis asked sunnily when he answered my delayed page. He took the bedpan away, returning a minute later to straighten my blankets and check my vitals. "How do you feel this morning?"

I decided I would be a trooper if it killed me.

"Better. I don't have as much pain, and my head feels clearer."

"That's what I like to hear! Did you sleep all right?"

"Like a baby." I waited patiently while he finished giving me the once-over, then asked the question now uppermost on my mind. "When's breakfast?"

"Hungry?"

"Starving! What's on the menu?"

"Let me check. Hmm. I thought so. Piping hot, pureed rice cereal and a delicious protein shake. Yum!"

To hell with being a trooper.

"You're kidding," I said.

"No way. Those protein shakes rock."

"Can't I have some real food?"

"There's no pleasing you this morning, is there?"

Before I knew it, he was announcing his intention to give me a sponge bath. This time the blush went clear to my toes. I'm no prude, but I had never laid eyes on this person. Granted, he was a nurse and all, but nobody had given me a sponge bath since I was two. From where I lay, this situation went way beyond awkward.

I tried to reason with him. "Trust me, Dennis, I can do this."

"No, you can't."

"I've been washing myself for years, big guy."

"Blindfolded, with an IV in one hand and the other arm in a cast? And how are you going to change your gown?"

He had me there.

I sighed. "You win. But close your eyes, all right?"

"There's no need to be embarrassed." He was trying not to laugh, I could tell. "I do this kind of stuff all the time."

Maybe half an hour after my bath I was feeling almost human. Amazing what getting cleaned up and donning fresh duds could do. Not only that, but Dennis had actually let me brush my own teeth, tossing a much-appreciated crumb to my dwindling sense of self-sufficiency. By now I was so hungry even pureed rice sounded good, so when I heard the rattle of dishes and the clatter of silverware against tray tables, I pressed the button to raise the head of the bed a bit more.

"Good morning, Ms. Gregson." The woman's voice was soft and sweetly girlish. "I brought your breakfast."

"Thanks," I said, smiling widely. I would have rubbed my hands together, if the one arm hadn't been in a cast and sling.

"Here, let me help you set up your tray. There you go. The cereal is directly in front of you, spoon at nine o'clock. The protein shake is at eleven o'clock."

Her detailed description only served to drive my sightlessness home, but reminding myself this was all temporary, I ruthlessly nipped blossoming self-pity in the bud. Return of the trooper.

"Thanks again, Ms. ....?"

"Terrance. Katy Terrance. Can you manage on your own, or would you like help?"

"I'm sure I can handle it, Katy. I'm so hungry, I could eat a horse!" Or pureed rice.

"All right. Press the call button, if you need assistance."

Finding the spoon was easy, but the process got trickier from there. I felt like a goof for resorting to the toddler fist-grip, but I wasn't going to bet my breakfast on my ability to hold my spoon like an adult, because I didn't trust the fine motor skills in my left hand. I inched hand and spoon carefully across the tray table until my knuckles touched the bowl, then scooped clumsily, pleased as punch when I got the spoon to my mouth without spilling anything. That shining sense of accomplishment died a quick death when I discovered there was nothing in the spoon to spill. Blowing out a breath for patience, I reacquired the bowl and dug deep. Got the spoon to my mouth again, this time with a payload—slightly sweet, mostly tasteless gruel. Unfortunately, the warm glow of success was somewhat dimmed by the fact that a dollop of said gruel could be felt soaking through my gown an inch north of my belly button.

Reluctant to admit defeat, I kept giving it the good old college try, until I realized I was getting more food *on* me than *in* me. I shuddered to imagine the mess I had made of the tray table. If I was this hopeless with cereal, how on earth would I manage more challenging delicacies like Salisbury steak, powdered mashed potatoes, and rubber peas?

Time to face facts. At some point during the next six weeks I could and would learn to feed, dress, and bathe myself. I would probably learn to get around more or less on my own. But I needed help to get from here to there. Wanting to stand on your own two feet is admirable; cutting off your nose to spite your face is dumb. Laying the spoon on the tray table, I sighed, swallowed my pride, and capitulated to the inevitable. I pressed the call button.

Chapter 6

"How do I know if she's awake?"

"Hey, A.J.?"

"Yeah, Dennis?"

"Mr. Maxwell here is wondering if you're awake."

"Depends on what he wants."

"What do you think I want?" growled Tug, doing his best imitation of aggrieved innocence. Unfortunately for Maxwell, innocence of any kind isn't his forte. "Can't a man drop in to cheer up a hurt friend? Here. I brought you flowers, you ingrate." He dumped a florist's box in my lap.

I fumbled the lid off the box, releasing a sweet perfume that made my jaw drop. "You brought me *roses*?"

"What? You don't like roses?"

"Sure I like roses. But since when did you start spending a hundred credits a pop on flowers? Or anything else, for that matter?"

"Now, is that any way to talk? You're gonna have Nurse Baker here thinking I'm some kind of cheapskate."

"If the shoe fits, Tug."

"You hear that, Baker?" he groused, dragging up a chair. The scent of rose petals didn't stand a chance against the ever-present cigar smell that clings to him like a pungent aura. "No respect. No respect at all."

It wasn't true, of course. We enjoy baiting one another, that's all. I actually have a boatload of respect for my editor. Even consider him a sort of mentor in my less judicious moments.

Tug Maxwell is a short fireplug of a man with steel-wool for hair and a mustache to match. His wardrobe runs to rumpled suit coats he wears unbuttoned over creased shirts straining to cover a belly that overhangs his belt buckle. He's got a face like a bulldog—pugnacious, flat, and heavily jowled—a mug that telegraphs his personality long before he opens his mouth. One look at that face and you sense it would take an act of God to keep Tug Maxwell from getting the story. He doesn't know how to take *no comment* for an answer. Of course, that's the brand of moxie it takes to work your way up from copy reader at some Podunk weekly to editor-in-chief of World News Network, the largest news organization on the planet.

Most of what I know about reporting I learned from him, starting the day I walked through the doors of WNN for an internship during my last semester of college. Maxwell was captain of the West Coast police beat, I was full of vinegar and gunning for my first byline. Day one on the job, he sent me for sandwiches. Not exactly the foot in the door I had in mind, but I kept my disappointment to myself and trotted off to the deli. After two weeks of scut work and gofering, Tug figured I had paid my dues and let me tag along when he visited the precinct houses. A month later, he gave me my first shot at a story, then bullied me until I got it right.

Rewrite it, Little Miss Got-Rocks. Lead with the meat this time.

You call that a sound bite? Hell, I've seen commercials with bigger teeth!

Bad neighborhood? What does that have to do with the friggin' price of potatoes? Listen, Rocks, you wanna be a police reporter, you gotta get to know the man on the street. Every John Doe out there is a potential source.

Nobody was more surprised than I was when he offered me a job after graduation. He's been my boss ever since, mentor and dictator all rolled into one.

The day he hired me, he ordered me to work on my name.

"You ever hear of a hard-hitting crime reporter named *Amanda Joy*?" I guessed his sandpapery rendition of a girlish falsetto was supposed to emphasize the point. "Listen, a cutesy moniker like that might be okay for high-school cheerleaders, but it'll kill you in this business."

The same thought had already crossed my mind. Not that I would admit it and give him the satisfaction.

"So what do you suggest?" I asked.

Well, Tug is big on initials: M.T. for Mark Tong, K.C. for Kenseisha Caroline, and so on. Efficient, he says. So while he still calls me Rocks, my fans know me as A.J. Gregson.

At last count, said fans numbered around four million. It has taken ten years, but I've worked my way up from sound bites on fender benders and shoplifters to covering the big, the bad, and the nasty. Bloody murder. Serial killers. Major swindles and organized crime. Even the occasional cold case, when an unsolved's anniversary rolls around. I've got a syndicated, bi-weekly column and a weekly hour-long talk show, both called *Crime Watch*.

Tug has been behind me all the way. But while I like and respect him and owe him more than I can say, I'm not gullible enough to take his every word and gesture at face value.

Today's roses smelled fishy, because the story *always* comes first with Maxwell, and he was there to get one by hook or by crook. Never mind the fact that I had been conscious for three lousy days. It was only a matter of time before he started in.

Right on cue he said, "Thanks for showing me in, Baker. I'm sure you have plenty to do. We can take it from here, right, Rocks? I'll stop by the nurses' station to check out."

"No need to stop by the nurses' station," said Dennis.

"I don't have to check out?" Tug sounded surprised. "I thought CIIS wanted every visitor to check in and out."

"That's the protocol."

"Oh, I get it. Listen, that's real nice of you, but I don't need any special favors. I put my pants on the same way as your average working stiff; I don't mind playing by the rules."

"Guess that's why everybody calls you a stand-up guy, Mr. Maxwell."

"I try," Tug replied with spurious modesty, rolling right over the sarcasm.

"And since you are such a stand-up guy," my nurse-watchdog continued mildly, "I'm sure you won't mind if I stay. It being required in this case, except when the visitor is family. Besides, somebody has to put A.J.'s roses in a vase."

The box was lifted from my hands. Seconds later the sink in the bathroom kicked on.

"Hold on, now," Maxwell sputtered. "Are you trying to tell me I can't have a few minutes alone with my own repor— ... ah ... with my good friend?"

Thwarted had never been part of my editor's personal vocabulary, but that was about to change. Thoroughly enjoying the prospect, I had to throttle a chuckle into a cough.

"Sorry. Tickle in my throat. Can I have a drink, Tug?"

"What? Oh, sure. Here you go." He shoved a plastic cup into my extended left hand, predictably oblivious to the water that sloshed over the rim and into my lap. The cigar smell got stronger as he lean in close. "So, what have you got for me?" he muttered *sotto voce*. "Must have been one hell of an explosion, huh?"

"Must have been," I agreed, matching his tone. "Too bad I can't remember it."

"You don't remember *anything*?"

"Not so far."

I toyed with the idea of passing along the few details the doctor had given me, but decided against it, mainly because they were second-hand, vague, and would unleash a barrage of questions I couldn't answer yet. Besides, if I gave him anything at all, he would run with it. But nobody was going to tell *this* story but yours truly.

"Damn," said Tug, as the sink in the bathroom cut off.

"Tell me about it."

"Watch it," he muttered. "He's coming back. Whatever happened to privacy?" he groused as Dennis' footsteps approached the bed.

"You'll have to take that up with CIIS. Meanwhile, pretend I'm not here. There you go, A.J. I put the roses on your side table, so you'll be able to smell them."

I lifted my nose for a sniff, smelled nothing but Panatelas. Still, it was the thought that counted, so I said, "Nice. Thanks."

Tug's "Now, look here, Baker," was punctuated by the scrape of a chair as he shoved to his feet.

His usual MO would be to get in his opponent's face, intimidating by sheer force of Maxwell's infamous indomitable will. That strategy worked with most people, but from what I had heard, Dennis wasn't most people. As tempting as it was to let Mister Pushy find that out the hard way, I figured there was no use *both* my editor and me being hospitalized.

"Tug!"

"What?" he snapped impatiently.

"Did you know Dennis here used to be Special Forces?"

Silence. Then, "That so?"

"Six years," Nurse Baker assured him happily.

"Huh. Well, then, I guess he's gonna stay." He dragged back the chair and sat down. "So, Rocks, how you feeling?"

He left ten minutes later. Without the story.

Chapter 7

I jolted awake, heart pounding a mile a minute, those frustrating mists swirling in my head as I fought to calm my breathing. Desperate to reach beyond the darkness and ground myself in reality, I groped for the short sections of bedrail framing my pillow. With my fingers wrapped around cool, solid metal, I fought to recall the dream. But by the time my cardio-vascular system leveled off, I was forced to admit defeat. Again. Ten days since I came around, and there was still a blank wall where those memories should be. Maybe Doctor Ramirez was right, maybe I would never remember.

Physically, I was doing great. IV-free and no cast. Plenty to be thankful for, but I wanted more. I wanted it all. I always do, even though I know life doesn't usually work that way. Still, it never hurts to aim high, and giving up gets you nowhere. *Maybe tomorrow.*

"I wonder what time it is," I sighed.

"Sixteen fifteen."

I yelped and levitated an inch off the mattress, because that's what you do when you think you're alone, and a voice as deep and dark as midnight pipes up from right next to your bed.

"Four fifteen p.m.," the voice explained.

"I know that." I clapped a hand over my jackrabbitty heart. "Who are you, and what are you doing here?"

"Name's Eagan, Ms. Gregson. Special Agent Jack Eagan, with CIIS. I didn't mean to startle you."

"Uh-huh. How long have you been sitting there?"

"Not long. Fifteen minutes, maybe."

Watching me sleep. Watching me surface from my obscure nightmare like a drowning swimmer. I felt almost indecently exposed.

"Don't be embarrassed," he said. "Anybody in my line of work understands about nightmares. They're nothing to be ashamed of."

Doubly flustered because he had read me so easily, I snapped, "Yeah? Well, it's disconcerting to wake up from one and find out you have an audience."

He thought about it. Then, "I can see where it would be."

More than ready for a change of subject, I said, "What can I do for you, Agent Eagan?"

"It's Jack, and I would like to talk to you for a few minutes, if you're feeling up to it."

"I feel fine," I replied, flipping back the covers. I located the left-hand rail again and held on as I sat up and swung my pajama-clad legs over the left edge of the bed. No way was I having this conversation flat on my back like some helpless female. I heard him scoot back his chair to give me room. "There's just one problem, *Jack*."

"What's that?"

"You have me at a disadvantage. You *know* who I am," I waved an index finger between us, "but how do I know you're who you say you are?"

"Sharp lady," he murmured approvingly. "Tell you what, why don't you ring for Baker? He can vouch for me."

My eyebrows shot toward my hairline as I groped for the buzzer. "You know Dennis?"

"For years. We served together."

"On the Teams?" Silence, which I took for a yes. "Don't tell me, let me guess: You would confirm that, but then you would have to kill me."

That surprised a chuckle out of him. "I wouldn't go that far."

Dennis' voice broke into our conversation. "I see you two have met."

"I take it you *do* know Agent ... uh ... Jack?"

"And all the skeletons in his closet. Don't worry, A.J., Eagan's one of the good guys. I hope you don't mind my letting him in to see you?"

"No, I don't mind. Thanks, Dennis." Right then, my stomach gurgled hungrily. "That reminds me. As long as you're here .... What's for dinner?"

"Woman eats like a truck driver," my nurse informed my

visitor. "Not that you would guess it by the looks of her."

I beamed a smug smile in his general direction. "I have terrific metabolism. So give. What's on the menu?"

"Chicken a la king. Now, if you don't mind, I've got patients who actually need me. You two have a nice chat."

"Chicken a la king!" I groaned. "I don't even want to know. What I wouldn't give for a fat, greasy cheeseburger with the works!"

"That can probably be arranged," reckoned my visitor with a smile in his voice.

"I've got news for you, Special Agent Jack Eagan. If you think for one minute you can get on my good side by bribing me with junk food ... You're probably right."

"I'll keep that in mind." He paused, and when he continued, the smile had left his voice. "Now about the reason for my visit. I was here a couple times before but never managed to catch you. You were either out for tests or roaming the hallways. I have a few questions about the night of September fourth."

He might as well have doused me with ice water. I nodded slowly. "I have a few questions about that night myself."

"Such as?"

"Such as, what happened?"

"You still don't remember?"

"Not for lack of trying. That nightmare you walked in on? I have it at least every other day, but so far, nothing sticks. The only detail I've remembered is a man's face: young, African-American, dreadlocks, a gold stud in his left ear."

"Evander Cuey. He was one of our best agents. Left a wife and two kids — six-year-old twins. Girls."

"Oh, no. God. I'm so sorry!"

"Yeah. It's tough on the families."

And the friends, I added silently.

"I'm told two agents were killed that night. Who was the other?"

"Sammy Michaels. Tall, skinny kid with red hair. Good with computers, electronics, that kind of thing."

"Did he have a family, too?"

"No wife or kids, but his seventy-two-year old grandmother is taking the death of her only grandchild hard.

She's in a room two floors down, recovering from a stroke."

"Doesn't seem fair, does it? Why them and not me? How did I earn a pass?"

"Don't go there, Ms. Gregson."

"A.J."

"All right, A.J. You shouldn't feel guilty because you lived and they didn't. Believe me, 'Vander and Sammy wouldn't have had it any other way. If you want to honor their memories, you'll get well and live to a ripe old age."

"If you say so."

"I do. Okay, you don't remember that night. What about the days leading up to it? Is there information you didn't share about the tip you gave us, for example? Details you might have kept back for journalistic reasons, like the name of your informant?"

My brow knit as I scrambled to shift gears. "Tip? What tip?"

"The anonymous tip the three of you were following up on when Cuey and Michaels were killed."

I grabbed the edge of the bed as my dark world spun crazily. "I gave them a tip? You're saying they went to the Port because of me?"

"No," he replied calmly, "I'm saying they went to the Port because that's where the van was. Because it looked like we had finally caught a break, thanks to you. Don't forget, you thought so, too. You were right in the middle of the action. Despite the fact that Special Agent in Charge Ito strongly advised you to keep your nose out of it, I might add."

"I'm a reporter," I murmured absently, trying to process this new data. "My nose was right where it belonged."

"You think so?"

"Yeah."

"I'll tell you what *I* think. I think you're damned lucky to be alive, A.J. Gregson."

No argument there.

"I don't remember the tip, either. Based on what you've told me so far, it mentioned the location of a van. Why was that so important?"

"The Ferrymen. Ring any bells?"

Chapter 8

The alley was wet, and it smelled. Damp pavement, soggy boxes, and ... urine?

I wrinkled my nose and glanced over my shoulder, trying to spot the forlorn cardboard condo lying in sodden ruins beyond the nearest streetlight's anemic, blue-white glow. I could barely make out that misshapen lump now that darkness had swallowed three-fourths of my surroundings. Not that I was worried about lurkers. Cuey and Michaels had scanned the alley before sentencing me to wait here more than two hours ago. Nobody was home at the recyclable hovel ... or likely to be any time soon, given the miserable weather.

At least the downpour had stopped. A fine mist hung fuzzy haloes around the heads of the few widely scattered streetlights, blurred the edges off buildings, and shed tears on blankly staring windows. It also kept me blinking and swiping my hand across my eyes in an effort to see clearly. Of course, visibility would have been limited even without the mist, thanks to the impenetrable shadows enveloping the maze of blackly towering warehouses. A little more than a block away, the van was reduced to an indistinct silhouette crouched silently, almost sullenly, in front of warehouse one nineteen.

The wind kicked up, dank and smelling of the Bay. A gust knifed into my alley, moaning through the narrow space as it pressed my jacket and clammy black turtleneck against my skin. I shoved dripping black bangs off my forehead and squinted, trying to pierce the gloom behind the lifeless windows and the dark pools breaking up my sightline. I hadn't seen hide nor hair of my escorts since they left me here with or-else orders to, "Sit. Stay." Funny guys. Anyway, I knew the CIIS agents were out there ... somewhere.

When are they going to make their move? I wondered impatiently.

Supposedly, they were reconning the area. Riiight. I imagined them set up in a nice, dry warehouse, drinking coffee from a thermos, and chuckling over the expression on my face when I caught my first whiff of the alley. I growled in frustration.

Well, a deal was a deal, and I had agreed to do this their way. Yes, the person claiming to be an innocent duped into making deliveries for the Ferrymen had chosen to make contact with me instead of the feds. Yes, I had, out of the kindness of my heart and a highly developed sense of civic duty, passed what I considered an iffy tip along to CIIS, the premier intelligence-gathering, law-enforcement agency on the continent. I had still had to do some fast talking to get the SAC, a taciturn guy named Ito, to see the situation my way and let me tag along.

Truth be told, he had been within an inch of tossing me out on my ear, when I reminded him my anonymous tipster might decide to contact me with last-minute information that could immediately, significantly impact the mission in progress. Since Citizen Unknown made no bones about the fact that he or she would break off all communications the first time any face but mine appeared on screen, I ought to be on site. Each second counts, right?

I probably hadn't sold the whole load of bologna, but I had planted a seed of doubt. So that was one argument in my favor. Second argument, I had a reputation for giving cops and feds a fair shake and keeping my cool in tight spots. But the argument that won them over was my refusal to tell them where to go unless they took me with.

Once I got my erstwhile teammates past the arrest threats by convincing them I would rather be behind bars than left behind, we managed to come to an agreement.

Movement down the block and across the street from the van caught my wandering attention. I braced my left hand against the rain-slick concrete wall, leaned around the corner, and snuck a peek. I didn't see anything at first and was tempted to chalk up that flicker of so-called movement to wishful thinking, when I glimpsed a lithe form ghosting through the deep shadows cast by the warehouse opposite the loaf-shaped "target vehicle." In the blink of an eye, the figure vanished, merging with the darkness again. Two or three minutes crawled by before another figure, shorter and huskier, materialized near the back of the van. A signal was given, and the taller individual darted out of the shadows and across the street to join his partner.

After a brief consultation, the shorter of the two — that would be the dreadlocked Cuey — squatted and reached underneath the rear bumper, planting the first tracking device, a chip the size of your average pinhead. The plan was to follow the van, ID the small fry, tail them to bigger fry, and so on, until the authorities reached the top of the world's most murderous food chain. Cuey and Michaels would plant a backup device equipped with audio/visual capabilities inside the van. Providing they could bypass the anti-intrusion measures, of course.

Unfortunately, I hadn't been able to get the specs on those, because my source hadn't left a callback number, and the subject hadn't come up in our earlier chats. But if the tip was on the level, and the cargo was as advertised and belonged to the gang it reportedly belonged to, that security system would be well-nigh impregnable.

Possibly lethal, I mused, rubbing a hand over a persistent prickle at the nape of my neck. Now that we were here, this deal was beginning to feel way wrong. Seized by a sudden, almost overwhelming urge to call the whole exercise off, I took a half-step toward the mouth of the alley before I managed to rein in the impulse. These guys were pros; they didn't need me to tell them this might be a trap.

As soon as Cuey stood up, he and Michaels went to work on the cargo-bay doors. The tiny red eye of their scanner cast a diffuse glow as Cuey ran it around the seams. I had it on good authority Michaels was the Investigative Division's resident computer whiz kid-slash-wonder boy. Supposedly, the system he couldn't hack had yet to be invented. I pictured his freckled fingers dancing across a haptic interface, searching for the command or series of commands that would temporarily reprogram the anti-intrusion system to open Sesame. Once he succeeded, if he succeeded, the scanner's indicator light would flash green.

Five minutes later, it did. Michaels pumped a fist in the air, and Cuey leaned in close to the van.

Retinal scanner, I thought. Probably mounted at eye level to the left of the small, tinted back window. Michaels must have fooled it into recognizing Cuey's retina. I held my breath, bracing for the big bang, but the door slid up into the roof with a pneumatic hiss not much louder than my sigh of relief. Cuey drew his weapon and climbed cautiously inside, closely followed by his partner.

By now, I was weighing the pros and cons of moving in for a closer look myself. I wanted to see the inside of that van so bad I could taste it, but there was no question in my mind about what would happen if Cuey and Michaels caught me within fifty feet of them when they had specifically warned me to stay put. Despite my bravado back at headquarters, incarceration wasn't an attractive prospect for any number of reasons. In addition to all the pesky legal hassles and bad food involved, Dad's press secretary, Carolyn Mayer, would have a cow. And her reaction would be mild compared to Mom's. But the con that trumped them all was the fact that I had given my word. End of debate. I would stay where I was, as comfy as a wet cat, in the mouth of an alley with severe halitosis. I only hoped the story would be worth it.

I had no sooner made my decision, when the nerves in my wrist hummed, scaring me out of half a year's growth. Swearing silently, I tore my eyes away from the van and pushed up my left sleeve. UpLinks. Can't live with the phone-computer combo, sure as hell can't live without one, now that the nuts and bolts of life are stored in the Cloud. The nearly weightless black band tickled my wrist again as I read the crimson crawler, **Urgent call, caller unknown**. Now, as we all know, Caller Unknown is the favorite ID of telemarketers and anonymous tipsters the world over. Since tonight's ticklish operation was based on information from the one of the latter, I issued a mental **answer call, closed caption** command to the thought-activated software.

The three-dimensional color image that materialized on the flex-screen took maybe five seconds to register. Five merciful seconds before I realized what I was looking at, moaned, "Nooooo," dropped to my knees, and vomited. I threw up until I hit empty, then managed to unfold at the waist. Still on my knees, dizzy and shaking, I wiped the back of my right hand across my lips, shoved up my sleeve again, and forced myself to take a closer look.

I had never seen anyone flayed alive but had no doubt this would be the result, if someone was. There was no way to tell whether the raw, bloody corpse had been male or female, Caucasian, Asian, or Martian; it had been peeled like a grape. The lipless mouth was frozen in an agonized scream. No tongue. The caption read, **This is what we do to traitors**.

My stomach pitched again, but a second message vibrated "incoming," so I sucked a steadying lungful of air and called up the transmission. **And inquisitive reporters.** I quickly flicked to the next screen to read the rest. **You're out of your league, Ms. Gregson.** Flick. **Suggest you stage a tactical retreat.**

They know, I realized, as my heart catapulted into my throat. And if they know they have a leak, they probably guessed I would tell ....

My head whipped up. My eyes locked on the van. I scrambled to my feet, letting my sleeve drop over the UpLink as I stumbled toward *the street, screaming a warning. I was still screaming when the van erupted with a deafening roar in a blinding flash.*

Chapter 9

Memory and I woke up together for a change, the events of that night crystal clear, complete in every detail, so sharp they cut like a knife. Heart thudding painfully in my ears, I lay perfectly still, horror rolling over me like a malevolent tide.

The van had been an ambush after all. Armageddon on a long fuse, the end delayed just long enough to lure prospective prey well into the trap. Cuey and Michaels hadn't been blown up, they had been vaporized.

My stomach knotted and rolled. Laying a hand on my abdomen, I breathed slowly and deeply, waiting for it to settle. It was a long wait, but I eventually managed to level off. Or come close to level, anyway.

"Time check," I croaked.

From the nightstand next to my bed, my new UpLink—the old one had been reduced to a Dali clock-melt—replied in a pleasant male tenor, "The time is twenty-three-oh-five. Date: thirty September."

Drawing a shaky breath, I sat on the edge of the bed and mentally accessed the visualization program embedded in the walls of my room and linked to my implants. They had been activated a week ago, when the docs decided it was safe for me to be up and about on my lonesome. The black screen behind my eyelids bloomed with blue, three-dimensional shapes—chairs, walls, doorways, windows, even the slippers I had kicked off midway down the left side of the bed. Not the way you want to see the world twenty-four/seven, and vizzing for more than a few minutes at a time will give you a worse headache than a six-margarita hangover. But the program is great for short stretches, when you're blind as a bat bereft of echolocation and want to get from point A to point B without crippling yourself because somebody moved the furniture.

I slid my feet into the mules and stood, waiting for my legs to firm up before scuffing across the room and into my private bath, where I nudged the door closed with my hip. Wrapping both hands around the edge of the sink, I dropped my chin to my chest. Just when I had begun to doubt I would ever remember that night, total recall in one fell swoop. It was almost more than I could take. So I stood there, trying to ride out the storm and navigate a chaotic flood of emotion.

When the waves calmed to choppy-but-navigable, I straightened and shoved my hands under the motion-activated tap, letting water tumble over my wrists and forearms. I soaked a washcloth and ran it over the back of my neck, across my lips and chin, down my throat. My hair was matted with sweat, but as tempting as it was, sticking my head under the tap, bandages and all, didn't seem like such a bright idea with surgery scheduled for six a.m.

Yes, today was the day. By this time tomorrow the worst would be over, and I would be halfway home. Three weeks from today people and furniture would no longer be Euclidean. I would be able to see my family again and get my first look at newcomers who had become major players in my small, dark world. Doctor Marisol Ramirez, Nurse Dennis Baker, Katy Terrance, even the mysterious Jack Eagan.

Speaking of Eagan, I need to talk to him. Now that memory had returned, I had important information to share and almost no time to arrange a briefing.

Folding the washcloth, I draped it over the sink. Once my hands were dry, I shuffled out of the bathroom and over to the lounger angled in a corner to the left of my bed. I sat and studied the blue jumble atop my nightstand until I managed to pick out my UpLink and slide it on.

Then I hesitated. I wanted to keep this call confidential, but as nonsensical as it sounds, you have no actual privacy in a private hospital room. No such animal in a hospital, period. You never know when some medical weenie will pop in unannounced to listen to your heart and lungs or take your temperature or cop a scan. My best shot at keeping my chat with Eagan under wraps was to head back to the bathroom, so I did.

Thank God Jack decided to program his number into my unit. *Call Eagan, Jack,* I thought, activating the UpLink from my seat on the throne. After a ring and a half he picked up. Not being able to see him, I forgot that he *would* be able to see me.

"A.J. Are you calling from the ... never mind. What are you doing up so late?" I could tell he was tired—his midnight voice was a bit rough around the edges. "Don't you have surgery tomorrow?"

"Today, actually. Oh-six-hundred." Briefly distracted, I shook my head. "Have you been keeping tabs—" I broke off mid-sentence when I remembered the clock was ticking. "Forget it; it's not important. Where are you?"

"On my way home. Why?"

"How long would it take you to get here?"

Silence. Then, "You remembered something." No fatigue in his voice now.

"I remembered *everything*. I'm not sure how much it will help, though. You probably know most of it. But I do have a wrinkle or two to add, and I want to do it while the details are still fresh in my mind. Besides, who knows how long they'll keep me doped up after the surgery?"

"All right, if you're sure you're up to it, I can be there in fifteen minutes."

"I'm sure. Oh, and Jack?"

"Yeah?"

"Do me a favor."

"What's that?"

"Can you get in without anybody seeing you? I would just as soon not give anyone reason to wonder if I've remembered. Word might get out to the wrong people."

"Good thinking. I'll see you soon."

Chapter 10

How does that old song go? "It's all coming back to me now?" As I sat waiting for Jack, it all did.

The Ferrymen. My not-so-magnificent obsession for more than a year. Only a cataclysm could have made me forget.

I guess you could call them hitmen. You could also call Einstein a math whiz. Think ruthless. Think unstoppable. Think killers so proficient "caught the ferry" was fast replacing "bought the farm" in common usage, and you have the Ferrymen in a nutshell.

They made their debut about eighteen months ago, taking out a cardinal as he enjoyed a private dinner with the Pope, in the Pontiff's apartments on the third floor of the Vatican. A month later, they knocked off the capo of the Ferramo family, despite the fact that he had been closeted in his private retreat, a penthouse ninety-five stories up and accessible by a single, biometric elevator nobody but Gino himself could operate.

The Ferrymen had racked up more than a dozen kills since. Nobody was safe. Not the cardinal or the capo or the Afghan warlord. Not scientists or businessmen or the Secretary of the Air Force.

Their methods were as varied as their targets. Causes of death catalogued so far included designer toxins that had been ingested, inhaled, even worn. A marble-sized chunk of plastic explosive that assembled itself out of nanobots embedded in aspirin, then blew the quarry inside out. One victim's death was logged as "an apparent case of spontaneous combustion caused by an unknown chemical reaction."

Evidence was a pipe dream. All the cops had were bodies, means, and a fistful of dead ends. If it hadn't been for the obits, nobody would have guessed the murders were linked. But within a minute of each hit, up popped this obit. Always on some small-town news site—I figure there must be fifty thousand of them in Tri-America alone—always the same design. A ferry ticket made out to the victim and listing his or her "time of departure" to the minute. Above that, a sketch of Charon—that's right, the Grim Reaper himself, right down to the black hood and skeletal grin—surrounded by a shadowy collection of similarly garbed homeboys. Each clutched a coin, a Greek obolus, in boney fingers. Payment for ferrying a soul from this world into the next. Hence, the Ferrymen. Or, as they were sometimes known, Hell's Boatmen.

I had been snapping at their heels since the first calling card showed up in the WaKeeny, Kansas, *Weekly Watchman*. Between contacts in law enforcement and sources on the street, I managed to stay neck and neck with the federal task force. Even sniffed out some of their secrets. Like, for example, the fact that the press hadn't seen all the obits, because CIIS managed to intercept three before mass media got wind of them. I got that gem off the record, of course, and promised to keep it off. Why? Because a) I understood the feds had to hold back a tidbit or two, in order to weed out copycats and cranks; and b) my source promised me an exclusive when they were ready to make the information public.

I put word out on the street, and that word spread quickly. A.J. Gregson was offering cold, hard credits for leads. A hundred per. But the information had to be solid. CIIS offered financial incentives, too, but let's face facts. Certain types don't get nearly as nervous about talking to a reporter as they do talking to the Man. Especially if the reporter in question has been known to go to the wall to protect her source. Which I have. More than once.

Credits for confidences usually works for me, but this time I got zip. Either nobody knew anything, or they were too scared to talk.

Okay, I thought, *nothing is going to happen unless I make it happen.* And I got an idea.

I ran it by Maxwell, together we ran it by the network brass. Convinced them to turn up the heat with a full-court press. We took the hunt to the people, started a public crusade with a million-credit reward "for information leading to." We didn't actually expect anybody to take us up on the offer, but we hoped the attention would get the pot simmering. My editorials practically wrote themselves.

Meanwhile, nobody was more surprised than me when the million netted us a nibble.

I got a call. From whom? Search me. All I saw was a talking-head-in-a-hood in front of a solid black background. Electronically modulated voice. So no way to gauge height, weight, or gender. He or she never used words that would raise red flags with government eavesdroppers. I wasn't crazy about dealing with the Masked Marauder but decided to go along for the ride and see where we wound up.

We spent the first few weeks feeling each other out. Me to verify the caller was on the level, the caller probably trying to decide if I could be trusted. I guess I passed the test, because I finally got the whole, sad story.

I didn't know. Swear to God, I didn't. I'm not a crook, okay? Strictly on the up and up. You know, law-abiding. I don't even cheat on my taxes, for God's sake!

About five years ago, I went into business for myself. Overnight courier. Gypsies, they call us. Most of my runs were penny ante, delivering rush orders for local vendors, prescriptions for old ladies, stuff like that. Sure, I would wangle an uptown gig once in a while. Like manna from heaven, those jobs. Delivered a bunch of uncut diamonds once, made enough to get new thrusters. But most of the time? Most of the time I was just getting by.

Until one day, this guy calls. Nice suit, big office, the whole nine yards. Says he got my number from one of those uptown clients I told you about. Hears I'm reliable and discreet, willing to take the odd job on short notice.

"I would like to offer you a contract," he says.

"With who?" I ask.

"I'm afraid that's classified," he says.

Classified. Has to be the government, right?

"What would I have to do?" I ask.

"Remain on call for the occasional rush delivery," he says. "Vital cargo. We're prepared to offer substantial compensation if you'll agree to drop whatever you're doing when we call and take the jobs with no questions asked."

And I think to myself, "Only a dope would turn down a deal like this." So I sign on.

Only pretty soon, I'm smelling a rat in the woodpile, you know? I mean, maybe a top-secret government agency would get its packages at an abandoned farmhouse a hundred miles northeast of

Podunk. Or a half-gutted warehouse down by the docks. Maybe.

But would the feds set up an off-shore account for me? Would they shell out this much dough? Substantial is substantial, but brother, these fees were fat! *When you're in business for yourself, you learn. If a job seems too good to be true, there's gotta be a catch.*

So I start to look for it. The catch, I mean. I pay close attention, and what do you know? I spot a pattern.

Dates. It was all about the dates. What do I mean? Well, it was like this. I make a delivery, less than a week later, a major player catches the ferry.

I didn't know about those ads — the ones with the Grim Reaper? — yeah, those. I didn't know about them until I caught your show one night. That's when I finally put it together. I almost had a heart attack when I realized I was working for these guys! I was afraid to call the cops. What if they didn't believe me? What if they thought I knew the score all along? I could end up in the jug. Isn't that what they call prison? The jug? I decided to call you instead.

I no sooner reached that stretch of Memory Lane, when my inner radar registered a bogey in my room. I tensed. "Who's there?"

"Jack."

"Perfect timing," I said, relaxing. "Pull up a chair, and I'll tell you the rest of the story."

"So the tip about the van was supposed to prove your source was righteous. Then he or she would come in and talk to us."

"That was the idea. But honestly? I only half-expected to get that far. I wasn't a hundred percent sure I didn't have a crackpot on my hands. I passed the information onto Ito, because I knew I couldn't afford to guess wrong."

"Sounds like you feel guilty for doubting this character." I shrugged. "Aren't you forgetting an important detail?"

"Like what?"

"Like your 'innocent' courier set us up. Set *you* up."

"I don't think so."

"Because?"

"Because of two messages I got right before the explosion."

"Messages?"

"Um-hm. The first was a photo. Of a corpse." I shook my head slowly. "I've been to crime scenes. Seen more than my share of bodies, including vics who were beaten up, hacked up, and shot up. What I haven't seen in person, I've seen in CSI photos. But I've never seen a corpse reduced to raw meat. It looked like ... I swear, Jack, it looked like the victim had been skinned alive. You could barely tell it was human. The caption said, 'This is what we do to traitors.'"

"What did you do?"

"Threw up all over myself. Twice. I was on the verge of a comeback when the second message came in."

"Another photo?"

"No, text. 'Same goes for inquisitive reporters.' Or words to that effect. The sender suggested I take my nose for news elsewhere. That's when it hit me. The Ferrymen knew what the courier told me. They had to know I would take that information to the Service. I'd had a wrong feeling all night, but I kept shaking it off. Sat on my hands until I got those transmissions. By then Cuey and Michaels were inside the van. I tried to warn them ...."

"I told you. What happened to them wasn't your fault."

"I know what you told me. I'm still trying to believe it."

"Try harder. And remember. If not for you, we wouldn't be this far."

"How far is that?"

"Well, we know the Ferrymen outsource. Deliveries, for sure. That might give us a clue about their organizational structure."

"Like it could be extremely compact?"

"Right. A tight nucleus of operators farming odd jobs out to bit players. Subcontractors kept in the dark, probably contacted through a series of virtual cutouts. If an errand boy gets picked up or turns, he doesn't know enough to do any damage."

"So the breach is self-sealing. Makes sense."

"We've been working on that angle since you first brought the information to Ito. Put some agents undercover to fish for contracts or hook up with a courier who already has one. Like I said, the subs won't know much, but every piece of the puzzle helps."

"Too bad we can't locate the body in the photo. Forensics

might be interesting."

"Forensics haven't helped us so far. And the Ferrymen have gotten rid of the corpse by now. I know I would have."

"I wonder if they destroyed the image they sent."

"Probably, but we'll sweep the Cloud, to make sure."

"At least I know the pilot was the real deal."

"Not necessarily. You've been riding this Ferrymen story hard for more than a year. Your one-woman crusade really put CIIS in the hot seat. Pressure on us means more pressure on the Boatmen. Your snitch could have been on the company payroll, tasked with drawing you out so they could take you out. This bunch is long on tying up loose ends and short on conscience; they wouldn't hesitate to get rid of an asset that's outlived its usefulness. So there's no know way to know for sure. I'll tell you what we do know."

"What's that?"

"You got their attention."

"So I noticed. I wonder what happens now?"

"They try may again, but I think they'll wait and see for a while. You know we leaked word that you have amnesia?"

"Yeah."

"Well, as long as they believe that, you should be fairly safe."

"*Fairly* safe."

"Like I said, they may decide to finish the job. Especially if you pick up where you left off." Pause. "So maybe you should leave it alone."

Leave it alone when two agents were dead and two children fatherless because of information I supplied? Leave it alone while the Ferrymen were still in business? Not in this lifetime! Of course, I wasn't dumb enough to tell him that.

"At least I have time to figure out my next move," I said.

"What's to figure? You need to drop out of sight for a while."

"Hah hah. Very funny."

"I'm serious."

"You said I was fairly safe."

"Fairly isn't good enough, and an ounce of prevention never hurt."

"I guess I could spend a couple weeks at my parents' place in the foothills. I'll need at least that long to get up to snuff again."

"Gotta be more than a couple weeks. And forget your parents' place."

"More than a couple weeks? How much more?"

"I don't know. It could be months before we're sure it's safe for you to resurface."

"Months? Are you out of your mind?"

"Keep your voice down. Unless you want to read the night nurse in on this discussion."

I throttled back the volume, pushing the words through my teeth instead. "I can't disappear for months! I have a job to do!"

"Can't do it if you're dead."

"And what's wrong with my parents' house?"

"It's not safe."

"Says who? We've got state-of-the-art security. *And* Bart Dickson."

"Okay, but are you sure you want to drag your family into the middle of this?"

I sat up straighter. "What are you talking about?"

"What if the Ferrymen think they have to go through them to get to you?"

"I *told* you, we have—"

"Oh, I get it. The whole clan is going to barricade themselves in the foothills until this is over. Your father, too? Your brother, the DA?"

I was going to lose this one. I knew that now. Have I mentioned how much I *hate* to lose? Ever? At anything?

"You're right. Dad can't just up and disappear when the Assembly is in session." I sighed. "Fine. You've made your point."

"Meaning you'll do this my way?"

"Meaning I'll think about it. I assume you have a hiding place in mind?"

"Yeah, but I need to run it by someone else before I make definite plans."

"Uh-huh. Well, let's hope the Ferrymen don't decide to *finish the job*, as you so tactfully put it, before you get your ducks in a row."

"I'll know tomorrow. And the Ferrymen can't get to you here. You're protected twenty-four/seven."

"Really? By whom?"

"That's need to know, and you—"

"—don't want to hear that song and dance."

"All right, how about this? We'll do our job, you do yours. Get well. Sound fair?"

"Huh."

"Now I better get out of here before the nurse makes her rounds. Hang in there and don't let anyone know you got your memory back. Not even your family."

"No problem." I suddenly remembered how tired he had sounded over the UL. Reminded myself he was only trying to protect me. Felt like Kate the Shrew and didn't like it. I cleared my throat. "Thanks, Jack. I appreciate your help. Seriously."

"You're welcome. Talk to you soon, and good luck with the surgery."

After he left, I lay back, hands stacked behind my head, trying to decide if I was as fairly safe as he claimed. Maybe he was full of hot air. Didn't seem to be, but I had only known him for what? Two weeks? Could I trust him? My gut said yes, and I hoped it was right as usual. Because I was trusting him with my life.

Chapter 11

"Ya couldn'a *paid* me to undergo general anesthesia back then!"

"Really?"

"Heck, no! Talk about *primitive*! Pumpin' the patient full'a drugs that paralyzed the lungs and every other darned thing? *Geez*! *That* kind'a medicine we can do without, right? Hey, am I right?"

"Huh? Oh, yeah."

Angie DiNapoli sounded way too young to be a nurse anesthetist and far too perky for five-thirty in the morning. A real chatterbox. Normally, I make it my mission in life to encourage flapping gums wherever I find them. I mean, you never know where your next story will come from. But today wasn't normally.

"Did you know up until fifty years ago surgeons operated with *knives*? *Knives*, for cryin' out loud!"

"Really?" *God, I'm tired. But too wired to sleep without drugs, especially after talking to Eagan. Hope he's right about being safe here. Be a shame if the Ferrymen punched my ticket before I get a chance to see again.*

"No kiddin'. 'Course *lasers* were in their infancy then, so it wasn't *all* their fault. I mean, it's not like they *knew* better."

"Mm." *I can't believe I let him talk me into running. God only knows where he plans to dump me.*

Angie's fingers grasped the catheter for my IV. "Okay, we're ready to add the anesthetic to your drip. Don't worry, you won't feel a *thing*!"

Up to that second, I had been too preoccupied to pay much attention to her. My contributions to the conversation had been limited to a few absent-mined *Wows*, a sprinkling of *Reallys,* and one *Is that so?* Not that she seemed to mind. Or notice, for that matter. To tell you the truth, I'm not sure she even paused for breath. Angie obviously had her spiel down pat. Talk fast and keep talking, because it was the only way she could get her two cents in before her patients lost consciousness.

As of this moment, however, she had my complete attention. I tensed slightly. "So, this is it? You're putting me to sleep now?"

"What am I, a *vet*? *Geez*! *Strays* get put to sleep, not *people*! We render the patient *unconscious*. Sounds much nicer, right? More professional. But we won't actually knock you out until we get you on the table."

My lips twitched in spite of the circumstances. *Putting me to sleep* offended her professional sensibilities, but *knock you out* was okay?

"You remember how it works?" Not waiting for my yay or nay, she launched into the details. "When we switch on the nanochips, they'll disrupt the electrical activity among key structures in your brain, and *out* you'll go. When the surgery is done, we'll send the termination signal. Not *your* termination, o'course! *Geez*, that'd be like a scene out of one of those science *fiction* movies, ya know? *Anesthesia* termination. The chips'll cut off, break down into organic *components*, and exit your body through the *lymph* system."

"Sounds simple enough."

"Well, it's actually much more *technical* than that." She sounded slightly miffed but bounced right back. "I just wanted'a make sure you got the *drift*. Best of all, there are *no* nasty aftereffects. You'll wake up," she snapped her fingers, "like *that*. Bright-eyed … uh, I mean, really *alert*."

"Should I expect some pain?"

"What? You think we *torture* people? *Geez*! The OR nurse'll add targeted, time-release analgesics to your IV. You won't hurt a *bit*, not even for a *minute*."

"That's good to know."

"You bet! Most patients say they never felt better in their *lives* than they did when they woke up." Her fingers released the catheter, and she patted my hand. "You're all set. I gotta pop up to get stuff ready in the OR. I'll let your nurse know I'm *done* here. Cute guy. Kind'a *intense*, though. I like 'em fun-loving, ya know? Well, been nice talking to you. Bye for now."

"Bye."

Whoever said silence is golden wasn't wearing an elasticized paper bonnet and contemplating her first date with a surgeon. Angie's departure left a vacuum my imagination was all too ready to fill with lurid speculation involving eyeballs and blood and gloved fingers poking into places angels fear to tread. I needed a distraction in a hurry.

Angie said my nurse was cute. Also intense. Did she mean Dennis? He doesn't get in this early. Is Dennis cute?

Okay, that held the willies at bay for all of ten seconds. Now what? I went back over the morning so far and hit replay on the conversation that had taken place in this room a scant half-hour earlier. My family had rolled in on a sunny tide of optimism, showering me with hugs and kisses and words of encouragement. The gathering was totally copacetic until Mom made her big announcement.

"I have a surprise for you, Amanda."

"Okay," I said. Cautiously, because I was remembering her last surprise.

Mom has never given up on putting me in touch with my more feminine side. The last time she surprised me, I got shanghaied for a makeover at the swankiest salon in New Frisco. By the time I caught on, it was too late to run, so I bit the bullet and sat in the chair. After six hours of torture at the inhuman hands of Mister Marc and his merciless minions, Daphne and Fawn, I had three-inch nails and hair that looked like it had been combed with a blender. Memories of the facial peel could still make me flinch.

"Don't you want to know what it is?"

"Hm." *Probably not.*

"A trip to France! Just the two of us!"

"*And* Mrs. Gregson's security detail," Dickson added pointedly. His tone brooked no argument, and he didn't get one.

"France?" I echoed.

"Paris, actually. Think of it as a recuperative vacation. We'll leave as soon as the doctor says you're well enough to travel."

"Does this vacation involve *haute couture*?" I asked suspiciously. Not that it mattered. I doubted France would fly with Jack Eagan. "Because I'm telling you right now, Mom, you're not shoehorning me into one of those dresses shaped like a lampshade."

"Of course not," she replied disingenuously. "I've given up on reforming you." Dad cleared his throat. "Well, I *have*," Mom insisted, then sighed. "All right, I promise. We won't do anything you don't want to do, Amanda. Cross my heart. But imagine the fun we could have — strolling through the Louvre, lunching at that quaint little café on the Rive Gauche, taking an evening cruise down the river."

"Sounds great," I admitted, adding more wistfully than I would have liked, "I would love to go to Paris with you, Mom."

Except Eagan's plan was going to blow hers right out of the Seine. In a moment of abject cowardice, I decided, *Let him bust her champagne bubble.* I didn't have the heart.

"Then it's settled!"

Blissfully ignorant of the disappointment awaiting her, Mom continued to flesh out our itinerary. The more she talked, the worse I felt. Which is why I was pitifully grateful when Angie babbled in, and Dad herded the fam up to the waiting room outside the surgical suite.

My musings were interrupted by a familiar voice. "Ready to try those new baby blues on for size?"

"Dennis! What are you doing here? I thought you didn't come in until seven."

"You thought right, but we've got a busy floor this morning — your surgery and two others. The super asked me to come in early to help out." He sighed theatrically. "Gonna be a long day, thanks to you."

"Think of the overtime," I suggested. "Besides, what's a couple extra hours to a battle-hardened ex-commando like you?"

"Maybe civilian life has made me soft."

"Yeah. And maybe Lincoln is buried in Grant's Tomb."

He walked over to the bed. "Seriously, A.J., how do you feel? Excited? Little nervous in the service?"

"Well, I want to see again. But I don't know what creeps me out more — the thought of Ramirez removing my old eyes, or the thought of Klein popping in new ones." I grimaced self-consciously. "Silly, huh?"

"Nah. As common as they are, organ transplants are still a

big deal for the patient. Quite a load to handle, psychologically. And the eyes? Well, they carry their own mystical freight, don't they? Windows to the soul, and all that."

"So you don't think I'm a wuss?"

"Not even."

"Don't look now, Nurse Baker, but your sensitive side is showing."

"God, I hope not. I have my macho image to consider."

"Speaking of your macho image, you do realize I'm a few short weeks away from finding out what you look like?"

"Well, hell, I'll tell you that now. Short, fat, bald, and bowlegged. Three good teeth, and a wart on the end of my nose. Now pipe down and let me check your vitals."

What do *you look like?* I wondered, as his fingers found my wrist.

People almost never match the mental pictures I paint of them before I meet them face to face, so chances were, Dennis wasn't the lean, dark soldier of fortune I had been imagining over the past few weeks. Had I even come close?

You know that old saying about not missing the water 'til the well runs dry? Well, color me living proof of that! When I could see, the world just was. Every now and then a sunset would stop me in my tracks and take my breath away, but day to day the world served as my backdrop. I never appreciated the wonderful details. Textures and colors. The way the sky looks in that deep-blue hour before dawn. The flash and glint of sunlight off thousands of windows in the Financial District. The expectant blank wink of the cursor against a white background waiting to be filled, or the chaotic ballet performed by the reporters swarming the miasmic WNN newsroom affectionately known as The Swamp.

In a way, I even overlooked the faces I loved. Until I couldn't see them anymore.

Why are we so backwards when it comes to sight? Blind to what matters while we trust our eyes in all the wrong ways. We live as if idiotic clichés like *Seeing is believing* and *What you see is what you get* make perfect sense. Even though human history has proven otherwise, again and again. People see and refuse to believe all the time. How else can you explain smokers? As for getting what you see, any conman worth his salt can make swampland in Florida look like the real estate steal of the century. And let's not even get into used car salesmen.

Obviously, it takes more than a working pair of eyes to see clearly. Not that a working pair of eyes is anything to sneeze at.

Neither are the rest of our senses, for that matter. I mean, who knew hearing, taste, and smell had so much to add? Layers upon layers. I hoped I wouldn't lose that richness, that depth of perception, when I could see again.

"What's with the Mona Lisa smile?" asked Dennis.

"I was exploring the pros and cons of not being able to see."

"There are pros?"

"Surprised me, too. But besides figuring out what's worth looking at and what's not, I've learned to pay attention to my other senses. I considered myself fairly perceptive before, but this experience has taken my awareness to a whole new level."

"You need a whole new level," he said seriously. "From what Jack tells me, you're not out of the woods yet. The only way you're going to stay safe is to maintain complete situational awareness twenty-four/seven. Keep your antennae up, A.J. Tune in with all you've got."

As sobering reminders went, that one was a doozy.

I nodded slowly. "I hadn't thought that far ahead, but you're right."

He laid a hand on my shoulder. "And remember, you're not alone. Iceman's got you covered."

"Iceman?"

"Eagan. Iceman was his call sign in the Teams, and it stuck."

"Yeah? Why Iceman?"

"Well, for one, the guy's got ice water in his veins. Nothing, and I mean *nothing* rattles him. There's another reason we called him Iceman, but you'll figure that one out as soon as you see him."

"Wait. You're going to leave me hanging for *three weeks*? That's low, Baker, really low."

"No need to get testy. I'm only trying to give you something to look forward to."

"Gee, thanks."

"Ready to get this show on the road, Amanda?" Doctor Ramirez.

I turned my head toward the sound of her voice as a flight of giant butterflies lifted off in my stomach. "As ready as I'll ever be, I guess."

"You'll be fine. There's no more skilled ocular surgeon in the world than Doctor Klein."

"He seems to know what he's doing," I conceded nervously, remembering my interview with him a few days earlier. "He said he's probably done a couple hundred of these transplant surgeries."

"At least. Aaron actually teaches the procedure at Hebrew University. Nobody does it better."

"And it'll be over in a tic," said Dennis.

"I thought the surgery took six hours."

"Six hours or six days, *you* won't know the difference. You'll be asleep."

"Hm."

"Did they give you the mild tranquilizer I authorized?" asked Ramirez.

"I turned it down. Wanted to keep my wits about me as long as possible."

"All right. Well, we might as well get going. The two gentlemen who came in with me will bring you upstairs. I'll meet you in the OR."

"Thanks, Doc."

"Mike Tindal, Ms. Gregson." His voice was warm and friendly and thick with the Bronx. "My partner's name is Hamid. You let us do all the work, okay?"

"Okay."

Strong hands under my legs and shoulders, a quick lift and shift to the hover gurney. "No sweat, right?" Mike said cheerfully.

"You guys are pretty smooth."

"Ready to take a spin?"

Not on your life. But I opted for a doughty, "Drive on, McDuff," reaching up to adjust my bonnet as the gurney started to float toward the door.

"Sleep tight," said Dennis.

"Try not to get in any trouble while I'm gone."

"Who, me? I plan to sit right here and moisturize my

incredibly manly nose wart."

"Wart?" murmured a new voice I took to be Hamid's. "What wart?"

Chapter 12

As Dad likes to say, it was all over but the shoutin'.

Doc Klein popped into the recovery room a few minutes after I woke up to announce the transplant had been a complete success. He didn't expect any complications, he said, and aside from a few bruises collected as I learned to get around without the viz program, none had cropped up in the three weeks since. The blinders were due to come off tomorrow morning.

But that was tomorrow, and this was tonight, and old Father Time was dragging his feet. Since I couldn't sleep, I had no choice but to wait him out. Fortunately — or unfortunately, depending on your point of view — I had plenty to occupy my mind.

This side of my September date with destiny, it was easy to see I had led a charmed existence. Smooth sailing, baby, for thirty-two years. Blessed with wealth, health, and a terrific family to back me up, there hadn't been much I had wanted that I hadn't been able to get. I traveled whenever and wherever the spirit moved me. Graduated from the college of my choice and landed my dream job. Had friends all over the world, including a double handful I could count on through thick and thin.

Lovers? A few. But being on call twenty-four hours a day, hanging out in precinct houses and seedy neighborhoods, and working late six nights out of seven because you're trying to make deadline and be first with the story aren't conducive to romance. Plus, men tend to get grumpy if they're pillow talking in one ear, and a micro-bud scanner squawks, "One eighty-seven on Geary," in the other.

So far, nobody remotely resembling Mister Right is on the horizon, but I'm not crying in my beer. If he's out there, he's worth waiting for. If he's not, I can always get a cat.

Either way. As long as I can keep doing my job.

See, I love my job. I loved it when I was chasing fire engines, and I love it even more now that I've graduated to major crime. One unlamented former boyfriend claims I'm married to the job. In all honesty, I can't say he's wrong, even if he is a jerk.

I've also been called an action junkie. Another undeniable truth. Nothing lights my fire like that first whiff of a story. Pitting myself against perpetrators unknown—including, sad to say, the occasional crooked cop, CEO, or politician—is the highest high I know. But that's not the main reason I do what I do. As corny as it sounds, I do this job because I believe somebody has to speak up for the victims, lend a helping hand (or give a hard shove) to the long arm of the law, and turn over the rocks to expose the creepy crawlies of this world. If you ask my opinion, the work I'm doing is important and worthwhile, and I hope I'm making a difference.

But if the night of September fourth taught me anything, it taught me the world has a way of grabbing you by the throat when you least expect it. I was cruising along as smooth as silk until the Ferrymen entered the picture, and my life erupted in fire and blood. Now life and I never would, never *could*, be the way we were before the explosion. But if Hell's Boatmen had hoped to get rid of me, their plan had backfired.

Not that the memory of that night didn't have the power to rock me. Now that my memory was back, I woke up in a sweat more often than not, heart pounding like a kettle drum. The faces of Evander Cuey and Sammy Michaels never left me. I could still picture the mutilated corpse of my informant. I was a smidge less cocky and a lot more aware of the price to be paid, and the chill of my close brush with death stuck with me like a shadow. Everybody says experience is the best teacher, but nobody tells you how ruthless she can be. Take it from me, an up-close-and-personal run-in with pure evil will leave you in a world of hurt.

Unfortunately for the black hats, physical and emotional wounds weren't the only souvenirs I had taken away from our last skirmish. That explosion in the warehouse district ignited a short, hot fuse in my gut. I was more determined than ever to do whatever I could to bring the Ferrymen down. All the way.

Was I afraid? Am I a moron? Of course, I was afraid. The thought of a rematch turned my knees to tofu. And there was my family to consider. Threats against my own life were daunting enough, but would I be able to live with myself if the Ferrymen came after one or, God forbid, *all* of my family members because of me? I wouldn't dodge the question. Denial wasn't an option. Either I went to war with my eyes wide open, counting the possible cost beforehand, or I didn't go at all.

Bottom line, I wasn't sure I could survive a strike against my family mentally intact. But after hours of agonized soul-searching, I reached an iron-clad conclusion. I couldn't let anything stop me, not while Murder, Incorporated was still running rampant.

Knowing my family would agree took the edge off my guilt. Some, anyway. Oh, the entire clan would argue both themselves and me blue in the face when they found out I was headed back into the fray. But they would come around in the end, because Mom and Dad were the ones who raised my brothers and me to believe the world can only work the way it's supposed to if we all watch out for one another.

When Dad was first elected to the Northern Continental Assembly, he had a framed parchment hung on the wall of his office directly across from his massive mahogany desk, where he would see it while he worked. He told us the quote from Edmund Burke was a reminder. It said, "All that is necessary for the triumph of evil is that good men do nothing."

Or as I like to say, when it comes to standing for the right and against the wrong, nobody gets a pass.

I've never admitted it to a living soul, but that quote is one of the reasons I became a crime reporter. I wasn't going to turn my back on that guiding principle at this late date, simply because the evil in question was armed and dangerous and knew my name.

Jack Eagan wanted me to drop out of sight, and I would. For a while. During the next couple months I would give myself a chance to heal and get back in shape physically. I would regroup psychologically. But while I was at it, I would dig deeper for information I could use against Hell's Boatmen and come up with a strategy. When the time was right, I would warn my family, so they could take steps to protect themselves.

Then I planned to come out swinging.

Chapter 13

"Curtain down, kill the lights!" Doctor Klein chuckled merrily. "A small play on words inspired by the sizable audience gathered in this room. As a member of the Oxford University Drama Society, I once imagined I would go into the theater. That was before medicine seduced me away from the footlights, of course."

"Well, you certainly haven't forgotten how to make an entrance," Dad drawled.

"Thank you. It's nice to know I haven't lost my touch." I heard footsteps approach the lounger where I sat on the proverbial pins and needles. "And how is our patient this morning? Ready for the grand unveiling?"

I nodded. "More than."

"All right, we'll take it step by step. Blinds closed." I heard them hum quietly in response as Klein commanded the lights to dim and continued, "We don't want too much light. In fact, I'll ask one of the family members to close the door."

"I'll do it," said Jim. Then, "I'm sorry, this is a private room."

"I know." Jack's voice. "My name is Eagan, Counselor. Jack Eagan with CIIS."

"I see." Jim's tone dropped a degree or two below friendly. "Well, you've come at a bad time, Agent Eagan. My sister can't answer questions right now. The doctor is about to remove the bandages."

"I'm not here to ask questions."

"Why exactly *are* you here?" Dad asked.

"I invited him," I interjected.

"Why?"

"It's complicated, Bri. Look, I'll explain, I promise. But can we please wait until *after* the bandages come off? I'm tired of dark."

Mom jumped in. "Of course you are. Please come in and close the door, Agent Eagan."

"Thank you."

"Apparently, I'm not the only one who knows how to make a dramatic entrance," said Doctor Klein. "If this were a play, I would have to say, 'The plot thickens.'" Without missing a beat, he shifted gears. "Nurse Baker, would you bring me that stool and the instrument tray? Thank you. Now, young lady, I'm going to remove the bandages, but that will *not* be your cue to open your eyes. Do you understand?" I nodded. "Good. We'll first cleanse the area—gently, of course—to remove any dried discharge. I'll tell you when to open."

"Okay."

His touch was feather-light as he gently peeled the adhesive away from my left cheek. He worked slowly, patiently loosening the edges before carefully lifting the patch from my eye. He repeated the painstaking procedure on my right eye. Cool air kissed my eyelids for the first time in almost two months. They felt nearly weightless without the dressings, and I had to fight a sudden urge to let them drift open.

Doctor Klein must have read my mind.

"Not yet," he murmured. "A little more patience. Gauze pad, please."

The damp, chilly caress of the pad felt heavenly.

"She appears to have healed nicely," Klein decided, delicately swabbing the area around my right eye. "Do you agree, Marisol?"

"Absolutely," said Rodriguez.

"Another pad, please." He shifted his attention to the left eye. "There. That's good." His touch vanished. "All right, Amanda, listen carefully. I'll count to three. When I say, 'Three,' I want you to open your eyes. Don't be concerned if your vision is blurry for the first minute or two; that should clear quickly. Do you have any questions?"

I licked my lips. "No."

"All right, on three." You could have heard a pin drop on a cotton ball as the doctor counted, "One ... two ...."

A million thoughts raced through my mind in the breath

between *two* and *three*. Irrational fears that maybe the transplant didn't take. Fleeting thoughts about how a few weeks spent in darkness could seem like a lifetime. Brief mental snapshots of cherished faces taut with anticipation.

"Three," said Klein.

I slowly opened my eyes.

And there was light.

It spilled softly between the slats in the blinds, bathing the room in faint, cool early-morning-white and forming a pale nimbus behind the head of the man seated on a low, wheeled stool directly in front of me. I put him a year or two on the far side of sixty. Except for bushy eyebrows and a small gray goatee, he was as bald as a billiard ball. He was dressed in a white lab coat over a dark shirt and slacks. His rounded features were gently blurred, almost as if I were seeing him through a gauzy veil.

My gaze shifted to the petite woman standing behind him, leaning toward me as she peered over his left shoulder. Her eyes were warm and dark under black, angel-wing brows. Flawless complexion, full lips, and a mane of black curls swept up on the sides and cascading down her back. If it hadn't been for the scrubs and white lab coat, I would have taken her for a model. No wonder Kev wanted her number. Doctor Marisol Rodriguez was drop-dead gorgeous.

Right beside her stood a man who could only be Dennis. For once my mental portrait was close. He *was* dark and lean and looked dangerous, but he wasn't as tall as I had imagined. Around five-eight, if I had to guess. His hair was short and black. When he realized I was staring at him, he bobbed his eyebrows and grinned.

I grinned back, then turned my attention to the two people standing a few feet to my right, their backs to the bed. Mom was leaning against Dad's side, hands clasped nervously at her waist. The electric-blue silk of her jumpsuit contrasted vividly with his long-sleeved red polo. Dad had one arm around her shoulders, his hand absently caressing her upper arm. Had she always looked so tiny standing next to him?

My heart swelled. Unable to take my eyes off my parents, I offered them a wobbly smile. "Hi, Mom and Dad. Long time no see."

Mom released a sound that was half-sob, half-laugh. "Oh,

Amanda!"

"That's my girl," Dad chuckled.

"Like I said, a tough nut."

I tracked Dickson's voice to his position at the foot of the bed. He was wearing his signature outfit: black suit, white shirt, black tie, and black five-o'clock shadow. I couldn't see clearly enough to be sure, but his usual stern expression might have been softened by the barest hint of a smile.

"Hey, Dickson," I said, and he nodded.

Next I transferred my attention to the two beaming men flanking him. Both Kev and Bri wore jeans, but where Kevin wore a blue button-down shirt, Bri had opted for an unbelievably loud tie-dyed t-shirt under a black windbreaker.

"Hi, guys. Nice shirt, Bri."

"I thought you would like it," he said, smoothing a hand down the front. "I wanted to give you a chance to road test those new peepers on something with a hint of color."

Kevin arched a brow. "You call neon pink, fire-engine red, lemon yellow, and lime green a *hint* of color? You practically blinded *me* with that get-up."

"Yeah, but you're a pansy," Brian smirked, and I was so darned happy to be able to see that smart-aleck grin again, I almost broke my own rule and bawled like a baby. Thankfully, I chose that moment to glance back at Doctor Klein. He winked.

"Where did you pick up that relic, anyway?" Jim asked, drawing my attention stage left.

Dressed in a beige crewneck sweater and brown slacks, he leaned against the corner where the wall behind my lounger formed a ninety-degree angle with the short stretch of wall that ran back toward the door. I couldn't actually see the door from where I was sitting, but I had groped my way around this room often enough to know where it was.

Jim's arms were folded across his chest, his head cocked in critical appraisal as he stared at Bri. "Clearance sale at the Smithsonian, right?"

"Uh-uh. I found the instructions online."

"You *made* it?"

"Do I look like the crafty type?" Bri grinned like a pirate. "Bambi took care of the hands-on stuff."

"Blonde Bambi?" asked Kevin in obvious disbelief. "Long

legs and an MBA from Rutgers? *That* Bambi?"

Eyes dancing, Klein turned to face the room and held up a hand. "I hate to interrupt this extremely interesting discussion, but I still have a few pesky medical details to take care of before we can release your sister."

"Of course, Doctor." Dad shot a patiently amused glance at each of my brothers before turning back to the surgeon. "Please go ahead with your examination."

"Thank you. I'll try to be quick." He turned back to me. "Now, Amanda. How does the world look to you?"

"Better and better. Coming into focus pretty quickly now."

"Excellent." He held up an index finger. "Please watch my finger. Don't turn your head as I move it, but follow it only with your eyes. All right?" I nodded, tracking the finger as he moved it up, down, right, left. "Ah, yes," he murmured, "muscle attachment appears to be good, motor functions are normal." He lowered his hand and picked up a slim, silver device from the instrument tray to his right. "Please look over my right shoulder. Yes, like that. Now keep your eyes steady, while I scan the internal structures."

He did a slow pass in front of each eye, then poked the scanner's minuscule touch screen. Two colorful, three-dimensional images materialized in the air between us, rotating slowly under gentle flicks of the doctor's fingers.

"Look," said Bri. "Anti-grav eyeballs."

Focused intently on the images, Klein smiled. "*Beautiful* eyeballs. I should know, I made them myself!" He examined the images a while longer, then dabbed the screen again. The holograms vanished as he turned to me with a wide smile. "As a matter of fact, I would say those eyeballs are close to perfect."

Doctor Rodriguez was smiling, too. "Congratulations, Amanda."

"The only task remaining," said Klein, lifting a soft case from the instrument tray, "is to give you your aftercare instructions." He reached into the case and pulled out a pair of glasses with wire earpieces and smoky, rimless lenses. He held them up. "In any light brighter than this, yes?"

"For how long?"

"Two weeks, at least. After that, you can try going without them. If you experience sensitivity, wear them for another week, then try again." He slipped the glasses back into the case and handed it to me. Next he picked up a white bottle. "Your medication, formulated to strengthen the regenerated optic nerves. Two drops in each eye, three times a day for two weeks."

"Got it," I said, as he passed me the prescription.

"Well, then." He slapped his knees and got to his feet. "My work here is done."

I stood, too, offering my hand, which he took. "I don't know how to thank you," I said.

Patting the back of my hand with his free one, he said, "If you want to thank me, take care of yourself. Avoid explosive situations."

"*Amen!*" Mom seconded with feeling.

"I'll sure try."

Doctor Klein moved over to shake hands with Mom and Dad, and Doctor Rodriguez took his place.

"You've been a terrific patient, Amanda," she said, then turned to Kevin before I could answer. "I'll see you later."

"Pick you up at eight," he agreed, and nobody seemed surprised but me.

"How long has this been going on?"

Rodriguez gave me a very *un*-doctor-like grin. "Since you told me he wanted my number."

"The patient is always the last to know," I decided with a sigh, then wrapped her in a quick, light hug. "Let me know if he gets out of line," I murmured for her ears only. "We'll gang up on him."

"Deal," she whispered, tossing Kevin a smug smile as she followed Klein out.

"What was that all about?"

I turned to see my youngest brother eying me suspiciously. "None of your business."

Mom shook her head, but she was smiling ear to ear. "Some things never change." Her smile softened as she crossed the space between us to take both my hands in hers. "Get dressed, Amanda Joy. We're taking you home."

"I'm afraid that won't be possible," said Jack, speaking for the first time since he had arrived and sparing me the need to come up with a reply.

Dad drew himself up to his full senatorial height. "I beg

your pardon?"

"She can't go home yet, Senator."

He had been standing by the door where I couldn't see him, probably trying to give the family as much privacy as he could. But now that push was about to come to shove, he moved into the center of the room, giving me my first look at him. He turned to face me, and my breath caught. Dennis was right. It was easy to see how Jack Eagan got his nickname.

Iceman.

Chapter 14

Slipping my fingertips into the back pockets of my jeans and tucking my tongue firmly in cheek, I rocked back on my heels and sized up the faded gray sedan parked near UCSF Mount Zion's rear loading dock. *Tired* was the first adjective that came to mind.

"Nice ride, Agent Eagan."

Jack opened the passenger-side door and gave the small of my back a climb-in nudge. "I wasn't after *nice* this trip. I was more in the market for *nondescript.*"

He waited for me to angle my legs in, then closed the door before turning around for a last word with Jim. Watching them together, I couldn't help but shake my head. They were roughly the same height and build, but Eagan had a look about him, an indefinable quality that put him in a class all by himself.

In his black jeans and a white long-sleeved t-shirt, he could have been the Norse god Thor incognito. His hair and eyebrows where white-blond, his features chiseled and angular—strong jaw, slightly cleft chin, firm lips. His eyes were his most striking feature by far. They were a pale, icy blue, and when he turned them on you, it was like getting zapped with a laser.

Or maybe that was just my reaction.

The two men shook hands. My brother nodded to me as Eagan rounded the hood and slid into the driver's seat.

"Ready to go?" he said.

"I guess." I was still gazing at Jim. I smiled as we traded a thumbs-up. "Wish I could have had more time with them."

"Soon," he promised and started the engine.

Jim gave me a final wave and ducked back through the service entrance to join the rest of the family in my hospital room. News of my release had been withheld and the hospital staff sworn to secrecy, in order to give Eagan a chance to sneak me away.

"Cheer up." Jack swung the coupe out of the access drive and hung a right on Divisadero. "You'll be back with your family before you know it."

Maybe, maybe not. Once I made my next move against the Ferrymen, all reunion bets would be off. Of course, Jack wasn't aware of the fact that I was planning a return engagement, and I didn't intend to enlighten him. Eagan struck me as the protective type, the *let's lock her up in a safe house for her own good and throw away the key* type. So I smiled and nodded and kept my mouth shut.

"Let's take the scenic route to the outer loop," he said as he slipped neatly around a Metro-Hover pulling over to the curb, where two men and a woman waited in the enclosed bus stop. Earlier in the evening the stop would have been crowded with commuters, but it was after eight on a Friday night, and the nine-to-fivers had all gone home to the burbs. "I swept for tracking devices, but I want to make sure nobody decides to do the job the old-fashioned way and tail us."

I angled around to face him. "Any reason to think somebody might try?"

"Nope. But I didn't live to the ripe old age of thirty-eight by making assumptions and taking chances."

"Guess not."

He hung two more rights, followed by a quick left into the heart of the shopping district, where I immediately got distracted by the passing scenery, devouring the sights like a visitor to a strange new world. Columbus had nothing on me as I rediscovered light, color, and motion. My eyes drank in wide, bright windows framing kinetic displays peddling chocolaty mink coats or canary-yellow parasails. The end of October was still nine days off, but buildings on both sides of the street were already breaking out in cheerful splotches of red and green. Rivers of pedestrians streamed down the sidewalks. I saw a woman in a black cashmere coat pushing a stroller and found myself smiling at her bright-eyed, apple-cheeked baby as the kiddo gleefully gummed the tuft of yarn at the tail-end of her hot-pink stocking cap.

"Your family took it well," Jack said. "The fact that you

had to go away for a while, I mean. They never even asked where I'm taking you."

"Because they understand the whys and wherefores. This isn't the first time the Gregsons have had to deal with death threats, you know. Not that anybody has specifically threatened to kill me," I hastened to add. "Not in so many words."

His lips quirked sardonically. "You don't think so? I would be interested in hearing exactly what your definition of *being threatened* is, then."

"Dad gets it all the time," I continued, ignoring the jab. "There's always some whack job ready to vote his or her least favorite politician out of office with a lucky headshot. Jim gets his share, too."

Jack slid the coupe into the left lane. "Stands to reason in his line of work. It's not unheard of for an ex-con with blood in his eye to go after the prosecutor who put him away."

My oldest brother is district attorney for the city-state of Columbia, a global hub of political power even before the unification. In its heyday, D.C. was the capital of the old United States. Now the District has to settle for being one of three capitals for Tri-America, the other two being Ottawa and Mexico City. The government rotates between them, meaning the executive, legislative, and judicial branches switch their collective base of operations once every two years. Sort of like musical chairs, except everybody gets a seat. The locations are symbolic, anyway, since most federal business is conducted electronically, but the symbolism helps keep the constituents happy.

"Speaking of your brother Jim," Eagan continued, "I half expected him to insist on tagging along. I'm glad he and I didn't have to go a round before I could convince him that would have been a bad idea."

"Bart gave your plan his seal of approval. If he says a plan is all right, then it is." I paused, brow furrowed. "I get why they agreed to my going away; what I don't get is the enthusiasm. Nobody in my family ever ran from a fight. How come they're so gung ho about *me* running?"

"Come on, A.J., you know why. They nearly lost you."

"But they didn't, and I'm all right now."

Jack shook his head. "You're still not a hundred percent.

Until you are, and until we're sure the Ferrymen aren't actively hunting you, your family wants you to play it safe. What's so strange about that? And don't think of it as running, think of it as staging a strategic withdrawal."

"Uh-huh."

A comfortable silence settled between us. The show outside my window recaptured my attention when Jack took another left and cruised into the theater district. Not even my tinted glasses could dim the jewel-like brilliance of marquees glittering in the crisp October air. Streetlights dropped soft circles on sidewalks, washing pedestrians in a soft white ebb-and-flow. Lines snaked up to the brightly lit doors of restaurants, people laughing and chatting as they waited under canopies for their tables. Limos and taxis swarmed the curbs, dropped their passengers, and glided off again. Details leaped out at me: a coat collar turned up against the first nip of fall; a scrap of white paper skittering down the sidewalk; a red silk scarf, fringed at the end.

Eventually, the bright lights and bustle fell behind us, and we rolled into the Tenderloin, where darkness stalks the gaps between buildings. Here the night is barely held at bay by the tentative glow from corner mom-and-pops and the garish auras of massage parlors, bars, and adult bookstores. These are the city's mean streets, where windows are barred and the NFPD maintains a constant, visible presence.

Where street people with no warmth to go home to at the end of the day fold in, wrap themselves in their bony arms, and hang on with chattering teeth.

Where sharp-eyed packs of angry young men lurk in doorways and stake claims on street corners, taunting one another from a distance and talking trash to the ladies.

Where girls troll the sidewalks wearing a yard of fabric, skyscraper heels, and a brittle shield of forced bravado. Their too-old eyes are haunted by dark memories, darker fears, and the tattered remnants of stolen innocence.

Watching a scrawny black-and-white dog scavenge in the gutter, I told myself a person would have to be nuts to want to see this, let alone miss it when she couldn't. But I did, and I had.

Because out of sight is out of mind, and I don't want to forget.

The job takes me to neighborhoods as bad this and worse on a regular basis, and the people I meet there have taught me three lessons you can't learn anywhere else. One, we're all cut from the same flawed cloth. Two, no human life is more important than another. And three, if we could learn to care about other folks as much as we care about ourselves, streets like these wouldn't be nearly as mean.

Jack drove on. Next stop, Nob Hill. Imagine going from Hades to Mount Olympus in one short hop, and you'll get a general idea of the contrast.

We passed Huntington Park—top-of-the-world, green, well-manicured—nestled between the Grace Cathedral and the recently completed reincarnation of the Union Pacific Club. Down the arrow-straight sidewalk bisecting the park's center, I could see the softly lit, twice-restored Fountain of the Tortoises, streams of water from cherubs' cheeks arcing into the luminous basin below. An elderly couple strolled toward Taylor Street, hand-in-hand. Both were gray-haired and wrapped in expensive taupe all-weather coats, but where he was tall and thin, she was short and softly rounded. Ditto the dachshund waddling at the end of the thin leash loosely held in the man's left hand.

"You all right?" Jack asked.

I glanced over at him. "Fine, why?"

"You're quiet. I thought something might be bothering you."

"No, I was just looking at ...." I shrugged. "Just looking."

"I guess you've got some catching up to do," he said with a smile.

I smiled back. "Seems like." I watched him check the rearview display and straightened in my seat. "How are we doing?"

"Looks clear. We'll double back and loop Union Square again, to be sure. If we're still clean, we'll be good to go."

Thirty minutes later, we veered onto an exit for 80, heading east. Jack gave the voice prompt for flight mode and the SkyCoupe's scissor wings swung smoothly out from the vehicle's belly as the tires retracted into the wheel wells with a muted *thump*. When he engaged the thrusters, the worn sedan leaped toward the outbound tier like a high-strung filly bolting from the starting gate, pressing us back against the seats as we rapidly gained altitude.

I stared at Jack, both eyebrows raised. "Pretty spry for a middle-aged coupe."

He patted the dashboard. "She may be middle-aged on the outside, but she's state-of-the-art at heart." He activated the flight display. Speed, altitude, air traffic, and navigational data materialized in color, forming a heads-up hologram on the windshield. "We'll head up to fifteen thousand feet," he decided. "Traffic looks light clear across the heartland. It'll pick up some as we approach the Pennsylvania border, but we'll exit before we get tangled up in that mess around the Metroplex." The computer took over the piloting chores. Jack leaned back in his seat and pinned me with that glacier-blue gaze. "How are you holding up?"

"Who, me? I'm in great shape."

"The important thing now is not to get ahead of yourself. It's easy to get carried away at this stage and think you're stronger than you are, but you need time to heal. The physical injuries are bad enough, but a hit like you took leaves wounds that don't show. Fear, maybe — the kind that gives you nightmares and wakes you up in a cold sweat. You have to learn to deal with it. Then there's the second guessing. You go over each decision you made — once, twice, a hundred times — asking yourself what you could have done differently. It takes a while to trust your instincts again."

I searched his face. "The voice of experience?"

He smiled faintly. "I've been around that block a few times."

"You seem to have rebounded all right."

"So far," he agreed, but his tone made it clear he didn't intend to elaborate.

The reporter in me was dying for details, but the fresh bruise in my own soul wouldn't let me push for them. I decided to change the subject. "Tell me about this place you're taking me. I never heard of Hobson's Hope."

"Neither has anyone else, and the town council would just as soon keep it that way."

"How come?"

"It goes back to the reason the town was founded in the first place. It was the brainchild of a group called Salvage Our Collective Karma, or —"

"SOCK? As in, argyle?"

"Yeah. I guess they didn't think that one through. Anyway, SOCK was started by an eccentric billionaire named Whitfield Hobson and his wife, Abigail. Seems Mr. and Mrs. H blamed overcrowded cities and modern architecture for," Jack sketched quotes in the air, *"the dehumanization of the individual, resulting in a serious decline in the moral and intellectual fiber of society.* They figured society's only hope was to get back to its grassroots. Scrap the big, nasty cities in favor of friendlier, more intimate communities capable of nurturing the human spirit. The only problem was, their crusade to win hearts and minds fell flat. So about fifty years ago Whitfield and Abigail and the handful of likeminded folks they *did* manage to recruit built Hobson's Hope on the banks of the Monongahela. Current population around three thousand.

"Town's a throwback. Well, except for a few instances where the old technology would cause more problems than it solved. Computers and transportation, mostly. Even Hopers aren't purists enough to waste time and money putting up factories to build and maintain equipment that could only be used within city limits and would never meet modern environmental guidelines. They've settled for a compromise— tolerate quantum computers and limit inner-city traffic to the ground tier. But the rest is pure twentieth-century. Broad, quiet, tree-lined streets; mismatched assortment of old-fashioned houses with white picket fences. Nobody is in a hurry, and everybody knows everybody else." He paused. "You might feel like you've fallen headfirst through a time warp, but it's the perfect place to drop out and get some legitimate R&R."

"Wouldn't I be better off in one of those big, nasty, overcrowded cities?" I suggested wistfully. Hobson's Hope sounded like Dullsville on a slow day. "Someplace where I could lose myself among those poor, dehumanized masses?"

"You would never see the Ferrymen coming. I don't care how good their operatives are, it's almost impossible for a stranger to blend in and move freely in terrain like Hobson's Hope, and that's assuming even they know the place exists. It's not on any map I know of."

"*You* know about it."

"Only because an old friend of mine is descended from

one of the founders and decided to run the family boarding house when she retired. Trust me, A.J., this town is the best-kept secret of the twenty-first century. You couldn't find a safer place."

Chapter 15

The sprawling Philadelphia/New York Metroplex was a glow on the horizon when we started our final approach, banking south over Pittsburgh. Jack took manual control and dropped us smoothly through the ever-present smudge-pot overcast before merging with traffic on the Beltway. As we turned east again, the radiant grid of the city slid out from under our wing tips, the lights growing fewer and farther apart until nothing but dense, dark landscape rolled beneath us. We descended almost to street level, skimming ten feet above a two-lane ribbon that wound through thickly forested hills.

The headlights snared a mother raccoon and four kits strung across the road ahead. I caught a fleeting glimpse of eyes glowing an otherworldly yellow, then a flurry of movement as the coupe swept overhead and sent the whole family scrambling for the brushy shoulder.

"Wouldn't it be quicker to take the inbound loop?"

"We're on the inbound loop, such as it is," said Eagan. He lowered the tires, waited for them to kiss the pavement, then retracted the wings. "The good citizens of Hobson's Hope don't want to make it too easy for outsiders to find them. They don't even broadcast standard navigational coordinates."

Gazing out at the tangle of trees and bushes crowding both sides of the road, I was reminded of the old country lanes that snaked through the foothills back home. "This burg *is* out in the middle of nowhere, isn't it?"

"That was the general idea. Whitfield and Abigail bought up every available acre for fifty miles around and bequeathed it to the town with an ironclad prohibition against development outside prescribed city limits."

"What about development *within* prescribed city limits?"

"Tightly controlled to the point of being nonexistent."

"So to recap, we're talking about a community with serious aversions to publicity, tourism, and civic growth." I lifted one hand, palm up. "What keeps this town from dying on the vine?"

"When people want something badly enough, they'll do whatever it takes to find it. There *are* people out there — probably more than anyone realizes — who feel lost. Overwhelmed by our high-rise, high-tech rat race. They wish they could go back to a simpler way of life, dream about a place where their lives seem to matter. A thin but steady stream of those types finds its way to Hobson's Hope. It's almost like they've got a homing instinct." He shrugged. "As hokey as that sounds, I can't explain it any better. However it happens, the population stays pretty constant."

"Hm."

"What?"

I shrugged. "Sounds like you've given it some thought. You obviously like this town. I would even go so far as to bet you've been there more than once."

"Your point?"

"I don't get it. You're no more cut out for the peaceful, small-town life than I am. Lost-and-overwhelmed people yearning for the simple life don't go into the Teams. They don't join CIIS."

"Maybe not, but even people like us need a break in the action now and then — a place where we can get away, let down our guard a little, and pretend we're regular folks. Hobson's Hope is that kind of place. Speaking of which ...." He swung the coupe into a left-hand turn. "We're here."

The woods opened onto a street lined with houses. I saw three ranchers and two Cape Cods before Jack eased the SkyCoupe down in front of a three-story, brick Dutch Colonial. The car's safety locks disengaged, and we climbed out, Jack heading for a gate that swung open on well-oiled hinges, me pausing by the black wrought-iron fence for a look-see.

The narrow walk beelined to a front door flanked by twin lanterns glowing a soft, welcoming yellow. Two dormers jutted from the third story above an overhang that shaded a broad, wrap-around porch where five slat-backed rockers sat behind a rail strung between four plump wooden pillars. The neat lawn was lushly bordered by mums and canopied by the branches of two graceful sugar maples shedding a light carpet of leaves. The air was crisp and clean, the silence unbroken until Jack used the brass knocker, cuing a dog down the street to bark twice.

Almost immediately a light popped on behind the frosted glass panels set in the top half of the door. I hustled through the gate and up the walk, arriving on the porch as the door opened to reveal a small woman wearing red leggings, an oversized Philadelphia Phillies sweatshirt that hung almost to her knees, and fluffy white bunny slippers. Her café au lait complexion was unlined, despite the light frosting of gray in her close-cropped hair. Her nose was freckled, her eyes wide and almond-shaped, her lips generous. Big gold hoops dangled from her ears. I guessed her height at around five feet, weight at around a hundred five.

That made her maybe eighteen inches taller and fifteen pounds lighter than the dog at her side, an oversized pooch I judged to be a terrier-biker mix. Fido was brindled and shaggy, with a flat-top haircut, gunslinger's eyes, and a snazzy goatee. His black-leather collar bristled with heavy metal studs. Well, of course it did.

"It's about time," the woman said. "Come on in out of the cold." She and the dog backed up to let us pass.

We stepped into a narrow entryway with gleaming oak floors and buttery walls. A stairway rose to the right, an archway to our left opened onto a spacious, high-ceilinged parlor. All I could see of that room from where I stood were two tall windows framed in white lace and fitted with louvered shutters, the curve of a braided-oval rug, a cane-backed rocker draped with a moss-green afghan, and a short stretch of fireplace mantle.

Our hostess closed the door and turned to face us, hands on hips. "We thought maybe you forgot how to get here," she said, flicking a glance toward her pet. "Didn't we Cosmo?"

The dog said, "Urmm," and gave an infinitesimal wag of his stubby tail, but his hooded gaze was locked on me. Sizing me up.

"He knows better than that. Don't you, buddy?" Jack said, squatting to give him an ear-rub. Without looking away from me, Biker Dog leaned into the caress. Eagan stood and gestured toward our hostess. "Amanda Gregson, meet Saditha Carter, owner and operator of Hobson's Hope's finest boarding house."

"Hobson's Hope's *only* boarding house." I broke eye contact with the dog and shook the offered hand, intrigued by the combination of flawless French manicure and hard calluses. "And you can call me Sadie."

"A.J."

"I know who you are." Sadie tipped her head toward her dog. "This here's Cosmo."

"So I gathered," I said, bending at the waist to hold out my hand, palm down, fingers tucked. "Hey, boy."

Cosmo stepped up to give my hands and jeans a thorough sniffing-over. We were almost nose-to-nose when our eyes met again. Was it my imagination, or had that steely gaze warmed slightly? The tail-stump twitched. Once.

"He likes you," said Sadie.

"How can you tell?" I rubbed Cosmo's brush cut and straightened.

"You've still got all your fingers," said Jack.

"Naw, he wouldn't bite you. At least, I don't think so. But you got the wag. You two are going be *good* friends. I can tell." Sadie waved toward the living room. "Go on in and take a load off. I'll be right back." She headed down the hallway, leaving Jack and me to trail after Biker Dog.

"Cozy," I said, glancing around the parlor.

The home fire was burning, the built-in floor-to-ceiling bookcases were packed with books, four cushy wing chairs were grouped around a table, and the sofa had big, rolled arms. The wall above it was a mosaic of three-dimensional stills in recessed frames.

Cosmo thumped down in front of the fireplace as I wandered over to look at the photo gallery. The collection included shots of every kind of scenery imaginable. Golden, grassy plains undulating beneath a cloudless, faded-denim sky. The bleak, green-and-tan moonscape of a high desert, thick with lemon sage but devoid of a single tree. One long rectangular frame captured a tangled green struggle for sunlight as tree ferns, lianas, and pitcher plants pushed up through rotting leaves on a rainforest floor toward the unseen canopy towering overhead.

I peered into the bright-aqua translucence of an egg-shaped ice cave and asked, "Did Sadie take these?"

"Yeah," Jack said, coming over to stand next to me. "Good, isn't she?"

"They should be hanging in a gallery. Has she sold any?"

"No, she has *not*," replied the woman in question, striding through the archway. The wooden tray she carried held three heavy stoneware mugs, a jar of honey, and a cream pitcher. "And I don't intend to, either. It's a hobby that's all." She set the tray on the coffee table.

"Some hobby." But recognizing the *subject closed* tone, I left it at that. "This is a great house, Sadie."

She smiled fondly, revealing a narrow gap between her upper front teeth. "It is, isn't it? I inherited it from Great Aunt Elise. The perfect retirement plan." She pointed to the sofa. "You two come on over here and have some tea. It's chamomile with a touch of vanilla, and it'll make you sleep like babies."

As Jack and I obediently sank into the sofa's deep leather cushions, I realized the day was starting to catch up with me. On second thought, it was miles ahead of me. Damn. Since when did riding shotgun for a measly two hours leave me wrung out like a well-used dishrag?

Since you almost got blown to pieces?

Well, there was that. Choosing a mug, I spooned honey into my tea and reminded myself to cut me some slack.

Sadie picked up her mug and settled into the rocker. Using the toe of her right foot for leverage, she rocked gently and said, "Okay, Jack. What's up? All I know at this point is, three weeks ago you called to ask if I would have a room available—the one I reserve for *special* guests. When I said I would, you told me I was about to get a tenant, maybe for a couple months."

"That about sums it up."

"Uh, uh, uh," she disagreed, wagging a finger at him. "You show up at *two* in the morning, and you're not flying solo like you usually do. This time you've got a good-looking woman with you, but it's as plain as paint you two aren't an item." She shot me a semi-apologetic glance. "He always was kind of slow off the mark that way." Jack choked on his tea as she explained, "Not that women don't fall all over him, but he's married to the Service."

I hid a grin by lifting my mug to my lips. "Is that so?"

"Believe it, sister." She refocused on Eagan. "So my new tenant is a Pulitzer Prize-winning crime reporter. But not just *any* Pulitzer winner. Oh, no. You bring me the daughter of the Speaker of the Senate, a woman whose family has enough money to make a hefty dent in the national deficit. What gives, Jack?" She jabbed the index finger at him. "And *don't* try to tell me she's on vacation. You're no travel agent."

Eagan's lips curved. "Been doing your homework. Nice to know you haven't lost your touch."

"Lost my touch!" She snorted. "You *know* that'll be the day. Now stop trying to change the subject and tell me what's going on."

"A.J. needs to keep a low profile for a while."

She considered this as she sipped her tea. "How low?"

"No need to get drastic." His eyes lit with humor. "Don't break out the surveillance cams and motion detectors. I don't think she's in any immediate danger at this point, especially not here." He looked at me and cocked an eyebrow. "Not as long as you don't try to contact anybody back in the world and keep your byline to yourself until we're sure they're satisfied with a warning."

"They who?" Sadie asked.

"The Ferrymen."

She gave a soft, low whistle. "I wondered." She eyed me with a curious mixture of respect and pity. "I followed your series. Nice work, but you went up against some heavy hitters."

"The heaviest," I agreed.

"So what happened?"

Unsure about how much I should let on, I looked to Jack to take the lead. He started to fill her in. I kept waiting for him to block her next question with the All-purpose Junior G-Man Need-to-know Copout. He didn't. Not once. Twenty minutes later, Sadie Carter had the whole, unedited story.

I may have been asleep in my seat, but the old intuition was vibrating like a tuning fork. What did this uncharacteristic chattiness tell me? Eagan's trust in her ran deep. Furthermore, she knew exactly what questions to ask. Taken separately *or* together, those facts said there was more to my new landlady than met the eye. I suddenly had a hundred questions, but I knew neither of them would give me answers. Yet. I would, of course, get answers eventually. Reference rule number two: *Dig until you find the truth.*

Sadie gazed at me thoughtfully before turning back to Jack. "Okay, they've got to think they put the fear of God into her. So maybe the situation isn't that serious."

"That's what I keep telling him."

He gave me the laser eyes. "And I keep telling you it's serious enough to be careful. You know the drill: If anybody asks, you're still recovering, you don't remember the accident, and you're here for a few weeks R&R. Right now, it looks like the Ferrymen aren't in any particular hurry to finish what they started. Don't give them any reason to change their minds, okay?"

"Okay."

I went along because the truth would have been messier. No telling what Eagan would do if I announced my intention to give the Ferrymen as many reasons as it took *to* change their minds, but it wouldn't be pleasant. Much tidier to tell him what he wanted to hear and remain a free agent. Meanwhile, if I played my cards right, the Ferrymen would elevate me to the number one spot on their hit parade in no time.

The tricky part would be surviving the upgrade.

Chapter 16

The truth breaks over me in an icy wave, and my gaze flies to the van. It's a setup! Gotta warn Cuey and Michaels!

I fling myself toward the mouth of the alley, but my feet have turned to cement; I can barely lift them. Straining every nerve and muscle, I manage a Quasimodo lope, heart hammering wildly as I lurch down the wet pavement. I try to scream a warning, but nothing comes out. I try again, the veins in my neck bulge with the effort, but the best I can do is a guttural, "Unnnhhh!"

The alley telescopes ahead of me, the dimly lit entrance receding until it's a faint pinpoint. I push on, push harder, push myself to the breaking point, but the distance between me and the street grows with each lumbering step. The warning shrieks in my skull, and I try again to force it out, straining so hard my head feels ready to explode. Finally, my lips part on a high, thin, wordless wail.

Too little. Too late.

The van erupts.

Space-time collapses, and suddenly, I'm a step and a heartbeat away from the onrushing holocaust. The fireball engulfs me, incinerating my eyes as the pressure wave slams me against unforgiving concrete, catapulting me headlong into oblivion.

My eyes popped open. I stared at the creamy expanse overhead and fought to get my bearings. *Not the alley, not the alley, not the alley,* looped desperately through my brain.

Not the alley. Sadie's boardinghouse.

I relaxed my white-knuckled grip on the comforter as the unbearable tension started to ebb. I sat up, folded my legs, and tucked my chin. Stayed that way for a couple minutes then tunneled my fingers through my hair, running my hands over the crown of my head and down the back of my neck. Palms clasped over my nape, chin resting on my chest, I waited for the dream to release me. When it finally did, I unbent with a sigh and stuffed two pillows behind my back, leaning against the sleigh bed's gently curved headboard, letting my gaze wander the room that was a world away from the alley of my dreams.

Two tall windows were set in the wall to the left of the bed, French doors to the right. Diffuse sunlight edged between heavy bronze drapes, fanning thin rays across golden-oak flooring, French-walnut furniture, and walls painted a delicate spring green. On the nightstand next to the bed, a colorful mix of mums filled the mouth of a squat glass vase. The arched mirror on the bow-front dresser against the far wall reflected the print hung over the bed. I tipped back my head and studied Chagall's *I and the Village*, a whimsical portrait-in-profile of a green, white-lipped man nose-to-nose with a smiling, doe-eyed sheep. Or maybe it was a goat. If only the world were that happy and innocent. Just me and my nonspecific farm animal trading sappy smiles and goo-goo eyes.

Of course, if the world *were* that happy and innocent, I would be out of a job.

Feeling calmer, I allowed my mind to circle back to the nightmare. Not being able to prevent or change what happened that night was the worst part. Watching Cuey and Michaels die over and over again left me feeling battered and haunted by failure.

Now, I realize good versus evil isn't a popular concept these days. Ninety-nine percent of us consider ourselves too sophisticated, educated, nonjudgmental, and scientifically advanced to believe in moral absolutes. We've grown comfortable living in the gray areas, where we never have to point a finger and say, "That is wrong."

Problem is, those gray areas exist mostly in our heads. Talk to the victim of a brutal gang rape or a child who has been beaten, starved, and locked in a closet for years on end, and you're faced with the truth. You can't hide behind moral ambiguities. You have to come down on one side or the other, because unadulterated, unrepentant evil does exist, and it eats away at mankind like a cancer.

My nightmare was a vivid reminder that two good men had died battling that malignancy. At least dreaming their sacrifice over and over again kept my determination to carry on their fight honed to a razor's edge. I ached to even the score. An eye for an eye? Maybe, but I preferred to think of it as answering a cry for justice. And no time like now to start.

Stretching my arms over my head, I flipped off the comforter and climbed out of bed. Padding across a square area rug veined with shades of green, I entered the elegant bathroom and leaned across the marble vanity to check my reflection in the mirror—a mistake that prompted a pained grimace. During my timeout at Mount Zion, the hair I usually wear pixie-short with a moderately spiky crown had grown into a bantam black busby. Granted, I'm not one-tenth as fashion-conscious as Mom, but even I draw the line at helmet hair. A trip to the nearest salon was definitely in order.

I whipped off the 2-X gray jersey that doubles as my bathing suit cover-up and sleep shirt, let it puddle on the floor, and stepped into the tiled overhead shower. Dialing up a hot, gentle stream, I tipped back my head and closed my eyes. Holy kamaole, but the water felt good! I would have stood under it until my fingertips pruned, but my stomach rumbled a demand for breakfast.

Or would that be lunch?

On a normal day, my feet hit the floor at around five a.m., so I can get my morning run in before work. But the legs were still short of al dente, and yesterday's breakout had sucked the oomph right out of me . Add it up, and you had one late-rising newshound who wasn't sure how long she had slept and hadn't thought to check the clock on the nightstand when she got up. Had I missed the eight o'clock breakfast cutoff?

Newly motivated, I hopped out of the shower, brushed my teeth, and broke out the makeup. (In a perfect world, I wouldn't waste my time, but I've gotten into the habit, because I never know when I'll have to do an impromptu standup, and even I like to look decent on camera.) I was about to apply my usual drive-by swipe of taupe eye shadow, when I paused to peer at my reflection, searching my new eyes for some telltale difference in color or maybe a scar or two. Nada. Same indigo blue I had inherited from Mom, same baby crow's feet earned from too much fun in the sun and way too many late nights on the job. I shrugged, slapped on the shadow and wrapped up my toilette with a half-hearted dab of lip gloss. Thank God I've never needed mascara. You could lose an eye.

That chore taken care of, I climbed into my jeans, pulled

on a pale-blue cashmere sweater, and shoved my feet into a pair of well-worn, black ostrich-skin cowboy boots, silently thanking Mom for packing all the right gear. She even sent my lucky Naval Academy baseball cap, that scruffy excuse for a fashion accessory she detests but tolerates, because years ago it had been a Christmas present from Dickson.

By the time I slicked back my wet hair and covered it with the faded cotton hat, the bedside clock showed ten minutes past breakfast. Chewing my lower lip, I toyed with the idea of playing the convalescent card with Sadie, but nixed the ploy for two reasons. One, I'd had enough sympathy in the past two months to last me a lifetime. Two, my new landlady was too sharp to fall for it. Resigned to finding the nearest restaurant, I slung my black leather jacket over my shoulder and headed for the door, remembering my glasses at the last second.

My third-story room was situated at the end of a narrow carpeted hallway running down the back of the house. I shut the door and checked to make sure it was locked. Passing the closed door to Sadie's personal apartment across the hall, I came to the stairs and started down, fingers skimming the polished wood banister. Pausing on the second-floor landing, I peeked down the hall, counting four rooms between me and the tall window set in the end wall. Having gotten the lay of the land, I continued down to the first floor.

The clatter of dishes drew me to the dining room tucked between the parlor and the kitchen. Sadie had her back to me as she cleared the long, dark-chestnut table, so I hovered in the doorway, wistfully eying the generous remains of what had obviously been a five-star breakfast. I was fixated on a three-bite cloud of scrambled eggs liberally flecked with spinach and tomato, when Cosmo announced his presence by way of a gentle head butt to my right hip.

I grinned down at him. "Hey, Cosmo."

He acknowledged my greeting with a chin lift. It was like, *Yo.*

Without turning Sadie said, "I wondered if you were going to speak up or stand there lusting after my eggs all day." She turned to face me. I laid my right hand over my heart and gave her a *moi?* lift of the eyebrows. "*Mm-hmm,* you. I guess you're hungry."

"I could go for a bite." My stomach seconded the motion with a feed-me groan that prompted a chuckle from my landlady.

"All right, I'll make allowances, this being your first day and all. But you're gonna have to earn it." She hefted a tray loaded with silverware. "Help me clear away, and I'll fix you a plate in the kitchen."

"Deal," I agreed instantly, slinging my jacket over the back of a shaker chair and reaching for the closest platter.

In record time I was perched on a tall stool at the breakfast bar in the roomy kitchen. Cosmo sat at attention on the floor next to me, his armed-and-dangerous squint riveted on the plate Sadie was loading with eggs, apple bacon, and hash browns. She slid the dish across the counter, then added a homemade oat muffin and a small bowl of melon chunks mixed with red grapes.

"Eat," she ordered.

She didn't have to tell me twice.

When the eggs hit my tongue, my taste buds sat up and sang the "Hallelujah Chorus." "*Mmm*." I swallowed and said, "These are great, Sadie! Is that feta I taste?"

Obviously pleased, she nodded. "Elise's recipe. Jack likes 'em, too. Ate three big helpings this morning. You want some coffee?" she asked, as I dug into the hash browns with gusto.

"I'm not much of a coffee drinker," I admitted, after another swallow, "but I'll take some tea, if you have it. Speaking of Jack," I said, as she scooped loose leaves from a ceramic canister into a stainless steel tea ball, "did he get off on schedule?"

"Oh-six-hundred on the dot. Honey, that man is *punc-tu-al*." She poured hot water into the cup and set it in front of me, then crossed the kitchen to lift a deep purple apron off a peg mounted on the wall next to the back door. She pulled the bib strap over her head and tied the strings around her waist. "Said to tell you he would be in touch," she added as she pushed up the sleeves of her burnt-orange turtleneck and started to load an under-counter dishwasher.

"Glad to hear it, but what if I need to reach him before he contacts me? I don't have my UpLink. He confiscated it."

"Girl, this is Jack Eagan we're talking about. The man who thinks of everything?" She wiped her hands on the apron and pulled a silver UpLink out of her jeans' pocket. "He left this for you. Transmits on a secure Sat-Net frequency with end-to-end quantum encryption. His number and mine are the only ones programmed in, and you can't program in any of your own."

"You saying he doesn't trust me?"

"Not one-eighth of an inch."

I smothered a smile as I pushed up my left sleeve and slipped the device onto my wrist. Once it had self-adjusted, I tugged the sleeve back into place, making a mental note to get downtown as soon as possible to pick up a throwaway, so I could call whomever I wanted to and slip into the Cloud on the sly. I picked up a slice of bacon and started to take a bite, when Cosmo shifted. I looked at him. He looked at me, then stared pointedly at my bacon, then looked back at me. I broke the bacon in half and gave him his share.

"Have you known Jack long?" I asked Sadie.

"About ten years, I guess."

"I take it you were on the Teams together?"

She bent to transfer a fistful of silverware to the machine's cutlery tray. "Oh, I wasn't on the Teams." Her lips curved as she glanced over at me. "I was what you might call a consultant."

I ran my tongue around the inside of my cheek. "Consultant, huh?" Spook-speak for a CIIS field operative attached to the unit. Unless I missed my guess.

"Mm-hmm."

"But you *did* work with Jack."

"I knew him in a professional capacity, yes." Dishes loaded, she started to wipe down the gold-brown granite countertops.

Like trying to nail fog to a tree, I mused. *My kind of challenge.*

"So why did he quit the Teams to join CIIS?" I ate a bite-sized chunk of melon.

Again with the smile. "You would have to ask Jack about that."

Okay, what we had here was your typical irresistible force—i.e., my overdeveloped professional curiosity—meeting an immovable object—i.e. again, the professional spook's penchant for stonewalling. Did Sadie *know* she was tossing down a gauntlet? Based on the twinkle in her eye, I would say, yeah. She probably did.

Already planning my campaign to wear her down, I pulled the cup and saucer toward me, set the tea strainer on the saucer, and added a spoonful of demerara sugar and a dollop of cream to my tea. It was still piping hot, so I sipped gingerly, savoring the wake-up punch of a hearty black with hints of malt and caramel.

Then I changed the subject. "So how long have you been in the boarding house business?" Smooth, right?

"Four years," she said without missing a beat. Smooth.

She went on to tell me how much she liked cooking for people and taking care of them. She briefed me on Hobson's Hope, filling me in on public transportation, giving me the name of a good hairdresser, and suggesting I try lunch at Roma's Sidewalk Cafe, home of buttercup iced tea and the freshest focaccia in town. In the meantime, Cosmo inhaled half a muffin and most of my bacon.

Half an hour later, I left the house feeling jazzed. Between my plan to make life miserable for the Ferrymen and my battle of wits with Sadie Carter, the next few weeks should prove interesting.

As it turned out, *interesting* didn't come close.

Chapter 17

Dawn was a rosy glow behind the treetops when I slowed to a walk a block from the boarding house. I paused in front of a two-story brownstone, jammed my hands on my hips, and cocked one leg. Chuffing palm-sized clouds into the frosty morning air, I examined my mental score card.

Two measly miles and they hadn't been pretty. Well, at least I was running again. Had been for more than a week. Okay, I was still going less than half my usual distance at half my usual pace, but I was making progress.

Give it time, I reminded my ego as a trio of bright red maple leaves swirled onto the sidewalk to dance around my beat-up Nikes. *Two weeks ago you were in the hospital.*

The chill seeping through my damp, black-and-gold Chandler U sweats put a period to the inner monologue and got me moving again. When I reached the house a minute later, Cosmo met me at the front door.

Shoving back my hood, I gave him a noogie. "Getting stronger every day, pal. Another two weeks, I'll be doing five miles again." He snorted. "Okay, three weeks. You should come with me sometime." The cool, flat stare I got in return made me laugh out loud.

I inhaled deeply, drinking in the yeasty aroma wafting from the kitchen. Sadie was going to deliver on her promise of whole-wheat blueberry pancakes. My stomach gurgled happily as I gave Cosmo a quick, later-dude ear scratch and jogged up the stairs.

Sorry excuse for a morning run notwithstanding, I felt strong and energized. Ready for a fabulous breakfast, then a few hours' work. My research on the Ferrymen hadn't turned up any new leads yet, but my gut was telling me the chink in their armor was there, and my gut was seldom wrong. Shamelessly mixing my metaphors, I wondered if this would be the day I found their Achilles heel.

The rest of the morning followed the routine I had fallen into since my arrival. After my shower I scooted downstairs for breakfast with Sadie, Cosmo, and Sadie's four permanent tenants, an eclectic bunch I had taken an instant liking to.

Pert, curvy Fannie Jordan was a waitress who never met a stranger or a man she didn't like. Her sparkling eyes were hazel, but her hair color changed weekly—powder blue one week, hot pink the next, and so on. These rainbow dye jobs spilled over onto her dog, Jacques, a haughty teacup poodle evidently unfazed by the fact that he changed colors more often than your average chameleon. At least once a day, Jacques would assert his imagined alpha-dog status via a soprano snarl at Cosmo. Biker Dog did his part by totally ignoring Jacques's existence.

Systems analyst Connie Eller was curvaceous, too, but where Fannie curved in all the right places, Connie curved once—like an apple. She was short, wore her pale brown hair in a blunt pageboy with a zigzag center part, avoided makeup like the plague, and apparently had a closet full of boxy, mouse-gray pants suits. When she squinted, and she squinted often, she reminded me of a brilliant but slightly disgruntled mole.

Next we had Byron Waxman. Tall, lanky, and stoop-shouldered, hands perpetually stuffed in the pockets of faded blue jeans, he gazed at the world through soulful brown eyes set under an unruly mop of dishwater blond hair. He had advanced degrees in world lit and philosophy and taught both subjects at Whitfield Hobson High. In his spare time, Byron—never By—composed rambling nature poems and wrote the occasional theater or art review for the *Hobson Herald*.

Last but not least, my personal favorite, Ted Li. The town's pocket-sized deputy sheriff wore his black brush cut at attention, his khakis creased to a razor's edge, and his black shoes spit-shined. He tended to rock back and forth on the balls of his feet while he talked, giving you the unsettling impression he was about to launch. His ever-present toothy grin and upbeat attitude had earned him the nickname Happy. Happy Li. If you're going to go by an adverb, there are worse ones you could pick.

As soon as breakfast was over, I nipped upstairs, grabbed my jacket, and headed for the nearest hover-bus stop three blocks off. It was still a picture-perfect fall morning. The air had a pleasant bite, the sky was as blue as a robin's egg, and the sun bathed the world in translucent, burnished gold. The surrounding hills blazed with color. It was almost like Mother Nature wanted to give my eyes a treat on this first day without my dark glasses.

I caught the 8:30 Mid-Town Express, found a window seat near the back, and settled in for the twenty-minute ride.

As near as I could tell without an aerial view, Hobson's Hope was laid out like a wagon wheel, with downtown being the hub and residential neighborhoods radiating out like spokes knobby with cul-de-sacs. Thick forests of oak, hickory, maple, and pine hugged the outskirts of the city and filled the spaces between neighborhoods, giving each tree-lined residential area a secluded, living-on-the-edge-of-town feel.

Center City, as the natives grandiosely dubbed downtown, consisted of an orderly grid of clean, broad streets fronted by well-kept buildings in the trademark twentieth-century style. (Although I noticed the town fathers had unbent enough to opt for high, wide, solar-collection windows over old-fashioned glass.) The skyline was low, no construction higher than five stories, all the buildings static. Personally, I preferred the dynamic, shape-shifting skyline of New Frisco, but unto each his own.

As Jack had said, within city limits transportation was ground-bound. From seven to eight a.m., then again from five to six in the evening, traffic slowed to the forty-five minutes of polite, orderly stop-and-go Hopers called rush hour. I had seen worse snarls in parking lots.

Life-sized statues of Whitfield and Abigail Hobson were all over the place. They didn't look like a fun couple. More like a variation on *American Gothic,* except he had hair and the Missus was always portrayed sitting down, leading me to suspect Whitfield had been shorter than his wife and touchy about the fact.

You couldn't walk ten blocks without coming across an undersized park, but my favorite nook was a cobblestoned alcove sandwiched between the headquarters of the *Hobson Herald* and Mocha Joe's Coffee Shop. A narrow, covered passageway between the two buildings opened into a tear-shaped courtyard bounded on the far end by a curved, ivy-covered wall. With just enough room for a couple petite tables and four chairs, it was a perfect place to work undisturbed and unobserved, weather permitting. I headed that way when I got off the bus at Main and Prince, swinging by Joe's for my usual caffeine fix.

Joe Stephanopoulos appeared to be in his late forties, a dapper little guy who parted his wavy black hair on the left and waxed his mustache. He handled traffic at the counter, greeting regulars by name with a cheery, "Hallo!" Meanwhile, his plump daughter, Diana — as painfully shy as her father was outgoing — pulled barista duty, doing her level best to disappear into the cappuccino machine. Despite the differences in their personalities — or maybe because of them — father and daughter worked together seamlessly. Their steady stream of customers came and went in a smooth, uninterrupted flow.

Joe lifted one hand in a wave as I came through the door. "Hallo, Ms. Gregson, Mr. Ellison! What can we get for you today?"

"Good morning, Joe. Diana. Large organic chai, please." I smiled at the rail-thin redhead who had followed me into the shop. His long, horsey face was lined with fatigue and his gray overcoat looked like he had slept in it. "How's it going, Hank?"

The *Hobson Herald's* lifestyle correspondent rolled bloodshot green eyes. "Don't ask."

"Late night?"

"Those Garden Club ladies are killing me! Would you believe last night's meeting didn't break up until after midnight? Hydrangeas as a hot-button topic. Who knew?" He glanced at the proprietor. "Espresso, Joe, and make it a double."

"You got it, Mr. Ellison."

Hank leaned against the counter, facing me. "So what are you up to?"

"Not much. Enjoying the life of leisure, soaking up the local ambience."

"Nice work, if you can get it. I'll bet it comes with all kinds of benefits. Like sleep, for example."

I punched him lightly on the shoulder. "Come on, Hank. Real reporters don't need sleep."

He snorted derisively as Joe handed me a cup.

"Three credits, Ms. Gregson."

"Thanks, Joe." I pressed my index finger to the biometric pad mounted on the counter, authorizing the debit from the numbered account Dickson had set up for me at the National Trust Bank of Nassau. Untraceable, he said. Hopefully, nobody was trying.

"Have a good one, Joe and Diana," I said as I turned to leave. "You, too, Hank. Good luck with that Garden Club piece."

"I'll need it," he sighed. As I went out the door I heard him ask, "So, Joe. What do you know about hydrangeas?"

Chapter 18

According to my stomach, it was a quarter 'til lunchtime when I logged off the computer function on my disposable UpLink. The holographic interface vanished as I leaned back in my chair, stretched out my legs, and closed my eyes, mentally reviewing my progress.

I had been combing my private slush files, this reporter's equivalent of a Swiss bank account, except I deposit information instead of money. Thanks to a hacker acquaintance, my special stash is heavily encrypted, triple-password-protected, and registered under a numerical alias. You can't be too careful when it comes to private property in Cloud Land.

My file on the Ferrymen was massive, a couple hundred gigabytes, at least. It included the police reports for each hit, as well as any piece ever written or broadcast about the Ferrymen and/or their victims. I had notes from all my interviews, be they with law enforcement, law breakers, witnesses, or next of kin. Some of the information would never see the light of day—stuff like anonymous tips, off-the-record information, and the few unsubstantiated rumors I managed to pick up. But it was all there. I probably knew as much as about the Ferrymen as the high and mighty CIIS did. Maybe more.

My plan in was to scour the files item by item and line by line on the off-chance I would spot some commonality or clue I and who knew how many highly trained professionals had previously overlooked. Not saying it was a *great* plan, but it beat doing nothing. I had been batting a big, fat zero for a week now, but I was nowhere near ready to give up. Which is why I wanted to take a minute to go over today's assignment one more time. The Yanos case.

Dirk Yanos. Thirty years old, Greek-god handsome,

fabulously wealthy. He'd had it all by anyone's standards—a brilliant mind for business, a heaping helping of élan, and a globe-trotting lifestyle guaranteed to inflame both the imagination and benign envy of your average working stiff. Dirk's chiseled features routinely appeared in business journals, posh monthlies, and fanzines alike. And that was *before* he threw the fairytale wedding of the century in Monaco, hitching his already blazing star to that of stunning Rita Winston, a watercolorist renowned for paintings of simplicity and grace. Her works were regular fixtures in museums from the Louvre to the Metropolitan.

To say Yanos had a lot to live for would be akin to saying water is wet, and he had been poised to sweeten that pot in a big way. Yanos Pharmaceuticals, one of a hundred subsidiaries of DY International, was hot on the trail of a new medication designed to wipe out the scourge of drug addiction now and forever, amen. The company had been holding its cards extremely close to the vest, but rumor had it the new treatment worked on the genetic level, switching off the genes that kept the addict hooked, regardless of the drug of choice. An instant cure without the agony of withdrawal or threat of relapse, to be distributed free of charge? Dirk had been a Nobel shoo-in, guaranteed to go down in history as one of the greatest humanitarians of all time.

Predictably, South America's five major drug cartels were less than thrilled to hear their fat, healthy demand curves were about to flatline. Equally predictably, they didn't intend to let that happen without a fight.

So nobody was particularly surprised when Yanos Pharmaceuticals' main research lab was broken into, twice. Delicate equipment was trashed, electronic files wiped clean. All this despite the facility's top-of-the-line security system. Fortunately, Dirk had been several steps ahead of the opposition, stockpiling reserve equipment and creating hot- and cold-backup systems with continuous data protection capability and redundant storage—all discrete and off-site. The research forged ahead.

A couple scientists went missing. Yanos promptly packed up the rest of his people and their equipment and moved the whole kit and caboodle to an undisclosed location. He had started to receive death threats by then, but instead of joining his employees in hiding, Dirk went right on living his life, although he did unbend enough to let CIIS surround him with a hand-picked security detail. Somebody had to stand up to the cartels, he said, and it might as well be him.

A noble sentiment, but one morning Dirk's wife woke up to discover her young husband lying stone cold dead over on his side of their massive round bed, not a mark on him. The Ferrymen obit popped up in the Badger, Iowa, *Bugle* before the echo of her screams died away.

According to the autopsy report—the unexpurgated version I managed to sneak a peek at—high concentrations of an extremely potent synthetic poison were found in the victim's bloodstream and respiratory system. *Elegantly engineered* was the phrase the medical examiner used to describe the sophisticated toxin formulated to react exclusively with Dirk's DNA. A thousand other people could have sucked it in by the lungful, no harm, no foul. This stuff was designed to kill one man, and one man only, but not right away. The assassins had micro-concentrated the poison and packaged it in nanobots programmed for remote activation according to their personal timetable. In point of fact, said the ME, it would be all but impossible to determine when and where Yanos had actually inhaled the concoction.

Dirk was a high-profile, heavily guarded target already alert to the threat. Far from an easy hit, but the Ferrymen pulled it off. The imagination, expertise and technology needed to dream up the plan, then produce and package the toxin, hadn't come cheap. The Ferrymen's client or clients had deep pockets.

Nobody seriously liked Dirk's obviously devastated widow as the contractee, but the feds had to rule her out, since at least six murders out of ten can be traced back to an enraged spouse. Rita was cleared quickly. Ditto the fifteen house servants. They all passed the background investigations and truth scans with flying colors.

Nice, but not too startling, because investigators had already narrowed the list of probable clients to five major players, i.e., the cartels. Following the money was the obvious next step. If only it were as easy as it sounds.

Now that the world's economy runs exclusively on digital currency, billions upon billions of electronic financial transactions take place every hour of every day. Yes, international drug cartels constantly shuffle massive sums, but filtering even one day's transactions takes a few minutes—more than enough time for an army of pros to make the money trails vanish almost at their points of origin. With the right encryption, dirty deals can disappear (*Now you see them, now you don't!*) into a labyrinth of offshore accounts. The launderers keep the funds moving, washing and rewashing them until they trickle out of some distant branch in the pipeline, whiter than snow, in the form of untraceable diamonds or perfectly legal bearer bonds or profits from Pappy's Sporting Goods Store.

All of which put the odds of following the credit stream between the obvious suspects and the Ferrymen somewhere around a million to one.

Rita Yanos had gone into seclusion, but I dug until I came up with the law firm handling her affairs and asked them to pass along my request for an interview. Sure, I know how that sounds, but part of my job is putting crime into context. Take murder, for example. Homicide doesn't end with the corpse; there's always collateral damage. Call it the ripple effects of man's inhumanity to man. We've got to understand that, if we're going to learn anything at all. But if the press doesn't show the world the stunned, shattered survivors, who will?

Broaching the subject of an interview during some poor soul's darkest hour isn't easy or comfortable. My least favorite bullet point on the job description, for all kinds of reasons. I can charge up San Juan Hill with the best of them, but walking softly makes me feel clumsy and inept. And, yes, I do feel like an intruder.

Plus, if friends and family decide to talk to me, I have to keep what happens between us real. Drop the shield and admit I care. Day to day, I can't operate on that emotional plane. Without the shield, I would either burn out or go crazy or both. But whether I allow myself to acknowledge it or not, I always care. More than I can say. The day I don't will be the day I know I've been on the job too long.

So here's the way I go after an interview with a survivor. I make the offer, back off, leave the door open. You would be surprised how many grieving relatives jump at the chance. They want to speak for the dead and put a face on the dearly departed. I let them. Flesh out the vic, you make it harder for the viewing public to write him or her off as one more unfortunate statistic. Numbers are easy — digest and dismiss. Some creep wastes a waitress who reminds you of your neighbor or some old guy who reminds you of your Uncle Al? That's tougher to ignore.

Dirk Yanos was nobody's uncle Al, but he *was* one of our favorite sons. He and Rita were glamorous, exciting, the romance of the century. Icons of the good life. They were also human beings, and I wasn't going to let Dirk's murder be reduced to a tabloid sensation. Killing him was a crime against flesh and blood, his death a bitter loss that shattered at least one heart. I wanted Mr. and Mrs. Tri-America to get that. Rita must have wanted it, too, because she accepted my offer with an invitation to meet her at Pinnacle House, the couple's Rocky Mountain retreat and, as it happened, the final scene of the crime.

My videographer, Fast Eddy Cho — so called because the long, lean Asian is a wunderkind with the camera who never, ever misses the perfect shot — set up for the interview while Rita and I waited in chairs set catercorner to one another. She watched him, I studied her. The famous heart-shaped face, surrounded by a cloud of auburn hair, was pale to the point of translucence. Her eyes looked swollen and sodden, hazel irises swimming in a sea of pink. She was probably around five-six, but she seemed smaller. Fragile. Like she might break in pieces if you bumped her.

When Eddy gave us the thumbs-up, Rita's eyes shifted to my face.

"I'm so sorry for your loss, Mrs. Yanos."

"Thank you. And it's Rita, please."

"Did you and your husband come here often, Rita?"

"Not often enough." Her fingers plucked at a damp, balled-up tissue as she smiled a sad, secret smile. "This trip was supposed to be a romantic getaway. We'd had so little time together ... just the two of us, I mean ... since we got married two years ago."

"Busy people."

"Too busy. If we had known ...." She shook her head and pressed her lips together, as tears beaded her lower lashes. She brushed at them with her fingertips. "But there was so much to do, and it seemed so important at the time. My art. Dirk's research."

"Making the world a better place is always important."

"Is that what we did?"

"You doubt it?"

"I doubt everything now. Our priorities, our decisions ... even God."

"Most people would, in your place." When she didn't reply, I moved on. "I don't know if it's any comfort, but the outpouring of public grief and sympathy has been unprecedented."

"It helps—of course, it helps—to know so many people welcomed Dirk and me into some corner of their hearts. That, on some level at least, they care about what happens to us." Tears welled again, again she swiped them away. "It gives me hope that Dirk will live on somewhere beyond my personal memories."

"I'm sure he will." Inching closer to the heart of the interview, I said, "But the adoration came at a price, right? Life in a fishbowl."

"You get used to it. Catching the public eye is bread and butter for artists and research companies. Reporters, too," she added with a tiny smile. "Besides, we were having fun."

"Sure, but we all need a break from the unrelenting stare now and then."

"If only for a short while."

"So you came up here."

"It was my idea," she admitted. "Dirk wanted to wait. He was afraid people would think he was running away. Hiding out."

"Because of the threats on his life."

"Yes. But I pleaded until he gave in."

And blamed herself for it. Would until she could think clearly enough to realize Dirk had probably been exposed to the toxin before they got within a thousand miles of the Rockies.

"You didn't leave the grounds at all during the past two weeks?"

"No. But we *weren't* hiding out!" she insisted. "I hope you'll make that clear. It's important. To both of us," she finished softly.

"I'll be sure to include this segment in the broadcast." Then, "Can you tell me about that day?"

"I … I'm afraid I don't remember much. Just … waking up next to him. He was so cold. So absolutely … *inert.*" A tremor shook her. "The body I knew as well as my own—eyes, lips, hands, that tiny mole on his left earlobe—it was there. But *Dirk* wasn't."

"No indication that he hadn't been feeling well? He didn't moan or seem restless during the night?"

"No. We made love; it was wonderful. Afterwards, he wrapped me in his arms and we fell asleep." The tears she had fought so hard to contain finally broke free on a ragged sob. "I don't understand this. He was so full of life and … and … *joy!* Dirk never hurt a living soul! He only wanted to help people! What kind of animals murder a man like that?"

The worst kind.

Chapter 19

"Still soaking up the local ambience, I see."

Ellison's voice snapped the thread between past and present, transporting me from Pinnacle House to Hobson's Hope in the blink of an eye. Unfortunately, the bleak anger that ate at me during the interview with Rita came along for the ride. But that was private business, and I intended to keep it that way.

I forced my lips to curve lazily. "You know what they say, Hank. It's a dirty job, but somebody's gotta do it." A tantalizing aroma reached out to pry my eyes open. "That smells good," I said, zeroing in on the white sack dangling from his left hand.

"One of Rodney's special Southwestern Chicken Wraps." When my stomach rumbled with its usual greedy enthusiasm, Hank grinned evilly and waved the sack in my face. "Succulent chicken breast. Smothered in red peppers and onions. *Guacamole and greeeeen chilies.*"

"All right, Ellison. Either hand over the bag or point me towards Rodney."

"Place is called Half-Wrapped," Hank said, plopping his lunch on the table. "Turn left out of the alley, take another left two blocks down on Orange. But don't let the grass grow. He closes at two." I was on my feet and half-way to the street when he called after me, "Hey, if you're interested in local color, Rodney's your man."

I lifted a hand in acknowledgement.

Half-Wrapped was a warm, yeasty cubbyhole opening off a canopied entrance on the ground floor of a three-story building. The retro, greasy spoon décor included a scattering of cheap tables and chairs, a rack crammed with bags of chips in front of a wide counter, and a well-used grill tucked under two massive ovens set in the back wall.

The man behind the counter was big and potbellied, his black hair pulled into a ponytail that corkscrewed halfway down his back. Even in the dim light I could understand how Rodney rated the tag *local color*. He was a walking PSA, inked from the tips of his toes (I assumed) to his hairline. The tats lit up in random sequence. "Recycle Space Junk." "Earth to Earthlings: Am I Getting Warmer?" "Get A Life: Clone Now."

I was admiring a sad-eyed baby seal perched atop the words "How Could You?" when Rodney trilled in a surprisingly high voice, "What'll it be?"

"Southwestern Chicken Wrap with chips and a large iced tea."

"For here, or to go?"

"To go." In no time at all he handed me a fragrant bag and a tall Styrofoam cup. "Thanks. Nice ink," I said as I paid.

He glanced down at a beefy bicep. "You like it?"

"Sure. It's ... thought provoking."

He looked gratified. "Right. People see body art like this, they're gonna think long and hard. They're gonna remember."

"Absolutely."

"Guy's gotta take a stand for what's important, ya know?"

"You bet."

"Hey, wow! Was that your stomach? I better let you go so you can feed it. Besides, don't want that wrap to get cold. Stop by again sometime."

I hefted the bag. "Count on it."

The day was radiant, and the temperature had climbed into the fifties, so I decided to dine *al fresco* in the tiny green quadrangle located a block beyond the *Herald* building. Heading back the way I had come, I sauntered along in no particular hurry, perversely prolonging the anticipation as I savored the delectable *je ne sais quoi* Rodney's Southwestern added to the fall air. The windows I passed danced with sunlight and the ghostly doppelgängers of my fellow pedestrians.

Saunter slowed to amble when I spotted a curbside fender-bender in front of the *Herald*. Aside from the vehicles involved, it didn't look like much of an accident. Of course, any time an extremely pricey Grimaldi meets a boxy rattletrap, resulting in a deep crease in the former's rear aerodynamics, *somebody* is going to be unhappy. In this case, *somebody* was a middle-aged gent in an impeccably tailored gray, Glen plaid suit. The object of his wrath was a Caspar Milquetoast in off-the-rack khaki slacks, a white button-down shirt, red bow tie, and shapeless chocolate brown cardigan.

The sidewalk was clotted with gawkers. Happy Li and his partner, Sheila Preston, were already at the scene. She was mid-intersection, directing traffic in an attempt to speed up the rubberneck crawl of motorists ogling the confrontation. Apparently armed with nothing more than his irrepressible smile, Happy had placed himself squarely between the antagonists.

Hank Ellison lifted a hand in a come-on gesture, inviting me to join him near the corner of the building. He nodded in greeting, then turned a rueful gaze on the accident.

"A Grimaldi, yet." He shook his head and sighed. "Bumbling Benjie strikes again."

"The guy in the sweater?"

"Yep. Full name, Benjamin Palmer. Works in our archives. A bigger doofus you never met. He's the butt of every practical joker on staff. Never so much as says boo about it. I can't help but feel sorry for him. Fifty-three years old, and he still lives with his mother, if you can believe that."

Eyeing Palmer's baby face, apologetic demeanor, and maiden-aunt hand-wringing, I decided I could.

"Why Bumbling Benjie?"

"Because the man is a born stumblebum. I swear, that poor klutz could trip over his two left feet sitting down." Hank gestured toward the hapless Palmer. "Take this latest disaster, for example. Seems Benjie bobbled his hot chocolate while parking. Burned the crap out of himself and rear-ended the Grimaldi." Hank grimaced like a man in pain. "A three-million-credit Grimaldi, for God's sake!"

A shout drew our attention back to the affluent complainant. Happy had him by both shoulders now, as the man shook a fist at Palmer.

"Do you have any *idea* what you've done?" Benjie darted a furtive, humiliated glance at the rapidly growing crowd and stuttered an apology. "*Sorry?* You're *sorry?* You moron! You pea-brained excuse for a human being!" The aggrieved party flung a hand toward his mangled vehicle. "Custom-made. Do you know what that means? Replacement parts will have to be ordered from the dealer! It will take months! We're talking *fifty thousand* in parts and labor! That's more money than you *and* that fly-by-night insurance agent you mentioned will make in your entire miserable lives!"

I don't know what Happy said to him then. Probably words to the effect of, *You're making an ass of yourself*, because the Grimaldi's owner suddenly seemed to notice his avid audience. He pulled away from Li, squared his shoulders, and tugged at the lapels of his suit coat. Straightening his silk tie and running a hand over his neatly barbered hair, he shot a parting glare toward Palmer.

"Look at him," he sneered. My gaze and everyone else's automatically shifted to the deathly pale *him* in question, now reduced to staring at his penny loafers. "The man is a joke. A living joke."

And that's when it happened.

Chapter 20

The earth moved.

That's how it felt, anyway—like the patch of sidewalk I was standing on took me on a slow glissade left. The smooth, swift sense of displacement made me dizzy. I blinked and shook my head as my vision blurred, shapes and colors blending into an indistinct smear.

I'm having a stroke. That was my first thought. Followed closely by, *Call 911.*

I opened my mouth to say it, but closed it with a toothy *click* when Benjamin Palmer snapped back into focus. The rest of the world remained a blur—like when you shoot a photo with the lens wide open so everything but the subject is in soft focus? Palmer alone stood in vivid relief; I could see him with hyper-clarity. The spot he had missed shaving that morning, his ragged cuticles, the pearly button hanging by a thread in the middle of the chocolate stain on his shirt. His red bowtie, brown sweater, and green eyes sizzled with color.

I almost swallowed my tongue when Palmer erupted, morphing from five-foot-six-inch mouse to ten-foot-six-inch monster faster than you can say growth spurt. Bug-eyed and slack-jawed, I watched his muscles bulk and swell until he had biceps like bowling balls and legs like tree trunks. His massive head swung between his antagonist and the onlookers as broad, powerful hands with thick fingers balled into pile-driver fists. His lips drew back, barring oversized teeth in a savage snarl. His eyes broadcast a murderous rage.

I felt my hair stand on end. Managed a strangled, *"OhmyGod!"*

"I know. Poor schmuck probably wishes the earth would open up and swallow him. Think I should go over there?"

Huh?

I dragged my goggle eyes away from Palmer to stare at Ellison, whose face reflected only pity. My gaze flew back to the *Herald's* archivist. I blinked, hard. Blinked again. But the hallucination hung on.

This is not happening!

" —wrong?" Hank's fingers wrapped around my upper arm. He gave it a gentle shake. "Hey, are you okay?"

The second Ellison touched me, Palmer downsized to Bumbling Benjie, and the world eased back into focus.

"Good question," I rasped.

"For a minute there, you looked like you saw a ghost."

"Or something," was my dazed reply.

"Maybe you should sit down for a while," he said, towing me toward the building's entrance. "Put your head between your knees."

Houston, we have a problem. And whatever it was, I doubted putting my head between my knees would make it go away. Maybe that concussion I had was worse than anybody thought. Like permanent-brain-damage worse.

The possibilities seemed endless and increasingly dire. When a tightness in my chest made me realize I was holding my breath, I grabbed the reins of my galloping imagination and hauled back hard.

"I'll take you to my office," Hank was saying.

We were almost at the doors. I planted my feet, forcing him to stop. When I tugged on my arm he let go, but his worried frown said he wasn't sure turning me loose was such a good idea.

"I'm all right, Hank." Not even, but I prefer my panic attacks in private.

He dipped his chin and eyed me dubiously. "You sure about that? I've seen skim milk with more color than you had a minute ago."

"I look okay now, don't I?"

"Depends. If by *okay* you mean you don't look like you're about to keel over right this *second*, then yeah, you look terrific."

He made another grab for my arm, but I stepped back out of reach.

"Look, I swear I'll go straight back to Sadie's." I held up my sack and jiggled it. My smile was probably on the anemic side, but it was the best I could do. "Got to reheat my Southwestern." When he grunted skeptically, I figured I had to go one better. "Okay, what if I promise to take it easy for the rest of the day?"

He mulled it over for a second. "All right, but I'm driving you back there."

"Hank—"

"It's either that, or I call Sadie to come pick you up."

Yielding to the lesser of two evils, I shrugged. "Hey, you want to play gallant knight to my damsel in distress, it's no skin off my nose."

He latched on to my arm again and started toward the nearest parking garage. "Anybody ever tell you you're a real smart ass?"

"All the time, Ellison, all the time."

By the time we got to the boarding house I had settled on *too much too soon* as the logical explanation for the Palmer-and-Hyde Show. I wrote the incident off as a bizarre fluke, an optical illusion caused by me pushing the research harder than I should have. (As anybody who knows me will tell you, pushing too hard is my default mode of operation.) I promised myself I would pare my work sessions down to an hour with an hour of rest between.

For added insurance I decided to start wearing the glasses again.

Then I tried to put the entire episode behind me, and for the most part, I succeeded.

Until it happened again.

Chapter 21

Wednesday it rained, so I decided to work at the library.

The building was four stories, limestone with a classical façade that included three Corinthian columns, a wide flight of steps, and enormous arched windows. Spacious, high-ceilinged rooms were seamed with tall shelving units dense with books. I didn't know how many volumes they had, but given the fact that hard copy publishers are few and far between these days, the Abigail Hobson Municipal Library's stacks had to be worth billions.

I had filched some of Sadie's baklava on my way out the door that morning and polished off the last bite before I pushed through the library's heavy double doors. Checking out the key to one of the fourth-floor study carrels, I jogged up the wide marble steps, key in my left hand, because the fingers on my right were sticky with honey.

The ladies' room at the top of the stairs was occupied by two teenage girls and the ten pounds of makeup they had strewn across the counter. My arrival didn't rate more than a dismissive glance as one of them, a cute, curvy brunette who wore her thick hair in a bob, leaned into the mural-sized mirror to touch up her lipstick.

The other teen reminded me of a nymph—slender build, silky blond curls, wide blue-green eyes, and skin like porcelain. She wore designer jeans and a form-fitting lime-green pullover, and her hands waved all over the place as she talked.

"I worked my butt off for that paper, and I deserved an A! Mean, ugly old witch! Who ever heard of taking thirty points off for a poorly structured bibliography?" She tossed up her hands. "*Thirty points? Not fair!*"

The brunette slid her lips together to even out the color,

then shook her head. "How many times do I have to tell you? Life isn't fair." She used her pinky to clean up the line of her lipstick. "You know what your problem is? You're an overachiever. Tina Nelson, Type A brainiac. Me? I would give my right arm for a C from old Mrs. Venable."

"Do you think it would help if I talked to her?" Tina sounded almost pleading.

The brunette rolled her eyes. "Give me a break, okay? It's one lousy C! Probably the first C you've ever made in your whole life!"

"I can't afford Cs. Not even one. Not if I want to get accepted by UC Davis."

"There are other schools."

"Not for me, and you know it. I want to get as far away from this town as I can. I'd go to college on the other side of the planet, if I had the money." She paused. "God, Margo, my dad will kill me when he sees that paper!"

Maybe it was the way she said it, but her words pulled my gaze from my soapy hands to her reflection in the mirror. As soon as my eyes locked on her face that sliding, shifting sensation hit me and the scene slipped out of focus. I almost groaned out loud.

Not again!

Then Tina's reflection popped into sharp relief, and almost immediately a rainbow of bruises blossomed on her face and neck, some fresh black-and-blue, a few aged yellow-green. A bloody seam widened to a fissure under her right eye. Her lower lip ballooned, then split like an overripe melon, sending a trickle of blood down her chin. I stared, torn between fascination and revulsion at the delicate features now bruised and bloody, battered almost beyond recognition. The eyes were the worst—blackened whirlpools of pain, terror, and resignation that threatened to suck me under.

"—staring at?"

At the sound of Tina's voice, the vision started to fade. A second or two later, it was gone. I blinked rapidly, then glanced from one young face to the other, trying to hide my *there are more things under heaven, Horatio* stupefaction. Both girls were eyeballing me like I was an escaped mental patient. And maybe they weren't far off.

"What are you staring at?" Tina repeated a tad

suspiciously.

The best I could come up with was the not-so-artful dodge, "Oh, was I staring?"

"Yeah. You were looking at me like ... well, like ...."

"Like she had two heads," Margo chimed in helpfully.

"Sorry. I was actually ... uh ... *thinking*. Thinking about something. Else." I gestured vaguely, water and suds running off my hands and down my forearms to soak the pushed-up sleeves of my dark blue sweatshirt. "I didn't mean to stare."

They weren't buying, and who could blame them? I sounded like a half-wit. Deciding to quit while I was behind, I got busy at the sink. The silence was deafening as I hurriedly rinsed my hands and shoved them under the radiant drier. I'm not the type to spook easily, but this business was throwing me into a tailspin, and it showed. No wonder Tina and Margo continued to watch me warily until the door closed between us.

The rain had let up while I was hallucinating and terrifying adolescents, so I decided to walk back to the boarding house. I was wound tight enough to snap, and the long hike home would both bleed off some of the tension and give me a chance to get my thoughts in order.

I had to see a doctor. That much was obvious. What I had to figure out was how to get to one and how to best describe what was happening to me.

If I had my druthers, I would set up an appointment myself, strictly on the QT, with nobody but the me and the doc in the loop. No use freaking out the family, right? But I was supposed to keep a low profile. Maybe the Ferrymen *were* looking for me. Maybe Klein's UpLink had been hacked. Maybe they had him under surveillance.

Maybe I should get a grip.

And help. I could definitely use some of that. Let somebody else worry about the integrity of Klein's communications. Lucky me, I knew just the man for the job.

Chapter 22

"His name is Bonner. Samuel Bonner. Klein swears he's one of the best. Retired, but he still takes the occasional referral, mostly for exceptional cases or as a personal favor to friends, which I gather Klein is."

Dressed in a royal-blue polo that set off his pale blue eyes, Jack sat facing me in a high backed chair, a telepresence I could almost feel. Even long distance, the man packed a punch.

"Okay. Where do I find him?"

"About five miles due west as the crow flies."

"He's in Hobson's Hope? No way!"

"Address is Forty-four Chestnut."

He accessed his UpLink, and a 3-D real-time satellite's eye-view of Hobson's Hope materialized between us, a virtual view within a virtual view. Jack palmed the image and spread his hands apart, initiating a dizzying zoom-in that leveled off to reveal ant-sized vehicles streaming between miniature buildings. He flicked to shift the focal point from Center City to the west-side, then zoomed in closer to tighten on the front of a pretty Cape Cod surrounded by a white picket fence.

"That's the house."

I studied the quaint cottage dubiously. "Far be it from me to quibble, but a one-and-a-half-story bungalow isn't my idea of a state-of-the-art medical facility." Not that I was eager for a return visit to the hallowed halls of healing, but …. "Wouldn't it be better if I met him at a clinic or hospital?"

Jack spun the image, revealing what appeared to be a small addition jutting off the back of the house. "Bonner may call himself retired, but he likes to keep his hand in. He managed to cut a deal with the U of PA Medical School. He donates his case files to their library and shows up for the occasional lecture, they fund his backyard eye clinic. Strictly a cutting-edge setup, according to Klein."

"All right. If it's good enough for Klein, it's good enough for me."

The satellite view dissolved.

"He'll be expecting you tomorrow morning at nine," Jack said.

"I'll be there. Thanks for setting this up. And thank Doc Klein for me." Word was my surgeon barely had time for a cup of coffee, what with transplants out the wazoo. Hence the need for a pinch-hitter. I cleared my throat. "You ... uh ... didn't mention this to my family?"

He shook his head. "Or Ramirez, either, since she's dating your brother, Kevin. Klein wasn't happy about leaving the doc out of it, but I helped him see the light. The last thing we need right now is to have the Gregson clan riding to your rescue."

"Right. No use getting the folks in an uproar; it's probably nothing anyway."

His ice-blue gaze searched my face. "Care to fill me in?"

Well, sure, Jack. It's like this: I'm seeing things. Yeah. That would go over big.

I shook my head. "Like I said, it's probably no biggie. Part of the healing process maybe. I would rather not go into it until I hear what the doctor has to say."

He nodded, reluctantly I thought. "Have it your way. But keep me posted."

"You bet, and thanks again." I ended the transmission, and Jack and his console vanished.

Washing a hand down my face, I stood and crossed to the French doors. It was nine p.m., and the temperature on the tiny balcony that opened off my room had already dipped below freezing, but I hardly noticed as I sank tiredly into a fan-backed chair and folded my forearms atop the wrought-iron railing. Dropping my chin onto the backs of my hands, I stared moodily across Sadie's densely shadowed backyard.

Tomorrow couldn't get here soon enough.

Chapter 23

"You want my professional opinion?"

Samuel Bonner was short and round and button-nosed, with skin the color of dark caramel and a bald pate fringed in close-cropped frosty white. His coffee-brown gaze, warm with gentle good humor when he had greeted me at the door, was currently unreadable.

Bracing for the worst, I nodded. "Let me have it."

"*Nada.*"

"What?"

"My professional opinion is *nada*." He got up to turn on the lights and raise the blinds. The abrupt transition from shadowed to bright made me blink. "No structural defects," he continued, as he came back to sit in the chair. "The optic nerve has completely regenerated, everything's healed and functioning exactly as it should be. I would say my old friend Aaron did his usual damned fine job."

I didn't want to ask but had to. "What about brain damage?"

"Diagnostics say no."

Bewildered, seesawing between relief and a completely irrational sense of letdown, I glanced around the high-tech lab. What it lacked in square-footage it more than made up for in advanced technology, all the equipment either hand-held or built-in.

I looked back at Bonner. "So what's causing my ... ah ... problem?"

He didn't answer for a minute, just sat there with his head cocked and his wise old eyes staring holes in me. I waited for some kind of pronouncement, but the one I finally got wasn't exactly enlightening.

He rubbed his hands together and stood. "You up for some hot apple cider?"

Without knowing quite how I got there, I found myself ensconced in a comfortable blue wing-backed chair in his study, listening to the doc putter around in the kitchen. Autumn sunlight spilled into the room through a pair of windows between my chair and an aged leather recliner, bathing the room's contents in pale gold. The beige carpet and sturdy pine desk. The books lining the wall behind the desk. The crazy quilt of photos on the wall to my right and the corpulent mass of butterscotch-striped fur draped limply across the back of a floral-print settee. If not for the intermittent twitch of the tip of its tail, I might have thought the cat was dead.

"Here we are," announced Bonner, arriving with two steaming mugs.

He had traded his lab coat for a red cardigan. Passing me a cup fragrant with apple, cinnamon, and nutmeg, he settled into the recliner, flashing a quick glimpse of old-fashioned tan suspenders bisected by a bright red stripe.

He took a drink and gave his lips an exaggerated smack. "Just what the doctor ordered."

My own gray stoneware mug was at half-mast when the cat launched itself into my lap, briefly kneading my thighs before it flopped down and oozed across my blue jeans. The amber eyes closed, the tail tip flicked.

"Make yourself at home," I suggested.

"Fat Murray," said Bonner with an indulgent grin.

"Nice to meet you, Murray." I scratched the broad, flat head right behind the ears and got his motor running in a throaty purr.

"He's got a lousy BMI," the doc admitted cheerfully, "but he's good company."

"How long have you had him?"

Bonner's eyes crinkled in amusement. "You're not a cat person, are you? Nobody *has* a cat; cats either condescend to live with you, or they don't. Murray's been with me about seven years. Since my wife, Katie, died."

He raised his cup toward an eight-by-ten of a woman surrounded by a lush garden bursting with colorful blooms. She smiled out from under the wide brim of a straw hat, one pink-gloved hand on her hip, the other loosely cradling the handle of a wide, shallow basket.

"She was lovely. Were you married long?"

"Fifty-five years," he boasted. "You know, if it weren't for Katie, you and I wouldn't be sitting here, drinking this fine apple cider. Retiring to Hobson's Hope was her idea. Said she was tired of neighborhood-surveillance drones and traffic jams stacked clear up to the clouds. Wanted life at a slower pace. Someplace quiet, with less crime. She loved it here. We both did." Gazing at the photo, he smiled fondly and shook his head. "Lord, I miss that woman."

"I'm sorry. It must be— Ow!"

Bonner leaned toward me as I hastily put down my cup to rub the back of my left hand. "Nipped you, huh?"

I cast a wary glance at my assailant, who had lifted his head off my leg to give me the evil eye. "Yeah. Maybe he had a bad dream. I wasn't even touching him."

"Well, there you go. Murray gets cranky if you stop petting him before he decides he's had enough." He beamed like a proud papa. "He's quite the character."

"So I see." Discretion being the better part of valor, I started petting again. Once Murray was purring, I felt safe enough to shift my focus back to Bonner. "Listen, Doc, about my eyes."

Leaning back in his chair, he regarded me thoughtfully. "You say you've been seeing double?"

"Well ... yeah." Silence, accompanied by a clearly skeptical lift of his left eyebrow that made my face heat. "Sort of," I mumbled.

"Define *sort of.*"

Go ahead, A.J., give it to him straight. I almost laughed out loud but caught myself. No matter how I described what I had seen, he would think I had a screw loose.

That would make two of us.

"I can't help you, if you're not completely honest with me," he said.

It was a bald statement of fact delivered too gently to be an ultimatum, too logically and calmly to be anything but the truth. With that one short sentence the doc put me smack dab between a rock and a hard place with only one way out. So, taking a deep breath, I told him.

I expected rank disbelief, possibly an SOS to the guys in the white coats, but aside from a slight sharpening of his gaze during my narration, he didn't immediately react. Once my tale was told, silence fell like a ton of bricks between us. I would have given a year's pay to know what was going on in his mind, but his face wasn't giving his thoughts away. Three minutes later the tension was approaching unbearable, and I was composing a retraction. *I'm kidding, doc!*

Then he put down his cup. "Well, now." He clasped his hands atop his chest and stared at me. "Well."

I grimaced self-consciously. "I know it sounds crazy— "

Unlacing his fingers, he held up a hand. "You say the first episode involved Benjamin Palmer?"

The way he asked encouraged me to take a shot in the dark. "You know him?"

"I've known Ben and his mother for years; we attend the same church. Wilma Palmer is a tall, sturdy, raw-boned woman and one of the unhappiest people I know. I never met her husband—he died before Katie and I moved here—but rumor has it, Edgar was henpecked to a fare-thee-well. Benjamin gets the same treatment. Has, I gather, ever since he was a little, bitty bump.

"Lord only knows how—Wilma keeps him on a short leash—but he managed to make a lady friend a few years back, and it looked like he might finally have a chance to get out from under his mama's thumb and have a life of his own. But as soon as the relationship got serious, Wilma ran the woman off. Katie passed not long after that, and Ben stopped by to pay his condolences. One thing led to another, and we got to talking, and out the story came." He paused meaningfully. "You wouldn't know it to look at him, but Ben Palmer is eaten up with rage. The man is a volcano waiting to erupt."

The implied connection sank in slowly. He hadn't said it in so many words, but I finally realized Bonner was suggesting I had developed some kind of freaky ESP. Murray must have felt me tense in reaction, because he jumped off my lap and stalked away in a huff.

"You're saying I somehow tuned into that?" I asked, hoping I had misunderstood.

"You tell me."

"Come on, Doc. That's ..." *Loony tunes.* But I settled for, "... impossible."

"You think so? Tell me, Amanda, did you happen to catch the news last night?"

"No, why?"

"Activate personal computer interface," he said. A pinpoint of light sparked in the air between our chairs, elongated vertically, and finally expanded horizontally, forming a virtual monitor. "The girl in the second incident. What did you say her name was?"

"Nelson," I replied slowly. "Tina Nelson."

"News search. Source: *Hobson Herald.* Date: yesterday. Keywords: *Tina Nelson.*"

The bronze starburst slowly spinning mid-screen was replaced by the image of a young female reporter. The stamp of shock clear on her face, the correspondent gazed solemnly into the camera, as a glittering background welter of red-and-blue lights thrown by an army of police cruisers splashed the walls of a white Colonial. Two more cruisers hovered over the scene, their spotlights bathing both house and yard in a stark white glare.

"Shortly after nine p.m. this evening," began the reporter, "police responded to a report of a possible domestic disturbance at the residence of City Councilman Peter Nelson and found the Nelsons' fifteen-year-old daughter, Christina, bruised and bloodied from an apparent assault. The first officers to arrive at the scene were met at the door by the Councilman's wife, Carla Nelson, who insisted everyone was fine and suggested they contact their dispatcher for an address correction. A request for permission to search the premises had no sooner been denied, when a woman's scream prompted the officers to force their way past the protesting Nelson."

A yearbook-style photo of Tina popped into the upper right-hand corner of the picture as the reporter continued, "Arrested on suspicion of felony child abuse and serious bodily injury to a child, both Councilman and Mrs. Nelson are being held without bond. Christina Nelson was transported to Hobson Memorial, where she is listed in serious but stable condition. We'll bring you more on this shocking story as details emerge. This is Nala Halawagi reporting for *The Hobson*

Herald."

"Exit," Bonner commanded quietly, but I barely heard him and hardly noticed when the screen dematerialized.

Staring into the now-empty space between our chairs, I had the distinct impression time and tide had ground to a halt. If not for the fact that I could hear it pounding deep and slow in my ears, I would have sworn my heart had stopped, too.

"That's ... I saw— " I broke off, my head wagging a feeble denial. "But that can't be." I focused on Bonner. "Please tell me there's a rational explanation for this."

He regarded me pensively for a moment before asking, "Are you a scripture-reading woman?"

After trying, and failing, to guess where this was headed, I shrugged. "Not since my parents made us go to Sunday school. Why?"

Opening a shallow drawer in the coffee table, he pulled out a Bible. Judging by its battered, brown-leather cover and the fact that Bonner almost immediately found what he was looking for, this particular Good Book had seen years of near-constant handling.

"Here," he said, handing me the New King James and indicating a verse with his index finger. "Read this."

The Bible felt cool and weighty in my hands as I focused on the line he indicated. *Man looks at the outward appearance, but the LORD looks at the heart.*

I slowly lifted my gaze to meet his. "Doctor Bonner—"

"Sam."

"Okay, Sam. I hope you're not suggesting I'm seeing .... I mean, you can't actually believe ...."

"You have a better hypothesis?" He relieved me of the Bible and put it back in the drawer, then leaned forward in the recliner, elbows on his thighs, hands clasped between his knees. "You're a reporter, look at the facts. You came across two perfect strangers. In each of these encounters you saw ... well, a kind of vision, I guess you could call it. A revelation of the person those individuals keep hidden from the rest of us. Today you got objective proof of that. What more do you need?"

Inspiration tossed me a lifeline, and I grabbed it with both hands. "It won't wash, Doc. If I could see people's—"

" —Hearts?" he offered helpfully.

"Whatever," I muttered, backpedaling warily. "If I *could* see that way, why those two? Why not everybody?"

"Good question. Let me think about it." Lips pursed and eyes narrowed, he did. "Right off the top of my head? Seems to me the emotional state of the subject could be the determining factor. Both individuals were pretty upset when you ran into them, right? Probably took every ounce of self-discipline they had to keep up appearances.

"Think of it this way: Under certain types of acute physical stress, we know the body diverts resources from one system to bolster another. Like when blood flow to the extremities decreases to preserve the vital organs. Maybe extreme *emotional* stress triggers the same kind of exchange, the psyche drawing energy from one quadrant to bolster another. When strong emotions force an individual to divert resources to shore up the *external*, the *internal*, that part of us scripture calls the heart, might be stripped of a layer of concealment. Most of us still can't see that innermost person, but for no physiological reason I can detect or fathom, you obviously can." He paused, clearly waiting for me to respond. When I didn't, "Well? What do you think?"

The realist in me, the reporter with a well-known disdain for the so-called paranormal, sneered. But a deeper part of me, the woman who believed in intuition and serendipity, couldn't dismiss his idea quite so easily. I made a desperate bid for professional skepticism, that thread of objectivity that's the life's blood of every good reporter. Came up twenty logical objections to his cockamamie theory. But they all died unspoken, as I was suddenly swamped by the disconcerting conviction that my whole life boiled down to this one surreal moment, this choice between belief and denial. I could have sworn the entire cosmos was holding its breath, waiting for me to decide.

I lifted my hands, palms up. "Assuming you're right, what am I supposed to do with this … this …."

"Gift?" he suggested, then smiled reassuringly. "Don't worry, Amanda. The Good Lord gave you this ability to discern hearts for a reason. You'll know what to do when the time comes."

Chapter 24

I've run into truth crazier than fiction more times than I can count. Seen stuff you wouldn't believe. So my shock-and-awe threshold is higher than most. Not high enough for this magnitude of crazy, though. This crazy blew my threshold to Kingdom Come. And kept on going.

Once the numbness wore off, both mind and body started to buzz with a spidery current that made every nerve ending twitch. All of a sudden, I needed to *get out of there*. Put some distance between me and … and what? The calm certainty in Bonner's eyes? My disturbing inability to blithely file his conclusion under "Crackpot Theories?" Can you distance yourself from your own uncertainties and fears?

Sadie's was six miles away as the crow flies, closer to ten by Shank's mare, but what the hell. Wearing through shoe leather was getting to be a habit. Sam didn't press me when I passed on his offer of a ride. Smart man. Smart enough to know I had to unravel this twist of fate on my own.

It was almost one thirty when I left. The wind had picked up, and the sun was playing hide-and-seek behind scudding tufts of steel-gray clouds as I trudged toward the heart of town, hands buried in the pockets of my leather jacket. Time to corral my chaotic thoughts and herd them into some kind of order. What, exactly, were we talking about here? Sudden-onset ESP?

Of course not. Only a complete numbskull would buy that.

So why, against all logic and reason, was I already half-convinced? Not in my head, but instinctively, down deep in my gut. A smart reporter learns to pay attention to hunches, especially when they have a proven track record, which mine do. Ignoring the gut leads to all kinds of missed opportunities and trouble. Case in point: The last time I didn't listen to mine,

Cuey and Michaels died, and I woke up minus two eyes.

But this? This was stretching gut credibility to the breaking point. I could only imagine the chatter if word of my latest hunch got out.

Hey, you hear about A.J. Gregson?

Heard she lost her mind somewhere in Pennsylvania. Claimed she was abducted by aliens.

I would be working the tabloids before I knew what hit me. "Farmer's Wife Has Bigfoot's Love Child," by Amanda Gregson.

And Mom thought *crime* reporting was undignified.

Absently sidestepping a toddler barreling down the sidewalk on a bright red trike, I made a last-ditch grab for common sense. Scolded, pleaded, and debated with myself for at least two miles.

Fact: I had evidently had a couple, for want of a better word, visions. Both turned out to be uncannily accurate.

But what if?

What if the Sight—as I was already starting to think of it, although I would have cut out my tongue before calling it that out loud—was temporary? A passing aberration? What if it fizzled as suddenly and mysteriously as it appeared?

The smart attitude would be *get a second opinion.*

I thought about it, I really did. But I couldn't shake the strong, gut-level hunch that Sam Bonner was on the right track. His theory about the *what, how,* and *why* of my predicament seemed to fit.

The only piece that felt wobbly was the God angle.

I mean, come on. We're talking *God* here.

Okay, push comes to shove, I'll admit I believe in Him. More so than not, anyway. Like most people I know, my impression of the Deity tends to be off-hand and fairly abstract. He's out there. You know, around. But He and I ... well, we're not what you would call close. Begging the question, why would He start bestowing gifts?

Assuming this *was* a gift.

Maybe it was a curse.

That slant rattled me for a few blocks, but I calmed down when I eventually decided I was probably no better or worse than the next person. In other words, either way you looked at it, I wasn't a likely candidate for special divine attention, be it a pat on the back or a rap on the knuckles. No, there had to be another explanation. Quantum physics, maybe—a subatomic glitch involving photons and quarks and the uncertainty principle.

In the end, I gave up trying to figure how it had happened. Some questions don't have easy answers, and going off on existential tangents is a great way to get lost. Better to focus on questions I at least had a shot at answering.

Like, did I actually believe I had experienced some kind of weird second sight?

Partly. I mean, *something* had happened to me. Twice. And since arguing myself out of Bonner's explanation and my corresponding hunch hadn't worked, I had no choice but to hang with my gut and see what shook loose. Wait and see if it happened again. Even I did feel like Alice must have felt when she took a header down the rabbit hole and found herself hobnobbing with playing cards and jabberwockies.

Moving right along to question two, I wondered, *If it's permanent, can I control it?*

Yet to be determined, but based on my experience so far, I had to say no. Or at least, not yet. If the Sight was going to stick around, maybe I could *learn* to control it. Certainly be smart to try. It was either learn to flip the off-switch or collect way too much information about way too many folks, up to and including friends and family. There were some secrets, I decided with a pained grimace, I did *not* want to know.

I had been walking for three-quarters of an hour by then, and having missed lunch, had worked up quite an appetite, even for me. So I stopped at a canopied lunch cart on the corner of King and Chestnut for a couple foot-longs and a large side of fries. Food for thought. I sat down on a bench, peeled the foil off one of the dogs, and took a healthy bite, moaning out loud as the combined flavors of beef, sauerkraut, onions, and relish exploded on my tongue.

Ambrosia, thy name is fully loaded frankfurter.

Maybe it was the grease and carbs ... or the exercise ... or the fact that I had at least partially suspended my disbelief ... but I wasn't nearly wired as I had been five miles ago. Which isn't to say I didn't still have plenty of issues with my new talent. The big picture, for example, continued to elude me. I had no clue how these visions, assuming I continued to have them, would fit into the grand scheme. But I was going to figure it out.

Chapter 25

The chirp of an UpLink in the wee small hours can jerk you out of Dreamland into anxiety in less time than it takes you to open your eyes. Probably an outgrowth of man's instinctive awareness that ringtones at three a.m. almost never mean you won the lottery.

When Jack's telepresence materialized at the foot of my bed, his expression was grim. He skipped right over the part about how sorry he was to wake me up and said, "There's been another hit."

"Ferrymen?" I asked, pushing myself into a sitting position.

"Yeah."

"When?"

"Late yesterday."

I scooped a hand through my hair and struggled to catch up. "How come I didn't see anything on the news?"

"We clamped a lid on it. I had to call in some markers and make a few threats, but the networks agreed to hold off on the story for twenty-four hours."

"Ohh-kay."

I stretched the word into two wary syllables, because I was finally awake enough to catch the drift. Eagan wasn't calling at this ungodly hour to deliver a courtesy brief to his favorite reporter. There was more. Then my brother Jim virtualized next to Eagan, and the most likely definition of *more* cannonballed into me.

My lungs seized. I grabbed the fistful of gray jersey directly over my heart and hung on. "Dad! Oh, my God, it was Dad, wasn't it?"

"*No!*" Jim signaled stop with both hands. "No. Dad's fine. The family is fine." He dropped his hands and paused, sorrow etching deep lines in his face. "Stretch .... It was Bugsy."

"Bugsy?" My emotions ping ponged from panic to relief to stunned as I scrambled to shift gears. "Why would anybody take out a contract on Bugsy?"

"Your brother and I have been comparing notes on that," Jack said. "The senator had some powerful enemies."

"The kind who'll do whatever it takes to get what they want," Jim added. "You know how she was when she got riled."

"Uh-huh."

In default mode eighty-year-old Agnes "Bugsy" Oppenheimer was a pussycat—soft voice, endearing smile, benevolent eye-twinkle. But try to play the bully or violate her solid sense of right and wrong, and the tabby turned pit bull. And as a long list of sadder but wiser opponents been unlucky enough to learn, once the elfin senator from California sank her teeth into you .... Well, you might get loose, but you would lose a pound of flesh doing it.

She was a born science teacher, not a born politician, but she had promised her husband, Darrel, she would try for his congressional seat in the event he couldn't serve. So when he suddenly dropped dead of a heart attack at age seventy, Bugsy reluctantly came out of retirement and hit the campaign trail. Much to the pundits' surprise—and maybe her own chagrin—she was elected. Politicians and media alike tried to cast her as a cuddly figurehead, Senator Grandma, but Agnes Oppenheimer refused to be relegated. Never one to do a job halfway, she dove into government headfirst and became a force to be reckoned with in no time at all.

"Bugsy was a thorn in the side of the International Climatological Consortium for the past three years," Jim said. "Scuttled their last geoengineering proposal almost singlehandedly."

"Because tinkering with the earth's radiation balance could turn Central Africa into a dust bowl." I released the fabric bunched in my hand, absently rubbing at the hollow ache in my heart as I added, "The last time the weather weenies monkeyed with the environment, it took European agriculture five years to recover. Africa wouldn't survive a disaster of that magnitude." I glanced from one face to the other. "You think the ICC had her eliminated?"

"We don't know who held the contract," Jim said with a

shake of his head. "I was using the Consortium as a for-instance."

Emotion threatened to break through the insulation of shock, but I shored up my inner walls by concentrating on the facts. "Where did it go down?"

"Kenya," said Jack.

"*Kenya?*"

"The bug safari?" Jim reminded me.

"Oh, right. With everything else that's happened, I forgot."

Insect or arachnid, didn't matter. If it had six or more legs, Bugsy was nuts about it, hence her nickname. She had been psyched about her Africa trip, the latest in a long line of expeditions to exotic (read: *wild and wooly*) entomological hotspots. She had described her plans in such minute detail, I could easily picture her wading through a tangle of vines, canvass bush hat held atop her flyaway silver hair by a chin strap, hazel eyes alight with the thrill of the hunt. I almost smiled at the image now. Until I remembered she was gone.

"How did they pull it off?" Eagan called up a photo, and I squinted to bring it into focus. "Looks like a squashed mosquito."

"Close. It's a mini-drone, *Anopheles* class. You can get them on the open market."

"Sure. A dime a dozen for anybody with a license: DOD, police, PIs, corporations worried about industrial espionage. Used for surveillance, right?"

"Usually, but this one was weaponized. Pretty sophisticated design, too." Jack flicked the photo, giving me another angle. There still wasn't much to see. "Obviously, what's left is in bad shape, but we salvaged enough to guess it was programmed to home in on the senator's scent fingerprint. She must have felt the 'bite' on the back of her neck, because she slapped it and mangled it, so instead of flying off into the sunset, it slid under her collar and into her shirt. Doubt we would have found the murder weapon, otherwise."

"What agent are we talking about?"

The image dissolved as Jack answered, "A potent combination of neurotoxins. ME says a two hundred-pound man would have lasted four minutes, tops. Given the senator's age and the fact that she didn't weigh half that much, paralysis of the respiratory muscles would have been almost instantaneous. Loss of consciousness in under a minute, death in less than two."

"Probably never knew what hit her," my brother concluded.

Maybe not—God knows, I hoped not—but *I* had an uncomfortably rough idea what had hit her, because I had boned up on neurotoxins not too long ago. I'm far from an expert, but I understand enough to know you're talking about an ugly, painful death. Quick, but without a shred of dignity. Your brain shuts down almost immediately. You start to convulse and foam at the mouth. Your bowels and bladder let go ....

I slammed the door on the image taking shape in my mind, because I didn't want to see Bugsy that way, not even in my imagination, not even for a minute.

"I'm sorry, A.J.," Jack offered after a short silence. "Jim tells me she was a close friend of the family."

I nodded. "The Oppenheimers never had kids of their own—not sure why. Always figured it was none of my business. Anyway, they made up for it by more or less adopting my brothers and me. Bugsy was like an extra grandmother, spoiled us rotten. You know, the usual: cookies, pony rides, totally off-the-wall science experiments. Remember the time she helped us build that ten-foot volcano?" I asked Jim.

We traded crooked smiles as the memory dawned in his eyes.

"Working model. Yeah. I also remember she forgot to warn Sheriff Perkins about the eruption. He thought the county was under terrorist attack when that baby went off. Dad and Darrel spent a good week working their connections to quiet the uproar."

"Darrel being the senator's husband," Jack guessed.

"Right. He was the one who convinced Dad to run for the Assembly."

The inner walls were crumbling despite my best efforts, shock giving way to a potent mix of grief and rage, heavy on the rage. Probably because mad is easier. Mad doesn't knock you down like grief will, mad makes you feel strong. But I didn't let my budding fury show, because both Eagan and Jim were already eyeing me like I was an abandoned backpack with a timer attached. One hint of blood about to boil, and they would have Happy Li throw me in the local deep freeze until I cooled off.

Thank God they didn't have my recently acquired gift.

"When's the funeral?" I asked.

"We'll get them, A.J.," Jack said.

"Glad to hear it, but that doesn't answer my question."

Jim stuck out his jaw. "Forget it, Stretch. You're staying right where you are."

"You think Hell's Boatmen will take a run at me at a state funeral? Security will be so tight it squeaks. I'll be in no more danger there than I am here in—"

Eagan threw up a hand to stop me. "Your brother doesn't need to know where you are."

"Since you conferenced him in, I assumed you had told him."

"He conferenced himself in."

"I was notified as soon as CIIS found the obit." Jim glanced at Iceman. "That was fast work, by the way."

"Only because we knew what to look for. The job had Ferrymen written all over it. I just wish we had managed to pull the blurb before the news got out."

"You did your best." Jim turned back to me. "You know how it is. Any threat or crime against the Assembly when it's headquartered in the District, my office gets read in. As soon as I found out what happened, I buttonholed Agent Eagan and told him to muzzle the press until we could break the news to you."

"You mean until *you* broke the news to her." Eagan shrugged. "I understood once you explained the relationship."

"So, I guess I owe you," I mused. "Both of you."

The smile Jim gave me then should have been wreathed in canary feathers. "Yes, you do," he said, "and I'm calling in the I.O.U. right now. Promise me you won't show up at the funeral."

"But—"

"No buts. You won't do Bugsy's memory any favors putting yourself and everyone else at unnecessary risk."

The *everyone else* was what cut me off at the pass. He had

known it would.

"I hate it when you do this."

"Does that mean you're going to pout, but you'll stay put?"

"Yes, I'll stay put." *For now*, I hedged silently, because a plan was beginning to take shape.

"And don't do anything stupid."

"Who, me?" When he scowled, I held up a hand. "Okay, okay. Nothing stupid, I swear."

An easy promise to give him, because I planned to stick with clever and cunning from here on out. Although I doubt my brother would have agreed, if he could have read my mind.

"We've got eyes on her," Jack said. "We'll make sure she doesn't go anywhere."

Eyes on her. It was all I could do not to roll mine. Feds. It's like they can't help themselves.

Not that this was a newsflash. Only a nitwit would believe Eagan had parked me with former spook Sadie Carter by accident or handed me a government-issue UpLink out of the goodness of his heart.

All the better to surveil you with, my dear.

Even though I had guessed as much, I mentally thanked him for the official heads-up. It would remind me I needed to step carefully, if I wanted to put one over on my keepers. (And I most certainly did.) I wouldn't be able to get away with squat as long as CIIS was in a position to block my slightest move.

But with the right skills you can get past any blocker, and as luck would have it, I grew up playing football with three older brothers.

One end run, coming up.

Chapter 26

According to Euripides, the tongue is mightier than the blade. I agree, up to a point. If I didn't believe words have power, I wouldn't be in the business I'm in. But the morgues are full of poor, dumb stiffs offering silent testimony to the fact that when it comes to a street fight, blade trumps tongue nine times out of ten.

And I wanted a street fight.

Assuming I could pick a fight at all. I wasn't sure I would be able to start a tiff with the Ferrymen, let alone the knock-down-drag-out I was after, but I had to try. I owed it to Cuey, Michaels, and now, Bugsy.

I only hoped the old Greek was right, because talk was all I had–no evidence, no leads, not even the *glimmer* of a lead to back it up. What I did have was the branding.

If Hell's Boatmen had an Achilles heel, it was their rep. The obits were the giveaway. Why leave a calling card when you've committed the perfect crime? Because you want to build your street cred. You want potential clients to know you're relentless, lethal, and available for hire. When you market yourself as death on wheels, reputation is everything.

So, my plan, such as it was, was to hit them in the brand. Tarnish the Ferrymen's aura of invincibility. While I was at it, I would lie through my teeth and claim to have what I didn't, namely, information that could hurt them. If I got lucky and struck a nerve, Charon might get worried. Get him worried enough, even the Angel of Death can make a mistake.

If I got *unbelievably* lucky, I might live to see it. Another big if, because jerking the tiger's tail hard enough to raise his hackles is a sure-fire way to shorten your life expectancy.

But while I was willing to play fast and loose with *my* life, I didn't want my family in the line of fire. There was probably no way to slide them completely out of the crosshairs, but I would do my best by giving them fair warning before I made my move. Two caveats: I couldn't let them get a fix on me when I called, and timing would be crucial. If they knew where to find me, and I warned them too early, my clan would move heaven, earth, and two divisions of Marines to protect me from myself. If I held off too long, Bart Dickson wouldn't have time to circle the wagons.

Make that three caveats. I couldn't let them sic Eagan on me. I would be facing *that* music soon enough, I admitted with a wince. Iceman would land on me with both size thirteens for pulling this stunt. Imagining his reaction was enough to give me heartburn, so I decided to take a page from Scarlett O'Hara and think about it later.

One other person had to be brought on board ahead of time: my editor. But again, not too far ahead. Discretion isn't Tug's strong suit. I would brief him in when I was ready to roll and not a minute before, then let the expletives fall where they may. Once he got all the cuss words out of his system, Maxwell would chomp down on his stogie, roll up his sleeves, and light a fire under the entire network, because there's nothing Tug enjoys more than a late-breaking chance to stop the presses.

But first things first.

Before I could start to put my pieces in place, I needed space to maneuver, and I didn't have an inch of wiggle room with Eagan and company keeping even closer tabs on me now that the Ferrymen had made it personal. So not only did I have to give my watchers the slip, I had to do it without them realizing the slip had been given. If somebody got to wondering what I was up to, Eagan would start sniffing around, a process that could only end with him putting the kibosh on my best-laid plan.

Neutralizing the CIIS UpLink seemed like a logical first step toward freedom of movement. ULs make tracking easy, and let's face it, sometimes people listen in. Suddenly leaving it home would be like tattooing, *Look, monkey business!* on my forehead. Fortunately, I had a couple ideas on ways to outsmart the technology. Whether they would work or not remained to be seen.

I devoutly hoped they would, because keeping CIIS in the

dark until my first salvo had been fired was crucial. After that, it would be too late for the feds to do much more than hang on for the ride.

Providing the Ferrymen took the bait, of course.

That would be me.

Chapter 27

"You sure had me fooled."

I glanced over my shoulder to where Sadie stood in the parlor doorway, sleeves of her tailored navy blue shirt rolled up to her elbows, arms folded across her chest. Cosmo ambled in to sit next to her, so they could *both* give me the fish eye.

"What do you mean?"

"I would have bet my pitifully small government pension we would have to hogtie you to keep you off the Ferrymen after they dusted Senator Oppenheimer."

I turned back toward the window and the sun-dappled yard outside. "I'll deal with the Ferrymen when the time comes."

"So you keep telling me. I hear a whole lot of *just you wait*, but talk is cheap, right?" She snorted. "Look at you! You are *no* kind of threat to *anybody*. When was the last time you even left the house? Went for a run?"

I shrugged. "Couple'a weeks, I guess."

"You guess right. You don't go out, you don't sleep, and you don't eat enough to keep a bird alive. Never thought I would see *that* day," she added under her breath. A second later, her hand was on my shoulder. "Look, I know the senator's murder hit you hard."

"Never lost anybody close to me before. Knocked me for a loop, I guess."

"It will do that. From what you've told me, she was quite a woman." She punctuated this iota of sympathy with a hard knuckle to my upper arm. "So you think a high-spirited lady like the senator would be proud of you now, Miss She Was Like a Grandma to Me? Miss Big-time Po-lice Reporter? Moping around, staring out windows and acting all hang-dog." Biker Dog grunted. "No offense, Cosmo. Oppenheimer was a scrapper, A.J., and I thought you were, too. Hard-charging journalist, and all that. Yeah, right! Well, you better snap to, if you plan to get payback!"

I turned to meet her gaze. "What do you want from me?"

Her eyebrows lifted. "Me? Not a thing. It's no skin off my nose if you want to take it on the chin. Long as the government pays your rent on time, I'm happy. On the other hand, you *might* consider getting off your butt to help Jack nail those creeps."

I frowned at her. "Eagan doesn't want my help."

"*Eagan doesn't want my help,*" she parroted through her nose. "Does the law *ever* want your help? You know how it is between The Man and the press. Since when do orders from headquarters keep a hot-shot correspondent like you from sticking her nose in?"

"Well ...."

"You ever turned the cops onto a lead they missed?"

"Once or twice."

"All right. Only one question left, the way I see it. You want that payback for Senator Oppenheimer or not?"

I narrowed my eyes. "You know I do."

"Prove it," she said. "But keep your snooping under the radar. Jack will kick my butt, he finds out I been putting ideas in your head." She shooed me with both hands. "Now go on and get busy. Just remember, dinner's at six. And you had *better* bring your hollow leg!"

Cosmo measured me with his trademark Johnny Ringo stare, huffed in disgust, and padded out after her.

When the fading sound of footsteps assured me they were out of earshot, I exhaled heavily. *About time!*

How do you pull the wool over a spook's eyes? Spies are worse than reporters, always looking at you sideways and dissecting your every word and motive. To tell you the truth, I almost gave up before I tried. But I had business to take care of.

Necessity being the mother of invention and all, it wasn't long before I settled on my strategy. It was called "Do What Comes Naturally."

The trick was to use the emotions I was actually experiencing without letting them stop me in my tracks. Give my audience the grief and anger they expected, so I didn't arouse suspicion, but avoid going up like a Roman candle, so I didn't wind up sedated or incarcerated. Not the easiest tightrope to walk when your moods are swinging like a well-oiled pendulum. Some days, the balance took all the self-control I possessed.

Per my own first commandment, the hardcore grief and rage were vented behind closed doors. Once I drained the tear ducts, I would take my bloodshot eyes downstairs, corner my landlady and talk about who Bugsy was and what she had meant to me and how awfully I would miss her. I chatted up my thirst for revenge. Added a dollop of fretfulness — "I hate being hamstrung!" — and a soupçon of dire promises about what I would do when my hands were no longer tied, *et voila!*

Two weeks. That's how long it had taken to erase the watchful glint in Sadie's eyes and replace it with concerned exasperation. Fourteen days. Not forever, but long enough. I was beginning to wonder if she would *ever* get fed up and kick me out of the house. I wondered if I would be too weak from hunger to go when she did. Waiting for her to relax her guard was no picnic, but eating like a fashion model almost killed me.

In the end, the sacrifice was worth it. The scene couldn't have played out better if I had written the script myself. I would still have to be careful, or I would wind up toe to toe with Eagan before I was ready, but I had filched my inch. Now to snatch the mile.

The blood was racing through my veins, plans buzzing in my head like a swarm of eager bees. I was psyched. Time to get the ball rolling.

What about me? moaned my stomach.

So who said I couldn't get the ball rolling over a large pizza with the works?

Chapter 28

Exile in Dullsville had it perks. The absence of official surveillance, for example. There were no patrol droids to broadcast your whereabouts or query the authorities about suspicious behavior. The only surveillance cameras in Hobson's Hope were local feeds unconnected to the big spy-eye-in-the-sky. Banks, convenience stores, like that. I knew this, because I checked the public records. You've gotta love irony. In his bid to keep me under wraps, Jack Eagan had stashed me in the one city on the planet tailor-made for my end run.

God bless Whitfield and Abigail Hobson.

Before I actually set the wheels in motion, I decided to at least *try* to figure out if Sadie was Eagan's only asset in Hobson's Hope. I thought she probably was, but it never hurts to be sure. An undercover babysitter popping up at the last minute would seriously gum up my works.

I had researched surveillance detection routes once for a piece on undercover agents tracking anarchists in Toronto. I'll be the first to admit three how-to sessions with Dickson weren't much to go on, but they would have to do.

I counted thirteen other passengers on the nine o'clock bus to Center City, but I was the only one who got off at the King Street stop. I lingered over tea and a blueberry scone at a closet-sized mom-and-pop. Stealing glances at a handful of fellow diners and folks passing by the window. Memorizing shoes and jawlines, because most tails don't remember to change the former and can't change the latter. After brunch I hit the stores, reversing course once or twice, abruptly stepping into the odd boutique, and surreptitiously checking reflections in various display windows. No repeat sightings. Nobody seemed remotely interested, or even suspiciously *disinterested*, in my movements. Best guess, no one was following me, and best guess was all I had. I headed for the library.

About the time I wrapped my fingers around the brass handle on one of the library's glass double-doors, another possibility dawned on me. If CIIS had tagged the library as one of my favorite haunts, they might have an agent in place, waiting for me to show up. Unable to decide if I was edging toward ridiculous or being canny, I gave the building a quick walk-through, lingering on the fourth floor. I slunk around four for fifteen minutes before concluding I was the lone skulker in the stacks.

Beginning to feel like a conspiracy theorist run amok, I unlocked the study carrel and closed the door behind me. Using my CIIS UpLink, I accessed the WNN morgue and pulled up the official file on the Ferrymen. I selected the Yanos hit, because there was more information on that job than on any other; ergo, the file would entertain government eavesdroppers longer, should any decide to tune in. Sadie was right, Eagan would probably raise Cain if he did tune in. Okay, let him. I've been known to raise some Cain myself.

The first 3-D clip swirled to life in the airspace over the desk. So far, so good. I slipped that UpLink off my wrist and laid it on the table. *Track that, Iceman.*

I sidled out the door and locked it behind me. Zipped across the still-deserted reading area between blocks of shelves to the ladies' room, planning to make my calls and get back to the carrel as soon as possible. Not that I expected Eagan to contact me, but you never knew.

Not soul in sight; odds were I had the restroom all to myself, but I tugged on each stall door to make sure. Then I perched a hip on the counter where I could keep one eye on the door. Firing up my off-the-books UL, I got to work.

Chapter 29

"Can you do it?"

Shuki Okazawa smirked. "Is there gold on Mars?" A view of the mines as seen from the Mars Orbital Assay Station swam onto the lenses of the opaque, wrap-around shades perched atop her button nose. "Pieceacake. Provided."

I bit back an exasperated, *Can we please cut to the chase?* The four-foot-eleven, ninety-pound techno-priestess known as Shady Lady—both because of her trademark headgear and her well-known rep for operating on the shifty side—was temperamental. If the petite Asian climbed on her high horse now, it would take days to cajole her out of the saddle.

We had first met five years ago. A counterfeiting operation was driving the feds crazy as they tried to follow a diffuse, masterfully encrypted funny-money trail that seemed to start everywhere and end nowhere. There was this one bank president, Lambert Gottschalk. Tall, silver-haired, dignified. Every time you turned around he was taking to the air waves to assure John Q. Public First Federal was working with the authorities to dam the flow. Guy was always front and center ... a little *too* front and center for my taste. My gut told me Gottschalk was dirty, but when I suggested law enforcement do some digging on Mister Clean, nobody wanted to hear it. That left me holding the shovel.

I needed a geek, but not just *any* geek. I needed somebody better than all the gifted-yet-stymied federal geeks combined. Shuki came highly recommended by one of my back-alley contacts—one of those *friend of a friend of a friend* referrals. It had cost WNN an arm and a leg, but she finally agreed to work for us. Trouble was, she came on board hell-bent on hacking into the bank, the Continental Reserve, and at least half the world's money markets.

"They won't even know I was there!"

But I was out to fix this deal, not break it worse than it was already broken, and I wanted evidence that would be admissible in court. Shuki was disappointed but rose to the occasion, designing a one-of-a-kind marker-byte she could slip into a counterfeit transaction mid-stream. In less than a week she had the goods on Gottschalk.

She and I have worked together enough times since for me to swear she's the slickest, quickest, most creative hacker on either side of the law. If she's not unstoppable, she's a baby step away from it. Unfortunately, Shuki knows all this, too.

Since I didn't have time to wheedle, threaten, or bribe my way back into her good graces, I held onto my patience. "Provided what?" I asked.

"Provided you got no problem with a touch of piracy." Her bright-blue, cupid's-bow lips curved in a nefarious grin as her lenses flashed hideously cackling Jolly Rogers.

"You know I like to keep it legal, Shuki-O."

"Yeah, so you keep telling me."

The Rogers shattered into colorful bits of confetti that arranged, then rearranged, themselves in a series of intricate patterns as she pondered, lips pursed. Watching her absently finger the thin, pink braid sprouting from her inch-long, blue-black buzz-cut, I could almost see the synapses firing. Finally, she shook her head, the lens confetti coalescing into twin abstract caricatures of Shuki's frowning face.

"Sorry, Goodie Two-Shoes, there's no other way. Unless you wanna leave a trail a third-grader can follow, I need a back door into the Cloud." Her glasses came alive with a rapidly shifting series of schematics laced with streaming lines of code. "We'll route the signal through a series of ghost terminals and sneak it in when the data flow is heaviest. Once I lose it in the other transmissions, I can bounce it between satellites, downlink to a heavy traffic terminal, pull it back out, and run it over an anonymous virtual. I'll delete the whole schmear the second the transmission ends. You're not gonna stay on long, right?" I shook my head. "Good. We should still triple-encrypt, though. Another layer of insurance never hurts."

"So the broadcast will be untraceable?"

"Nothing's untraceable, if you've got the right people on

it."

I was momentarily distracted enough to ask, "You're not tracing *this* call, though. Right?"

I had used the disposable's high-end quantum-encryption and anti-trace caller ID-alteration features. Programmed in a plain gray background to disguise my surroundings and placed the call via one of the thousands of anonymous call-routing services offered by here-today-gone-tomorrow providers based in Bangladesh or Timbuktu. Not bad for an amateur, but no defense against Shady Lady. It would take thirty seconds, tops, for her to pinpoint both me and the silk flower arrangement near my left elbow.

The scowling Shukies made a return appearance. In red. "I gave you my word, didn't I?"

"Sorry," I said, and held up a placating hand. "I'm sorry, all right? I'm a little on edge here."

"Yeah?" She sniffed. "Well, like I was saying, nothing's untraceable, if you've got the right people working on it."

I looked her straight in the UVs. "You don't want these guys to find you, Shuki. They play for keeps."

"So I hear. Don't worry, I'll drop off the grid as soon as we're done. Won't be the first time I erased my existence. Meanwhile, the *A.J. Gregson Show* will be on the air and off," she snapped her fingers, "like that. They might be able to trace it back to your general geographic location eventually, but it'll take them a day or two."

"A day or two is all I need." By that time I would have ditched the throwaway and found a safe, secure place to await developments. Heck, Jack would probably lock me up himself.

"All right," I agreed reluctantly, "we'll do it your way, just this once. But don't get caught, okay?"

"Do I ever?"

Chapter 30

"Threats, Amanda Joy?"

Nothing says you're on thin ice quite like a frosted Virginia drawl. I subdued a wince and forced myself to meet his gaze head-on. "Only because you won't listen to reason, Dad."

"Listening to reason assumes the party of the first part has said something reasonable."

Always the lawyer. "I have to do this."

His angry gaze softened slightly. "I know you do. I even understand your reasoning. I'm not sure I agree, but I respect your professional judgment and realize you've got to follow your convictions. That's the way your mother and I raised you, and I won't play the hypocrite now." He paused. "Much as it pains my father's heart not to."

"So, what's the problem?"

"The problem isn't what you want to do, but how you plan to do it. Alone and unprotected. There's no reason to risk your life foolishly. Tell me where you are. Let me send Bart."

My gaze shifted to the bodyguard making like the Sphinx behind Dad's left shoulder. Might be nice to have him watching my back, but .... "He'll have his hands full covering the rest of you. That's why I'm giving Dickson this heads-up, so he can make arrangements. You'll have to move fast," I told Bart, "but you should have time to get the pieces in place. I can't do this, unless I know the family's taken care of."

I got a tight nod in reply.

"For the love of God, Amanda," Dad said, and the rough plea in his voice almost broke my heart.

"Look, I probably won't get any reaction at all. Why would they bother? It's not like I can really hurt them." Seeing as how I had bluff and bubkes to work with. "A week from now, I'll probably have egg on my face. Dickson will grouse about all the unnecessary work I caused him. Better to be safe than sorry, that's all."

"At least let Agent Eagan know what you have planned."

Sure, Dad. Then I'll shoot myself in the other *foot.*

But I was taught to respect my elders, so I said, "He would never let me go through with it."

"Maybe if I had Bart talk to him."

"No. Nobody talks to him. Swear, Dad, or I'll drop off the grid right now. Then *no one* will know where I am."

"Better give her what she wants, Senator," Dickson advised. "At least this way she'll stay put, and Eagan will know where to find her, once the cat is out of the bag." He shot me a look ripe with promise. "He'll have her in protective custody ten minutes after the broadcast."

If that long.

"I don't appreciate being blackmailed by my own daughter," Dad fumed. "I don't like it one bit." He glared at me in clenched-jawed silence, before exhaling in defeat. "But it appears you have me over a barrel." Then, "Lord in heaven, how am I ever going to explain this to Ruth?"

"You'll think of a way." Better him than me, right? "So you promise not to rat me out? You won't try to find me and send the cavalry?"

"I promise, damn it." He skewered me with a wait-until-I-get-you-home glower. "Of course you know, you and I are going to have a sit-down when this is over."

"I figured as much," I admitted, smiling ruefully.

But the truth hung unspoken between us. If my scheme worked out as planned, Dad reading me the riot act would be the least of my problems.

Chapter 31

I was only two steps away from my goal now, but they were long steps.

One, I needed access to a studio—sans audience and crew, because I didn't want any innocent bystanders who might get in my way or become collateral damage later. The fact that the *Harold* had the only broadcast facilities in town narrowed my choices to three, according to the website. Like all news organizations, this one would man a night desk, but in a burg like Hobson's Hope, where they rolled up the sidewalks early, the after-hours staff wouldn't be big enough to play a hand of bridge. So, barring a local, national, or global catastrophe that would call all hands back on deck, those studios should be dark and pirate-able.

Two, I had to come up with a believable reason to go out after dark. Pitiful, but true.

On a scale of one to ten—one being a tea party, and ten being a Roman block orgy—Hoper nightlife didn't hardly crack the scale. Even the bar, singular, closed early. Since arriving, my social life could be summed up under the heading "Evenings at Sadie's." If I wasn't reading, I was watching documentaries with Byron or suffering through chick flicks with Fannie and Connie. On a good night, I got to talk cop-shop with Happy or play chess with Sadie and Cosmo. (Biker Dog was a world-class kibitzer. Sitting with his nose at board level, eyes glued to the action he critiqued each move, giving it either an *atta-girl* tail twitch or a derisive curl of the lip. Although how he ever learned to tell a rook from a pawn is anybody's guess.)

Anyway, thanks to the absence of anything remotely resembling after-hours entertainment, an unexplained excursion that lasted beyond eight p.m., no matter how brief, was bound generate innocent but unwelcome curiosity.

And I had to do this between eight and ten. Prime time, baby. Sure, Tug would replay the recorded version *ad nauseam*, but I was going for the big splash, live and in person. That meant prime time, and *that* meant I needed a hall pass. One so completely legit Sadie wouldn't raise an eyebrow. I was still wracking my brain for an idea two days after talking to Dad, when fate intervened. Hank Ellison and I crossed paths again at Mocha Joe's.

"A.J.," said Hank, "glad I ran into you. I would have called last night, but I don't know your number. I was going to ring the boardinghouse when I got to work." He flicked what struck me as a nervous smile across the counter. "Morning, Joe. Give me a jumbo coffee, black."

"Comin' right up, Mr. Elllison."

I squeezed a packet of organic honey into my chai and licked an errant dribble off my middle finger. "What's up?"

Obviously ill at ease, he straightened his navy blue tie. "First of all, I … ah … I wanted to tell you I'm sorry about Senator Oppenheimer. WNN said you two were close."

The ache in my heart throbbed as I answered softly, "Yeah, we were."

"So how are you doing?"

"As well as can be expected, I guess."

He nodded and lapsed into awkward silence. I was about to ask if offering condolences was the only reason he had wanted to get in touch with me, when he cleared his throat. "I know you're still …. I mean, I know this must be a tough time for you, but I was wondering …." He faltered again and ran a hand over his fiery cap of close-cut curls. "Damn, I hope you won't think this is out of line."

I snapped the lid back on my cup. "Spit it out, Hank."

"It's … ah … well, it's the Garden Club," he finished in a rush. "Thanks, Joe," he mumbled accepting his coffee. He glanced around. "Look, can we sit down for a minute?"

"Sure." I followed him to the window table, and we sat. "Now what about the Garden Club?" In an effort to put him out of his obvious misery, I smiled and asked, "Bloodshed among the hydrangeas?"

"Probably," he said, relaxing a bit, "but that's not what I wanted to talk to you about." He fingered the lid of his coffee, watching me out of the corner of his eye. "They're having their annual Petal Pushers' Gala tomorrow. Big black-tie to-do, their major fund-raiser for the year. They pull out all the stops — five-star catering, music, champagne, the works. My sister was supposed to go with me, but she had to back out at the last minute, because her son broke his arm at peewee football practice. I wondered if you might like to use her ticket. Not like a date," he hastened to add, "strictly professional. Malcolm Conover's going to give the keynote."

"You can't be serious. Heart of Gold Conover? Here?"

I couldn't see it. Malcolm Conover was both a multi-billionaire and a world-renowned philanthropist. His name was practically a household word. Universally admired for his compassion for, and commitment to, the less fortunate, he donated untold sums to found state-of-the-art hospitals in third-world countries, construct fabulous shelters for the homeless, set up cost-free training programs for the unemployed, and rush tons of relief to disaster-stricken areas.

I shook my head. "You're telling me an A-lister like Conover is coming to Hobson's Hope?"

"I know, right?" He forgot his discomfort long enough to look at me. "Everybody knows the man is a fiend for gardening, but why chat up Podunk when you would get the red carpet treatment at the Royal Botanic Gardens? I did some checking. Turns out our Garden Club president is his only living relative. Second cousin, twice-removed. On his mother's side, I think." Ellison took a quick sip of coffee. "So, you ... uh ... want to go? It might take your mind off your troubles. You can think about it and call me later, if you want."

What was to think about? This was like a gift from God. The perfect explanation for going out. The gala would give me a chance to do the broadcast. It would also keep me beyond the reach of the long arm of the law for a couple hours afterwards. Any plan that offered a temporary reprieve from the wrath of Eagan was a plan I could love.

"I can give you my answer right now. I'll go. I have a favor to ask, though."

I laid out the basics and suggested he hold his questions until the next night, when my request would become self-explanatory. Curious but game, he agreed and said he would pick me up at seven-thirty.

As soon as he was out the door, I slumped back in my chair and blew out a long, slow breath. Okay, the stage was set. All I had to do tomorrow night was walk out and say my lines.

Imagining how it would feel to spit in the devil's eye, and wondering what might happen afterwards, I found myself both raring to go and scared stiff. I felt dizzy and slightly winded. Closing my eyes, I fought to control my breathing. It took a good ten minutes, but my system finally settled down enough so I could finish my chai and be on my way.

When I left Mocha Joe's, I did something I almost never do of my own free will. I bought a dress.

After that, I called Tug.

Chapter 32

Shuki's disembodied voice: "Okay, bring up the lights."

An overhead spot popped on, illuminating me but leaving my surroundings shrouded in darkness. Hank was in the control room. Nobody else was around, because the *Herald's* lifestyle crew called it a day at five.

If Ellison was any kind of reporter at all, curiosity had to be eating him alive by now. First I borrow his set, then I draft him into service, all without giving him any specifics. Two mysterious, encrypted texts later, parties unknown remote-commandeer his system, and a sultry female voice invades his soundstage. And those were only the preliminaries. Hank didn't know it yet, but he had a box seat for the biggest broadcast of my life.

I only hope it won't be the last *broadcast of my life*, I thought, with a glance at the clock. Eight-thirty. Showtime.

Shuki said, "You're live in three, two, one—"

With a surreptitious breath to steady my nerves, I looked into the camera. And smiled. "You call yourselves the Ferrymen. I have a message for you.

"You haven't scared me off. I'm still on your case, and I'm going to stay there, now more than ever. You'll be sorry you missed your shot at me, because if you thought I was a can of worms before, that's nothing compared to what I'm about to become.

"I'm the one who got away. The one who's going to bring you down. I would move heaven and hell to do it, but to tell you the truth, I'm beginning to think orchestrating your downfall won't be the challenge I expected it to be. I mean, you botched your chance to take me out of the picture, right? Maybe you got careless because you've started to believe your own press, or maybe you're losing your edge. Bottom line, you're evidently not the big, bad, invincible wolves we all thought you were.

"I wonder if prospective clients are thinking twice about contracting with you. Now that they know you couldn't hit one unarmed reporter. I'll bet they are. If not, they will be. As soon as they hear what comes next.

"Our mutual friend? The one in the photo you sent? You figured him for some harmless schlemiel who didn't have the brains to tie his own shoes. Maybe you should have been more careful around him. It's always the small stuff that trips you up, right? The slip of the tongue, the minor lapse, that gives the game away? Our friend was more observant than you gave him credit for. We had an extremely informative chat before you booked that last photo shoot. I can get to you with what he told me. Might even share the scoop with my new pals in CIIS.

"Long story short, you blew it, big time, and your days are numbered. Trust me on that.

Meanwhile, I want you to remember three names. You might want to write them down. Not that all the other murders you've committed don't matter, but these made it personal for me. Special Agent Evander Cuey. Special Agent Sammy Michaels. Senator Agnes Oppenheimer. When you're on the run and looking over your shoulders, I want you to know why."

Then I drew a finger across my throat, signaling Shuki to end the transmission.

"*Oooh*," she crooned when the lights came up, "that had to hurt! And they say *I* like to live dangerously! Nice job, Goody Two-Shoes, but I am *way* out of here."

"Take care, Shuki-O." I didn't expect or get an answer; I had a feeling she was already gone.

"Holy crap!"

The quiet, almost reverent, exclamation drew my attention up the curved stairway to the right of the tiered audience seating. Hank stood outside the door to the control room, eyes wide, arms hanging loosely at his sides. His face was so white, both his freckles and his bushy red eyebrows looked like they had been glued on.

He shook his head and said it again, with feeling. "*Holy crap!*"

"Hank—"

The sound of his name seemed to snap him out of his daze. He sprang into action, loping down the aisle, two stairs at a time. "Are you out of your freakin' mind? I don't freakin' *believe* this!"

"Calm down, I—"

"*Calm down?*" He landed in front of me, slightly out of breath, cummerbund askew. "*Calm down?*" His index finger stabbed the air in front of me. "You call out the world's most efficient killing machine, *from my studio*, and you want me to *calm down*? I'm a dead man," he groaned, closing his eyes. "My life is over, and I never even had a chance to get married and father an heir to follow in the old man's footsteps." He opened his eyes to glare at me reproachfully. "You could have at least warned me before you set me up for a blind date with death."

I couldn't help myself. "*Blind date with death?*" The glare intensified. "Okay, forget I said that. But would you have helped me, if I had told you what I was going to do?"

The blood rushed back into his face with a vengeance. "I don't know, but it would have been nice to have a choice!"

Time to settle him down before the increased blood flow blew an aneurysm in that overheated brain. "Relax, Hank. There's no way anyone can connect what happened here to either you or the *Herald*. My technical expert is the best in the world, and she assures me this broadcast will be virtually untraceable."

"*Virtually* untraceable? Now why don't I find that reassuring?"

"Will you calm down? Even if the Ferrymen eventually trace it back to me, *you're* in the clear, and I'll be leaving town, probably later tonight. We planned this down to the last detail, covered all possible contingencies. Trust me, I would never put someone else's life at risk."

I paused, wondering if that was strictly true, given what had happened to Cuey and Michaels. I still wasn't one hundred percent convinced their deaths weren't my fault. Of course, this wasn't the time to wrestle my conscience. Instead, I told Hank, "You're safe."

He eyed me suspiciously for a long minute. "You're sure."

"Absolutely."

He stared at me some more, then heaved a sigh. Straightening his cummerbund and checking his tie, he muttered, "I hope you're right, but I guess we'll find out soon enough." He ran an unsteady hand over his hair. "Look, I don't know about you, but I could use a drink. You still up for the gala?"

"Sure."

Adrenaline was still pouring through my veins as we left the studio, each wrapped in our own thoughts.

Despite the way his eyes had lit up when he first saw me in my long-sleeved, floor-length gown—a black, beaded number that rose high in front and plunged almost to my waist in back—Hank was probably wishing he had never laid eyes on me.

As for me? I felt like an actor in some post-modern adaptation of the Cinderella story. My low-heeled, size-ten black pumps were hardly dainty glass slippers, but I *was* dressed up and on my way to the ball. I knew the clock was ticking, and midnight would come all too soon. But where Cindy married the prince, my storybook ending was still up in the air.

And living happily ever after was drawing long odds.

Chapter 33

The private drive leading to Treemont Country Club broke out of the surrounding woods to cut a sweeping curve through three acres of manicured lawn. Twin borders of luminaries flickered softly under a blanket of stars as a steady stream of luxury sedans and limos cruised between them, skirting a kidney-shaped pond directly across from the clubhouse where banks of windows two stories high blazed with light. The yellow-gold glow spilled across the driveway to dance on wind-ripples wrinkling the water's mirrored surface.

One by one, the vehicles ahead of us drew up to the curved portico to disgorge Hobson's Hope glitterati. Then it was our turn. We pulled up in front of the twin pillars supporting the canopy. One black-clad valet swept open my door and handed me out onto the red carpet, while a second slid behind the steering console. As Ellison's forest-green coupe pulled away, he took my elbow to guide me toward a pair of massive oak doors.

A trim man in a tux greeted us, his lips curved in welcome under a pencil-thin black mustache. "Ms. Gregson, what a delightful surprise! It's not every day I get to greet a famous correspondent. Henri Marceau, General Manager, at your service. Welcome to Treemont." He turned to Hank. "And speaking of celebrities, here's one of our own. It's been a while, Mr. Ellison."

"Didn't have time for golf this fall, Henri." The two men shook hands. "And it's too cold to play now. I'm strictly a fair-weather duffer."

"Well, at least join us for dinner now and then. Otherwise, Morgan will think you no longer appreciate her. You know how sensitive artists can be."

"I'll stop in soon. Morgan Garamond is the chef," Hank

explained for my benefit, as Marceau turned to greet the next group of arrivals.

We stepped into a grand entrance hall and went with the flow, passing under a massive crystal chandelier before we hung a left. The ballroom was a soaring space clasped between the arms of two curved stairways and crowned by a high balcony. Thick logs burned majestically in the big black-veined marble fireplace across the room. French doors to our right opened onto a flagstone patio bordered by a low wall. A string quartet tucked in the far corner was doing right by Mozart as guests chatted at the wet bar and eddied around the buffet tables, each of which sprouted a stunning, oversized floral arrangement.

We hadn't gone three feet before my stomach sat up and took notice of the enticing aromas wafting from those tables, gurgling a reminder that I hadn't fed it since noon. I was about to steer Hank toward sustenance, when I noticed the approach of a statuesque woman in a ruby silk gown. Silver curls trailed out from under the turban that matched her dress, flirted with the diamonds dripping daintily from her earlobes, and feathered down the graceful curve of her neck. She didn't so much walk across the room as sail, serene as an ocean liner on a calm sea.

She coasted to a stop directly in front of us and skewered Hank with a look. "It's nine. You're late."

He smiled, obviously unfazed. "Sorry, Lavonia. Something came up."

"My fault," I said.

She treated me to a queenly stare and haughty brow lift, that had me clamping my lips against a grin.

Hank hurried to make the introductions. "Lavonia Hammersmith, this is—"

"A.J. Gregson. I know. I've seen some of your work."

The *and didn't think much of it* was implied. She waited, possibly expecting me to squirm under her disapproving pewter gaze. I almost hated to disappoint her, but between being a reporter, working for Tug Maxwell, and having three brothers, I have a hide like a rhinoceros.

"Nice to meet you," I said with a smile, and glanced around. "Hank wasn't exaggerating when he said this would be an elegant affair. Reminds me of some state dinners I've attended." Only under extreme duress, but why clutter up the conversation with details guaranteed to cement her bad opinion of me? I gestured toward the closest table. "Did your club do the flower arrangements? They're incredible."

Her eyes widened slightly, a discrete but welcome signal I had caught her by surprise. "Yes, we did design the centerpieces." Her expression defrosted infinitesimally. "I'm pleased you noticed them."

"They're even better than last year's," Hank assured her. "Remind me to get some photos for the Sunday feature." Rubbing his hands together, he scanned the crowd. "Now, where's the guest of honor?"

"Malcolm just called. I'm afraid there's been a last-minute delay. Normally, he's quite punctual, but I gather an unexpected situation arose—an issue involving a business venture. One of his many *worthy* causes, no doubt."

"No doubt," I murmured.

"I expect him within the hour. In the meantime," she continued, with a regal sweep of her hand, "please avail yourselves of the buffet—it's *très magnifique*. Chef Garamond has outdone herself. Now, if you'll excuse me, I see Mayor Makomba has arrived. Since he's charged with introducing Malcolm, I'll need to update him on the schedule change." And off she sailed.

"Let's get that drink," Hank suggested. My stomach burbled a protest loud enough to be heard over the first dainty notes of the quartet's next selection, a Haydn piece in D minor. "Okay," he said without missing a beat, "*I'll* get the drinks, *you* hit the buffet tables. Name your poison."

"I'll stick with water, thanks. I need to keep a clear head for later."

"Yeah, I see what you mean." He hesitated. "But you're sure *I'm* okay, right? Not that I want to sound selfish or come off as chicken, it's just—"

"You'll be fine, Hank."

"All right, if you say so. Go ahead and fill up a plate; I'll find you."

He was back before I knew it, handing me a crystal flute of spring water. We spent the next forty-five minutes grazing on crab-cheddar polenta spoons, bacon-wrapped shrimp, pork tenderloin, grilled vegetables, quail, and raspberry cobbler with white chocolate sauce. With our plates in one hand and drinks in the other, we wandered from one lively horticultural debate to the next: hybrids versus open pollination, hot or cold composting, native versus imported.

Hank was in his element, dropping two cents and the odd question into each conversation, but the minute a full-figured type sporting cream satin and an impossibly black beehive mentioned hydrangeas, he latched onto my arm and hauled me toward the French doors, muttering words that sounded like, "get some air." We were half-way to the patio when a buzz of excitement rippled across the ballroom, drawing our attention to the man framed in the entrance.

If Santa ever decides to drop a hundred-fifty pounds and trade his fuzzy red suit for beige Italian silk, he and Malcolm Conover can pass for twins. Same grandfatherly twinkle in the bright blue eyes. Same rosy cheeked smile. Same snowy hair and beard, although Conover wore his whiskers trimmed and his hair in a neat queue.

The resemblance didn't stop with appearances. Like Saint Nick, the philanthropist delivered goodies on a global scale, by air. The big difference was Conover's gift list, which had nothing to do with naughty or nice, but was strictly needs-based. In a world where people had trouble agreeing on the weather, Malcolm Conover was unanimously regarded as a genuine prince among men, a reputation he earned after a less-than-stellar adolescence, according to his surprisingly candid official bio.

A privileged son of privileged parents, he had grown up spoiled, even by the standards of the silver-spoon crowd. Hard to imagine a wild, willful hellion with a name like Malcolm, but hellion he had been. He eventually got into a few scrapes with the law, one serious enough to earn him a couple hundred hours' community service in an under-developed village in Mexico.

Surprisingly enough, running headlong into real poverty and need turned out to be the perfect wrench for a serious attitude adjustment. Young Malcolm saw the light. By the time he finished his service and headed home to Toronto, he was determined to "alleviate human suffering when- and wherever possible." He was eighteen years old when he set up the Change a Life Foundation, a complex network of wide-ranging charities that currently drew tens of billions in donations annually and had a reputation for getting tough jobs done all over the globe.

I had never met Conover in person, but it seemed I was about to get my chance. Arm linked through his, Lavonia Hammersmith was homing in on Hank and me for the second time that evening. Then, they were standing in front of us.

"Ms. Gregson," began Lavonia, "Malcolm—that is, Mr. Conover—would like to make your acquaintance. As a matter of fact, he expressly requested an introduction the moment he found out you were here." Both her expression and tone bordered on mystified.

The famous philanthropist sent her a sheepish look. "Pardon me for acting like a star-struck schoolboy, cousin, but I'm one of Ms. Gregson's most loyal admirers."

"Please, call me A.J.," I said, handing Hank my glass so I could offer my hand.

Conover's attention shifted from Lavonia to me. The hand that gripped mine was unexpectedly strong and calloused, but that didn't surprise me nearly as much as what happened when our eyes met. I felt my surroundings tilt as I slid into that other dimension. Assaulted by the now-familiar vertigo, I dropped Conover's hand and took an instinctive step back, trying not to stammer when I told him it was always nice to meet a fan.

"Oh, I seldom miss your broadcasts," he said with a Kris Kringle-y smile, as lines blurred and colors ran. His gentle voice seemed to come through a long, dark tunnel as he added, "I was concerned when you disappeared from the airwaves a few weeks back. Yours is a dangerous line of work, after all. Then I saw this evening's editorial and realized you were in your usual fine fettle."

"Caught that one, did you?" murmured Hank.

My heart bucked violently when Conover jumped back into ultra-sharp focus. I could see every pore, each individual eyelash, each putrefying sore that erupted on his forehead, cheeks, and chin. His flesh grew rancid, then dry as parchment, pulling his lips into a grisly grimace as his face rotted right before my eyes. Watching the skin flake off his bones was like watching a corpse decompose in time-lapse. Conover was still smiling, but his pearly whites were pointed like fangs and caked with gore, and his gaze glowed like the coals of Hell. Then the last layer of skin vanished, and I almost fainted for the first time in my life.

Atop those narrow silk-clad shoulders sat the Death's Head, the visage of Charon himself. As I watched, spellbound, those soulless eyes locked on me. Instead of pupils, the irises were holed by the irregular Greek coins known as oboli. Charon's fare. And they were engraved with my name.

Chapter 34

The first-floor ladies' lounge was an estrogen oasis with all the frills. Very nice, if you're into Italian renaissance loveseats and gilt-framed Botticelli prints of Venus rising from a clam shell. I'm not.

I was scrubbing my hands like Lady McB, trying to wash away Conover's touch when the door opened inward, admitting a petite blond in an orchid sheath. We traded *nobody here but us girls* smiles—hers was better than mine—as I dried my hands. She joined me at the vanity, pulled a lipstick and compact out of a dinky clutch and started to freshen up. *When in Rome*, I figured with a mental shrug, and leaned into the mirror to fiddle with my hair, pretending to primp, while my mind worked overtime.

The hard lefts just kept on coming.

Three weeks since the first vision, and I still hadn't completely adjusted to the idea that I was having them. Some surprises are harder to take in than others, I guess. Harder to hide, too. Watching Joe Schmoe go *Portrait of Dorian Gray* is tough on your poker face. Witness my performances during the Palmer and Nelson makeovers.

Thank God I managed to project a reasonable facsimile of cool, calm, and collected tonight, even though this shockwave had been triple-strength, compared to the first two. Of course, self-preservation *is* a first-class motivator. So what if my composure was only skin deep? It was darned near miraculous, given the who and what involved.

The blonde stowed her makeup in her sequined postage stamp and closed it with a dainty *snap*. Giving me another polite smile, she swept out the door, leaving me alone. I crossed the room to sit on one of the richly brocaded loveseats and leaned my head against the silk-covered wall, estimating I had maybe five minutes before my absence provoked unwelcome interest. Long enough to go over the facts one more time.

Fact One: My come-and-get-me lure had paid off better, and sooner, than expected, netting me a bigger, wilder fish than I bargained for.

Fact Two (and this was the kicker): The most generous, loved, and admired man in the world was apparently the mastermind behind a vicious pack of assassins. I could hardly believe it. But I knew it like I knew my own name.

Fact Three: I couldn't prove it.

Both my conscience and my instincts chorused, *Do something! Stop him!* I told them I was open to suggestions. How was I supposed to get the word out, for example? Who would believe me? Whatever I decided to do would involve a mile-high limb and a laser saw.

I groaned in frustration.

What I wouldn't give right now for a smidgen of confirmation to reaffirm the accuracy of my so-called gift! Was that so much to ask before I went after an icon like Malcolm Conover armed with no more evidence than a bogeyman nobody else could see?

I had barely asked the question when the CIIS UpLink tickled my wrist with an incoming call. *Doctor Samuel Bonner,* according to the caller ID. But the face that materialized on the flex-screen held no trace of the easy-going old gent I had visited in the house on Chestnut. Gone were the relaxed smile and calm, kind warmth. He didn't bother with *hello* or *how are you.*

"I got your number from Agent Eagan. Did you hear?"

"Hear what?"

"Benjamin Palmer murdered his mother this afternoon. Strangled her with his bare hands."

You wanted confirmation, A.J.? Now you have it. Next time, be careful what you wish for.

I was itching to get out of Dodge, but I needed a ride, and so far, no Eagan. Why is there never a cheesed-off fed around when you need one?

Anxious to avoid another face-to-faces with Conover and his alter ego, I hovered behind the long, paddle-like leaves of a six-foot bird of paradise near the back of the ballroom. Hank stood about five feet in front of me, hands tucked in his pockets as he patiently waited for my return from the lounge.

Meanwhile, over in the far corner, the guest of honor, the mayor, and Lavonia Hammersmith mounted the stage recently vacated by the string quartet. As soon as the trio got situated, Makomba launched into a paean to Conover. His praises were punctuated by bursts of applause meant to honor the man of the hour, who demonstrated suitable humility with a becoming blush.

Don't look now, don't look now, I chanted silently. I didn't want Conover to see me as I slipped up behind Ellison and tapped him on the shoulder. "Time to go," I whispered.

He glanced from the stage to me and back. "What, now? Malcolm's about to make his remarks."

"I can see that. Look, I wouldn't ask, if it wasn't important."

He turned to study my face, then nodded. "Okay."

The ten minutes it took the valet to bring Hank's coupe around were the longest in my life. Waiting in the entrance hall, I could hear Conover wax warm and folksy about how great it was to get up close and personal with Mother Earth by doing our bit to beautify the planet. Wall-to-wall sunshine and butterflies. You had to hand it to the man, he knew how to work a crowd. He even sounded like he meant it when he singled out Hobson's Hope as "a veritable Garden of Eden in an increasingly denaturalized world."

I pictured him smiling as fondly as Tri-America's favorite uncle while he imagined filleting a certain police reporter, one drawn-out slice at a time.

When we were finally on our way, I turned to Hank. "*Malcolm?* Since when are you and Conover on a first-name basis?"

He grinned out the windshield. "That's right, you missed our get-acquainted chat. I know he's got all the money in the world, but Malcolm is a regular guy. Friendly, easy to talk to. And man, does he know gardening! Settled the hydrangea question once and for all. Turns out aged cow manure is the best way to maintain the soil acidity you need to get blue blossoms."

"You bonded over cow manure?"

"We talked about other stuff, too. Organics, hydroponics … you."

I sat up a little straighter. "*Me?* What about me?"

"He asked if I knew where you're staying. Guess he really is a fan."

My heart lurched into my throat. "Did you tell him?"

"Didn't get a chance," he replied with a curious sideways glance. "Lavonia showed up to drag him away for his speech."

"Oh." *Lavonia, I owe you. Big time.*

"Why? Is there a problem?"

"No," I lied, "no problem."

We rode in silence until he turned onto Sadie's street and asked, "So, where do you go from here?"

"I'm not sure yet." And wouldn't tell him if I knew. It was safer that way … for both of us.

As we approached the boardinghouse, Hank spied the vehicle parked in front and gave a low whistle. "Well, what do we have here? A Shrike Mark-VI! You don't see one of those babies every day. Now, that is what I call a *ride.*"

I had to agree. Silver, sexy, and low-slung, the Shrike's sleek, swept-back design screamed *fast-mover* even when the car was in park. If the cavalry had arrived, it had arrived in style. Not that I had time to *ooh* and *ah* over transportation. I had maybe ninety seconds to come up with a workable script for a possible showdown with Iceman.

Hank parked behind the Shrike, killed the engine, and popped the doors. "I'll walk you to the house," he said, climbing out. He gave the Mark-VI a covetous one-handed caress before we started up the walk. "What a night, huh?"

You have no idea. And unless I missed my guess about who held title on the Shrike, the excitement was far from over.

"Eventful," I agreed. "Thanks for your help, Hank. I couldn't have done the broadcast without you."

He smiled ruefully. "I don't know about that. From what I've seen, you're one gutsy lady. You would have managed. All I did was push a few buttons and fall apart afterwards. So much for my image as a stalwart member of the Fourth Estate."

"You did great."

"No, *you* did great," he countered as we started up the

porch steps, "and I hope you bring them down. Meanwhile, thanks for setting the broadcast up so I stay in the clear." His words no sooner registered when realization slammed into me. If Hank hadn't grabbed my arm, I would have planted a facer on the porch. "Whoa! You all right?"

No, no I wasn't. And whether he knew it or not, neither was he. Conover had seen us together, and I had a feeling he could add two and two quicker than most. Given the timing of the broadcast, he had to suspect we had come to the gala straight from the *Herald*, and that suspicion would be more than enough to get Hank killed. My eyes flew to Ellison's face. He would have to disappear, for who knew how long. Jack could make it happen, but God, how was I going to break the news to him?

"Hank—"

That was as far as I got before the front door opened and Eagan stepped out on the porch, dressed in black from head to toe. He ran a measuring glance over Ellison, before dismissing him to focus on me. The glow of the porch light warmed his white-blond hair but did nothing to thaw his glacial gaze. The arctic gleam in those pale-blues could have triggered a new ice age. I was ready with my explanations, but he got in the first word.

"Okay, exactly what part of 'don't do anything stupid' didn't you understand?"

Chapter 35

Pro that she was, Sadie took our unexpected departure for parts unknown in stride, no questions asked. Hank, on the other hand, threw a fit, forcing Jack to drag him out of the house. They played push-me-pull-you all the way down the walk, Ellison sputtering objections and demands for an explanation with each balky step. Finally, Jack whipped around, hit the lanky redhead with a subzero *I would just as soon kill you as look at you* glare, and tersely ordered him into the Shrike.

No flies on Hank. He climbed in, buckled up, and shut up.

Two hours later, we were in a high-tech hideaway among the pines foresting the Selkirk Mountains in British Columbia. The CIIS VIP safe house, shaped like a mushroom cap perched atop four squat legs sprouting from a square landing bay, could be relocated at will—sort of like a glorified RV. Thanks to some gee-whiz transformation optics and a micro-fine plasma skin, the house and its occupants were cloaked, veiled from prying eyes *and* sensors. Why we needed top-flight protective shields, intrusion detectors, and defensive weapons on top of that was anyone's guess.

If lying low at Sadie's had been like being grounded, confinement here would be like prison. Forget work. Eagan confiscated my disposable UL right off the bat. Forget going outside for a run. According to basic safe house etiquette, I was expected to meekly hunker between these four walls until Eagan decided I could get on with my life. But I'm not meek, I don't hunker well, and I had about had my fill of hiding.

The pump was primed. The Ferrymen were ready to rumble, and I had a *real* lead. Solid gold, hell, this lead was platinum. Inside information, literally, straight from the top. All I had to do now was figure out the best way to leverage the scoop. At least this peaceful, hopefully *brief*, Canadian interlude would give me a chance to figure it out. I could wait. For a day or two.

I had certainly waited in worse places. The décor here would have done a five-star hotel proud. Wide banks of one-way windows under the domed ceiling gave the roomy interior a light, airy feel. Thick oriental carpets were scattered across white marble floors. The living room—done in green and gold with ebony wood accents and the occasional splash of fuchsia—was furnished with plush sofas and sculpted armchairs. My assigned bedroom, powder-blue with white trim, included a private bath and a walk-in closet bigger than most apartments.

"*Nice,*" I said, doing a slow three-sixty.

"So, the room is all right?" asked my guide.

She was a nondescript woman, plain except for wide, heavily lashed brown eyes. She kept her sable hair shoulder-length, her smile deferential and eager-to-please. I guessed her to be in her mid-twenties. Like Ellison and I, live-in housekeeper Tanya Sidorov would be confined to quarters for the duration.

"It'll do in a pinch." Always on the lookout for odd, potentially useful scraps of information, I asked, "You're not cooped up here all the time, right? I mean, they *do* let you out once in a while?"

"Oh, yes," she assured me with childlike earnestness. I tried to place her accent. Slavic, maybe. "It is only sometimes I must stay, when we have guests. For the safety of all, you understand, myself included. It is not because I am not trusted," she hurried to add, boasting shyly, "I have a *clearance.* Almost *two years* I have worked for the agency. It is a very *good* job."

That had been an hour ago. Now four of us sat in high-backed chairs around an oblong conference table. Me, Jack, Hank, and Fred Stanhope.

Stanhope tended toward fat, balding, loud, and obnoxious. Smart mouth, always running. I knew enough about the Service to know you didn't earn agent-in-charge of a safe house by acing your last performance review. No, Stanhope had screwed up somewhere, and this backwoods baby-sitting job was his slap on the wrist. I might have dredged up an ounce of sympathy, if he hadn't volunteered the opinion that reporters ranked lower than pond scum. As it was, it didn't take me ten minutes to write the guy off as a bona fide jerk.

I had just dropped the Conover bombshell, and Stanhope was giving me that so-you-think-you're-Jesus smirk usually reserved for inmates at mental institutions.

Eagan said, "Run that by me again?"

"Malcolm Conover is with the Ferrymen. If you want to know the truth, I think he's the head honcho. Charon himself."

"And you know this, because you had some kind of vision."

I felt my face heat. Even *I* had trouble believing my story. These guys probably thought I sounded like one of those late-night infomercials. A.J.'s Psychic Hotline. No reading too bizarre.

Well, it was too late to change my story now. So I forced myself to meet his gaze and said, "Yeah."

Hank goggled in disbelief. "I'm still in a rented tux, more than two thousand miles from home without my toothbrush, because you thought you saw a *vision*?"

"I knew a guy who saw a vision," drawled Stanhope. "Little blue men riding pink elephants. We put *him* in a safe house, too. You know, the one with the pretty padded walls?"

Eagan silenced him with a look and turned back to me. "And you say this happened before, with two other people. It's the reason you went to see Bonner."

I nodded. "He's the one who figured it out." His probing gaze made me feel like a bug on a pin; I had to resist the urge to squirm like one.

"You went through hell the night we lost Cuey and Michaels," he reminded me matter-of-factly. "Post-traumatic stress can cause all kinds of problems, including hallucinations. Now, I'm not saying Bonner doesn't know his stuff when it comes to eyes, but maybe you need to get a second opinion from a doc who specializes in psychological trauma."

"*It's not post-traumatic stress!*" I snapped, then made a grab for my patience. "Look, I know this sounds crackbrained. As a matter of fact, that was my first thought. Brain injury. But Bonner says there isn't one, and facts are facts. I meet a teenager. Two minutes later, she looks like she went ten rounds with a Louisville Slugger and lost. Twenty-four *hours* later, she's in intensive care, battered to within an inch of her life by Daddy Dearest. Before her, Benjamin Palmer. Another complete stranger." I stared pointedly at Ellison. "According to you, known as a spineless klutz who couldn't walk and chew gum."

"Yeah. So?"

"So while you and Conover were talking manure, Palmer killed his mother. Strangled her."

Hank squawked, "*Whaaat?*"

"You heard me."

"*Bumbling Benji?*"

"You won't be the only one surprised. Almost nobody figured him for a homicide waiting to happen. But I saw the monster inside him."

"Why those two?" asked Eagan.

"Three," I shot back. "Don't forget Conover."

"Okay, why those three? Why not everybody?"

"I told you. We ... Bonner and I ... figure I can only see that way when a person is under psychological or emotional strain. Intense strain, so he or she has to siphon off some internal energy to maintain outward appearances."

"Emotional strain." He nodded. "You mean ready to blow a gasket like I was, when you pulled that brainless stunt tonight?"

"*Brainless stunt?* Listen, Eagan—"

"How about me?" Hank interjected. "I'm *still* under intense emotional strain." You wouldn't have known it by the way he glanced at his watch and announced, "And for the record, seeing as how it's now ten past two in the morning, Pacific Standard Time, she technically pulled that brainless stunt *last* night."

Jack ignored him to bore in on me. "Come on, A.J. What did you see when I caught up with you? Anything?"

"Other than the fact that you looked ready to kill me yourself? Not a thing."

"Okay."

"Not okay. Come on, Eagan, you're a smart guy. Try to keep up. I didn't see inside, because you *wanted* me to know how you felt. Same with Hank. No cover up, no need to tap inner resources, no vision."

"All right, let's look at it from another angle. There are millions of desperate, depressed, scared, lonely people out there. People who go through life barely holding it together. You pass thousands of them on the sidewalk every day. If this ... *sixth sense* of yours works the way you and Bonner say ...." He spread his hands.

"Why don't I see inside *those* people?" Good question, and this was the first time it had occurred to me. At that moment, my face had to be a snapshot of consternation. Caption: *Newbie clairvoyant ponders baffling gift.*

"Well?"

"There's obviously more to it. A second trigger, maybe."

Stanhope snorted and Hank rolled his eyes. Eagan waited patiently, no doubt expecting me to finally come to my senses and admit I needed therapy.

I tuned them out and ran the data. A minute later, the missing puzzle piece dropped into place with an almost audible click. "A crime," I murmured, mostly to myself.

"Say again?" said Jack.

My heart picked up a beat as I refocused on him. "What if the sight only kicks in when the person I'm looking at is either a victim, a perp, or a potential perp?"

"Oh, this just keeps getting better and better," Stanhope chuckled snidely.

"Can it, Fred."

Nice of Eagan to step on Fat Freddy, but if Jack's gathering frown was any indication, I was losing him. Oh. Like I ever had him to begin with. He didn't believe me, and who could blame him? Truth be told, *I* still wasn't as sure as I would have liked to be. If I hadn't experienced the visions myself, if I hadn't seen two of them actually born out ....

But I had, and I needed to earn some credibility here. I needed to earn it in a hurry. Because if my gift was real, then what I had seen was real. We had our hook. We could catch the bad guys and stop the killing. All I had to do was get Eagan to believe me. No pressure, right?

Will somebody please tell me how I'm supposed to convince this guy?

Sam would have called what happened next a case of *ask and ye shall receive*. I call it inspiration.

"A test!" I blurted.

Jack shook his head. "You lost me."

"We need to run a test." I barreled on, hoping to steamroll any and all objections before he could get them out. "Let's put our cards on the table, okay? Claiming to have visions is totally off the wall. You know that, I know that, even Hank knows that."

"Hey," said Hank.

"I can trot out one argument after another, but a controlled test is the only way you're ever going to believe me. You need evidence. You need to see me in action. Plus, a test will give me a chance to check my theory about triggers. Come on, Jack, you can set this up. What can it hurt? What have you got to lose?"

He scowled. "I don't think— "

"Good! *Don't* think! Listen to your gut." Like I was listening to mine. "What does your gut tell you?"

"*My* gut says you're a nut job," muttered Stanhope, but I ignored him. Only one man in the room had the power to make the test happen, and it wasn't this bozo.

"What if it's true?" I pleaded urgently. "What if I *do* have this crazy, impossible gift? What if I *did* see the real Conover? Do you know what that would mean? We've got them! We *own* the Ferrymen! We can shut them down. Get payback for Cuey and Michaels and Bugsy and all the others."

I paused to catch my breath and gauge his reaction. He seemed to be considering my proposition. He wasn't blowing it off out of hand, anyway. No use kidding myself, though. If he agreed, it would be because he expected me to fail. Then, he could force me to admit I needed to go a few rounds with Doctor Feel Good. Fine. Terrific. I could live with low expectations, as long as I managed to shove him across the line between *maybe* and *let's do it*.

"Your terms all the way," I offered. "Just give me a chance."

"And if you come up empty?"

Call and raise. He had me cornered. We both knew it, and we both knew there was only one way I could play it from here.

Drawing a breath and mentally crossing my fingers, I tossed my last chip into the pot. "If I come up empty, you name the shrink."

Chapter 36

Real estate agents and federal agents have at least one love in common—location, location, location. Like her two Tri-Am sister capitals, the District reserved her prettiest scenery for her most secretive citizens. I guess nothing says security to a spook quite like a cloak of woodlands and a single avenue of approach.

Headquarters Building for the Continental Intelligence and Investigative Service is a Babushka-doll nest of figure-eights resting on its side, high at both ends and low in the middle. Brick-red concourses ribbon inward in progressively smaller loops, eventually winding down to the central hub that houses the communications center and the director's office.

As Jack banked the Shrike, lining up for the approach, I gazed wistfully back in the direction of the Capitol building, picturing the way sunlight slides down the concave sides of that deconstructed glass cube. Was Dad in his office? Was he worried about me? Then I pictured the slender white needle of the Columbia Justice Complex, where Jim worked. What would my big brother say if he knew what I was up to? Would he believe in my gift?

Had it only been a month since I had seen them? It seemed like years. The family still didn't know where I was, only that Jack had, indeed, ridden to the rescue and taken me into protective custody. They wanted to be there for me, but we all understood why they couldn't be. Not that understanding made the situation easier for us. But we knew the reunion would have to wait until I took care of the Ferrymen.

Correction. Until *we* took care of the Ferrymen.

I slid a sideways glance at Jack as we touched down. His cooperation would be key. Without CIIS, I wouldn't be able to do much more than raise a stink and get myself killed.

All I had to do is make a believer out of the world's biggest skeptic.

As Shuki-O would say, *Pieceacake.*

Chapter 37

The observation broom closet—calling it a room would be hyperbole—was narrow, windowless, and dim. Then again, how much space and light do you need to sit and spy on people?.

The broom closet was also occupied. I stared at the man seated in one of three chairs facing the left-hand wall. "What are *you* doing here?"

"I work here," said Baker.

"I thought you were a nurse."

"I *am* a nurse." He shrugged. "Or was. Sort of."

"Sort of? You gave me sponge baths, and now you're telling me you're *sort of* a nurse?"

Eyes dancing, he raised his hands, palms up. *What can I say?*

"Relax." Jack nudged me into the chair next to Dennis. Eagan was in black again—leather jacket, t-shirt, and black jeans. Real mix-and-match kind of guy. "He was a medic with the Teams. More training than an RN but less than a doctor. Not much less," he qualified as he took the chair next to mine. Bracing his elbows on his knees, he turned his head to give me a slight smile. "I *did* tell you we had people keeping eyes on you twenty-four seven while you were in the hospital."

"I remember." But I absolutely refused to remember how much of me Baker *had* kept eyes on. "I can't believe I didn't at least suspect it was you," I told him. "It's enough to make me turn in my press pass."

"Don't be too hard on yourself. You had a load on your mind."

"Yeah, but still." I didn't ask who else had kept eyes on me. They probably wouldn't tell. Besides, ignorance is bliss when it comes to feds who have put you on the bedpan.

"I'm going for coffee," said Dennis. "Either of you want a cup?"

"Black," said Eagan.

"Can I get some water?" I asked.

"Sure."

"Make it quick," Jack said. "We go in ten."

Exactly what would happen in ten was his secret, and I had agreed not to pry. Eagan's terms, all the way.

After Dennis left, Jack and I fell into a prickly silence. What was left to say? Either I would pass the test, or I wouldn't. He was betting on the latter, had probably already written a mental referral to his friendly neighborhood psychiatrist. Yet, here he sat, ready to run an experiment he no doubt considered an embarrassing waste of time. Why? What made this guy tick?

Despite my skillful probing—conducted with undeniable finesse, if I do say so myself—Sadie had given me zilch to go on. But if I passed his test today—and if he wasn't too hard-headed to entertain the idea—Eagan and I would probably be working this case together, no doubt to our combined annoyance. That meant my life and the lives of who knew how many others might well rest on those broad shoulders. But aside from the obvious—i.e., that he was bossy, over-protective, and could paralyze people with a freeze-ray glare—what did I actually know about this character? What kind of man was he?

Too bad my quirky gift had its limitations. Be nice to get a sneak peek right about now.

Add up what you do know, and go from there.

Well, I knew he had been on the Teams. That implied some desirable qualities. Above-average intelligence. Exceptional tactical skills. Adaptability and cool-headedness, even under fire, and almost super-human endurance. Plus, the man could kill you six ways to Sunday before you knew he was there. I'm not a violent person, but given the mob we were up against, lethality didn't seem like a bad thing.

For all that, Jack apparently had a compassionate streak. He had, after all, gone out of his way to assuage my guilt over Cuey and Michaels. Even bent his own rules to let Jim break the news about Bugsy.

Sadie liked him, and she was good people. Cosmo liked

him, too. If a sharp lady *and* her dog like a person, he's probably okay. Right?

The one or two other data points I had collected on him weren't germane to my current situation. They were, however, impossible to ignore now that he and I were sitting shoulder to shoulder.

One, he smelled nice — like soap, leather, and citrus.

Two, he looked even better than he smelled.

Not that I had just noticed. A woman would have to be dead not to notice, and I am, after all, a professional observer. But when I first laid eyes on him back at Mount Zion, my life was a twenty-four karat mess. Eagan's looks registered — *Bam!* — but I didn't get much further than that, because we had to move fast, and before I knew it, he was gone.

Now he was back. My life was still a mess, but the more time I spent with him, the harder it got to ignore the fact that Iceman was hot. Chiseled and rugged are a combination I always find tough to resist, but this wasn't the most convenient time to be tempted. Didn't I already have my fair share of problems? Evidently not. Evidently, murder, mayhem, and the imminent threat of involuntary commitment weren't enough excitement for me.

"Problem?"

I glanced at him. "No, why?"

"You were frowning."

"Oh." I felt my cheeks heat and grimaced. "I'm keyed up, that's all. Anxious to get this over with. The sooner you believe me, the sooner we can move on Conover."

Doubt tinged with an emotion uncomfortably close to pity settled over his face like a cloud. "Listen —"

"I'm going to make a believer of you, Jack," I insisted, praying it was true.

He appeared far from convinced. "Okay. But remember your promise. If this doesn't turn out the way you expect ...."

"It will." I hoped. "And if it doesn't .... I never welsh on a deal, Eagan."

"Back just in time," said Dennis, coming through the door with a Styrofoam cup in each hand and a bottle of water tucked under his right arm. "They're on their way."

Jack's troubled gaze lingered on my face a second longer. Finally, he swore softly, stood, grabbed a cup, and headed for the door. "All right," he said. "Let's get this over with."

The wall in front of me was transparent on our side, opaque on theirs when three men and two women, all carrying takeout coffees, ambled into the adjoining conference room.

At first glance they came across as a mismatched hodgepodge of accountants, blue-collar workers, and college students. Averageness seemed to be the only trait they had in common. Average height and weight, average features, dressed in your average business suit, coveralls, blue jeans, and/or sweats. Pass one of them on the street, and you would never notice or remember. That's the way they're supposed to be — invisible.

I scanned for signs of tension and came up empty. The whole crew looked as cool as the other side of the pillow. They chatted and chuckled with easy familiarity. Jack arrived last.

A blocky Hispanic, who looked maybe eighteen years old in his faded jeans and gray hoody, greeted Eagan with, "Yo, Iceman. Didn't I see that black getup in a spy movie once?"

"Spies don't wear black, Juarez." This from an accountant type in a charcoal-gray suit with a fine pinstripe. He grinned out from under his neatly trimmed mustache. "*Ninjas* wear black."

"I like it," offered a strawberry blond in tan coveralls. Her hair was caught up in a long, heavy ponytail, and a pair of canvass work gloves lay on the table in front of her. "*Très* armed and dangerous."

"It *does* make a statement," agreed the petite brunette sitting next to her. Like Juarez, she was an erstwhile college student. Pink sweats, sheepdog bangs, and oversized hoop earrings.

"Black leather jackets are passé." The African-American at the far end of the table brushed an imaginary piece of lint from his narrow lapel. "Harris tweed is where it's at. Retro, baby."

Eagan held up a hand. "All right, settle down. You don't get paid enough to be fashion consultants."

Somebody muttered a wry *amen* as holographic monitors materialized in front of each of them, and Jack kicked off what was obviously a briefing. Three agents gave updates about ongoing investigations, then Jack handed out two new assignments. The brunette with the bangs, Stephenson, would run down a drug pipeline, possibly involving one or more tenured professors at a handful of Ivy League universities. The strawberry blond, Tracey Haskell, would work with Harris Tweed Retro—otherwise known as James Henderson—to uncover a military procurement ring diverting weapons for sale on the black market. He would infiltrate in uniform, posing as an E-5 procurement clerk; she would work the loading dock at the suspect shipping facility.

As they ironed out the details, I asked Dennis, "Do you think they know somebody's watching?"

"This is the Puzzle Palace, A.J. Somebody's *always* watching."

"Where's the trust in that?"

"There isn't any." He stretched his legs out in front of him and crossed his ankles. "Mind telling me why *we're* watching?"

That would require more explanation than I was ready to give at the moment.

"Did you ask Jack?" I stalled, still scrutinizing the faces in the conference room.

"He said I wouldn't believe it, if he told me."

Keeping my eyes on the agents, I grimaced. "Yeah, well, that about sums it up. How about this? I'll let you know when I see it."

"This is payback, right? For when I wouldn't tell you what Iceman looked like?"

My lips curved, belying the tension knotting my muscles. I had a bundle riding on this tryout. Half of me was already savoring the moment I served Eagan a man-sized helping of crow. The other half was suddenly wondering exactly how I was supposed to do that now that Jack had segued into a rousing discourse on equipment allowances. If I was going to see into that other dimension, *somebody* had to at least break a sweat. Five more minutes of this malarkey, and the entire room would go from calm to comatose.

"They're increasing the allowance," Jack was saying, "but they're tightening the audit process. The bean counters will nail you on the details, so dot all your i's, cross all your t's, and upload your five-twenty-threes within seven days of purchase. Any questions?" They shook their heads. "Okay, that's it."

I sat straight up. "'*That's it?*' Did he just say, '*That's it*'?"

The agents were pushing back their chairs, and I was composing an earful that would raise blisters on an Iceman, when Eagan added, almost as an afterthought, "Oh, one more item. The Director's Office handed down a new reg yesterday."

This announcement provoked groans all around.

"What are you moaning about, Stephenson?" said Juarez. "We're talking about the *book*, girl. You know you love it. Heard you keep a copy tucked in your panty drawer. You and the director. The two of you should get together sometime. You know, compare favorite articles and sub-sections and stuff."

"The director and the original Ms. Rules-Were-Made-to-Be-Broken?" Tracey wrapped the end of her ponytail around an index finger. "We could sell tickets."

"As I was saying," Jack interrupted pointedly, "The DO handed down a new reg yesterday. The inner loop wants more frequent truth-and-loyalty evals on all hands. Word has it, the head shedders beefed up the process—added some next-gen pharmacology and a deep-brain scan that picks up even unconscious deception. From what I hear, nothing gets by this combo."

"So much for Oakley's secret high-heel fetish," said Henderson. When the guy in the pinstriped suit flipped him the bird, he shrugged. "Hey, man, I don't think they'll actually terminate you for it. I mean, your pumps, your business, right?"

Again, Jack nipped the byplay in the bud. "We don't have all day, so let's wrap this up. About the evaluations. Bottom line, the sooner we make the inner loop happy, the sooner we can get back to fighting for truth and justice. I had to pull some strings, but we're on for tomorrow morning. Quick and painless, okay? Here's the lineup: Henderson at eight, followed at two-hour intervals by Haskell, Juarez, Stephenson, and Oakley."

He went on to give some additional details, listen to some gripes, and answer a few questions, but I was no longer tuned in to the conversation. I only had eyes for one person.

Chapter 38

"So where do we go from here?" Dennis wondered.

Jack scrubbed the back of his neck. "Damned if I know."

"Oh, for—" I tossed up my hands. "We go after Conover! What else?"

"Now, why didn't I think of that?" drawled Jack.

"We can't just *go after* Malcolm Conover," Dennis protested.

"Why not? I passed the test, didn't I?"

"Looks like," Eagan admitted.

"Forget *looks like*. I *nailed* it, Eagan!"

As soon as Jack hit the roomful of agents with the newsflash about the truth scan, we were off to the races. First that eerie sliding sensation, followed by the soft blur, then Tracey Haskell snapped in. Couple seconds after that, a fissure started at the crown of her head, gradually growing longer and wider until it split her face cleanly in half. One half peeled away from the other, rotating in a slow one-eighty until it faced backwards. So, two faces—one looking at Jack, white and wide-eyed, etched with fear bordering on panic. One facing away, foxy and deceitful, lips moving in concert with Jack's, apparently repeating his every word.

The Janus-faced apparition was beyond creepy. But beautiful, too, because she spelled *VINDICATION* in caps two feet high. I wanted to stand up and shout, "Hallelujah!"

By the time Eagan rejoined Dennis and me, I was locked and loaded and ready to fire. His buns no more than hit the chair before I launched into a detailed description of what I had seen and told them point blank what I thought it meant.

"Tracey Haskell is dirty. Well?" I prodded after short, supercharged silence. "Am I right?"

The two agents exchanged glances.

Finally, Jack said, "Yeah."

Not exactly the ringing endorsement I had been hoping for, but that was understandable. Iceman's logical mind had to be spinning its wheels trying to get traction on *this* slippery slope.

"So what's the story?"

"Haskell shared good information with a bad customer, and it's coming back to bite her."

"You knew this, but you gave her a new assignment anyway?"

"Complete with enough rope to hang herself."

I had nodded and left it at that. Any other time, I would have kept digging, but Haskell wasn't my main concern at the moment. I did, however, make a mental note to revisit this lead after we took care of Conover.

"I'm willing to admit you made Haskell," Dennis said now, "but that doesn't mean I'm ready to hotfoot it over to the inner loop to pitch Conover as a suspect. 'Hey, Director, did you know the World's Most Wanted fugitive also happens to be the richest do-gooder on the planet and one of the President's closest friends?'" He grimaced. "Like that's going to fly."

"It will after we explain it to her," I insisted. Baker's answering expression read, *Get real.* "I'm serious! If she doesn't believe us—and she probably won't—we'll convince her to set up another test."

"Not gonna happen," Dennis insisted flatly. "You start in on how you're seeing visions, she'll toss us *all* out of the building."

"So what do we do? Twiddle our thumbs and hope Conover gives himself up before the Ferrymen rack up a few more kills?"

Jack spoke up. "No. We're going to check this out."

Dennis raised both eyebrows. "We are?"

"Yeah. Discretely. *Very* discretely," he added under his breath, then focused on me. "You haven't made a convert out of me yet."

"But—"

"But what? You've been a crime reporter for how long? Ten years? I'll bet even *before* your accident you could spot a baby-faced felon in a room full of choir boys singing *Ave*

Maria. Nothing mystical about it. You probably had good instincts to start with, and plenty of street time has only made them better. I know, because it's the same for Baker and me and every other investigator worth a damn." He paused, rubbing his neck again. "Maybe fingering Haskell was instinct, maybe it wasn't. Maybe it was exactly like you said. Either way, I figure you've at least earned a shot."

"Thanks."

We both looked at Dennis.

"All right," he sighed after a brief hesitation, "I'm in. What have you got in mind?"

"Money," Jack answered. "Based on their level of sophistication and the choice of high-visibility targets, it's safe to assume Ferrymen contracts don't come cheap. We don't know who's been paying the bills so far, but we *do* know when the hits went down. That gives us approximate timeframes when money would have changed hands. We've never been able to trace the flow, but if A.J. is right about Conover, we know where the credits ended up."

"Change a Life," I agreed. "It's the perfect setup. Big donations pour in all the time. Lucky for us, the amounts are a matter of public record, even if the donors want to remain anonymous. The Foundation itself is like a clearing house. Or a spigot. Turn it on, and funds cascade down from headquarters until they're spread out among hundreds of subsidiary charities, some of them ten- and twenty-man operations."

"DIY money laundering," Dennis concluded. "Slick, safe, and easy."

"We might be able to match the hit dates with large anonymous donations," Jack figured. "If we can find a pattern ...." He shrugged. "It's not much, but it's a start."

"Not to be a wet blanket," I interjected, "but doesn't this kind of investigation usually involve major resources? An army of treasury agents? A phalanx of geeks?"

"Don't worry, we'll get what we need," Jack assured me.

Baker cocked his head. "Mind telling me how we're going to do that without the director's authorization?"

"Who said we won't have her authorization? Once I tell her we got a tip claiming drug cartels are washing dirty money through legitimate charities—unbeknownst to the nonprofits themselves, of course—she'll pull out all the stops. But we don't point fingers or name names until we've got solid evidence."

Like he said, it was a start. Too bad Shuki had taken herself out of circulation; she would have been the perfect bloodhound for this hunt. Unfortunately, nobody but *nobody* would find Shady Lady if she didn't want to be found, which, for obvious reasons, she didn't.

Jack was finally moving on the intel I had given him. I should have been doing my happy dance, but the Victory Waltz wasn't playing yet. What were we missing? I mulled it over while he and Dennis discussed the assets they would pull in—who was a team player, who might balk and ask too many questions. I turned the plan over in my mind, taking it apart and putting it back together again, trying to nail down what was bothering me. I was about to table my uneasiness until later, when I spotted the hitch.

"There's a problem," I announced abruptly.

Jack was ahead of me. "Conover hasn't missed a step so far, but he's too smart to forget Murphy's Law."

"Meaning?" said Dennis.

"Meaning he's hedged his bets," Jack replied. "Set up a healthy cushion of plausible deniability between himself and the blood money."

Dennis nodded. "I get it. You're saying even if we trace the hit money to Change a Life, so what? The Foundation employs thousands of people. Conover would claim he didn't know jack about those funds. Reputation like his, he would get away clean. Go underground, wait us out, and start all over again."

"There has to be a way to tie him in." I nibbled my lower lip for a second, then said, "And I think I know what it is."

"What?"

"Dangle some irresistible bait and nail him when he goes for it."

"Great idea," said Dennis, "except we don't *have* any bait."

Jack was tracking perfectly, as usual. He was already shaking his head. "Don't go there, A.J. Not again."

Too late. I had already arrived. "Sure you do," I informed Dennis, ignoring Eagan. "You've got me."

Chapter 39

"Tell me, Jack, are you always this pigheaded?"

We were two hours into our flight back to the safe house, nearing the final approach, and I hadn't made a dent. The man simply would not listen to reason.

"I would rather be pigheaded than have a death wish."

"I do not," I assured him through gritted teeth, "have a death wish!"

"Okay, how about more guts than sense?"

I swallowed a pithy retort and took hold of that last frayed thread of patience. "I don't understand your problem. The bait card is already in play. You *do* remember my broadcast?"

"How could I forget?"

"See there? If you can't forget, you can bet Conover won't. He's going to come after me. I saw it in those eyes. But he doesn't know I'll be expecting it, because he doesn't realize I'm onto him. Life doesn't hand you an advantage like this every day, pal. We need to make the most of it. Dangle me like a fat, juicy worm and trick him into coming for me on our terms."

"On our terms? This guy can take out—correction, *has* taken out—targets from thousands of miles away. He doesn't have to *come* for you."

"Thanks for reminding me." I stepped on the worm of vulnerability that tried to rear its anxious head, insisting, "There has to be a way."

"Maybe, but why dive in over your head, when you can sit on the bank and fish? Let the task force run the numbers. If the hit-date/donation connection turns out to be a dead end, maybe we'll revisit your idea."

"Meanwhile, we all cross our fingers and hope the Ferrymen don't murder anybody else," I muttered to the passenger-side window.

We started our descent, bumping through gunmetal gray clouds that thinned here and there to offer patchy glimpses of the forested slopes below. I spied a hawk circling lazily in the distance off to our right, wings canted slightly and held almost motionless as the bird rode invisible currents. The rocky spines of the Selkirks rose around us, dappled in snow and fir.

"I don't need your permission, you know."

"Don't make me arrest you, Gregson."

I turned to face him. "You wouldn't dare."

"Try me," he shot back, checking the rearview display. Whatever he saw behind us evidently caught his attention, because his eyes narrowed. A few seconds later, he nodded toward the 3-D image. "What do you make of that?"

I leaned in for a look and saw the hawk ghosting in and out of the clouds back in our wake. "The hawk? Yeah, I noticed it a while ago."

"Did you notice it's following us?"

I leaned in closer. "Maybe it's curious." He didn't answer. "Come on, you don't actually believe ...." I shook my head. "God, you're paranoid!" But I had to admit the hawk's course *was* uncannily straight. *Looks like we're towing the darned thing on a long rope*, I reflected uneasily.

"You know what they say. You're not paranoid, if they're really after you." He activated a scanner that wasn't standard equipment, even on the Shrike. Unless you're an overzealous fed, of course. "And they're really after us."

"So, you're saying—"

"I'm saying Mother Nature didn't give birth to our feathered friend back there. Hold on."

I wrapped my fingers around the armrests. "What are you going to do?"

"Try to buy us some time and space."

Between one heartbeat and the next, the Shrike arrowed heavenward, slicing through the clouds and slamming me back against the seat. What felt like twenty Gs later, the craft shot out of the overcast and into the sunlight. We nosed over, blue sky and clouds cartwheeling outside the windows as the Mark-VI went belly-up to the sun.

Jack nodded toward the display. "Check it out."

I had to uncross my eyes first. I blinked hard, my vision cleared, and I looked. The breath caught in my throat when I realized the "hawk" was mimicking our aerial back flip.

About the time that bizarre sight registered Eagan ordered me to, "Hold on!" again.

He threw the car into a screaming dive. As the Shrike pierced the clouds like a needle through cotton, the prefab ham-and-cheese cafeteria sandwich I had for lunch rose in inverse proportion to our descent, butted against the fear lumped in my throat, and hung there. Meanwhile, I kept my eyes glued to the display and the tiny UAV still back there on our tail. Eagan leveled out, juking right and left, up and down, as we flashed through the clouds wreathing the saw-toothed peaks. The diminutive hunter mirrored our every move ... only now it had company.

"Jack?"

"Yeah, I make it three in a narrow V-formation."

"All tailing us."

"I was wrong about that. They're not tailing us," Iceman countered, as the Shrike popped over a crest. Freezing rain slashed wetly across the windshield as we streaked over a river, Jack banking the car sharply to parallel a slab-stacked granite rock face. "They're trying to waste us."

He sounded cool and calm. Clearly, the man wasn't human.

Who *they* were was never in doubt. But how had they known when and where to strike? I quickly decided that answer would have to wait.

The burning question now was, "Then why haven't they?"

"According to the computer, the delivery vehicles are Falconiform-3Ls ... 'L' as in laser. Right now, the only thing standing between us and a one-way ticket to a one-point landing nobody walks away from is the weather. Rain and clouds scatter the beam. Long story short, we need to wind up this game of tag before it stops raining or they get so close the rain doesn't matter."

I darted a glance toward the sky, searching for unwelcome holes in the cloud cover. "Can't you shoot them down?"

"With what, my sidearm?"

"The house has a weapons system, but your car doesn't? Great! Just great." I forced myself to draw a calming breath. "Okay, we can't blast them. Got any other ideas?"

"Working on it," he said as the Shrike knifed into the

forest.

Eagan dropped the craft so low, I had to resist the urge to raise up in my seat as we blew over the forest floor. We whipsawed through don't-blink-or-you'll-miss-them gaps between tree trunks at the tip of an explosive rooster-tail of snow and pine needles.

"Stay with me," Eagan crooned to our pursuers. "This party is just getting started."

I flinched instinctively as something green and bushy slapped my window. "Either you've lost your mind, or you've got a plan."

"I wouldn't call it a plan, exactly." We banked ninety degrees, sliced between a pair of boulders, and leveled out again. "More like a half-baked idea. But it might work."

"I don't supposed you would care to share?"

"You'll figure it out." He checked the rearview, but our snowy backblast shrouded the scenery behind us. He eyeballed the scanner and nodded. "Still on our six. Come on," he muttered, "close up. Closer ... closer .... Okay, that's good, that's real good. Stay with me. Just a little farther now."

A little farther to what, I wondered as the world whipped by in a dizzying green-and-brown blur. I wasn't left guessing long.

Rilled and weather-beaten, the craggy wall of rock seemed to erupt out of the earth ahead of us. Skirted by tumbled boulders and sparsely blotched with olive-drab brush, its soaring gray bulk all but blotted out the sky. I no sooner registered its immovable presence dead ahead when the Shrike's collision alarm shrilled and red lights popped on all over the cockpit. I wondered when Jack would make a course correction, then realized he had nowhere to go with trees crowding in tunnel-close on both sides.

That's when it finally dawned on me. We were playing chicken with a mountain.

Ten seconds later we were practically on top of it. As tons of granite filled the windshield, I yelled, "*Jaaaaaaaaaaaaack?*"

"Hold on!"

"Oh, my God! Not again!"

I got a white-knuckled death grip on the armrests, Eagan whipped the Shrike's nose skyward, and we rocketed up the cliff face. My heart battled the ham sandwich for the right-of-way in my throat. I chanced a quick glance down. Bad move. Now I knew a few feet of air were all that stood between us and a fatal keelhauling. We were almost at the top when a detonation echoed through the valley and sent rocks clattering down the mountainside. I tore my gaze from the cheese-grater surface threatening to make mincemeat of our undercarriage and zeroed in on the rearview display. A trio of rapidly receding black-smoke mushrooms boiled off the rocky face behind us. A second later, the Shrike shot past the lip of the cliff into blessedly clear airspace.

I released the breath I hadn't realized I had been holding and peeled my fingers off the armrests, one by one. "Okay, that was interesting."

Eagan's lips twitched as we leveled off and resumed course toward the safe house. "Well, it worked."

"Yeah. Better yet, we lived to tell the tale. How did you know it would go down that way?"

"I didn't. Not for sure. I gambled on the precip and creating a snow-blower effect to generate enough interference to blind their weapons systems and topographical sensors. I figured the odds were better than fifty-fifty in our. Favor."

He had turned to look at me as he spoke and tacked the last word on almost as an afterthought when our gazes collided and locked. A charged silence spun out between us. We must have reached the same *Trouble with a capital T* conclusion at the same moment, because we broke eye contact by unspoken consent.

Jack cleared his throat and busied himself with the controls. "You did good, by the way."

I revisited the view out the passenger-side window. "You expected me to scream like a girl?"

"I wouldn't have blamed you. Hell, if I hadn't been busy dodging pine trees, *I* would have screamed like a girl."

"Umm." I surveyed the wilderness below, a thousand rugged miles of nowhere. "How do you think they found us?"

"Good question. Only three people knew we would be in the neighborhood."

"So Ellison, Sidorov, or Stanhope."

Fifteen minutes ago, a mole among us would have seemed farfetched. Now? Not far at all. Hard to believe any of the above-named suspects had opened a direct line to the

Ferrymen, but exploding UAVs didn't lie. So did the snitch sign *on* as an accessory to attempted murder, or was there some other motive for dropping a dime on us?

Maybe Hank hadn't been totally up front about what he had told Conover. Maybe after hearing about my vision, he decided to give his new, multi-billionaire gardening buddy a heads-up. Cement their burgeoning friendship. Loose lips have sunk ships for less.

Or maybe Stanhope decided to parlay a less than stellar career with the Service into a new identity and a beachside cabana in Pago Pago. He didn't have to believe my story to sell me out. All he needed was my whereabouts.

And what about Tanya Sidorov? How much did a civil-service housekeeper earn in a year? Answer: Not nearly as much as she could collect from Conover with a five-minute call. But how would she have known to call him in the first place?

"Which one of them gave us up?" I wondered out loud. "How? Why?"

Checking our coordinates, Jack signaled the safe house's computer. The structure did a slow fade-in ahead of us, remaining visible just long enough for Eagan to pilot the Shrike into the landing bay.

"No idea," he admitted, shutting down the engines. Then he turned to me and smiled. It was the kind of happy-hungry smile a great white might wear as it daydreamed about a school of plump bluefin. "What do you say we go find out?"

Chapter 40

I love it when it's easy.

Tanya Sidorov didn't turn pale or gasp or fall into a dead faint at the mere sight of us. No, she remained every inch the professional domestic in her long-sleeved white blouse, knee-length black skirt, and sensible black brogans, her arms forked under a stack of clean, crisply folded sheets. Her expression veered between concerned and attentive when Eagan ordered her to round up the rest of our suspects PDQ and meet us in the conference room. But when her eyes met mine a second later, space-time skated sideways, my head swam, and my pulse picked up a beat.

Showtime.

The vision started to play out per usual—colorful, soft-focus blur followed by the snap to the high-res close-up. Only this time, I caught no more than a flash preview—face breaking out in scales; flat, snaky gaze; neck flaring like a cobra's hood, tattooed with an obolus—before it all disintegrated like so much pixie dust. I was confused until I noticed Sidorov's relaxed posture and cynical smile. That explained it. She had decided to reveal her true colors in real time.

"Hel-lo," I said.

Eagan stared into Sidorov's suddenly cold, empty eyes and said, "Well, I'll be damned."

She, on the other hand, didn't say a word. Maybe because she was waiting for a question? I decided to ask one and see. "How long have you been with the Ferrymen?"

"I was recruited when I was fourteen." No start of surprise, no useless denials. Her jig was up, and we all knew it.

"You're under arrest," Jack immediately decided. "You

have the right to remain—"

"I know my rights, Agent Eagan. And waive them."

"And you admit involvement with the Ferrymen?"

She shrugged. "Why not?" And pointed at me with her chin. "She already saw the truth."

Jack's head slowly swiveled my way. Despite the combined weight of his stare and the *I told you so!* poised like a diver on the tip of my tongue, I kept my eyes on Sidorov. Was she guessing, or did she know?

"Did I?"

"Oh, please! I was listening," she informed Eagan, "when she told you about the Sight. You were too sophisticated to even consider the possibility, but where I come from we embrace the mystical. Not all of life can be explained. Some things one can only believe."

"Hmm," said Iceman.

I felt smug but tried not to get carried away with it. *Focus, A.J.!* "Where *do* you come from?" I asked.

"Sibiu, a city in the Carpathian mountains." She eyed me with professional curiosity. "It was the shock, yes? That was why I could not hide from you."

"Probably. You thought we were compost."

"*Da.* Your survival was inconceivable; the organization never fails to take down a target. What is it they say? First time for everything?"

"Except this is the second time you guys tried and failed with me."

"Ah, right. Well, under normal circumstances, I could have covered my reaction. I'm good, and it's not in my nature to panic or give up without a fight. But knowing you have the Sight …." She shrugged. "I concluded pretense would be useless, any attempt to maintain my cover a foolish waste of time. Much better to devote my energy to negotiating our deal."

Eagan spoke up. "No deals."

"Agent Eagan," she replied patiently, "I do not blame you for being angry. We tried to remove you, and you want to make me pay. I would feel the same. But the attempt failed, and no harm has been done. The question you must now ask yourself is, 'Do I want the foot soldier, or do I want Malcolm Conover?' Your ultimate goal is to destroy the organization, yes?"

His eyes narrowed on her face. "You're saying Conover *does* run the Ferrymen? And you're going to give him up? Just like that?"

"Not *just like that*. Do I look stupid? In addition to immunity, I want a new identity and enough credits to live comfortably in the country of my choice. Or perhaps I will settle in one of those luxury lunar colonies," she mused. "I have not decided." She cocked an eyebrow. "Well? Do we have a deal?"

"Jack?" I prodded, when he hesitated.

"I won't agree to fix a parking ticket until I hear what she has to offer. I want proof," he warned her, "the kind that will stand up in any court on the planet. If you can tie Malcolm Conover to the Ferrymen so tightly he can't wiggle free, then we'll talk."

Tanya weighed her options, then nodded. "It's fair." She hefted the towels slightly. "Let me put these away. Meet me in the living room, and I'll tell you my story. When I'm done, you'll give me whatever I ask for. You'll see."

Chapter 41

She had quite a story to tell—one part Dickens, two parts rap sheet.

Transylvania's answer to the Artful Dodger was born on the wrong side of the tracks. Mother a prostitute, father ... well, take your pick. Her early childhood was a study in benign neglect and bad examples until her tenth birthday. That was the day a light popped on in the drug-addled recesses of her mother's brain. Little girls like her daughter were a hot commodity.

Wise beyond her years, and not in a good way, Tanya understood more than any ten-year-old should have. So when she overheard Mama and the madam ironing out the details for her "coming out," she made up her mind that even a dog-eat-dog life on the street beat slow death in the brothel. She didn't bother to pack, simply walked out the door and never looked back.

Before the week was out, she hooked up with a gang of tweens and teens who didn't mind stealing what they couldn't get by panhandling, and who more or less watched out for each other. For the next two years home was a cavernous, trash-strewn freight terminal hundreds of years old, outer walls still black with the exhaust of the twentieth-century diesel locomotives it was built to service. That's where the forces of law and order finally caught up with Tanya's *kompania* less than twenty-four hours after the gang burglarized an electronics store. Owned, as luck would have it, by the mayor's son.

Most of her pals went directly to jail, but our heroine was young and plain and had gotten a less than idyllic start in life. In view of those extenuating circumstances, and the fact that this was her first (known) offense, a well-intentioned judge gave twelve-year-old Tanya a six-year opportunity to turn her life around at the Crina Antonescu School for Wayward Girls. Run by a charity called *Salvare*, or Rescue. A subsidiary, as luck would have it, of the Change a Life Foundation.

Well, you know what they say about good intentions.

The judge's gamble might have paid off, except Tanya didn't *want* to be reformed. She *liked* stealing. But she was canny enough to work the angles and bide her time. While the do-gooders congratulated themselves on saving her from a bad end, she went right on pilfering whatever she needed or wanted, mostly from the other girls, sometimes from teachers or fat-cat visitors. She only got caught once. By Malcolm Conover. As luck would have it.

It was a month before her fourteenth birthday, and young Ms. Sidorov had decided she'd had enough. Fed up with slim pickings, rules, and moral platitudes, she couldn't wait to put Antonescu's behind her. All she needed was traveling money and a chance to make her break. She could steal the money. The golden chance dropped into her lap when the headmistress announced the school would hold a folk music festival in honor of a group of important visitors from the Foundation. Tanya could well imagine the uproar. The regimental routine would fall apart while the teachers and counselors ran around like chickens without heads, distracted by details and kowtowing to the VIPs.

Perfect.

When the great day came, Tanya waited until all eyes were on the twelve girls fast-stepping a manic Romanian folk dance called the *Mărunțel*, then slipped out of her back-row, aisle seat. She ghosted through the hallways to the teachers' quarters, where she managed to exchange her frumpy gray uniform for jeans, a t-shirt, and a black hooded sweatshirt with deep pockets—which she quickly filled with the ill-gotten gains she had been hoarding for this very occasion. The gates were unlocked to facilitate all the comings and goings. Freedom was a leisurely stroll out the back gate away.

Good plan, she congratulated herself, simple yet bold. But she no sooner reached the gate, when a hand latched onto her upper arm. Her captor was none other than Mr. Change a Life foundation himself, the wealthy American philanthropist, Malcolm Conover. But far from reflecting the shock, sorrow, or moral outrage one might expect from such a pillar of goodness, his blue gaze was sharp, cold, and calculating.

He had watched her. Even followed her.

She was astounded. She had seen or sensed no one.

He was putting together a special organization, and he could use someone with her gifts.

What gifts? she asked.

Face nobody remembers, heart of a devil, and ice water in the veins. You stand to make a great deal of money ... eventually. But first you have to finish school. I can't use you if you're ignorant or undisciplined.

Finish school? That's all?

That's first. But you have to graduate with a record that won't raise a single eyebrow, or the deal is off. No more stealing.

"I had already decided to accept his offer," Sidorov admitted to Jack and me, "but I was curious. 'If I refuse?' I asked him. 'If I report your attempt to recruit me?' He reminded me unfortunate accidents happened to children all the time. Needless to say, I signed on. I would be the best student the school ever had, I boasted, and so I was." Her lips curved sardonically. "A miraculous redemption.

"I didn't see Conover again until I graduated four years later. He sent a woman to pick me up and take me to his ranch in Texas. There he reinvented me with a legend so detailed and well-documented, I almost came to believe it myself. I was trained in tradecraft, hand-to-hand combat, the use of biological agents and all kinds of weaponry. Very intense. Three years. So, obviously, I was bitterly disappointed when he finally informed me I would be working as a housekeeper for the government, but by then I knew better than to object. That was two years ago."

"And you've been with the Service ever since," Eagan muttered in disgust. "How did you manage to get a clearance? A first-class legend won't get you past the truth scan."

"Surely you realize such matters can be arranged. One only has to buy or threaten the right people."

His eyes narrowed dangerously. "I want a name."

She gave it to him, then dismissed the issue with an airy wave of her hand. "But she's dead. Hit by a hover-bus, I believe. The organization always ties off loose ends."

"Loose ends like you?"

She smiled, obviously unfazed. "I have every confidence

CIIS will take excellent care of me until the threat no longer exists."

"Are there others?" I asked with a glance at Jack. "At other safe houses?"

"No mechanics. Drones, perhaps."

"Drones?"

"That's what we call nonlethal assets who are ignorant of the identities of their true controllers."

"Like the couriers."

"*Da*. Most think they're working for some government. They pass information through virtual cutouts, who pass it through other virtual cutouts, et cetera. We are sometimes forced to use them, because the organization itself is small and tightly knit. Fifteen of us, all trained at the same time."

"If you're one of the inner circle," said Eagan, "what are you doing so far from the action?"

"You think I'm an incompetent like Stanhope? Or are you trying to shame me into bragging about my accomplishments?" Her smile was a twisted sister to coy. "Maybe I'll disabuse you of that notion after you promise me immunity. For the moment, I will only say even a housekeeper can take a vacation."

"This was the perfect base of operations," I realized.

Tanya nodded. "Hiding in plain sight. The boss decided the advantages would far outweigh the risks. CIIS would hardly think to look for one of us in its bosom. Still, one has to be careful. I was extremely careful, but ...." She shrugged philosophically.

"This was more than a base of operations," Eagan guessed. "Conover had another reason for planting you here, didn't he?"

"Correct. The boss is a great believer in luck, and a man who trusts his intuition. This house is used only to hide important people. He foresaw the possibility that here I could have access to a target we might not otherwise be able to reach."

"A target like me," I said.

"Exactly."

"What I don't understand," Jack interjected, "is how you set us up today. This place is in lockdown when it's in use, all communications restricted."

"Ah, but I've been in this position for two years. Ample time to put certain measures in place when no one is in residence."

"What kind of measures?"

"A tiny fragment of code uploaded to the communications system via an untraceable UpLink."

"Comms are scanned for malware on a regular basis."

"True, but the script I used masks its presence long enough to gain control of the scanning software, making the intrusion impossible to detect later on. The code enables transmissions—infrequent microbursts buried in normal traffic—then removes all subsequent traces. In this case, I simply told Agent Stanhope one of the water recyclers had malfunctioned—the glitch wasn't hard to arrange—and asked permission to call it in. My voiceprint and the use of a specific code word triggered a burst, transmitting my location to alert the organization to a previously designated high-value target at these coordinates. All they had to do was position the weapons and await developments."

Jack closed his eyes and pinched the bridge of his nose. "Terrific." He dropped his hand and opened his eyes to glare at her. "Were the coordinates all you managed to broadcast, or should we assume Conover is in on A.J.'s secret?"

"I told you. It was a microburst. Coordinates only."

"Now what?" I asked after a brief silence.

"Now we bring in the rest of the team and decide how to play this," said Eagan.

"And my deal?" asked Tanya.

"Depends. Right now, all we've got is a he-said-she-said, and Conover is the one with all the credibility. Justice will want more: names, dates, methods of operation. If you can give us that, and if it all comes out in the wash—meaning your boss goes down, and we put the Ferrymen out of business for good—you can probably write your own ticket." He froze her with a look. "But so help me God, if this is a setup, or if you ever cross the line again when this is over, I'll hunt you down and kill you myself."

Tanya studied his expression. "A dangerous man," she finally decided. "Like the boss."

"Keep it in mind."

"I will." She glanced between Jack and me. "So, it's

settled." Her lips curved disparagingly. "I have turned over a new leaf, joined the forces of good in the contest against evil. Good always triumphs in the end, yes?"

"I don't know about always, but I'm going to make damned sure it triumphs this time," Jack promised grimly.

I wanted to believe him, but my gut was warning me this particular match was going to be closer than any of us cared to admit.

Chapter 42

Three a.m.

Moon-washed sand rolled away in every direction. Here it lay pleated by the wind, punctuated by scabs of rock and tufts of dune grass; there it piled in whaleback dunes. The blue-black sky overhead was thick with stars. I stood in the darkened living room, hands tucked in the pockets of a government-issue white terrycloth robe, staring out the bay window of the cloaked safe house now parked a hundred feet above the Saline Dunes in Death Valley.

Sensing I wasn't alone, I glanced over my shoulder. Wearing a white t-shirt and pale pajama bottoms, Jack sat watching me, one hip perched on the arm of the sofa. His blond hair was brushed silver by moonlight, his long, narrow feet were bare.

"Up early?"

"Up all night," I said and turned back toward the window.

"Pretty view," he said, crossing the room to stand beside me. "Peaceful. Almost makes me forget the downside of my desert tours. Sand flies and saw-scaled vipers. Parasitic skin infections."

I grimaced. "Yuck."

"Tell me about it."

The conversation, such as it was, stalled there. The air between us vibrated softly with his unspoken invitation to talk, but I couldn't seem to start. He decided to help me out.

"What's on your mind, A.J.?"

"I'm having trouble with this."

"What?"

"This deal with Sidorov. I've been chewing on it all night, only the more I chew the tougher it gets. It kills me to know she's going to walk." And pocket a hefty payoff on her way out the door. "The woman practically confessed to cold-blooded murder, Jack."

"Um-hm."

"And that crack about turning over a new leaf? Rubbing our noses in it."

"She's a professional killer, probably a sociopath. Conscience isn't part of the job description."

"Yeah. I've been trying to remember how she got that way. Some people never catch a break. How much of who we are is shaped by our circumstances? Tanya—or whatever her real name is—popped out of the birth canal with two strikes against her. Maybe I would have turned out the same way, if I had started life in a whorehouse in Eastern Europe."

"Maybe. But life gets off to a lousy start for millions of people. Or turns sour along the way. Disease, poverty, abuse. Most folks still manage to stay in the right. Besides, catching the breaks doesn't always earn you a halo. Look at Conover. He had it all—money, privilege, great education. You can debate nature versus nurture until you're hoarse, but the truth is, we've all got it in us to go either way. Maybe the real question is, why does one go bad when the next guy doesn't?"

"There but for the grace of God?"

"As good an explanation as any, I guess. But luck of the draw or no, there's right and there's wrong, and unless you're completely psychotic, you damned well know the difference, no matter where you started. We all share that, too. That awareness."

"Yeah. That's where I keep ending up."

Good always triumphs over evil in the end, yes? She had asked the question mockingly, like the answer was so obvious only an idiot with a Don-Quixote complex could miss it. *Good almost never triumphs. Ninety-nine percent of the time nice guys really do finish last.* The man on the street would probably agree that was the way the world seemed to work more often than not. *Que sera, sera,* right? Well, I couldn't accept that.

"You know," I murmured, "as much as it embarrasses me to admit it, in my heart of hearts I believe justice always wins out in the long run."

"Oh. An idealist."

"Nope, a pragmatist. The way I figure it, if right didn't eventually even the score, mankind would have self-destructed centuries ago. Granted, the comeuppances can be a long time coming, and we don't always hear about them, but I've always figured justice was your basic irresistible force."

"What goes around comes around? You reap what you sow?"

"Pretty much, yeah."

"So deal or no, Sidorov will get hers in the end."

"If she doesn't turn herself around? I can hope."

"Well, while you're waiting for lightning to strike, remember. If she's on the level, we're one giant step closer to decapitating the Ferrymen."

"I know."

"We're letting the smaller fish go in hopes of catching the big one. You've been around long enough to understand how it works."

"Sure, I understand. I just don't like it."

"Nobody *likes* it."

"Except the fish that gets away." I shook my head. "Come on, Jack, you and I both know she'll hire out again the minute she runs through the credits." I rubbed the knotted muscles at the back of my neck. "What happens if she goes back into business a year from now? If somebody else dies because we gave her a free pass?"

"Who said anything about a free pass?"

I looked at him, surprised. "You would go back on your word?"

"No way. If Conover goes down, and the Ferrymen go down with him, Sidorov will be able to write her own ticket as far as immunity from prosecution, a new identity, et cetera." He paused before adding, "But we're going to keep her on a short leash. You've heard of SIRIs?" He pronounced it *series*.

"Submicroscopic intracranial rehabilitation implants? Who hasn't? Track the subject's movements, monitor neurobiology for indicators of antisocial or violent inclinations, and instantly correct brain chemistry as needed."

He gave me a *well?* lift of the brows.

"For Sidorov?" I snorted. "Never happen! You would have to convict her first, and if CIIS agrees to the deal, prosecution will be off the table. But for the sake of argument, say trial is an option, and she's found guilty. You would still have to prove she's a *Repeat Offender Incapable of Reforming.* Hard to do when she doesn't have any adult priors on record.

No priors, no ROIR classification, which means you'll never convince two shrinks and one medical doctor to recommend the implant. No recommendations, no court order. End of story."

"Only if we're talking about an involuntary procedure. What if we get her consent up front?"

"*Consent*? Fat chance!"

"You would be surprised what people will agree to when the stakes are high enough. Sidorov has plenty riding on this deal, and I'm not talking about money and immunity. What happens if word gets out on the street? You know, the story about how she rolled on her boss and joined forces with the feds? We may not know who Conover's clients are yet, but it's a lead-pipe cinch they won't be thrilled to hear one of his hired guns is talking. And neither will he. Bad for business."

I felt my lips curve. "You think word will get out?"

"In a heartbeat, if she doesn't play ball."

The SIRI wouldn't stop Sidorov from living the high life, but it would definitely keep her on the straight and narrow. If it wasn't justice, it was probably the next best thing.

"Okay," I decided, "that helps."

"Thought it might. And while you're looking for the silver lining, try this one on for size: I'm convinced. About your ... uh ... gift," he said in answer to my blank look. "Not that we need to run around yakking about *visions*," he added hastily, when I broke out in a delighted smile. "If you ask me, the fewer in the know, the better. Bring too many people in on the secret, and it'll be impossible to contain. Remember, A.J., you're only one up on the bad guys if they don't know you have the edge."

Finally, we were on the same page, although I had to admit Eagan was a paragraph or two ahead of me.

Sam Bonner had said I would know what to do with my gift when the time came. He was right. Once I figured out that crime, real or potential, was a trigger, using the Sight as a stealth weapon in the fight *against* crime was a no-brainer. I mean, what else would I do with it, open a carnival act? My job with WNN would provide the perfect cover and, for better or worse, more peeks at the ugly side of life than I could shake a stick at. Now Iceman was suggesting we keep my gift on the QT, all the better to nab the bad guys and protect my assets.

Good plan, but I had one question. If only a few people were going to be in on this, and Eagan was one of them, did that mean he expected us to work together on a regular basis?

If so, I wasn't sure how I felt about that. Mister Protect and Defend could definitely cramp my style. Not that he wasn't easy on the eyes and occasionally reassuring to have around, but he was a rules-and-regs type. A bossy, buttoned-up fed. I, on the other hand, preferred independence, improvisation, and serving the story while it was smoking hot. Not exactly a match made in heaven.

"I agree," I said, keeping my reservations to myself. "And thanks for telling me. That you believe in me, I mean."

"Yeah, well. Fair's fair."

"Right." I could see him clearly now. A glance out the window revealed a sky lightening to pearl gray, erasing the stars and leaving Venus to fly solo above the faintly gilded horizon. "Sun's coming up."

"You've got time to catch a couple hours' shut-eye before the day gets off and running," he pointed out. "Gonna be a long one."

"Probably, but I'm still too wound up. Maybe a cat nap later."

"All right, if I can't talk you into getting some rest, how about breakfast?"

Before he crossed the "t" on *breakfast*, my stomach grumbled, *Now you're talking!*

"Does that answer your question?" I said, sharing Eagan's grin.

I followed him into the kitchen and watched him dial up a batch of fresh, hot cinnamon rolls as big as saucers. He brewed a cup of oolong for me and coffee for himself, going through the motions with the relaxed, competent air of a man who knows his way around a kitchen.

Iceman was full of surprises.

Unfortunately, he wasn't the only one.

Chapter 43

The jogging path wound through sun-splashed fields stitched along both sides with split-rail fencing. Shadows pooled under clusters of live oak, the trees' olive-drab leaves barely stirring under the feather-light touch of a summery breeze. The sky was blue and cloudless. Pounding along a smooth, uphill grade at the five-mile mark, I was starting to feel the burn, and the endorphins were kicking in.

I was a hundred yards short of a runner's high when Hank Ellison stepped onto the path dead ahead and announced, "We need to talk."

My arms and legs kept pumping, but the magic was gone. Not because Ellison was apparently set on a heart-to-heart, but because he was standing still, making it painfully obvious the scenery was moving, and I wasn't. Holographic bells and whistles notwithstanding, I was on a treadmill, still stuck in the safe house, and going nowhere fast. I blinked the sweat out of my eyes and tried not to hold the unwelcome reminder against him.

I shook my head. "If this is about going home—"

"Just the opposite," he cut in and glanced around. "Look, can we dispense with the drive-by landscape? It's making me dizzy."

"Computer. End virtual and initiate cool-down," I commanded, resigning myself to the inevitable.

As the treadmill leveled off and slowed, my rural fantasy faded from sight, revealing beige walls, a set of free weights, and one of those insect-like exercise machines that are all rods and pulleys. So much for my bucolic interlude.

"Thanks," I murmured when Ellison tossed me the hand towel I had dropped on the incline bench. I continued my cool-down walk as I dabbed at my face and neck. "So, talk."

"I have a proposition for you."

"What kind of proposition?"

"A partnership-type proposition." He waited, probably trying to gauge my reaction. "As in, you and me," he added, in case I had missed the point.

I hadn't. "I don't need a partner."

"Okay, maybe partner is the wrong word. How about assistant?"

"Hank—"

"Sidekick," he interjected hastily. "Whatever!"

I eyed him in exasperation. His horsey face had *I'm not going to take no for an answer* written all over it. "What brought this on?"

"You, taking down creeps like the Ferrymen. That's what you're planning to use this new …ah … *talent* of yours for, right? Well, I want to help." I started to ask him how he thought he could do that, when he held up a hand and hurried on, "Hear me out. I've been a reporter for five years, ever since I got out of college, and what have I got to show for it? You do *your* job, and the world is a safer place. I do *mine*, and gladiolas bloom."

"The world would be pretty dull without gladiolas."

"And orchids and daffodils and forget-me-nots. I agree. But it's not like nature will wither and die without my input."

"Exit program." The treadmill coasted to a stop. I waited until the anti-grav cushion dissipated and the unit touched down before stepping off. "And now you want to jump from mild-mannered gardening guy to caped crusader?"

He blushed but didn't back down. "If by *caped crusader* you mean I want to work the crime beat, then, yeah. Problem is, the closest I ever came to that kind of reporting was an exposé on Millie Driscoll, a seventy-year-old retired librarian who tried to enter a ringer in the Festival of Roses. Turned out her Homegrown Blue hybrid was actually a clone from Hoboken."

"And now you're ready to tackle big, nasty baddies." Hands on my hips, I stared at him long enough to make him squirm. Finally, I nodded. "Okay."

He must have been expecting a put-down, because he blinked and said, "Huh?"

"Go for it. I'll even introduce you to two or three editors

who might let you get a foot in the door. But don't expect *me* to provide on-the-job training. I'm not going to have time. You'll have to find your sources and earn your byline the old-fashioned way."

His face fell. "You still don't get it, do you? This isn't about a byline! This is about making a difference!"

"As my assistant."

"Right."

I rolled my eyes. "Earth to Hank. Have you been paying attention? The Ferrymen are dead set … no pun intended … on murdering me and anybody unlucky enough to get within a five-mile radius of me. That's bound to be the case from here on out, no matter which 'creeps,' as you call them, I go after. Watching my back and making sure my will is up to date are going to be part of my job description. I'm not happy about it, but I've had that talk with myself, and I'm ready to accept the risks. Are you? No offense, but you practically had heart failure when you heard my broadcast the other night."

"Only because I didn't know what you had planned!" he insisted. "Look, it's not like I haven't thought this through." He smiled crookedly. "There hasn't been much to do *but* think since you guys kidnapped me." The smile faded. "I've had that talk with myself, too, A.J. I understand the risks. I admit my knees start to knock whenever I imagine the what-ifs, but here's the bottom line, as far as I'm concerned: You've got a gift. You're going to use it to hammer crooks. I want to be a part of that, weak knees and all."

There he stood, the expression on his freckled, horsey face a crazy combination of hope and the importance of being earnest, and I started to wonder if his was such a bad idea. Hank already knew about the Sight. Had apparently become a believer. He would probably keep my secret—provided some gorilla didn't track him down and wring it out of him. Of course, that could happen whether I hired him or not. So why not include him? What did I have to lose? He was a bright guy and a trained reporter. An extra set of feet, hands, eyes, and ears—not to mention a fresh, if naïve, perspective—couldn't hurt.

"What if the closest you get to the action is background research or fact checks?"

Recognizing capitulation when he heard it, he started to

smile. "I can live with that."

"Not very glamorous."

"Not very dangerous, either."

"Knock on wood. All right," I sighed. "We'll give it a try. God willing, neither of us will be sorry."

"Sorry about what?"

I glanced over my shoulder to see Jack standing in the doorway.

Tipping my head toward the now-beaming Ellison I explained, "Seems I have a new assistant."

"Good for you," he said, which wasn't even close to the *have you lost your mind* I expected, so I turned all the way around to look at him.

His expression was unreadable, but those ice blue eyes spoke volumes. And nothing they had to report was good news.

That quick, I knew. "Who is it this time?"

"Sadie."

Chapter 44

"She was found late last night by one of her borders," said Dennis, "a deputy coming off a double shift."

"Li," I offered. "Ted Li."

"Right. He found her on the living room sofa, fully clothed. At first glance, she appeared to be sleeping, but Li figured there were two problems with that picture. One, nobody has ever known the woman to take a nap; and two, she didn't move a muscle when he came through the door."

"Sadie always slept light, with one eye open," Eagan said. "That's one reason she survived more than thirty years in the field."

"And it's a hard habit to break," said Dennis. "Anyway, long story short, Li checked, discovered she was dead—had been for some time—and called it in. Because there didn't seem to be a mark on her, the coroner was leaning toward natural causes."

"She was only fifty-eight," Jack objected, "and in great shape. She had a complete physical six months ago. They didn't find any problems. No sign of potential problems."

"That's why the doc planned to do a routine virtopsy this morning to confirm. She might have developed a blood clot or something. It happens, even *with* genetic engineering. Anyway, lucky for us, all former operatives are flagged, so we got pinged as soon as he entered her info on the database. An hour later, we had control of the scene and custody of the remains, which were brought back here for special processing."

By *here* he meant the ultramodern morgue housed in the Forensic Science Center at CIIS headquarters. The lab spanned eight thousand square feet and sported two free-floating multipurpose scanners; a couple industrial-sized sinks; an acre of shiny white countertops dense with scopes, spectrographs, and computer stations; and a ceiling hung with a tangle of robotic arms and tracked, computer-controlled light fixtures. The rear wall was your standard checkerboard of square metal doors.

Jack and I were virtual visitors, a tense audience of two beamed in for the postmortem rundown. Exactly four sentences had passed between us since he told me about Sadie. I was chockfull of questions, but Eagan was tightlipped and taut-jawed. The rage rolling off him in waves couldn't have been colder if he had been transfused with liquid nitrogen. All in all, it seemed like a good time to put a lid on it, hope this briefing gave me some answers, and thank my lucky stars Iceman and I were on the same side.

"She didn't die of natural causes," he repeated tersely.

"No."

"What then?" Jack asked the woman standing next to Dennis. "Poison?"

Great minds, same wavelength, I mused. Poison would explain the absence of marks on Sadie's body.

Doctor Mary Smith was about five three with brown eyes, a button nose, and a chestnut-brown, chin-length pageboy. Dressed in jeans, a short-sleeved turquoise t-shirt, and beat-up white cross trainers, she looked more like a soccer mom than a hotshot forensic pathologist.

"Poison would have been easy," she said.

Jack slowly straightened in his chair. "What the hell does that mean?"

"I'll show you." She crossed to a seven-foot-high virtopsy tablet mounted on the right-hand wall. "Computer, recall final, with drape, case five-two-seven-one."

A figure coalesced deep within the tablet's screen and started to rise like a ghost ascending from the underworld. My palms started to sweat. So much for emotional distance. *Knowing* Sadie was dead was bad enough, but *seeing* her dead?

Like I told Jack that night at the hospital, I've seen dead bodies before. In my line of work, if you do your job right, you often arrive at the scene of a homicide before the victim is processed for transport. I can't speak for anybody else, but corpses don't inspire objectivity in me; I always have to reach for it. It's harder to come by when I know the vic, of course, but so far I've been able to maintain that slim margin of detachment I need to preserve my sanity.

This time, it was different. My first encounter with the remains of someone I had lived with and gotten close to. It was also my first virtopsy. In all honesty, I wasn't sure I was up to either first.

I wiped my hands on my jeans as the image levitated free of the screen's two-dimensional confines. Clothed in an off-the-shoulder, ankle-length white muumuu, it morphed into a three-dimensional cadaver atop the obsidian surface. Because the tablet was hung vertically, the "body" was upright, the soles of the feet suspended a foot above the floor.

I made a last-ditch lunge for objectivity, and missed it by a mile. Reminding myself this wasn't actually Sadie's body but a computer-generated composite built slice-by-slice from the inside out using a complex array of scans and photographs didn't help. The image was accurate to the last hair follicle, so seeing it was, for all practical purposes, the same as seeing the real McCoy. This was how Sadie looked now. Café-au-lait complexion waxy, freckles leeched to ashy beige; slack facial muscles; sagging jaw; neck faintly creped. But it was the eyes that got me—open and empty, like windows staring out of an abandoned house. Which, I supposed, in a sense, they were.

You want to be careful about indulging in similes and metaphors at inappropriate moments; they'll take your mind on a detour before you know what hit you. There I sat, peering into those nobody's-home eyes while the ME started her report, only instead of paying attention and getting my answers, I found myself wondering where my former landlady had gone. Given the fact that energy can neither be created nor destroyed, where was the strong, vibrant life force that had been the essence of Sadie Carter? What did it look like, now that it had been brutally evicted from its shell? Had it been reduced to a microscopic uptick in the cosmic microwave background radiation? Somehow, I couldn't picture Sadie blending in with the rest of the universe.

Well, one thing was certain. If consciousness did go on in some form or fashion, Sadie was one unhappy camper right about now. She would *hate* being on display under the morgue's unforgiving white lights, yielding her carefully kept secrets to strangers. A virtopsy had to be the ultimate invasion of privacy, and here I was with a front-row seat, getting an earful of Sadie's business. Imagining her reaction, I winced.

"Are you all right? Jack asked.

"What?" I blinked, dispelling the mental fog. I forced my attention back to the business at hand. "Yeah, I'm okay. Sorry, Doctor. You were saying?"

She waited for a nod from Eagan before continuing, "No evidence indicating physical restraints were used—no fibers; traces of adhesive; or marks on the wrists, ankles, or neck. There were no lacerations, abrasions, or contusions. Scrapings from under the fingernails didn't yield any transfer evidence."

Jack's brow furrowed. "So no signs of a struggle."

"None."

"Not like Sadie to go down without a fight."

"I'm sure you're right, but resistance wasn't an option in this case. Remember, I said no *physical* restraints were used. We found traces of KZ-14 in her nasal mucosa."

"Sleep agent," Jack explained in answer to my questioning glance.

"It's an odorless gas originally formulated for use in hostage situations," Smith added. "Fast-acting, extremely potent, dissipates quickly. In and of itself, it's harmless."

"Until it falls into the wrong hands," I guessed.

"Ah, but KZ-14 is tightly controlled," Dennis singsonged. "Designated strictly for law enforcement or military use." His lips twisted sardonically. "Of course, we all know how that song goes."

"Yeah," Eagan muttered. "All you need is one bright bulb—an inventory clerk, a crooked security guard, maybe even one of the chemists working for the company that makes the stuff—who decides to go into business for himself. Brains, access, and the right passwords, and you've got yourself a black market bonanza."

"Probably vented it in through the HVAC," Dennis figured.

Eagan nodded. "Okay, that's how they got to her. The gas wouldn't have kept her out long."

"Long enough," the doctor assured him. Cupping a hand on "Sadie's" left shoulder, she guided the image away from the tablet. The body hovered eerily in mid-air as Smith gently turned it face-to-the-wall. She traced a square on the nape of the neck with her index finger and double-tapped to call up a section. She nudged the section away from the body before tugging at the corners of the frame to enlarge the segment.

"Can you see it? Here, right above the third vertebra. I admit it's faint."

"That red mark?" Jack nodded. "What is it?"

"An injection site."

With a flick of her index finger she peeled away skin and muscle to reveal the spinal cord. Since I was the only virtopsy virgin present, I was probably the only one who got queasy at that point. Sucking in a covert breath, I fought to control the greasy roll of my stomach and focus on the tiny black fleck clearly visible against the whitish tissue.

Jack pointed to it. "And that?"

"A microchip," Smith answered, "designed to block select signals from the brain. Based on our analysis, it would have produced quadriplegia similar to that caused by spinal cord injuries."

It took a second for the obvious implication to niggle its way through my lightheadedness. "Oh, my God!"

Chapter 45

"She was interrogated." Jack summed up the obvious in an icy monotone. He looked at the ME. "How bad?"

"As bad as it gets." She closed the slice view, rotated the body so it was facing us again, and tenderly maneuvered it onto the tablet. "Computer, close case file." Sadie's digital double did a slow fade as Smith turned back to us. "Based on the indicators—brain lesions, evidence of cellular cavitation, the presence of certain telltale metabolites—we believe she was subjected to torture by means of focused, high-frequency, pulsed ultrasound."

"I've had ultrasounds."

I wasn't aware I had said it out loud until she answered me.

"We all have. At lower frequencies it's harmless, even therapeutic. Pocket devices are standard equipment for physical therapists working in home health settings. Psychotherapists routinely use ultrasound in behavior modification techniques that involve remotely altering brainwaves. But as Ms. Gregson pointed out, a good product in the wrong hands can be devastating.

"Unlike its low-freq cousin, focused, *high*-frequency ultrasound wreaks havoc with the human nervous system and internal organs. One of the ways nonlethal sonic and ultrasonic weapons incapacitate is by triggering intense pain. In Sadie Carter's case, that effect was multiplied exponentially. The location of the tissue damage and changes to brain chemistry indicate manipulation of the rostral anterior cingulate cortex, or rACC, the part of the brain responsible for the awareness of pain—or, more accurately, the emotional component of pain. This is the region that experiences pain as suffering and feels compelled to try to make it stop. When physical sensations surpass a certain threshold, the rACC is activated.

"Whoever did this kicked the rACC into hyper-drive, one prolonged burst at a time. Pain perception would have gone off the charts. During each burst, pain would have been her world, all she could think about. Anticipating the next burst would have been almost as excruciating. And since thinking about pain generates more pain ...." Smith shook her head somberly. "No amount of training and experience could have equipped her to deal with it, even marginally. The plain fact is, she would have told them whatever she knew."

Jack closed his eyes and swore pungently. "Our names. That was all she had to give them. No information on where we were going when we left town. Hell, she didn't even know *why* we left town. She wanted it that way." He opened his eyes and asked about the cause of death.

"Prolonged vibroacoustic stimulation disrupts the heart rhythms, sometimes resulting in atrial fibrillation, sometimes bradycardia—when the heart beats too slowly. Either way, the end result in this case was sudden cardiac arrest."

Eagan washed a hand down his face and glanced at Baker. "What did we find at the scene? Do we know how they got in?"

"Hobson's Hope, remember? The door opens with a key. All you need for a B&E is an electronic pick. She did have a high-end security system, but it looks like they hacked it beforehand. Trujillo in digital forensics is working on tracing the software they used, but it doesn't look promising. Jorge says it was slick and quick and didn't leave any digital fingerprints. We didn't find any useful forensics in the house."

"I don't suppose any of the neighbors saw anything."

"A marketing rep who lives two doors down—blond name of Marci Jentzen—remembers a heating/air conditioning company van parked in front of the boarding house when she came home to let her dog out at lunchtime. She was in a hurry, so she didn't pay much attention. She can't remember the name of the company, but she thinks the van was white, or maybe light gray."

"Great, that narrows it down to a couple million possibles."

"Speaking of dogs," I interjected, "what happened to

Cosmo? He wouldn't have let a stranger get within a city block of Sadie."

"Probably not, but he was at the vet," said Dennis. "Sadie dropped him off around ten yesterday morning. He was listless to the point of being unresponsive, and she thought it might have been something he ate. Apparently, our pal Cosmo has a history of snacking on the local flora, which doesn't always agree with him. But when the vet got through checking him out, he realized the dog had been drugged. They tried to call Sadie, but ... no answer."

"What time was that?" asked Jack.

"Shortly before noon. About the same time the van was spotted."

During the pregnant pause that followed, nobody mentioned the obvious—i.e., what had probably been going on in Sadie's house while the vet was waiting for her to pick up—but I was pretty sure we were all thinking about it. Or maybe we were all trying not to.

Eagan finally broke the silence. "Time of death?"

"I put it between three and four," said Smith.

Jack rubbed his jaw. "Okay, I get the fact that it didn't take a rocket scientist to figure out she would probably be alone during the day when her boarders were at work. The killers stake out the house the night before and hack the alarm system. Next morning, they watch the boarders leave, dose the dog, then wait for Sadie to come back from the vet. What I don't understand is why somebody didn't find her earlier. What about the other tenants? Are you trying to tell me they didn't see her lying there all afternoon and evening?"

"They weren't home," said Dennis. "One of the females, Fannie Jordan, had a hot date right after work and didn't get in until after two in the morning. The systems analyst was babysitting a sick friend."

"What about Byron?" I asked.

"Away at a three-day conference on existentialism in twentieth-century America."

Eagan shook his head. "So we're left with a big, fat goose egg."

"That about sums it up."

Eyes narrowed in thought, Jack drummed his fingers against the arm of his chair. "Okay, tell the others to keep after the van and the hacking software, but put Oakley in charge; I want you out here with us. We've got independent confirmation of A.J.'s … ah … eyewitness testimony, and we need to decide how we're going to play it."

"Do tell." Baker's eyebrows climbed as his dark gaze swung my way. "Now, that's a story I can't wait to hear."

Jack cleared his throat. "Listen, about Sadie." Pause. "She didn't have any family."

"Nobody but us," Dennis agreed. "Not to worry. She and Ito worked together quite a bit in the old days. They were even partners for a while. Rumor has it, he's already planning the sendoff. Gonna be a bona fide blow-out, from what I hear."

"Good. That's the way she would have wanted it. The Sprite always hated funerals."

"Don't we all," muttered Dennis. His eyes met Jack's. "Listen, I know you and Sadie were close, and I …. I'm sorry. If it's any consolation, the whole team is up in arms. She was one of ours. We'll get the bastards who did this."

"Dead or alive," agreed Iceman, and the arctic glint in his eye left no doubt about his preference.

Chapter 46

"He probably blames me."

Dennis ambled back from the coffee maker. He turned his chair around and straddled it, arms resting across the back, one hand wrapped around a steaming cup of French roast. The ruins of a bacon-and-egg breakfast littered the table between us. "Who?" he said.

"Jack."

"For?"

"Sadie."

"That's bull," he replied calmly, and took a sip.

I shoved my plate aside and folded my arms on the table. "Think so? If I hadn't boarded with her—"

He held up an index finger. "Remind me again. *Whose* decision was that?"

"Okay, dumping me in her lap was Jack's idea. The come-and-get-me broadcast wasn't."

"Nope, rattling the Ferrymen's cage was definitely your brain child. And it worked."

"Great. Wonderful. Except for the part where I skipped town and left Sadie to pay the bill."

"You don't give her much credit, do you?"

"What?"

"Sadie. You don't give her much credit."

I scowled. "How do you figure?"

"Did Iceman brief her on why he wanted to put you at her place?"

"You know he did. In detail."

"There you go. You reckon she was experienced enough to understand the risks involved? Hell, she probably understood them better than you did."

"Still—"

"She could have turned us down, told Jack to find

someplace else. She didn't. She made her choice, A.J." His lips curved slightly. "Knowing the Sprite, she was probably hoping to get a shot at the Ferrymen herself. Like I said yesterday, some habits die hard."

"Maybe you're right. Strike that. I *know* you're right." I ran a fingertip around the rim of my stoneware mug. "It's just ...."

"What?"

I blew out a breath. "Cuey, Michaels, Bugsy, and now Sadie. I feel like a Jonah."

"Well, shake it off and start feeling like the woman who's going to help us hunt down these bastards. We're going to nail them, and sooner rather than later, thanks to you. But you gotta keep your head in the game. If Sadie could get a message out from wherever she is now, she would second me on that."

"In no uncertain terms. I can almost hear the lecture." I smiled crookedly. "Thanks."

"Hey, no problem. You're part of the team now, right? Teammates take care of each other, keep each other focused."

"Uh ... right."

Part of the team. Teammates. When feds talk like that, it makes my teeth itch. I'm all for cooperation and working together for the common good, but you don't want to obliterate the boundaries. I mean, you've got the law and you've got the press. Lot of times we see eye to eye, but just as often we don't. The two sides have even been known to disagree on what the *common good* looks like. You want my opinion, when the story comes down to press versus police — and it usually does at some point — you're either a reporter or a *team player* (read: *parrot*). So, you've got to walk that fine line.

Not that I'm above using the other side's terminology when it suits me. As in .... "If I'm part of the team, maybe you wouldn't mind satisfying my curiosity."

"About what?" he asked warily.

Hah! So much for team spirit.

"Jack and Sadie. How did they meet?"

He relaxed enough to smile. "Never managed to worm the story out of her, huh?"

"Not for lack of trying."

"She tell you anything at all?"

"Only that they met when he was with the Teams."

His dark eyes narrowed as he ran the need-to-know

analysis. I half-expected him to stonewall and was pleasantly surprised when he shrugged. "The names and dates are still classified, but I don't see any harm in sharing the parts that aren't. Off the record."

My three least favorite words in any language, but sometimes you can't get around them, and I was curious. "Sure."

"Our squad was tasked with bringing in a rogue scientist last seen shopping WMD research around the Terror Triangle. Air dropped us into the sand about forty klicks from the Persian Gulf, and headquarters said wait there for our contact. We sweated through six miserable days, but nobody showed.

"Day seven, we spot a kid coming toward us, toting a man-sized burlap sack and herding three of the mangiest sheep you ever laid eyes on. So we activate our cloaks and settle into our hidey holes to wait him out. Well, wouldn't you know it, the grubby little beggar squats down eighteen meters in front of our noses and starts to eat lunch. Okay, that's a pain in the butt, but it's not a serious problem. Again, all we have to do is lay up until he moves on. Only the kid is taking forever with that lunch.

"Almost an hour goes by before he swallows the last bite of naan, dusts off his hands, and announces, 'I appreciate the lunch break, but what do you say we stop playing hide-and-seek? I hate sheep, I'm not getting any younger, and we've got a collar to make.'"

"Sadie," I guessed with a grin.

"None other. She was quite a surprise, and I don't mean that in a good way. We bitched and moaned at first, but the grumbling didn't last more than the day or two it took us to realize this middle-aged woman no bigger than a minute rated expert on any weapon from a blade to a sonic cannon, didn't mind being dirty, and always humped her share of the gear without whining.

"We spent three months tracking the target's mobile lab, waiting for a chance to snatch him and his would-be buyers. Three months dug into sand up to our eyeballs, with our heads on a swivel. Living like that strips you down to what's real. You get to know one another pretty quickly."

He paused for a drink of coffee before continuing, "Sadie told us CIIS tried to tie her to a desk when she turned thirty-five. She threatened to resign, knowing good and well they couldn't afford to lose her. How many agents can speak five or six languages or know the local customs of at least that many countries better than most natives do? Anyway, headquarters backed down. So there she was, middle-aged and still in the field, sent along to make sure us knuckle-draggers kept the grab nice and legal."

"I take it she and Jack hit it off especially well?"

"Are you kidding? Once they found out they both had degrees in criminology, the two of them were thick as thieves. Sadie filled Eagan in on what worked in real-world law enforcement and what wasn't worth a damn outside the covers of a textbook. Even gave him the back-story on the guy we were after. How CIIS uncovered his plans to defect and tagged his DNA so they could track him, then set up the op in a way that would let them net a couple other birds at the same time. Iceman ate that stuff up with a spoon." Baker shrugged. "Guess it was in his blood. His dad is a cop. So are both his uncles. Only one who didn't go into law enforcement was his twin brother, Sean."

I held up a hand. "Wait. Back up. Jack Eagan has a twin brother?"

"Fraternal. They don't look all that much alike. Sean is two minutes older and an inch shorter. Dark hair, brown eyes."

Eagan had a family. A twin, for God's sake. So much for my theory about him being chiseled off an iceberg. Promising myself I would find out more later, I gestured for Baker to go on. "What happened then?"

"We pinched our targets as planned. We went our way, and Sadie went hers, but she and Jack stayed in touch. She even called to let him know the twerp and his buddies got life without parole. Eagan was jazzed about being part of that."

"But he stayed with the Teams."

Dennis nodded. "For four more years. Then we worked with Sadie on another case, gathering intel on a sex slavery ring with players on three continents. Iceman picked her brain nonstop. She finally threw up her hands and told him anybody who liked to ask questions as much he did ought to sign on with the Service. When the assignment was over, he took her up on it."

"So did you."

"Yeah. The Sprite definitely knew how to bait her hook. Anyway, not long after we came on board she retired and moved to Hobson's Hope. Claimed with the two of us to fill her shoes — one for each boot, she said — she could leave with a clear conscience. Jack visited her whenever he got the chance."

"So she was his mentor, as well as his friend," I said. "Losing her, especially this way, has to be a blow."

He nodded again. "The stuff we do .... You know you're going to take losses. You tell yourself you're mentally prepared, but you're not. When one of your team goes down, it carves a hole in you. Every damned time. You can train yourself not to rehash the details and refuse to play What-If, but that hole never heals.

"Most days you can cage the emotions in some dark corner of your soul. But now and then — when you're alone or tired or sick or drunk — the memories break loose and tear you to pieces until you can beat them back. The dreams are the worst, because you're helpless all over again. But you deal with your demons and go right back out, because carrying the fight to the enemy is the only way you can lay those ghosts to rest for a while." He paused to study my face before adding , "Of course you already know all that, don't you?"

"Yes," I answered quietly.

How many times had I relived the explosion in my dreams? How many nights had I lurched awake with a gasp, drenched in sweat and drowning in survivor's guilt?

Dennis leaned toward me, his expression earnest. "Look, A.J., I know you want to do your part, but you better think long and hard about what you're getting into with this talent of yours. Like I said yesterday, losing friends and teammates never gets easier. The more of them you lose, the rawer it gets. If you stay at this, one way or another, you're going to bleed."

Truth didn't come any colder or harder, except there was more to it.

"I believe you, but it doesn't change my decision. I can't *let* it change my decision. How would I live with myself, Dennis? Knowing I could have made a difference but chose not to because I didn't want to pay the price."

"And if the price includes family?"

"You think I haven't faced that possibility?" I didn't mean to bite his head off, but that spot was still tender. Always would be. I forced myself to calm down. "It's not like I plan to hang out a shingle or advertise on the air. All I can say is I'll do my best to keep them out of harm's way."

"Keep whom out of harm's way?" Jack wanted to know, as he joined us in the kitchen.

"My family."

"Ah." He strolled over to the cabinet, pulled out a cup, and poured some coffee. Leaning against the counter, he took a leisurely sip. "Speaking of your family, I just got through talking to your brother."

My heart bobbled but only for a beat. Whatever he had to tell me couldn't be bad news, or he wouldn't be lounging against the counter, coffee in his right hand, left hand tucked casually in the pocket of his blue jeans.

"Which brother? Why didn't I get to talk to him?"

"The pushy prosecutor. And you didn't get to talk to him, because he was on his way into court and only had a second to pass along a message."

"Which was?"

"Malcolm Conover called WNN, looking for you. Maxwell gave him the story we agreed on. You're off the grid, probably Lone Rangering a hot lead. Conover left a callback number in case you came up for air."

My scalp prickled with that familiar mix of apprehension and excitement I live for. "I don't get it. Why would Conover try to contact me? There's no way he could have guessed I saw …. He left a number? That's all? He didn't say why he wanted to talk to me in the first place?"

"He claimed he has some information. Said he wouldn't share it with anybody but you."

"Multibillionaire philanthropist calls with a hot tip for a crime reporter?" said Dennis. "I'm surprised Maxwell remembered his own name, let alone the fact that Jim was his emergency point of contact."

"He definitely smelled a scoop. Records show he was on the horn to the DA's office a nanosecond after the transmission ended."

"Maxwell isn't the only one who smells something," Dennis muttered. "I do, too. And it's not a news story."

"A trap," I agreed, mentally running through my options. It was a quick sprint, because there was only one. "It doesn't matter. I have to call. So far, he's got no reason to believe I've made him. That'll change in a New York minute if he thinks I'm avoiding him."

Eagan nodded agreement. "Already put the wheels in motion."

"I wonder what his angle is?" I said. "What does he hope to accomplish?"

Dennis snorted. "Before or after he dumps you in an unmarked grave?"

"He's not going to lay a finger on her," Eagan promised.

Talk about famous last words ....

Chapter 47

It was like being in a play, except I didn't have a script, and a missed cue could be fatal.

"Thank you for getting back to me, Conover said.

He was perched on the corner of a burled-walnut desk, his snowy hair tied back with a leather thong. He wore a red turtleneck, stylishly faded blue jeans, loafers sans socks, and an Eagle Scout's smile. I had to admit he was good. No, better than good. Looking at that face, you would never guess the man's heart was set on death and dismemberment. In this case, mine.

The real Conover was nowhere to be seen. Either Malcolm wasn't riled enough for the shields to drop, or my visions weren't Cloud compatible. Apparitions probably don't digitize well. But since this wasn't the time or place to explore criminal psychology or meditate on the physics of the paranormal, I let my questions slide and delivered my line.

"Tug Maxwell … my editor … said you have some information for me."

"I do."

He didn't appear the least bit interested in my surroundings. Either he wasn't scanning for visual clues to my location — the call itself was untraceable — or having learned about my CIIS connections from Sadie, he suspected the no-tell-motel room was so much smoke and mirrors. In which case, he would have been right.

"Mr. Maxwell said you were out on assignment." Pause. "By any chance, does this assignment involve the Ferrymen?"

"He tell you that?" I asked. Guarded.

"No." His lips curved ruefully. "For a newsman, he was singularly uninformative." The smile faded. "But you've been crusading against them for a year and a half, and you don't strike me as the type to let go of a cause once you sink your teeth into it."

"Not so far."

He nodded. "That tenacity is one of the qualities I most admire in you. How close are you to exposing the Ferrymen? I have a legitimate reason for asking," he assured me hastily.

I decided to be blunt. Hit him with the truth and see which way he ran with it. "If I were any closer, I would be inside."

Maybe I hoped he would at least bat an eyelash. He didn't. "What if I could help?" he asked instead.

"Excuse me?"

"I may have stumbled upon some information about their supply lines."

"Mr. Conover—"

"Malcolm."

"Malcolm," I conceded. "I don't mean to sound cynical, but where would a nice man like you come up with a lead like that? Philanthropists and assassins don't usually move in the same circles." *Usually* rolled off my tongue without a hint of irony. Maybe I should take up acting as a second career.

"Amanda …. May I call you Amanda?" He waited for my nod before continuing, "Not everyone I deal with is a saint."

I pretended to consider this pearl of wisdom. "All right," I replied slowly, "given some of the third-world dictatorships you have to do business with, I can see that. Not that I'm convinced," I quickly added, "but I'm willing to be. What have you got?"

"I'm not comfortable divulging that information via UpLink. Could we meet? I'm afraid I can't come to you—my movements attract far too much attention. Maybe you could visit Foundation headquarters in Austin?"

"If that's what it takes. When do you want to do this?"

"The sooner, the better. Shall we say tomorrow?"

I paused, a busy woman mentally reviewing her schedule. "Tomorrow should work. What time?"

"Come for lunch, and I'll take you on a tour in the afternoon."

I lifted a brow. "And I need a tour because …?"

"Because you're a well-known crime reporter, and our staff will wonder why you're here. I thought we might explain your visit as research. You know, familiarizing yourself with legitimate not-for-profits as preparation for a piece on fraud involving charitable organizations?"

Nothing like lifting a page from your own playbook, Malcolm.

"Sounds plausible," I said. "Okay, we'll play it your way. I'll be at your headquarters at noon tomorrow."

"Thank you, Amanda. I promise you won't regret your visit."

Yeah. I should live so long.

"Let me get this straight," said Dennis. "You're *going*?"

"No," Iceman interjected firmly, "she's not."

He was lounging against the counter again, but his aura had undergone a subtle shift from casual to immovable. I swallowed the retort that leapt to my lips, because *Back off, Buster!* would only make him dig in his heels, and I hoped to coax him fully on board for what I had in mind.

"Yes," I said, also firmly, "I am. My gut tells me it's time we got in this guy's face."

"To hell with your gut," Eagan decided. "We've got Sidorov. Justice signed off on the deal this morning."

"Glad to hear it. But you know what they say about putting all your eggs in one basket." Especially if said basket was woven of a long, drawn-out, bureaucracy-heavy investigation with lots of anally retentive detail obsession. "What if Sidorov can't come through with concrete evidence against Conover? This guy is connected to all the right people. More popular than Santa Claus. The fact that he's been so upfront about his misspent youth only adds luster to his saintly glow. If it finally boils down to her word against his, we're sunk."

Eagan scowled, tacitly acknowledging my point.

Dennis said, "And you're betting you can string him along and .... What? Get him to incriminate himself?"

"Maybe. It's happened before. Guys who think they're smarter than the rest of us tend to trip over their pride. Put yourself in Conover's shoes. He runs the world's most elite band of assassins. They come and go like phantoms. *Nobody's* safe. You know it, I know it, the neighborhood dogcatcher knows it. He's got cops on three continents running in circles, and VIPs on both sides of the law shaking in their boots, wondering if they're next. Our boy is getting away with murder in spectacular style, *but he can't tell anybody!* I'll bet he's dying to brag a little."

"Fishing for information cuts both ways," Jack reminded me. "Conover wants to get you talking as much as you do him. He needs to find out how much you know."

"Then I'll have to watch what I say, won't I? It's not like this will be my first interview with a felon, you know. If nothing else, our chat will give me a chance to get him *really* worried about what I have. If I can stir him up enough, I can get another peek inside. I might pick up information we can use."

"Could be worth a shot," Dennis guessed after two endless minutes of silence.

"I suppose it wouldn't hurt to let her have another look," Eagan admitted grudgingly. "But one of us goes with her."

"Now hold on," I said, but they ignored me.

"Not *one* of us," Baker interjected. "*Me*. Ito wants you to debrief Sidorov. As far as he knows, the housekeeper is our one and only lead, and he wants you to do the questioning. So unless you're ready to chance a mandatory psych evaluation by briefing him in on A.J.'s visions, you're stuck."

Eagan swore softly. "All right, you go. But we take the usual steps."

"Can I get a word in edgewise here?" I asked, holding up an index finger. Seeing I had finally managed to snag their attention, I said, "Not that I don't appreciate your concern, but I've been doing this for years. I don't need—"

Iceman severed my verb from my direct object with an impatient hand-slash. "Yes, you do, and that's not negotiable. You've been lucky so far, but nobody's lucky forever. Conover will pull out all the stops to get you dead, *after* he pumps you about what you know and where you got the information and who you shared it with. And he isn't into asking nicely. Or have you forgotten what they did to Sadie?"

"You know I haven't."

"Then let us do our job. Call him back and tell him you're bringing your assistant."

"Sadie told him I left Hobson's Hope with CIIS, but he's going to accept Dennis as my assistant?"

"Not for a minute, but he won't let on."

"Because," Dennis cut in, "the only guy who would *expect*

you to have a CIIS bodyguard *posing* as your assistant—"

"—would be the guy who tortured Sadie," I finished.

"Make the call," said Eagan.

Did I have a choice? No, but I didn't have to like it. "Fine," I sighed, "have it your way."

"I usually do."

Chapter 48

Two tiers of traffic crawled bumper-to-bumper. We rolled at a snail's pace between cobblestone sidewalks already thick with pedestrians — rat racers in three-piece suits, holiday bargain hunters mobbing early bird door-busters, sleep-deprived college students doing the zombie shuffle in burnt orange hoodies and flip flops. Long-necked patrol droids with lollipop heads and three-sixty perspective drifted through the crowd, scanning for pickpockets, purse snatchers, and wanteds. Apparently oblivious to the fact that the mercury hovered shy of forty, a man wearing nothing but a matted gray beard, purple thong, and light-up platform shoes had set up housekeeping on the corner of Sixth and Congress in a fan-backed chair that put the *rat* in rattan. He was arguing with a pal only he could see.

At the light we pulled up next to a massive biker, a regular Goliath. The red-paisley kerchief around his broad, flat forehead couldn't tame the explosion of salt-and-pepper curls that trailed to his shoulders. His hog was tricked out with a flames-of-Hell paint job, hand-tooled-leather saddle bags emblazoned with skull and crossbones, and ape-hanger handlebars. When he caught me looking, a *Well, hello, pretty mama!* grin dawned beneath his greasy Fu-Manchu, revealing the gap where his two front teeth used to be. I chuckled as the light turned green and traffic started to inch forward again.

"What's funny?" Dennis asked.

Still smiling, I shook my head. God, it was good to be back.

"Oh seven thirty," he announced. "We made good time, no thanks to Ellison."

"I still can't believe he went off on us like that."

Baker and I had decided to fly to Austin early to get the lay of the land and the local lowdown on Conover before walking into the lion's den. We were on our way out the door when Hank threw a major conniption fit, all because he had somehow gotten the harebrained idea *he* would be the one going with me. Him being my *real* assistant and all.

"At least he listened to reason," Dennis said.

"Uh-huh. I must have missed the page in the thesaurus where *reason* is listed as a synonym for *threats*."

"More like promises." He nosed our nondescript white van into a parking garage. "Look, the thought of facing Conover obviously scared the hell out of him, but he was ready to step up and do his part. Got to give him credit for that, even if it was a dumb idea. Iceman figured he needed a way to back down without losing face, so he gave him one."

He pulled into a vacant slip, we got out, and the van sank out of sight as the elevator ferried it underground. We emerged from the shadowed overhang onto the sidewalk, squinting like a couple of troglodytes seeing daylight for the first time in a month.

"Is it my imagination, or is the sun brighter here?" I slid my shades out of the breast pocket of the black photographer's vest I wore over a lilac cowl-neck sweater, and put them on.

"It's your imagination." But he slipped on his own sunglasses. The silver frames and narrow mirrored lenses completed his ensemble for the day: backward-facing black ball cap, faded jeans, Steelers jersey, black fleece jacket, well-worn running shoes. He spread his arms, palms up. "Well? How do I look?"

"Like somebody's gofer."

"Don't sound so surprised," he said, dropping his arms. "I do this for a living, you know."

"Sure." I glanced around. "Okay, where to?" My stomach rumbled a suggestion you could hear from three feet away. "Breakfast?"

"You're kidding, right? We had breakfast not more than two hours ago."

"Brunch, then."

"Nobody actually eats *brunch*."

"Tell that to my mother."

The Congress Avenue Café was a weathered-brick holdout wedged between the smoked-glass façades of the

Austin Museum of Art and the obviously trendy Sushi Lou's. Tan shades at half-mast in the café's two wide windows complemented a saggy brown awning to give the building a heavy-lidded, beetle-browed scowl. Both the craggy exterior and the bake sale flyers scrolling along the windows suggested this was a hangout for the hometown crowd. Dennis' eyes met mine in unspoken agreement. Local haunts draw regulars, and people get talkative when they feel at home and everybody knows everybody else. In short, the Congress Avenue Café suited our purposes to a T.

An antique bell jingled when we opened the door, its anemic tinkle quickly swallowed by the murmurous tide of overlapping conversations and the rattle of dishes. The five booths along the right-hand wall were taken, as were most of the square tables packed in the room's center. There was widespread visiting between tables and some spirited flirting with waitresses, of which there were two—a middle-aged blond and a sassy, college-aged redhead.

As near as I could tell, the café was two-thirds eatery, one-third gift shop specializing in Texas kitsch. Shelves covering the far left wall displayed merchandise ranging from pralines packaged as armadillo droppings to t-shirts sporting sentiments like *I wasn't born in Texas, but I got here as fast as I could,* and over the silhouette of a handgun, *We don't call 911.* A waist-high glass display case was filled with turquoise jewelry and silver belt buckles the size of dinner plates.

Baker spotted an empty table in the back left corner, and we waded in, threading a course between retirees asking about the senior special and ranch-hand types shoveling down man-sized helpings of steak and eggs or beans and breakfast tacos. I caught a whiff of bacon, and my mouth started to water.

The red-and-white-check vinyl tablecloth was still damp from the busboy's rag when we sat down. We silently studied a sprig of silk bluebonnets sprouting from a milky vase and salt and pepper shakers shaped like cowboy boots.

"Cowboy boots?" said Dennis.

"This is Texas. They don't do subtle here."

"Or tasteful?"

"Don't be a snob. Taste is in the eye of the beholder."

"If you say so."

I slid a hand-printed menu out from between the Tabasco and Billy Bob's Liquid Fire Habanero Sauce but barely had time to glance at it before the older waitress stepped up to take our order. With her star-of-Texas earrings, sharply creased jeans and western shirt that resembled the Texas flag, she was a walking postcard for the Lone Star State.

"Mornin'," she said, setting two glasses of ice water on the table as the overloaded silver charm bracelet on her right wrist dingled musically. "Y'all ready to order, or you need another minute?"

"Coffee for me," said Baker.

"How about you, honey?"

"I'd like some hot tea and …. Hmm. I don't know." I quickly scanned the menu. "It all looks good. What do you recommend?"

She didn't hesitate. "Hill Country Biscuits and sausage gravy. Guaranteed to melt in your mouth and stick to your ribs."

"Sausage gravy?" My belly gnarled enthusiastically. Dennis cleared his throat and pretended he wasn't dying to comment. I ignored him and told the waitress, "Okay, bring them on."

"Bless your heart! You won't be sorry," she assured me and bustled off to place the order.

"She left in a hurry," I said.

"It's that low, menacing growl."

"What low, menacing—" My belly rumbled again. Loudly. "Oh, *that* low menacing growl."

"She's probably afraid you'll keel over before she can feed you."

He must have been right, because the waitress was back a minute later with Dennis' coffee, a mug of Earl Grey for me, and a basket of bite-sized muffins.

Setting the food and drinks on the table, she said, "You eat up now; these muffins are on the house."

"Thanks. That's very nice of you."

She folded her arms and eyed me expectantly. Realizing she intended to hover until I took nourishment, I chose a warm poppy seed muffin and popped it into my mouth. Light, airy. A delicate blend of lemon and butter that was practically a religious experience.

"Mmmm," I said.

"Aren't they good?" She waited for my swallow, then cocked her head. "This your first time here? You look familiar to me." She snapped her fingers. "I know, you're that murder reporter. WNN, right?"

"As rain," I said, offering my hand. "A.J. Gregson."

"I didn't recognize you at first; you're taller in person. Thinner, too. I'm Bobby Mae Tolliver. I own this place."

Judging by the way she cocked her hip and settled in, Bobby Mae was inclined to chat. I narrowly resisted the urge to punch a fist in the air and holler, *Jackpot!* Her affability made our job that much easier. All we had to do was steer her in the right direction.

"Nice to meet you, Bobby Mae. This is my assistant, Denny."

"Howdy, Denny. Are you sure you don't want somethin' to eat?"

"I'll stick with the coffee for now, thanks."

"Well, you let me know if you change your mind. Leroy — the cook? — he can whip up some huevos rancheros that'll make you swear you've died and gone straight to heaven."

Baker smiled into his cup. "I'll keep that in mind."

Bobby Mae nodded, then turned back to me and lowered her voice conspiratorially. "I don't mean to pry, but are you in town to do one of your stories on that Boatmen bunch? Because if you are, I've got to tell you, I don't think we have any of that around here."

Guess again, Bobby Mae. But so much for steering her in the right direction. She was already going our way.

"I'm working on another story this trip."

Her ruby-red lips turned down at the corners. "Not one of those 'Cities with the Lowest Crime Rate' pieces, I hope. Every time somebody sings Austin's praises, the damn Yankees come runnin'. We sure don't need more people from up north comin' down here to tell us what we're doin' wrong." She paused, eyes widening as she belatedly noticed Dennis' jersey. "Oh, Lord! Y'all aren't from up that way, are you?"

"Nope. I'm from California, he's from —"

"New Mexico," Baker finished smoothly and plucked at his shirt. "This was a birthday present from an old girlfriend."

"Oh. Well, that's all right then. It's not that I'm prejudiced, you understand, but Austin hasn't been the same since *those people* started movin' in. They just can't leave well enough alone! Used to be, you could swim in the Barton Springs pool; now they've got the whole place under a dome. To protect it, they say. I say, what good's a swimmin' hole if you can't swim in it?"

She paused, her gaze expectant, so I said, "Right," and earned an approving nod.

"Half the locals are fed up. Leavin' town. Even the bats moved out. Used to be millions of them under the Congress Avenue bridge. Little, bitty brown things no bigger than your thumb? Folks would come from miles around to see them whoosh out in a big cloud at dusk. Looked like a biblical plague," she recalled dreamily.

"Well, Austin is safe from me."

"Thank God for small mercies. So why *are* you here? If you don't mind my askin'."

"No big secret. I'm working on a piece about fraud involving charities. Denny and I are meeting Malcolm Conover this afternoon. He agreed to provide some background material."

"Malcolm Conover?" Judging by her grimace, Bobby Mae was fonder of the recently departed bats. "Oh, Lord."

Dennis and I exchanged a quick glance.

"You don't like Conover?" he asked. "I've seen him on the networks, heard him speak a few times. Seems like a nice guy. Concerned. Compassionate."

"When he's in the limelight, maybe."

"Are you saying he's different in private?"

"Put it this way. He's not real popular around *here*."

"How come? The foundation he started spends billions on charity; they help a lot of people."

Bobbie Mae nodded once. "They do for a fact."

"Having his headquarters here has to be good for the local economy," I added.

"Maybe so, but we don't set as much store in that as we do in a man's character. The way he treats ordinary folks. Mr. High and Mighty Conover looks so far down his nose at the locals, you'd think he'd go cross-eyed! Lives way out in the hills up near Drippin' Springs, miles away from anybody. Clamped a force shield over his property, blockin' traffic up to fifteen thousand feet! Acts like that ranch of his was Fort Knox!"

"Could be he's trying to protect his privacy," Baker suggested. "He must have money-hungry crazies coming out of the woodwork looking for handouts."

"Might have, but that's no reason for his hired guns to chase away the neighbors. His security yahoos have been known to rough up a few of the more persistent ones." She sniffed indignantly. "Not that the law does anything about it. Money talks."

So did the neighbors, evidently.

"That level of security does seem like overkill," I offered.

"There you go! Why, nobody has ever *seen* his house, much less visited. They say he designed the place himself, brought in laborers from somewhere down in South America to build it, then shipped the hired help back where they came from. At least, that's the story. You ask me, those poor souls are buried in a gully out there." The tablet in her hand chimed softly, drawing her attention to the readout. "Your order's up. Just as well. I don't need to be preachin' from my soapbox when I've got a house full of hungry customers. I'll be right back with your biscuits."

As she bustled off toward the kitchen, I looked at Dennis. "Care to bet she's wrong about those construction workers?"

"Not a chance."

Chapter 49

Change a Life's headquarters building was an accordion of triangles stacked one behind the other, stark white points piercing a sky blue enough to break your heart. The glassed-in front soared ten stories, the slightly narrower section behind it nine, the next eight and so on, until the structure tapered to a slender waist four stories high. From there it gradually broadened again, stair-stepping back up to eight stories. The cornucopia metaphor was impossible to miss. Especially with oversized marble gourds, nine-foot concrete ears of corn, enormous bunches of plump stone grapes, and giant bronze apples littering the broad flagstone courtyard like so much overflow from Conover's horn of plenty. An immaculately manicured lawn shaded by crepe myrtle and live oak rolled down to the edge of Lady Bird Lake.

Automatic doors slid silently open as we approached, ushering us into a football field-sized lobby floored in gleaming black granite. Plush, royal blue area rugs framed cozy conversational groups made up of black coffee tables tucked in rainbow arcs of colorful wrap-around chairs. Over against the right-hand wall, brass benches with black-leather seats stitched a broken line between eight-foot potted ficuses.

A soft *bong* to our left drew our gazes to a bank of elevators. One of the doors slid up, revealing a gangly, fresh-faced, jeans-clad twenty-something with a shaved head and skin like ebony. He bounded out of the elevator and across the lobby toward the closest conversational group. Two men in colorful dashikis stood to greet him, smiling broadly. Hands were shaken and backs slapped as greetings echoed under the vaulted ceiling.

"How was the flight?"

"Late leaving Dodoma, as usual," answered the taller of

the two visitors. His vowels were round, his consonants clipped.

"The Tanzanian concept of time continues to play hell with our western schedules. Well, come on up. The group is waiting to hear your report on the orphanage project."

As the next elevator arrived to whisk them away the visitor said, "We're making progress, thank God. The district council finally approved the plans."

"May I help you?"

The voice belonged to an older woman seated behind the low, sweeping curve of a granite console that appeared to have sprouted seamlessly from the floor. She had gray-blue eyes, silver hair cropped in a stylish pixie, and silver teardrops dangling from her ears. Her nameplate read, "Receptionist."

"We have an appointment with Malcolm Conover," I said, as we crossed the lobby to stand in front of her. A hint of patchouli wafted across the console.

"Of course, Ms. Gregson; we've been expecting you. If you and your assistant will have a seat, I'll call up to let him know you've arrived."

"Thanks."

We ambled over and sat down. People came and went in a steady, energetic stream that gave the five elevators a constant workout. Expressions tended toward cheerful and sincere, modes of dress toward casual-eclectic. The atmosphere was laden with warmth and good will toward men.

Sentiments in direct contrast to those displayed by CAL's founder, if you could believe Bobby Mae Tolliver. I found it hard not to, given the fact that her opinion had been seconded by the two cab drivers, three store clerks, and one off-duty traffic cop we had also talked to that morning. If word on the street was any indication, our boy Malcolm wouldn't be voted Austin's favorite son any time soon.

Speak of the devil, I mused as our host strolled out of the far-right elevator, and we stood to greet him.

"Amanda." He was all smiles. "Good to see you again."

I plastered on a fake smile of my own. "Thanks." Tipped my head toward Baker. "This is my assistant, Denny Barker. Denny, Malcolm Conover."

The two shook hands. "Welcome to Change a Life," said Conover.

"Quite a place." Dennis glanced around. "Busy."

"Oh, this is merely the tip of the iceberg. Come on, I'll show you." He started toward the elevators, and we followed. "I thought we would have lunch in the cafeteria; it'll give you a chance to meet some of our staff before we adjourn to my office. I hope you like veggie burgers? We try to keep expenses down here at headquarters."

"One of my favorite food groups," I lied. The door slid down, and the elevator started to climb. "Listen, no offense, but I hope this tour won't take too long. I'm curious as a cat about this information you have for me. Not only that, we have to be in Philly by seven."

He nodded. Mr. Understanding. "Trust me, Amanda, the tour will only last as long as it takes to establish appearances. I'm as eager for our talk as you are."

Eagan's point, exactly. One I would do well to keep in mind.

"And you're convinced your material will help us break up the Ferrymen?"

"Oh, yes. I never would have asked you to make the trip, otherwise. Please believe me when I say I believe you'll get more than you bargained for when all is said and done."

Not if you get yours first.

We ate lunch family style, twenty of us sitting at a long, gray table in the sunlit dining room on the fourth floor in the cornucopia's narrow waist. The veggie burgers, tasting only slightly of sawdust, were served with a side of bright ideas liberally seasoned with boundless enthusiasm and a passionate desire to help the helpless. After lunch we toured the building. The offices were divided into various theaters of operation: Africa, South America, the Sino-Russian Confederation, Tri-America.

Contrary to expectations—mine, at least—not everybody who worked at Change a Life was young and naïve. A few of them had clearly hoed long, hard rows in their days. But regardless of age or experience, every staff member we met appeared to be on fire with the vision and willing to give it his or her all. I got the impression the CAL team would make the world a better place or cheerfully die trying.

To a man and woman, they idolized Malcolm Conover,

hanging on each utterance with starry-eyed devotion. Earnest and dedicated themselves, they couldn't imagine him as less than he appeared. Never dreamed the compassion he wore on his sleeve was all for show, couldn't begin to understand the mindset of a man who would play the world's misery like a violin, as long as it suited his filthy purposes. I didn't look forward to disillusioning them, but I would do whatever it took to stop the killing. I only hoped CAL's best and brightest managed to bounce back and pick up the pieces afterwards. Millions of desperate people were depending on them.

We finally made our way to the tenth floor. Conover told his secretary to hold all calls and waved us into his office and a pair of black-leather studio chairs angled in front of a desk I recognized from our recent call.

His office was roomy but fell short of spacious. The décor was quality without being over the top—small walnut conference table ringed by six chairs, powder-blue carpet, a healthy rubber plant in the far corner. Photos lined the walls to our left and right, aid-in-progress shots taken all over the globe—wells being sunk in arid plains, medics setting up shop in jungle clearings. If Conover had been what he claimed to be—namely, the well-to-do CEO of a charitable organization that spent eighty percent of every credit on the people it served—the office would have been perfect.

He closed the door behind us and crossed the room, shucking the tweed jacket he wore over a plain white dress shirt and draping it over the back of his high-backed swivel-chair. Then he turned to face us, the glass wall behind him, the sky his brilliant blue backdrop, the sun haloing his silver head. Imagine a stained-glass window starring the devil in drag as an angel of light, and you would get the general effect.

"Can I offer you some refreshment?" he asked. "Coffee? A glass of iced tea?"

"Not for me, thanks."

"Denny?"

"I'm good."

Conover sat, folded his hands atop the desk and regarded us soberly. "I think the tour went well. Our staff seem to have accepted our explanation for your visit. You've been wonderfully patient. Now, where should I begin?"

"Your information is only as good as your source," I said.

"So let's start there."

"All right. Until a week ago, my informant was a small-time arms dealer operating out of the Horn of Africa. I won't give you her name, because she's trying to make a fresh start, and I believe everyone deserves a second chance. Given your profession, I'm sure you understand and sympathize with the need to protect a source."

Every reporter's soft spot. Nice touch.

"Sure, Mr. Conover ... *Malcolm*," I amended before he could correct me. "Problem is, singles bars are full of losers who claim to be arms dealers. It's their favorite pickup line. Sometimes it even works. How do you know your contact is legit?"

"We were introduced by a personal acquaintance of mine, an ex-policeman from Djibouti-Somalia. The two evidently crossed paths more than once during his career, and although their relationship was adversarial, she learned to respect his integrity.

"A few weeks ago, she decided to get out of the illegal arms trade, before, as she put it, 'one of the gangsters I do business with decides to gnaw off the hand that feeds him.' Her plan was to trade amnesty for her client database, but she needed a middleman she could trust to broker the deal with the authorities. She remembered my friend and managed to track him to one of our medical clinics, where he now acts as head of security. He refused to represent her until he had proof her files were current and would be useful. Because she trusted him, she agreed to let him examine a limited number of transactions. He sent the files to me, and I had my people go over them. I also had them scan the Cloud for peripheral chatter amongst the buyers listed, for traffic that might support her data. We found a great deal of corroborating evidence."

"Okay, so chances are, she's on the level. Now tell me about the Ferrymen connection."

"It isn't direct, but it is compelling. While combing the sample files, we came across a special order for a toxin that could be bioengineered to interact with a specific individual's DNA."

"The Yanos hit," murmured Dennis.

"That was our thought," agreed Conover.

He tossed out this potentially explosive nugget with an expression of complete sincerity. If I hadn't been wise to his act, a lead like this would have launched me halfway out of the frying pan. Then again, given the way my inner antenna was vibrating, maybe I was already airborne. I angled my upper body toward him, doing my best imitation of a sucker about to bite. At least, I hoped it was an imitation. "Did your source fill the order?"

"She didn't have the resources, but she recommended someone who did. BioWep, Incorporated."

"I've heard of them." My voice hinted at suppressed excitement. It wasn't totally put on. "Privately owned. Believed to work both sides of the fence."

"Does the information help?"

My mind raced. BioWep as a supplier was totally believable. What was going on in that twisted mind of his? Give me the scent with a solid tip, then sit back and let my nose lead me into an ambush like the one that took out Cuey and Michaels? Not the quickest way to resolve his problem, but then, a pro like him probably had the patience of a spider. He might even enjoy the anticipation.

If that was the plan, why did this whole conversation feel way out of whack? Because I could *feel* the menace radiating off Conover, and the threat didn't feel distant or spider webby. It felt danger-close, like a trapdoor under my feet. Time to rattle the monster's cage and see what jumped out.

"The information is interesting, but it could take weeks to follow up. Not that I don't appreciate the tip," I hastened to add. "It will definitely help us tie up the loose ends."

"Loose ends?"

"That's about all we have left at this point."

"I don't understand."

I sat back and stared at him like I was trying to decide how much to let on. Let the suspense build, then leaned forward again. "Confidentially, Malcolm, I'm ready to make my move now. In less than forty-eight hours, the Ferrymen will be history." The words no sooner left my lips, when space-time started to slide. I braced against the now-familiar vertigo and said, "I've got an inside source."

"Carpathian chick," Dennis added. "One of their mechanics."

We had agreed to give up Sidorov to prove we weren't blowing smoke. Also as incentive to keep her in line. But since Jack had her safely tucked away in the bowels of CIIS headquarters, and her new identity—including face and fingerprint transplants—was already in the works, the risk was minimal.

"That's …. I don't know what to say. Are you sure this woman is who she claims to be?"

The room and all of us in it were blurry now, but I fought the instinctive urge to try to blink it all back into focus. Wasted effort, and it might make him wonder. "Absolutely. We caught her red-handed, and she's been unloading like a dump truck ever since. Clients, hits, methods." Each individual nerve ending in my body was tingling. I managed to keep that energy out of my voice as I delivered the coup de grace. "That's why we have to be in Philly by seven. She's ready to name the entire crew. Claims the who's who of the Ferrymen will rock my world."

The monster leaped out at me so suddenly, I almost fell out of the chair.

Chapter 50

"Did you see anything?"

"Hmm?" Reaching into my pocket to toy with Conover's business card, I mumbled a distracted, "Excuse me," when my shoulder collided with a heavyset man wearing a Santa hat and unwieldy bracelets of shopping bags.

Baker and I were back on Congress, about three blocks from the parking garage. The crisp kiss of the breeze, the velvet softness of a purple-blue twilight, and the multi-colored glow of a street lit up like a Christmas tree registered peripherally. My feet were on autopilot, my brain in high gear.

"I said did you see anything?"

"What? Oh. Yeah." The question was what to make of it.

"Well?"

"Hmm?"

"For the love of—" He grabbed my arm and hauled me back on the curb, yanking me out of the path of a half-ton delivery truck. Breaks squealed and horns blared as Baker spun me around and jumped on my case while my heart did the close-call two-step. "Wake up! We didn't go to all this trouble so you could wind up a hood ornament for Tri-Am Parcel."

"Sorry. I've been trying to make sense of it."

"What's the problem? Did he ... it ... look different this time?"

"Still your basic Grim Reaper, but his expression bothers me."

"How so?"

"That's what I'm trying to figure out. He seemed ...." I pictured gory, yellowed teeth stretched in a rictus grin. Eyes alight with unholy satisfaction. "Smug, almost triumphant." I shook my head. "I can't get a clear read on it. It was almost like he was gloating because he knew something we didn't."

"He knows plenty we don't, but we're catching up. You think the BioWep connection is on the level?"

I nodded as we started walking again. "Could be. Remember what you said about Sadie knowing how to bait the hook? Same goes here."

"Best way to reel you in is give you something legit."

"Something plausible, anyway. But if BioWep *is* involved, he only gave them up because he was sure giving them up wouldn't hurt him."

"He expected you to bite hard and run with it."

"Yeah, but we didn't. Instead, we threw Sidorov into the mix. The meet didn't play out the way he planned, so why the grin?" I turned it over and over in my mind as we walked. "I don't like it," I decided, as we climbed into the van.

"And I'm starting not to," Dennis said, shifting into reverse. "Let's get out of here."

We spent the next thirty minutes zigzagging through Austin, then lifted into the outbound tier of Texas One South. We climbed to fifteen thousand feet on a beeline for the safe house.

Baker checked the rearview display for the umpteenth time. "Still no sight of a tail, human or otherwise." He leaned back in his seat. "Maybe the Ferrymen are on their way to Philly."

"Maybe."

As the distance between Conover and us grew, I should have been able to relax. We were forty short minutes away from home free. Or as free as you can get when you're in protective custody, anyway. But the miles made no difference at all. That feeling of wrongness clung like wet mohair.

"The trip wasn't a total waste," Dennis offered.

"No, but we didn't hit a bonanza, either. We gave him Sidorov, a leak he can't plug, and he dangled BioWep, a poisoned apple we didn't taste. I would have to call it a draw, at best."

Then why the crocodile smile? It didn't make sense.

"So we keep nibbling at him," Dennis said, "eat the bear one bite at a time."

"And hope nobody dies while we're chewing."

"Conover has you zeroed in, at least for now. I'll get Hell's

Boatmen don't get back to business as usual until you're taken care of. Lucky for us, his guys are oh-for-two on pest control."

"So far. Let's hope their slump holds." I leaned my head against the seatback, closed my eyes and replayed the vision, still digging for the root of my uneasiness.

Smile like that says, "Gotcha!" What makes him think so? Dennis says nobody is following us. Conover can't be tracking us, because he had no way of knowing which car was ours.

Maybe the grin was because he bought the Philly yarn and was planning to get there ahead of us. He would have to move fast, but he's got the resources. He could arrange an uncomfortably warm welcome in no time. Glad we're flying west while he's looking the other way.

Then again, Conover didn't get where he is by being stupid or trusting. No way he would bet his whole setup on information he hasn't confirmed. Besides, that was not the smile of a guy who had spotted his chance. He looked way too complacent. Like we were already in the bag.

Conover hadn't been able to find me, so he got me to come to him. Golden opportunity, right? Maybe his last chance to swat the gadfly. But if he wanted to save his fairy-godfather cover and protect the Change a Life Laundromat, he had to get rid of me in a way that couldn't be traced back to our visit.

Variation on the Yanos hit? Be easy to do. Slip a designer biotoxin in the food, one with that delayed release feature to create a comfy interval between time of death and our visit to Change a Life. End of story, right? Except he would need samples of our DNA to work with. Getting mine wouldn't be impossible, but he would have had no chance to get Dennis' ahead of time.

Besides, Conover needed information from us. He wanted to know what I got from the courier, how much Sidorov had already told me, and how much I had shared with CIIS and/or my editor. He also wanted us to give him Tanya, so he could shut her up permanently. All of the above required live input from both Baker and me.

I cycled through the vision again, freeze-framing the bogeyman's victory leer. Between one heartbeat and the next, the answer hit me like a brickbat. All those flawlessly executed hits. Every detail nailed down, every contingency covered. Of course Conover wasn't the trusting type. Of course he was tracking us. But he hadn't known about the van, so the device had to be planted on either Dennis or me.

My brow furrowed. But when? And how? Apart from shaking hands, nobody had so much as brushed against us. Nobody had given us anything, either, except ....

My eyes popped open and my breath caught as my gaze crawled down the right side of my vest. I stared at the lowest pocket, before gingerly reaching in with thumb and index finger to fish out the cream-colored rectangle embossed with Conover's name and the number of his private line. My fingers were icy. The business card wasn't. It was warm and getting more so.

"Dennis—" I croaked, but he wasn't listening.

"What the hell?" I turned my head to find him frowning at the readouts. "We're off course. Must be a glitch in the navigation software. I'll switch to manual control."

My eyes danced between him and the card. "No. It's Conover. He's doing this."

"*What?*"

I held up the card and started to explain, but the words shorted out between my brain and my tongue. My hand and arm, which suddenly weighed about a thousand pounds each, dropped into my lap. I watched helplessly as Dennis blinked and shook his head. He shook it again, slowly, before slumping in his seat, head lolling towards me. Brown eyes met blue in a flash of grim but fading awareness.

Our gazes were still locked when my vision dimmed, and a last shot of adrenaline set my already racing heart slamming against my ribcage like a trapped bird.

Darkness swallowed me.

Chapter 51

The closer I swam to the light, the more reluctant I was to get there. I couldn't *see* the light yet, but I sensed it drawing nearer and understood *a very bad thing* was coming with it. I couldn't remember what. Didn't want to find out, but apparently, I wasn't going to have a choice. The comforting darkness was rapidly receding, like a wave that tosses you ashore then ebbs out from under you.

I came to in spite of myself but kept my eyes closed, instinctively playing possum while I fished around in the mental murk, groping for the source of a nameless and growing dread. I chased memories through the foggy corridors of my brain, catching them one by one, struggling to put them in order.

The visit to Conover. Charon with a victor's grin.

Dennis: *What the hell? We're off course.*

Conover's business card, locking stares with Baker as darkness closed in, not knowing if we were dying or ….

Oh, my God!

My stomach clenched like a fist, pushing bile up my throat. I forced myself to breathe through it. Panic was a luxury I couldn't afford.

Okay, the good news was, I was alive. I suspected Dennis probably was, too, mainly because Conover wasn't a bonehead. Nabbing an active-duty CIIS agent would be like getting his hands on the other team's play book. He would want to study Baker cover to cover, and that would take a while.

The bad news was, Conover had us, which meant there was even worse news in store. Since I wasn't dead already, I figured we had called it right. Charon wanted a chance to interrogate me before he ferried me over to the south forty and a shallow grave alongside those South American construction workers. But our conversation would have to wait until I was awake, so I kept pretending not to be, hoping to buy some time.

I checked in with my body, cataloging aches and pains from the top down. Piercing headache, the kind you might get if someone shoved a knitting needle into your right temple and out your left. Cotton tongue. Dry, mildly scratchy throat. Nausea. Okay, no serious damage so far.

I didn't feel any restraints around my wrists or ankles. That was a relief until I realized I couldn't *feel* my wrists and ankles. Couldn't feel my hands, feet, arms, or legs. It was like they weren't there. I blanked for a second, then I remembered.

A tiny black chip. "*Designed to block select signals from the brain.... Quadriplegia similar to that caused by spinal cord injuries.*"

This time, the fear hit me like a freight train. I couldn't breathe. *OhGodohGodohGod!*

Still feigning unconsciousness, I willed myself to move—a toe, my pinky, *anything!* I strained until my heart hammered in my ears and a fine sweat broke out on my forehead. Forget it. I might as well have been buried up to my neck in sand. Conover could do whatever he wanted to me, *whatever he wanted,* and I wouldn't be able to lift a finger to stop him. A primal scream, ninety percent terror, ten percent outrage, boiled up my throat, but I gritted my teeth and locked my jaws to hold it in. Started to hyperventilate, got dizzy, and came close to passing out.

Came even closer to losing my mind.

Eternity passed, but I eventually burned through the panic and crashed, wrung out and breathless. My heart was still skipping a beat now and then, so I focused on my breathing and waited for my pulse to regulate. Meanwhile, I clamped an iron lid on my imagination and fought to harness the power of positive thinking.

I told myself any chip that could be surgically implanted could be surgically removed.

I pictured my family's faces and promised myself I would see them again.

I reminded myself over and over and over again that while my body might be paralyzed, my brain wasn't. Right now, my mind was the only weapon I had, so I damned well better hold onto it.

Inch by inch, I clawed my way back from the edge. Not that I wasn't still scared. I was terrified. But I was determined to control the fear, instead of letting the fear control me. No more freaking out. Winston Churchill would have been proud.

I finally calmed down enough for curiosity to get a word in edgewise. Several words, as a matter of fact, starting with every reporter's standards: *who, what, when, where, why, and how?*

The *who* and *why* were obvious.

When remained a mystery. No telling how long I had been out.

I had a leg up on *how* – the business card – and could make an educated guess on the general *where.* Dripping Springs, because Conover would feel next to invincible back at the ranch.

But the specific *wheres,* the most immediately critical *wheres,* I had yet to figure out. Where on the ranch was I? Where was Dennis? Where was Eagan? And last, but certainly not least, where was Conover?

If the answer to that final question was *three feet away, cranking up the ultrasound,* all other *wheres* were irrelevant. *So, step one, open your eyes and find out if you're alone.*

Except the decision wasn't nearly that simple. Being awake when the opposition thought I was out cold wasn't much of an advantage, but I would take any break I could catch for as long as I could hold onto it. In other words, I had no way of knowing if opening my eyes would get me in more trouble than I was already in.

I was stuck in neutral, unable to decide what to do, until I belatedly remembered I might be able to tell whether or not I had company *without* opening my eyes. When I hadn't been able to see, I had developed a fairly accurate radar system. Did it still work? Would I be able to *feel* Conover's presence, or the absence thereof? Might as well give it a shot. Mentally crossing my fingers, I focused on making my breathing slow, deep, and regular and tuned in to my senses.

Judging by the reddish glow behind my eyelids, the lights were strong and directly above me. The air on my face was cold and clean. *Cold, bright, and sterile. Like an operating room.* Ruthlessly quashing a fresh squirt of panic caused by the simile, I concentrated on my other senses. I didn't smell anything. Hadn't Conover been wearing cologne? Yeah, I remembered thinking the scent was all wrong for a fiend. Lightly floral instead of acrid brimstone.

I listened hard. It was quiet. Deathly ... no strike that. Let's say eerily quiet. No muffled opening and closing of doors, no subdued voices or distant footsteps, not a whisper from the HVAC system. The overhead lights didn't buzz. The only breathing I heard was mine. I stopped for a minute to make sure.

Ninety-nine point nine percent convinced I was by myself, I slitted my eyes, waited for them to adjust to the light, and shifted them from side to side behind the screen of my lashes without turning my head. Listened some more, checked my inner radar, then sighed quietly in relief and opened my eyes all the way. Lifting my head, I craned my neck for a looksee.

The room's only occupant was me, lying prone on a gurney in an eight-by-ten space painted wall-to-wall, floor-to-ceiling, bare-bones white. There were no windows and only one door, with a control panel set in the wall next to it. A black leather armchair sat about four feet away, facing the left side of my gurney. I didn't see a camera, but belatedly figured there had to be one and immediately wanted to kick myself for not thinking of that before I gave my game away. Hoping to recoup my losses, I let my head fall back and closed my eyes. *See? I passed out again.* Meanwhile, my mind raced.

Realistically speaking, my future looked brief and none too rosy. Dennis was probably immobilized the same as me. Neither of us was wired to go down without a fight, but we had been trussed up like chickens before we could throw our first punches. Our only real option now was to stall like crazy and hope Jack Eagan came through.

Well, maybe there *was* one other option. No atheists in foxholes, right?

God? I messaged silently, *You up there? Can You hear me? If You are and You can, maybe You could lend Iceman a hand? I don't think we have a whole lot of time here.*

I had no sooner made the suggestion when I heard the door activate with a quiet hiss. So someone *had* been watching, and thanks to my camera blooper, he or she knew I was awake. No use pretending now, so I opened my eyes and watched Conover stroll into the room, king of his castle and all he surveyed. He was wearing the same outfit I had last seen him in. Okay, same day. Or more likely, that night. He wouldn't have rushed off on our heels. Somebody might have noticed.

I eyed him warily as he ambled over and sat in the armchair. He leaned back, crossed his legs, and stacked his hands on his knee. "Let's talk," he said.

Never let them see you cry; never let them see you sweat, I reminded myself staunchly. But for once in my life, I wasn't sure I could pull it off.

Chapter 52

End game, and we both knew it. We were on his turf and to say he had the upper hand would be the understatement of the century. That didn't mean I intended to roll over and play by his rules.

Not as long as I had a choice, anyway.

The minute he turned Grand Inquisitor on me—a mood swing I expected sooner rather than later—and made with the ultrasound, heroic resistance would die a quick and painful death. Followed by the rest of me, ten seconds after I spilled my guts. That being the case, my best shot was to postpone the inquisition as long as possible. Draw out the prologue and pray for a miracle. Not the most proactive survival strategy, but it was all I had.

I ignored the invitation to blubber like a baby and beg for mercy embedded in Conover's opening gambit and asked, "Where's Dennis? Is he all right?"

"For the moment. Of course, that could change, if you don't cooperate."

"Give me a break, Malcolm. You and I both know that will change no matter what I do."

He acknowledged the truth with a shrug, as he studied my face. "You don't seem surprised to see me. How long have you known?"

"Long enough."

"Sidorov." He pronounced the name like a death sentence.

"Before." I wanted to knock him off balance and wipe that smug smile off his face. I awarded myself a homerun when said smile melted into a half-frown.

"Impossible. How? Who told you?"

I slowly shook my head. "You know me, Malcolm. Never reveal a source."

"You might as well; you will eventually."

Fear coiled heavily in my belly, but I battled it down and changed the subject. "It was the business card, right?"

Come on, Charon, impress me. You know you want to.

It took him a heartbeat to follow my course change, but the *I've got you where I want you* smile gradually reappeared. "Figured that out, did you? You have to admit it's a great gimmick. Designed in-house. We sandwiched nanocircuits between two layers of cardstock and built in the capability to activate the circuits remotely via satellite."

"That's how you tracked us."

He was really enjoying himself now. "I didn't track you. I didn't have to. You flew straight into my arms."

"You wish." But we *had* been off course. "How did you pull it off?"

"Let's just say I have a business arrangement with NavStar's chief systems designer."

I had to fight to keep the shock off my face. The NavStar Corporation holds one of the few monopolies allowed by international law. With billions of John Does piloting vehicles ranging in size from subcompacts to semis, world governments finally decided a universal navigation system was the only way to standardize air-traffic control and avoid intercontinental chaos in the skies. NavStar won the contract, gave the world UniNav, and the rest is history.

I narrowed my eyes. "You expect me to believe you got to NavStar's head geek?"

"With the right intelligence and/or the right incentives, you can breach any system or organization. We've proven that time and time again."

No argument there. Their ability to hit targets the rest of us considered unreachable was one of the Ferrymen's main claims to fame.

"So that's why our van changed course."

"Um-hm. My operative at NavStar built a trapdoor into the software according to my exact specifications. As soon as we activated the nanocircuits embedded in it, the business card transmitted the appropriate signal to your onboard computer and co-opted the navigation system."

"You hijacked the van, then knocked us out."

He nodded. "Otherwise, you might have ejected over New

Mexico and lived to fight another day."

Implying that was now out of the question. I shoved the fear that he was right out of my mind and rolled on. "KZ-14?"

"Yes. The cardstock was impregnated with it. Heat generated when the circuits activated kicked off a chemical chain reaction, and the gas was released."

"Couldn't have been a very big dose, packaged in a business card."

"Barely measurable," he agreed. "But in an enclosure that small, three hundred micrograms of super-concentrated KZ were more than enough."

We were running out of topic in a hurry, so I frantically wracked my brain for a fresh tack. "The chip. On my spinal cord." A slight widening of his eyes told me I had surprised him again. "I was at Sadie Carter's virtopsy."

"Ah."

"So about the chip."

"What about it?"

"Can it be removed? If it can and is, will the effects be reversed?"

He stared at me like I was nuts, then shook his head and stood. "I know what you're trying to do, but you're only postponing the inevitable. Last chance. Tell me what I want to know, and I'll make the end quick and painless."

I swallowed hard, but managed to keep my voice steady. "No, you won't. This is personal, right? I want to make you pay, you want to make me pay. Same as the courier."

"Of course I want to make you pay, but it's not personal."

Oh, like that made it better. On the contrary, I felt irrationally slighted. Like if it was personal for me, it should be personal for him, too. Maybe I *was* nuts.

"Payback is never personal," he explained patiently, "it's simply good business. Make someone an example, you send a message. The stronger the message, the more likely it is people will think twice before crossing you. But I might be willing to trade public relations benefits for expediency."

"No dice." He shrugged and took a step toward me but paused when I blurted, "You won't get away with it, you know." B-movie line, but the best I could do.

"I won't?" If the twinkle in his eye was any indication, my melodramatic warning amused him all over again. "Who's going to stop me?"

"CIIS. They know all about you."

"They may know about me, but they won't arrest me."

"I wouldn't bet on that, if I were you."

"Bets are for suckers. A few hours from now, this ranch house will burn to the ground, apparently with me in it. By the time the feds sift through the ashes for my remains—which, of course, they'll find, complete with the proper DNA—my Boatmen will have scattered to the four winds, and I'll have slipped into one of a dozen prepared identities. I've got twenty billion credits spread over fifty numbered accounts. I'll lay low for a week to heal from the cosmetic surgery, then quietly revamp the organization. We'll reopen for business before you know it."

"You don't have a few hours." I tried to sound more certain than hopeful. "The cavalry is already on its way."

"I hate to disappoint you, but you're wrong."

"You sure about that?"

"As sure as I am of the fact that the same device that assumed control of your navigation system broadcast a downed-vehicle code, too. Your would-be rescuers are too busy scouring the Sangre de Cristo Mountains to search for you here. I'm afraid you'll be a far-from-fond memory long before your so-called *cavalry* arrives. Besides, they would never get past our defenses."

"Armed guards and a force shield up to fifteen thousand feet. Yeah, we know." His annoyed frown marked another small victory. "I'll admit you've got an impressive setup," I continued, "but I've heard that with the right intelligence and/or the right incentives, you can breach any system or organization." A satisfying zinger, but it backfired on me.

"Then I had better not waste any more time," he said, starting toward the gurney and sliding his right hand into his pocket.

Visions of peewee ultrasound devices flashed through my brain. Shackled by my own body, panic and despair crashing through me, all I could do was shake my head. By the time my lips formed a soundless, "Wait!" he was on me.

Chapter 53

It wasn't what I expected.

The gizmo Conover pulled out of his pocket had nothing to do with sound waves and everything to do with high-pressure jets of pharmaceuticals. The common injector—favored by doctors and junkies alike—was a bit longer than my index finger. With a plump black body and a stubby barrel, it could have passed for one of those old timey derringers, if you lopped off the downward-curving grip and stuck a square, clear-plastic syringe in the business end.

I teetered between weak-kneed relief that I wasn't in for the ultrasonic torture treatment and a fresh surge of alarm as I watched him push up the sleeve of my pullover and shoot me up.

"What was that? What did you give me?"

"Harpatinol," he said, re-pocketing the injector. Sitting back down, he crossed his legs and smiled. "Known in the vernacular as a truth serum. A few short minutes from now, you'll be semi-conscious, unable to initiate conversation, but ready, willing, and able to provide honest answers to any question I care to ask." He cocked his head. "What?"

"I thought you would do me like you did Sadie."

"Who?" His brow furrowed briefly but cleared when he gave an absent wave of his hand, almost like he was shooing a fly. "Oh, her. Federal agents are inoculated against psychoactive medications. You weren't."

"Lucky me." Was it my overactive imagination, or did I already feel the drug's silky tendrils unfurling in my bloodstream? It couldn't possibly work that fast, could it? Instinctively steeling myself against a (real or imagined) creeping urge to relax, I blurted, "Why are you doing this?"

"And to think they say there are no stupid questions. I *did* give you a chance to volunteer the information."

I shook my head. "I don't mean this, with me. I mean the Ferrymen. Why? It's not like you need the money."

"You're right, I don't."

"Then why?"

"What good will it do you to know that now?"

"What harm will it do you to tell me now?"

He pursed his lips and narrowed his eyes, probably deciding whether or not to humor me. Finally, he shrugged. "Killing is human nature. Has been ever since Cain dropped Abel. Every minute of every day somebody, somewhere, offs somebody else. Or wishes they could. We're all killers at heart."

We've all got it in us to go either way.

"Maybe," I granted grudgingly, "but we don't all give into the urge and the ones who do aren't usually cold-blooded murderers for hire."

"What you call cold-blooded, I call professional. Of course, realistically speaking, every hit is a crime of passion. On some level, at least."

"How do you figure?"

"Well, on the one hand, you've got your amateurs. Somebody sets them off, and in a fit of passion, they do the deed themselves. Nine times out of ten they make a mess of it and get caught.

"On the other hand, you've got your wishful thinkers. They either don't have the guts to get their hands dirty, or they're smart enough to admit they don't have the skills to commit murder and get away with it. But they still want somebody dead, and they want it *passionately* enough to pay big credits to make it happen. That's where professionals like us come in. We can satisfy their bloodlust by proxy, because we've got the nerve, the skills, and/or the tactical ability they lack." He paused before concluding, "So I suppose you could say I do it because I can."

"That's the bottom line? You murder people because you *can*?" The fact that my outraged disbelief was muted, hazy, and short-lived spoke volumes about the Harpatinol's progress.

"And because I love it, have ever since my first safari at

age ten. The hunt. That heady sense of power you get when you take a life. By the time I was sixteen, I realized I had a unique skill set. I started looking for a more challenging and rewarding way to use it."

"Hunting humans. For money."

"Wiliest prey there is, and the market was certainly there. Demand grew so quickly, I knew the day would come when requests for my services would outstrip my individual ability to supply. I decided to put together a team. Handpicked each operator. Recruited them young and trained them myself. My Ferrymen are the best in the world. Nobody is beyond our reach. And nobody can stop us."

"Omnipresence and omnipotence?" My voice sounded way too mellow, but I couldn't seem to work myself into a sweat over it, and the will to even try was slithering through my fingers like a greased rope. "See wha' happens when you start ta believe your own press? Think you can play God."

"Who's playing?" He stood, leaned over me, and thumbed up my eyelids. "Your pupils are dilated." Straightened and laid two fingers on my wrist. "Pulse is slow but steady."

I was drifting now, distant and disconnected. "Was'sat mean?"

"It means it's time for our chat."

"I don't wanna talk to you."

"No, but you'll talk anyway. So, let's begin. Question number one: How did you find out about me, Amanda?"

My last conscious thought was, *No comment.* But I never stood a chance.

When the curtain rose again Malcolm Conover was sitting in the armchair, staring at me like I was an alien life form. *Did I talk?* floated up from the groggy depths, but given the way he was ogling me, I figured the answer was obvious. Like a magpie.

So I settled for a hoarse, "What happens next?"

"We wait."

"For what?"

When he smiled slightly in reply, a voice in the still-hazy recesses of my brain whispered a reminder that Cheshire Cat smiles like his almost never bode well for the recipient. "Not what. Whom. One of my people. A specialist. He's flying in from Denver."

"Specialist?" If the Harpatinol hadn't already left me dry-mouthed, the prospect of Conover bringing in some kind of expert would have done the trick. "I thought ...."

"That I wanted to kill you myself? I do, and I will. Eventually."

Still a bit woozy, I tossed around the word *eventually* and concluded my final countdown was temporarily on hold. I had been trying to buy time, and now I had some.

So what's the catch?

"Why not now?" *Please tell me I didn't just say that.* But I needn't have worried.

"You have something I want."

Don't ask! yelled that inner voice, but I couldn't help myself. "What's that?"

"Your eyes," he informed me cheerfully, then stood. "Now, if you'll excuse me, I have some arrangements to make."

My horrified gaze was still riveted to the door five minutes after it closed behind him.

Chapter 54

Why me?

Deep down, each one of us believes, *I'm the exception.* We live our lives in the unconscious certainty that the brick walls that fall on other people will never flatten us. That's why we rant and rave and shake our fists in God's face when life suddenly goes south.

Why me?

I had been asking that question over and over ever since Conover left the room. Asking for what seemed like hours.

Dying with my boots on I could accept, at least in concept. Guarantees of personal safety had never been part of the job description or listed among the bennies. I had known from the get-go my chosen career could be dangerous; and if I was honest, I would have to admit that element of risk was part of what attracted me to police reporting in the first place. Of course, accepting death in the line of duty as an abstract idea isn't quite the same as looking it in the eye.

Not that I was resigned to dying. Far from it. I would fight and hope right up to my last breath. Still, if this was it, I figured I had no legitimate gripe.

But mutilation was never part of the bargain. Wouldn't be now, if not for my crazy gift. *That's* the *Why me?* I was struggling with. Thousands of people have eye transplants every year, and as far as I know, not one of them has ever complained of bizarre supernatural complications. So why me? The only answer that came to me was as unsatisfying as it was inescapable. Why *not* me? Why anybody else? Aside from maybe a cop or a spook, who was a better candidate?

I finally decided the *why* didn't matter much this close to the final whistle. My predicament was what it was for whatever reasons. I needed to stop chasing answers I would probably never get. Keep my wits about me and watch for a chance to make some kind of move.

Worst case, that chance wouldn't come, and I would die. Conover would cut out my eyes and chuck the rest. Incinerate it or dissolve it in acid or bury it deep in the heart of Texas. However he decided to handle the disposal, I was fairly sure nobody would ever find my remains, and I had covered enough stories about missing persons never seen or heard from again to understand how Mom, Dad, and my brothers would suffer. Knowing the truth deep down but hoping against hope for the rest of their lives.

And me? What would happen to me?

Not the flesh-and-blood me, but the me who has ideas and dreams and a burning, if embarrassingly naïve, desire to put the world right in any small way I can. If I believed there was more to life than our physical existence, believed there was some kind of *afterwards*—and in spite of my hard-won cynicism, I did—was I ready for it? The question threw me for a loop steeper and higher than any I had ridden so far, and given my circumstances, that was saying a mouthful. It scared me enough that I took a panicky mental step back from the abyss that suddenly seemed to yawn at my feet by reminding myself all wasn't lost yet.

Eagan, that poster boy for mistrustful, leave-nothing-to-chance feds everywhere, was out there. He had great instincts. The kind of gut that would sniff out a red herring faster than you can say kippers. Not only would he have been tracking our progress, but ten seconds after our unscheduled, unannounced course change—about as long as it would have taken to call us and get no answer—he would have sounded the alarm and whistled up the troops.

So what if Conover had fixed it so the van's distress signal read New Mexico? It might be a strong feint, but Eagan wouldn't put all his faith in technology. Sure, he would check out the signal. He would also tap CIIS's considerable manpower to cover all other possible bases, because that's what extremely suspicious people like him did. And needless to say, Conover's ranch would be high on the list of bases to cover.

Conclusion? Help was on the way.

A comforting thought, but Conover had been off making his "arrangements" for a couple hours now, and my gut was telling me he would be back any minute. *Just in the nick of time* was right around the corner, and *better late than never* wasn't going to cut it for me.

Then the door opened. Conover and another man stepped into the room.

The gut calls it again.

Chapter 55

Look for Einstein on a bad hair day. That's what I would tell Iceman, if I lived long enough to put him on the trail of Conover's specialist. Unfortunately, that scenario was growing less likely by the minute.

"Who's this?" I asked. But while I may not have known *who* Conover's plump companion was, I was afraid I knew exactly *what* he was.

"You can call him Doctor," answered Conover, confirming my worst fear.

My flesh crawled as the man with the bushy eyebrows stepped up to the gurney and eyed me with impersonal fascination—sort of inquiring scientist to exotic specimen. I pressed my head back into the pillow when he bent over me, but he didn't seem to notice as he peered into my eyes, then checked them out with a palm-sized scanner.

"No obvious abnormalities," he concluded, then straightened, tapping a blunt index finger against his cheek. A few seconds later, he nodded pensively and said, "In addition to both eyes, I suggest we remove the optic nerves, and take a cross-section of the lateral geniculate nucleus, the brain's primary processing center for data received from the retina."

"You're the expert," said Conover.

My heart jolted then sped up as I lost sight of the doctor, who had stepped to the head of the gurney to disengage the electronic tether. Before I knew it, the bed was floating gently down a long, white hall with me in it and Conover strolling by my side.

Knowing it would fall on deaf ears but unable to help myself, I urged hoarsely, "Don't do this, Conover! You heard what he said: No abnormalities."

"No *obvious* abnormalities."

"There are no abnormalities, period! One of the best

ophthalmologists in the world went over me with a fine-toothed comb, ran tests your guy can only dream of. I don't know where the Sight comes from, but it's not structural."

"There *must* be an anomaly," my own personal Doctor Frankenstein insisted from behind me, "if only on a molecular level. Whatever it is, I promise you, we'll find it."

"And replicate it," added Conover with evident satisfaction.

"Why?" I asked. "What good will it do you?"

"As is? No good at all. But if we can modify it? Imagine a world in which my Ferrymen were able to identify undercover agents, for example. The possibilities would be endless."

And too horrible to contemplate.

"It won't work."

"We'll see. Meanwhile, look at the bright side," he suggested as the gurney pushed through a set of swinging doors into a fully equipped operating suite as cold as a meat locker. "You're going to die painlessly after all."

They shifted me onto a table overhung with robotic arms and bright lights, then went to scrub up, leaving me in an agony of fear punctuated by flashes of panic, unable to so much as shiver. That last-minute rescue I had been counting on started to seem like a fairytale written by self-delusion.

All too soon my captors were back in full surgical gear. While the doctor positioned the necessary equipment, Conover draped a sheet over me, covering me to my chin. The blue gaze above his mask cool and dispassionate.

Nothing personal, just good business.

As far as he was concerned, I was already dead.

By now my breath was coming in short, shallow gasps. The thunder of my heart was all I could hear. When the doctor slid an IV needle into my inert left arm, I knew the clock had run out for me. With luck, Eagan would come in time to save Dennis, but I was going to die, right here, right now.

A few seconds later, my world went black for the last time.

EPILOGUE

Yes, Virginia, there is a heaven.

"Aren't you going in?"

"I don't know if I'm ready. Guess I didn't really expect to wind up here."

"There's no hurry. Take your time."

I continued to stare. Paradise, pure and simple. Light all around me. Trees twinkled with it. Watery exclamation points leaping from a luminous reflecting pool glittered with it. Even the lofty towers glowed, erupting like luminous crystals two hundred stories high from streets paved with light. As I watched, the nearest tower started to morph from the top down, its sides slowly segmenting, shifting, and rotating.

"I can't believe it's over," I murmured.

"Most of us feel that way at this point."

"It *is* over, right?"

"Right."

"You're sure it was him?"

"Positive," said Eagan. "Like I told you, I ID'd the corpse myself, then had Baker confirm. We ran both the DNA *and* the microbiome after you told us how he planned to fake his own death. It never hurts to be sure, and now we are. Trust me, A.J., it was Conover."

"Okay."

"I wouldn't lie to you."

"I know, but you have to admit, it's a hard story to swallow if you didn't see it for yourself. I mean, what are the chances?"

"That Conover would get skewered by a live oak while he was trying to steal one of our ATVs? A million to one. *Two* million."

"Maybe there's such a thing as divine retribution after all."

"You won't get any argument from me. What happened

that night ...." He shook his head. "Stuff I still can't explain. Like that damned winter thunderstorm that blew in out of nowhere. One minute the reading is clear skies for a hundred miles, the next all hell breaks loose. Craziest thing is, we couldn't have timed it better ourselves. Conover's crew didn't bat an eye when their systems shut down. They assumed the storm knocked them off line, when it was actually our UAV blanketing the area with high-energy microwaves to disrupt the compound's electrical grid. We caught them with their shield down while they stood around flatfooted, waiting for the emergency generator to kick in."

"I'm still not clear on how Conover wound up outside, dressed in CIIS tactical gear."

"With a six-foot sliver through his heart?"

"That, too."

"Nobody actually saw what happened, but we managed to piece together a rough sequence. After the firing died down, we found one of our agents in the library. He went down on the threshold of a priest's hole tucked behind a moveable section of floor-to-ceiling shelves. A hidden compartment not much bigger than a closet. Except this one was packed with high explosives."

"Conover's failsafe."

He nodded. "Rigged for remote detonation. But by the time he realized he was going to need it, his systems were down and our guys were already conducting the room-to-room. Best guess is, he was trying to salvage his getaway plan by jury-rigging a bypass when Mike Morrison caught up with him. I don't know how the old guy managed to come out on top, but he slit Morrison's throat, dressed in his gear, and strolled right out the front door in all the confusion. Judging by the fact that we found him straddling the ATV, hands wrapped around the grips and a surprised expression on his face, I would say he was ready to lift off when lightning struck, literally. Blasted the live oak to Hell and gone. Nothing left but a smoking pile of bark and our pig on a spit."

"Gives me goose bumps every time I hear about it," I muttered, rubbing my arms.

"Not as big as the ones I got when I saw it."

"Wish I could have caught some of the action."

"So brushing shoulders with the Grim Reaper wasn't excitement enough for you?"

Remembering my close encounter with the hereafter had me rubbing my upper arms harder. "Now that you mention it, you *did* cut it pretty fine."

"Not by choice, A.J. We launched the raid as soon as we could."

The posse had actually mounted out in record time. Conover's plan to lure Eagan and company off on a mountain-top wild goose chase had one teensy drawback: It would only work if CIIS was tracking the van. They weren't. They were tracking Dennis. Nobody was parting with the super-secret details, of course, but I gathered the process involved material injected under an agent's skin—a chip or isotopes, maybe— some thingamajig so tiny and finely tuned it took a specially equipped satellite to pick up the signal.

I was tempted to thank Eagan again for the rescue, but the last time I tried, he all but broke out in hives.

"Hey, far be it from me to complain!" I said instead. "I'm alive and kicking, aren't I? Heck, I can even wiggle my fingers and toes." Except in my dreams.

"Baker's happy about that, too. I don't think he's stopped wiggling them since the chip was removed."

Eagan and company tracked Dennis to Conover's high-tech basement. His cell was ten doors down from the operating room where they found me, out cold, and Conover's butcher, standing in the dark with his thumb in his ear. Tough to do an enhanced lobotomy when you can't see your hand in front of your face.

"Conover planned to give Dennis the same treatment he gave Sadie," I said.

"Yeah, but you distracted him. Baker says he owes you."

"Hey, it's not like I planned it that way." Still, there's a lot to be said for holding a federal cop's IOU. Never hurts to have that ace up your sleeve. "So did we get all the bad guys?"

"Not sure yet. The techies were into Conover's private corner of the Cloud five minutes after they got their hands on his UpLink, but they're still trying to decrypt his files."

"I might know somebody who can help with that. Her name is Shuki Okazawa, and she can make an UpLink sit up and beg to tell you its secrets." If I could manage to track her down. Maybe she would catch my upcoming broadcast and realize it was safe to come up for air.

"I don't think it will come to that," said Eagan, "but I'll keep it in mind. On the plus side, Sidorov claims the hit men trained at the ranch when they weren't in the field, so we know we got some of them. She'll be able to identify the bodies. Headcount came up three short of fifteen, so we've got stragglers, but they're operating without a network. We'll get names and descriptions from our Transylvanian snitch and track them down."

"So for all practical purposes, the Ferrymen are history."

"Pretty much. We've still got some mopping up to do, of course. The NavStar issue, for example. Intel services all over the world went bananas when they found out about that little debacle. Needless to say, the company is feeling the heat. They've got all their employees working twenty-four/seven on a patch to close the trapdoor in their software."

"And Conover's mole?"

"Got helpful in a hurry when we confronted him. Same with the psycho-surgeon, Wentzler."

"Both angling for a plea deal?"

"Chances are. Meanwhile, we're still following the money. We've made some progress, but word from the backroom is, it'll take another week to identify and untangle all the accounts and shell companies. With any luck, we'll be able to scoop up some of the Ferrymen's customers and suppliers while we're backtracking."

"What are the feds going to do with the money?"

His lips curved a bit. "What do you think we should do with it?"

"Give it to Change a Life. Just because Conover was a fiend in philanthropist's clothing doesn't mean everybody who works there is. Those charities do a ton of good."

"The director had the same idea, and she's already working on a solution. First order of business is to do background checks on all the CAL staff members." He paused. "We might need some special help with that."

"You got it."

"Baker and I will keep your participation on the QT, of

course. Ito's got high blood pressure as it is. Meanwhile, we managed to pull the names of enough donors whose contributions are probably untainted to let the director channel their money into a special fund to keep the milk of human kindness flowing until we can sort out the rest."

"That sounds like a—" I lost my train of thought when a cold, wet object landed on the back of my neck. I looked over my shoulder and met Cosmo's flinty gaze. "You got a problem, pal?"

"Probably needs to stretch his legs," Jack chuckled. "Come on, I'll walk you to the door. If you're ready."

"I'm ready. But why to the door? I was planning to give you the VIP tour."

He grimaced at the bright red WWN logo perched over the entrance to the nearest tower. By now the building had rearranged itself into a shape vaguely resembling a spiral staircase. You've gotta love dynamic architecture.

"Thanks, but I'll pass."

"Suit yourself," I said, climbing out of the car and stepping back to make room for Cosmo, "but it's not like I was planning to throw you and a bucket of chum into the deep end of the reporters' pool."

The frosty air was refreshing. I looped Biker Dog's leash around my wrist as the three of us started toward the building. As we drew even with the near corner of the reflecting pool, I stared at the fairy lights winking in the trees and shook my head. "I feel like I'm coming home after a year on another planet. Hard to believe it's only three weeks 'til Christmas."

"Going to spend the holidays with your family?"

"You bet. Oh, and speaking of my family, thanks for not telling them about my Dripping Springs detour." As far as the Gregson clan was concerned, I had spent the last few days fat and unhappy in the safe house. "If Mom knew how close she came to arranging my funeral, I would never hear the end of it. I'll have to do girly stuff with her for a week as it is."

"Bet that's the first time need-to-know ever worked *for* a reporter."

We walked a bit farther, then stopped to let Cosmo baptize the leg of a wrought iron bench.

Jack said, "Are you sure about this, A.J.?"

"About what?"

"About this gift of yours. How you want to use it. Sooner or later, you could find yourself in another tight spot. What if Baker and I aren't around to pry you out of it?"

"What's your point?"

"I'm just saying nobody would blame you if you changed your mind."

"Wrong. *I* would blame me." He sighed and shook his head. "Seriously. You know, Jack, I had plenty of time to think while I was lying there like a beached whale, waiting for Conover to do his worst. I asked myself, 'If I had known the story would end this way, would I have acted differently?' Keep in mind, I was ninety-nine percent sure I was about to become another Ferrymen success story."

"*Ninety-nine* percent sure?"

"I bet the other one percent on you."

"Thanks. Thanks a lot."

"Hey, at least I didn't lose *all* faith. Anyway, like I was saying, I went over it again and again. And each time I asked, I came up with the same answer. Yeah, I would. I didn't audition for this sideshow, but I'm stuck with it, and I believe things happen for a reason. Gotta make the most of the talents we're given, right?"

"I guess. Be nice if you could get the credit you deserve."

"Credit's not all mine. If you hadn't believed in me, Conover would still be murdering people right and left, and I would be wearing a jacket with sleeves that cross in front and buckle in the back. Trying to get somebody to listen to me. If you hadn't ridden to the rescue, I would be dead. We stopped them *together*—you, me, and Dennis." My lips curved. "Besides, credit is nice, but a byline's better. I may not be able to tell the *whole* story, but I've still got one hell of a scoop."

Cosmo interrupted with a grumble and a pointed tug on the leash.

"Not to mention one hell of a dog," Eagan added.

"You sure you want me to keep him?" I asked, way too hopefully, as we started to walk again. God help me, I was already attached.

"The boarding house will be headache enough." So he

said, but I could tell Sadie's bequest meant the world to him. "Luckily, her lawyer already found a retired schoolteacher to manage it for me. But a dog? I'll settle for visitation rights. Besides, he likes you better."

We were thirty yards from the building when a lanky redhead bounded through the doors and loped toward us. Biker Dog stopped us dead in our tracks and growled low in his throat.

"Easy, pal." I patted his head. "He's harmless, remember?"

Ellison skidded to halt a few feet away. He and Cosmo eyed each other warily. There had been no love lost between them since their first meeting at Sadie's.

"What's *that* doing here?" asked Hank.

"Cosmo's my dog now."

"Wow, a consolation prize." But Hank's sarcastic grin faded quickly under Cosmo's cool, unrelenting stare.

"Listen, I've got to get going," said Eagan. "I'll keep you posted on the case. Take care of her," he added.

"I will," Hank promised.

"Thanks, but I was talking to the dog."

"That guy scares the crap out of me," Ellison admitted as we watched Jack walk away. "He scare you?"

"No, but he tries." When the Shrike pulled away, I turned and started for the building. "I see you managed to get through the door."

"Yeah. Mr. Maxwell didn't believe me at first ... you know, about me being your assistant." *I'm having trouble believing it myself,* I thought, as he added, "But Agent Eagan straightened him out."

My lips twitched. "Now *that* I would have liked to see. By the way, nobody calls him *Mr. Maxwell.*"

"What do they call him?"

"Lots of things, most of them profane. Try Tug."

"If you say so," he agreed doubtfully.

As we pushed through the double glass doors, Burt Thompson smiled a welcome from behind his desk. "Ms. Gregson! I sure am glad to see you back!"

"Not nearly as glad as I am to *be* back, Burt. Arrested any trespassers lately?"

Burt is a retired cop turned security guard. The job isn't as tame as it sounds, mainly because knuckleheads with gripes against the media have a habit of trying to bull their way into the building to air their complaints in person. Once in a while, they bring firearms along for punctuation. Either way, they run into an immovable, six-foot-two-inch, two-hundred pound Thompson. Or Sam Kingsford, his equally large daytime counterpart.

"Not lately," he admitted, "but I live in hope. Nice dog you've got there."

I almost beamed like a proud parent, but caught myself in time. "Thanks."

"What do you think Maxwell will say when he sees him?"

"Dunno, but it's bound to be colorful. Wanna come along?"

Burt's dark face broke into a wide smile. "Nah, I figure I'll be able to hear it fine from here. He's in the Swamp."

"Okay. See you on the way out."

Hank and I caught an elevator to the fiftieth floor and exited into a wide hallway. Iconic news photos of historic events lined one cream-colored wall. A three-foot-high crawler trailed breaking headlines down the other. The hall opened into the Swamp, a sunken, cavernous, almost circular room where reporters work UpLinks in cubbies crammed cheek-to-jowl. Day and night the room simmers with the raucous babble raised by hundreds of journalists shedding sweat, blood, and tears to get the story. Any story.

"Why do they call it the Swamp?" wondered Ellison. "Because it smells like one?"

"No." Although he had a point. "We call it the Swamp because working here is like being up to your ears in alligators all day, every day." I paused to drink it in. "God, I love this place!"

"Rocks!" Tug Maxwell stood in the center aisle, feet spread, arms akimbo, unlit cigar clamped between his molars. *Maybe I can't smoke 'em in the building, but I can sure as hell taste 'em.* "About time you showed your face around here!" he yelled, his foghorn voice barreling through the hubbub. "Well, don't stand there gawping, get in here and get to work. And lose that damned dog!"

"The dog goes, I go!" I hollered back.

I had never seen the newsroom screech to a complete standstill before, but it did then, all heads swiveling in my direction. People pushed back their chairs and stood. Someone, Mark Tong maybe, started to clap, and before I knew it, every newshound in the place was on his or her feet, giving me a standing ovation. Welcoming me home.

Never let them see you cry, I scolded myself as my eyes started to sting. Fortunately, the sight of Tug Maxwell bearing down on me was enough to keep the tears at bay. He planted himself in front of us and glared at Cosmo. Cosmo curled his lip and glared back.

Finally, Maxwell blew out a defeated breath and clapped a hand on my shoulder. "Good to have you back, kid."

I let my gaze stray through the Swamp before it settled back on him. He could be an insensitive, bullheaded SOB, but he had taught me what it meant to be a reporter. He taught me to dig and keep digging until I uncovered the truth. Then he taught me how to tell it.

"All in one piece, too," I said, although it had been close. Shoving the memories away," I broke out a slow grin. "Now let's give the world an exclusive it will never forget."

Acknowledgements

To paraphrase John Donne, no author is an island. I want to acknowledge a few of the wonderful folks (and animals) who make up my support and safety net.

My sons, Leo and Nick. Creative forces that you are, you never cease to inspire me. When I grow up, I want to be as talented as you guys.

My brother, sister, nieces, nephews, and all their assorted spouses and offspring. Thanks for loving me.

Patty Kelley. Thank you for being my friend, confidant, and sommelier.

The ladies of the HDQLSG. Your love, prayers, and support mean the world to me.

Jan Esher. Thank you for walking alongside me, showing me God's grace, and making it possible for me to do anything at all.

Emily and Travis Gasper. Thanks for visiting when I needed it most.

Joy Abella. We haven't worked together for a couple decades, but you taught me so much about writing and editing.

Molly & Lucy. Thanks for the love, slurps, exercise, and belly laughs.

And last, but never least, thank God.

Special Thanks

This paperback edition of *Amanda's Eyes* would not have been possible without the help of some special "angels." Heartfelt thanks go out to Jennifer Mellott, Davanna Minter, Boomer Wadąska, David Parrott, Lynn Worton, Timothy Soto, Sandy Briers, and Cathy Scott. I will always be grateful for your generous support!

www.ingramcontent.com/pod-product-compliance
Lightning Source LLC
Chambersburg PA
CBHW031259170626
46807CB00001B/230